THE MELODY BEHIND THE WORDS
WHERE PERSONAL VALUES AND ANCIENT MYTHS COLLIDE

A NOVEL

BY

SÉAMUS LANGAN

Published in 2015 by FeedARead.com Publishing

Copyright © Séamus Langan.

First Edition

A CIP catalogue record for this title is available from the British
Library.

To

Lucia and Tony

For your patient persuasion and more

Phoebus for thee too, Hyacinth, design'd
A place among the Gods, had Fate been kind:
Yet this he gave, as oft as wintry rains
Are past, and vernal breezes sooth the plains,
From the green turf a purple flow'r you rise,
And with your fragrant breath perfume the skies.
(Ovid Metamorphoses
Translated: Sir Samuel Garth, John Dryden, et al.)

Prologue: In the Time of Trajan

A sea voyage—fractured reflections of the summer sun dancing on the undulating water, giving it the appearance of a cache of diamonds—lends itself to recollection. The sail swells as it catches the wind that propels the ship away from the coast of Cyprus towards Palestine. I am departing my home of the recent past and returning to that of the distant past, my native land, Judea. I gaze up at the straining mast and wonder if, after more voyages than I can count, this would be my last. After years of journeying, teaching the Way—the New Covenant as envisaged by our beloved founder, the Teacher of Righteousness, many generations ago—I settled in Cyprus, as the Episkopos to our followers. I never took a wife. I loved once, that was sufficient. I have taught our faithful ones to wait patiently for the *Parousia*—the coming of the Lord in power and majesty. It seems that I, the teacher, have run out of patience. Now, I am moving again, no longer to preach and baptize, but to think and to die.

Born in the time of Tiberius, I have lived through the reigns and attempted reigns of many emperors and now, in my final days, Trajan rules the world. I think it unlikely that I will see his successor, despite the myth that, having once died, I would not experience death again but live on to witness the coming of the Lord in glory. I share responsibility for that myth. What a caricature the writings have made of me! What folly they have made of faith! Perhaps faith itself is the folly.

Alone on the prow of the ship, the waters parting before it, as they did before the rod of Moses, immensity below, infinity above and ocean vastness all around, I meditate on my life, my Master, and our founder, the Teacher of Righteousness.

1: Modern Rome

Who was the Teacher of Righteousness? Who might he have been? Was there any indication within the ancient texts that he or his later followers were the forerunners of the Christian community? These questions, like an importunate mosquito, teased Marc as he made his way from the Convent of Santa Ana towards Saint Peter's Square. The conclave for the election of a new pope was underway and, while he did not expect a result this early in the procedure, he wanted to be present for the smoke signal that would announce the result of the final ballot of the second day. In this age of instantaneous global interaction, a smoking chimney seemed an odd method of communicating information; it did, however, lend a certain mystique to the occasion. As the evening was damp, reminding the young Irish priest of his native climate, he wore a black hooded raincoat over his cassock. Small knots of sightseers were scattered here and there throughout the vast expanse of Bernini's gracious space, but he expected that the numbers would increase as the hour for the expected signal approached. As well as the rain, webs of light mist from the massive fountain were streaking the fresh features of the young priest. It must be after six o'clock, he thought, his mind still preoccupied with the research he was pursuing into the Dead Sea Scrolls, his chosen topic for his doctoral dissertation. Against the advice of his supervisor, he was searching for evidence that might link the group that produced the scrolls with the first Jerusalem Christian community. Living in the past for much of every day, he was not too sure, at times, if he lived in ancient Israel or present-day Rome. His

3

assignment to the Convent of Santa Ana was supposed to correct that imbalance.

The position of spiritual director to a dwindling community of nuns was not a demanding one—in truth they needed no direction. In fact, he felt that the nuns, with a spirituality deepened by years of dedication, should have been guiding him. However, the Church judged that priesthood, however young, possessed its own special charisma. His assignment provided him with a place to live and time to work on his thesis; it also afforded him a gentle introduction to pastoral care. He did not like to admit, even to himself, that the pastoral side of the priesthood did not appeal to him. He chose the priesthood primarily as a vehicle to study, particularly ancient texts. He considered himself to be an archaeologist or palaeographer more than a priest and longed to get his hands dirty in the dust of ancient sites. So far, the closest he got to dust was blowing it off old documents. That is not to say that he was not committed to the priesthood, he just felt awkward engaging in the social interaction that pastoral work entailed. He was deeply spiritual and the mystery that surrounded priesthood fed his poetic temperament. If it were not for the lure of a possible archaeological dig, he might have opted to join a monastic order.

Father Marc Harris, born in the west of Ireland, was 28 years old. He had been a quiet child, a reserved, perhaps inhibited, youth and a cloistered adult. His parents had experienced enough of the normal adolescent angst from their two older children, Luke and Rose, to appreciate the tranquillity that their youngest child afforded them. Still, they worried that underdeveloped social skills would hamper him in later life. It would have been very easy for him to make friends, since he had a pleasing personality that drew people to him without any effort on his part. However, his interest lay elsewhere and there was little his parents could do. So, their son developed intellectually, but virtually died socially.

He was younger than most when he graduated from second-level education with enough points to qualify for any number of his favourite

4

university courses. However, in spite of his quiet disposition and studious nature, it came as a shock to his family when he decided to study for the priesthood. His decision troubled his parents, especially his mother—the Church was facing challenging times. With allegations of sexual and physical abuse mounting, the priesthood was no longer a popular career choice. However, Marc stood by his decision and was ordained a priest after pursuing his theological studies at the Pontifical University in Rome. After his ordination, much to Marc's delight, his bishop had assigned him to further studies in Rome. He hoped that investigating the Dead Sea Scrolls would afford him the opportunity to visit the location of their discovery and to sink his hands, at last, into the dust of the ancient site. Such a visit seemed an obvious and necessary part of his investigation and he intended to broach it with his supervisor. In the meantime, to provide some pastoral experience and without impinging too much on his studies, his bishop had appointed him to the undemanding chaplaincy of the convent.

A surge of excitement in the crowd around him brought him out of his reverie.

'It's white.'

'No! No! It's black. It's far too soon. It's only the fifth ballot.'

Cardinal electors from all over the world were ensconced in the Sistine Chapel, engaged in perhaps their single most important function as a group—the election of a pope. Strange to think that way in the future this day's event would seem as archaic as the events he had been studying all morning in the ancient documents section of the Vatican Library. In the far-flung future, would the massive grandeur of Saint Peter's be as decrepit a ruin as were the ancient basilicas in the Forum today?

Marc instinctively turned his gaze up to the chimney stack that rose above the papal apartments, its only purpose to act as semaphore to the outside world. The smoke did indeed look white, but it could hardly be—it was early days. As he pondered the possibility of a speedy decision, the bells of Saint Peter's rang out. Because of the confusion that sometimes arose regarding the colour of the smoke, a 1996 Apostolic Constitution decreed that, as well as the smoke, the bells of Saint Peter's should ring out. The chimes confirmed the election of a pope.

Giant screens highlighted the view of the chimney stack on which the television cameras and the human eyes in the piazza were focused. Perhaps it was the confirmation of the pealing bells that rendered the smoke indisputably white. The cameras lingered for a while, and then panned out over the crowd that, like a microbiological culture, was swelling by the minute, in spite of the damp conditions. The roving electronic eye, randomly spanning the piazza, captivated Marc. He followed its casual sweep of the crowd, which transported his image and those of his fellow observers of history into homes around the globe. He was virtually omnipresent. It was extraordinary to think that in this technological age, this was a mundane event. He could not help wondering what the copyists of the scrolls would make of it. They would surely think that humans had become gods. Marc lowered his head self-consciously as he spotted his image gazing out from the large screen.

A few moments later, a familiar voice whispered into his ear, 'Just saw you on the screen.'

Marc knew the voice and was surprised to feel a little rush of pleasure. 'I'm surprised you found me among all the umbrellas,' he said, as he turned to face a smiling Carlo Soler, one of the junior librarians in the Vatican Library. He was a handsome young man about Marc's own age, with a well-defined body that owed as much to determined effort as to nature. Carlo was efficient at his work, so Marc usually sought him out when trying to track down a particular file of ancient documents. But Marc realized that the main reason he did so was because he liked Carlo. In spite of the fact that they met regularly, this was their first meeting outside the library.

Now, all eyes were moving from the chimney to the balcony over Saint Peter's main entrance where the protodeacon of the College of Cardinals, according to custom, presents the new pope to the people of his diocese and to the world. There would be an inevitable delay as the panoply of Church and State rolled into action. The rain failed to dampen the pageantry as bands and guards from various Vatican and Roman corps marched in and took their places in the piazza under the balcony, among them the Swiss Guard.

'There's Luigi,' said Carlo, as a Swiss Guard, carrying the Vatican Flag, appeared on the big screen. Two other guards holding their Halberds flanked him. Because of the rain, long dark blue capes covered their colourful uniforms, only the white ruff protruded above the collar. For this ceremonial occasion, silver morion helmets replaced the regular black berets. As the standard-bearer lowered the flag, it snagged on the metal peak of his helmet and he had to raise his hand to free it.

The image passed too quickly for Marc to identify any individual in the group. 'Who is Luigi?'

'A friend,' replied Carlo. 'A very good friend,' he added tellingly, leaving Marc to ponder the extent of their friendship.

'Was he the one carrying the flag?'

'No,' replied Carlo. 'Luigi was beside him.'

As they waited, the rain lightened. Umbrellas were lowered, as the various military groups marched in formation until they arrived at the spot chosen by the organizers of the display, directly below the balcony. An hour must have passed before the stage was set and the cardinal messenger made the familiar pronouncement, *Habemus Papam*. Marc tensed to catch the name as the applause from the piazza died down. The new pope, in a break from tradition, asked the blessing of the people before pronouncing his own over the city and the world. It was a small but significant shift of emphasis by the new pope, and Marc wondered if change would categorize the new pontificate.

When it was all over, the new pope disappeared back into the immensity of the basilica. People stayed on, looking at the façade of the great church and at each other as if unwilling to depart. Marc too felt like lingering.

'Don't you think that our new Papa might have popped the Prosecco? The latest emperor has been chosen.'

Up to now, they had conducted their conversations at a purely professional level, so Marc knew Carlo the librarian very well, but Carlo the man, he did not know. He was not too sure what to make of his comment. After all, the pope was the Vicar of Christ, not the latest of a long line of emperors.

'The remaining rump of the Roman Empire now has a new *Pontifex Maximus*. How about toasting him with a little Prosecco of our own?' Carlo persisted in equating pope and emperor.

'I don't drink wine.' Marc was apologetic and slightly annoyed. He had never developed a taste for alcohol, probably because of his lack of social interaction. He had nothing against it, it was no big thing; he just did not like having to explain himself.

'Sure you do. Every morning, I suspect.' Carlo's eyes sparkled with mischief.

'Oh!' Marc was nonplussed, unsure what to make of this new Carlo. He liked Carlo the librarian, so he decided to give Carlo the man a chance. 'I could join you for a coffee,' he offered tentatively. Social skills were never his gift.

'No! No! The occasion calls for something more, *Buona Fortuna*, *Papa*! You have a new Lord and Master, Father. Life is for living. Go on, live.'

Instead of encouraging him, Carlo's exhortation made Marc feel like bolting, but in spite of his mounting misgivings, Carlo's magnetism held him—he wanted to get to know this man better. 'Please Carlo, call me Marco.'

'Marco,' Carlo rolled the syllables around his tongue, as if savouring their flavour. 'Marco,' he repeated, a satisfied smile forming on his lips.

The singular crowd in the piazza, united by common purpose, had begun to fracture into smaller groups and disperse with the rain. However, Bernini's magnificent space was rarely empty. After the

8

momentary excitement of seeing the new pope, tourists began to revert to more normal tourist pursuits, while locals began to dissolve into the secular nightlife of the city. Carlo, the native of the city and the extrovert, guided Marc to his favourite trattoria. The priest had an uncanny feeling that this was the beginning of something. For a moment, apprehension prickled his spine. Should he draw back? Possibly, but he felt comfortable in Carlo's company. Perhaps there was more to life than ancient manuscripts and libraries. The thought surprised him, considering his all-consuming interest in study. By the time they reached the trattoria, the time for drawing back had passed.

Prosecco

Carlo led the way. They passed through an empty patio area, where tables were stacked and protected from the earlier rain, into the inviting wood-panelled interior to a window table that provided a view of Michelangelo's dome above the roofs of the surrounding buildings. The two young men sat facing each other, the street and the dome to their side.

'Something to eat,' suggested Carlo.

'My supper will be waiting.'

'You live at Collegio Irlandese?'

'I did, until recently. My bishop decided that I needed a challenge, so he appointed me chaplain to the Convent of Santa Ana.'

'That's a challenge!'

Marc smiled shyly and fidgeted with the napkin. 'The nuns are considerate. They realize that study is my main task.'

'I've noticed. You will exhaust the resources of the Vatican Library. Where is all this study leading?'

'I'm working on my thesis.' Marc mumbled the words; shy of his academic prowess.

'A doctoral thesis,' suggested Carlo, as Marc looked away self-consciously. 'Something to do with the Dead Sea Scrolls,' ventured Carlo, conscious of Marc's discomfort.

9

Marc smiled assent. It was an easy deduction for the librarian engaged in hunting down the material he wished to study.

'You should talk to Giuseppe, Giuseppe Rossi. He is an authority on the scrolls, but you must know that.'

The name confused Marc. He was about to admit that he had never heard of him when he realized who Carlo must be referring to. 'You mean Joseph Ross? I suppose you know that he is Irish.'

'Yes, but I am so accustomed to the Italian version, I sometimes forget.'

'I would like very much to meet him,' said Marc. 'He is such a famous scholar that the thought is daunting.'

'I could introduce you, if you like. He is one of the library's most constant patrons. We have become good friends.'

'Thanks, Carlo,' Marc's eagerness was genuine. 'It might be just the push I need.'

'Have you discovered who the Teacher of Righteousness was? Some experts think he might have been Jesus.'

'I do not think that likely.'

'Why is that?'

'One can't be dogmatic ...' began Marc.

'Good,' interrupted Carlo. 'I don't trust belief that is above and beyond the facts.'

Marc was nonplussed. For a Vatican employee, Carlo was proving to be a surprise. 'There are indications in the scrolls that the origin of the Qumran community was earlier.'

'Before the time of Jesus?'

'The group existed in the time of Jesus, of course, but the Teacher goes back to the time of Jonathan Maccabee, around one hundred and fifty years before Jesus. There are many suggestions as to his identity, but as the scrolls never name him, simply refer to him as the Teacher of Righteousness, we will probably never know for sure.'

'What is your topic?'

'I am researching a possible link between the people of the scrolls and the early Christian community.'

'I would have thought it obvious considering their similarities: rituals with water and meals of bread and wine. Many of their sayings are replicated in the gospels, and both expected a 'messiah' to sort out their lives.'

'You are very well informed,' commented Marc with admiration. 'Few non-professionals would know that.'

'I'm a librarian,' replied Carlo, as if the profession were a cabal harbouring the secret of universal wisdom.

'There were also significant differences between the groups,' offered Marc tentatively, as if reluctant to dismiss Carlo's conclusion out of hand.

'That is because they were changing, in my humble opinion,' added Carlo, with uncharacteristic diffidence.

'Changing in what way?' asked Marc, conscious that Carlo was an informed observer.

'They were progressing in their understanding of whatever it was they were trying to understand. Mind you, I think that they were wasting their time, but that is another matter. What emerged was a group that later generations would call Christians. Only those sold on the idea of the uniqueness of the Christian message could refuse to see that progression.'

'Do you think I am wasting my time?'

'Not if you produce something that will shake things up a bit.' Carlo's inquiring glance challenged Marc.

'You should be writing this thesis,' said Marc with sincerity that chastened Carlo.

Carlo shook his head, 'I don't have your expertise. You chew on the bones of the ancient symbols, savouring their flavour and sucking out their marrow.'

'You make it sound revolting,' said Marc.

Carlo chuckled before continuing. 'My understanding is superficial. I am the glossy magazine, you the scholarly tome. All this talk about chewing reminds me,' he picked up the menu. 'You will have something to eat?' Marc hesitated, but before he could reply, Carlo added, 'With the excitement of the election, the nuns have probably forgotten your dinner.'

'I doubt that,' said Marc, with a smile. 'Very well, I will have something, but I insist on paying my share.'

'No! The inviter pays, the invitee accepts. What would you like?'

'Whatever the inviter is having,' said Marc, taking stock of Carlo's healthy appearance and well-developed physique. 'He evidently knows about food.' Embarrassed by his remark, he shifted his admiring gaze from his impressive host to the imposing dome.

Ever alert to compliments, Carlo preened himself. Humility was not high on his list of virtues.

'Orandum est ut sit mens sana in corpore sano.
Fortem posce animum mortis terrore carentem,
Qui spatium vitae extremum inter munera ponat.'

'A Latinist,' said Marc, with admiration.

'Latin is our mother tongue.'

'Is that also your philosophy of life? *A healthy mind in a healthy body, a brave soul that does not fear death, that puts length of days last among nature's gifts.'*

'Yes! Life is for living. Forget death; when it comes we won't even know it.'

'As you are so familiar with Juvenal, you will remember that he asserts in the passage you eloquently quoted that the one path to a tranquil life is through virtue.'

'This conversation may be nourishing the mind, but my body is hungry for food. Where is Sergio?'

As if by magic, the waiter suddenly appeared by their table.

'Ciao! Sergio. The Padre here is starving. Sergio is my very good friend,' he directed the final comment to Marc.

12

'*Buona sera*, Sergio.'

'*Benvenuto, Padre*, I am sorry to have kept you waiting.'

'Call me Marco, please, and you did not keep us waiting.'

'Sergio, let us add a few kilos to Marco's figure.' Carlo evidently relished rolling the R. 'I guess it is just skin and bone under that cassock. We will have some of your risotto con zucca e tartufo and a carafe of your very best house wine. I did promise Marco a Prosecco to toast the new pope, but...' He gave a defeatist shrug. As Sergio left to carry out their order, Carlo looked apologetically at Marc, 'Sorry about the Prosecco.'

Marc dismissed his concern with a shake of his head. 'It would have been wasted on my uneducated palate.'

'I imagined all priests were connoisseurs.'

'Some are, no doubt, but I was never that interested.'

'More interested in ancient writings? Like the community of the scrolls, wine is also important in Christian ritual.'

'Yes!' Marc knew where the conversation was leading. There seemed to be an endless fascination with mystery.

'Do you really believe that...?' Carlo faltered, and then continued, 'Of course you do, otherwise you would not be a priest.'

'Do I really believe that the wine in the Eucharist becomes the blood of Christ? Yes, I do.'

'Ask a stupid question. I did also ... once upon a time.'

Silence descended on the table, broken when Sergio materialized like a genie. He placed two glasses on the table and a bottle of Prosecco. 'On the house,' he said, and departed into his bottle before they could comment.

'He must be a very good friend,' observed Marc.

'He is,' replied Carlo, smiling wistfully at some memory Marc's comment evoked. 'His family owns Trattoria Sergio. It will be his one day.' There was a pause as Carlo began to pour the wine.

'What happened?' asked Marc.

'*Scusa!*'

'You said that you believed in the mystery of the Eucharist once upon a time. What happened to change your mind?'

Carlo raised his glass, inviting Marc to do the same. They clicked and sipped, the bubbles rising and exploding, like expectant hopes.

'What happened?' Carlo repeated, meditatively. 'Life, I suppose. Like your bishop, I thought I needed a challenge. At some stage, it occurred to me that we were taking a hell of a lot for granted, without very much evidence to back it up. Prompted by what I considered my native good sense, I started to read the opposition. They made a lot of sense, the sensible ones at least. There are also many airheads in the opposition. The gospel advises against building a house on sand. The bible is not even sand; it is a quagmire, and Christianity is built on that.'

'Not just that,' suggested Marc cautiously. 'There is also tradition.'

'Don't get me started on tradition! You would need a surgical scalpel to separate authentic tradition from legend, especially in the vital first century. In my opinion, that is,' added Carlo apologetically. 'You have an expression in English for *in poche parole*?'

'In a nutshell,' suggested Marc.

'In a nutshell, Christianity has no foundation.' Carlo's English words, that in another age might have condemned him to the stake, mingled with the chatter of the restaurant and were lost in the air of a more tolerant age. He looked apologetically at Marc. 'I don't want to offend you, Marco, but you did ask.'

'You have not offended me, Carlo. I admire you for searching for answers.'

'There was something else.' Carlo paused, as if reluctant to continue, but did not get the chance. Their meal arrived. '*Bene*, Sergio. *Grazie!*'

'*Grazie molto*, Sergio. The Prosecco is very good.'

'*Prego, Padre. Scusami ... Marco. Buon Appetito!*'

Sergio departed, leaving them to savour their meal. Outside, Rome was putting on her evening apparel. Marc loved the many aspects of

Rome, but among his favourites was his evening stroll by the Tiber. However, this moment, sitting opposite Carlo, munching his risotto, with Michelangelo's dome keeping watch over them, was liable to become his favourite memory of Rome when he looked back in years to come. Perhaps the Prosecco gave a glow to the evening. It is true that he did not make a habit of drinking wine, but he did not shun it either. It never made him feel like this before. Perhaps it was the quality of the wine: it was delicious. But was that all it was?

'There was something else.' Marc spoke quietly.

Carlo stopped eating. He slowly raised his eyes from the plate. They were as black as his hair, but sparkling with interest. He stared across the table at Marc. 'You don't want to know.'

'Tell me.' Marc spoke with a forcefulness that was not usual.

'It's no big deal.' Carlo was more relaxed. He paused to take a sip of wine. 'It did make me think.'

'Yes!' Marc was willing him to continue.

'I am homosexual. I could not reconcile my feelings with the moral teaching of the Church—love and be damned—so I investigated. Some people would say that I left the Church because of my sexual orientation. That is not true. Because I am gay, I researched rigorously. That is the truth. I had the facility to do so. I am a librarian, after all,' he added with obvious pride in his profession. 'My study led me to abandon belief in the Church, in Christianity, in religion. So there you have it, in a nutshell,' he concluded with an engaging smile.

They continued eating, savouring the food and wine in silent companionship, as if they were friends of many years' standing, each at ease in the other's silence.

Garret

By the time they left the restaurant, night had descended. Marc loved Rome, but he was in awe of Rome by night when he considered it a magical city—illuminations transforming ancient ruins into mystical mounds that made the city seem like a constellation fallen to earth.

'I will walk you home,' offered Carlo.

'Is that out of your way?'

'No place is far in Rome.'

'Where do you live?'

'I have an apartment just around the corner from Pulcino della Minerva.'

'Bernini's *Elephant*,' said Marc, visualizing the quirky monument of an elephant supporting an Egyptian obelisk. 'It stands in front of the Basilica of Saint Mary over Minerva.'

'Santa Maria sopra Minerva,' said Carlo, thoughtfully. 'It is significant, don't you think? The Church built on Paganism.'

'Or the Church that surpassed Paganism,' suggested Marc quietly, enjoying the walk and the company too much to engage in polemics. 'An apartment sounds impressive,' he continued.

'It's small. A garret; makes me feel artistic. Would you like to see it?'

'Are you an artist, as well as a librarian?' asked Marc, avoiding the invitation.

'No, Luigi is the artist.'

'Luigi? I thought he was a Swiss Guard.'

'Not for much longer. His term of duty finishes in May, and then he intends to follow his heart.'

'A painter ... or a poet, perhaps?'

'An opera singer, aspiring!'

'I thought that a Swiss Guard was impressive.' commented Marc, who loved music. 'But an opera singer...!'

'He is more impressive in the flesh.'

Carlo's double entendres amused Marc. They also made him uneasy.

'Do you live alone?' Marc immediately regretted his question. It was none of his business and might indicate too great an interest in Carlo's lifestyle, which perhaps he had, but did not think appropriate to entertain or explore.

'For now,' replied Carlo. 'Luigi will probably move in with me when he has to vacate the barracks. At least until he wows the world. Then I hope to live off him. Well! What do you think?'

'About living off Luigi?' Marc knew that Carlo was harking back to his invitation, but tried to dodge it.

'No! Would you like to see my garret?'

'It's getting late. The nuns will be sending out a search party.'

'It's not far. We could make it a quickie,' added Carlo with a cheeky grin.

In spite of his apprehension, Marc felt like prolonging the encounter. He nodded, and they made their way towards Bernini's *Elephant* and Santa Maria sopra Minerva. Arriving at the church, Carlo sprinted over to the base of the monument and tried to replicate the elephant's expression, which seemed to indicate complicity in some enormous joke. The innocent enactment moved Marc profoundly; he looked at his companion as if seeing him for the first time and felt a quiver of something beyond delight. He wanted to hold on to the moment, but Carlo turned his attention to the building.

'As you know, the city is predominantly Baroque, but this is a notable exception. Behind the nondescript façade, its interior is Gothic. The adjacent convent was the seat of the Inquisition. There they forced Galileo to deny the evidence of his eyes.'

'It was an unfortunate error of judgement, but understandable at the time,' commented Marc.

'An error of judgement,' repeated Carlo, with a questioning tilt of his head.

'To put the sun at the centre of the solar system with the earth spinning around it could seem to undermine the authority of the Bible,' continued Marc in vindication of an event that he did not feel like justifying. 'Now, apart from the "airheads" you mentioned earlier, all accept that the Bible is not a study of cosmology, and is indifferent as to which cosmic rock orbits another.'

'Could the Church not have studied the evidence before jumping in and flexing its muscle?'

'At the time, the Bible was the evidence. I don't think it fair to judge the past by present scholarship.'

'Perhaps you are right.' Carlo did not wish to be confrontational on their first social meeting.

The ground floor of the building that contained Carlo's apartment was a restaurant, beside which was a door to the upper floors. Carlo unlocked it and stepped back to let Marc enter. They made their way up four flights of stairs to the top floor. There was a wide landing and just one door. Carlo unlocked it and once again let his companion go first. Marc could not stifle a little gasp of surprise and delight. Carlo's place was indeed a garret, but not the dismal one of *La Bohème*. Even in the night light, it was cheery. In contrast to many Italian homes, there was no clutter. There was not a pope or saint in view. What objects there were on shelves and tables were well chosen and thoughtfully placed. The main room was not large, but adequate. Marc could visualize it as an artist's space, but there was no easel in sight. However, an impressive abstract painting decorated one wall. The windows looked out on the surrounding roofs. Carlo opened one, which led onto a ledge—it was barely wide enough to justify calling it a roof terrace, which Carlo did with a smirk that reflected on his grandiose label. There were no curtains and no overlooking windows. Marc turned his attention from the windows, looked around the room and a family photo drew his attention. He looked closely and thought he saw two Carlos, indicating that Carlo might be a twin. A handsome Swiss Guard looked out from another photo frame and Marc concluded that it must be Luigi. Perhaps the uniform flattered his figure, but Marc concluded that Carlo's earlier comment regarding Luigi was understated. Carlo was physically arresting, but Luigi was something else, the all action hero, ideal for the role of the sword-wielding Sigmund in *Die Walküre*. He turned his attention back to the room. A closed laptop computer lay on a table, and close by an iPod stood poised on a futuristic-looking external player.

Noticing Marc eyeing the iPod, Carlo activated it. *La Bohème* was playing. Marc smiled. He should have known. Carlo, like most Romans, loved opera.

'You live in a garret. Would I be correct in thinking that *La Bohème* is your favourite opera?'

'I have many favourites, but it is one of them,' said Carlo. He then leaned over and whispered into Marc's ear, echoing the words of the opera's heroin, '*Mi chiamano Mimi.*'

Surprising himself, Marc took hold of Carlo's hand. 'Your hand is neither tiny nor cold,' he said with a laugh. A moment later, he had reason to regret his uncharacteristic impulse when Carlo turned the tables on him and grabbed his hands.

'You know that I like you, Marco, and I think you like me.'

'I do like you, Carlo, as a friend. I should go, before the nuns alert the Carabinieri. Thank you for the dinner and showing me your garret. I love it.'

Carlo released his hold. 'Can we meet again? Outside the library, I mean.'

'Of course, I would like that.'

Carlo insisted on walking Marc home. 'Some cheeky Roman stud might run away with you,' he offered as an explanation. Marc was silent, thinking that Carlo's words might be a classic example of transference. But why? The question puzzled him, considering that the desirable Luigi was already an obviously much-loved friend—more than a friend perhaps. Whatever the reason, Marc was comfortable with and at ease in Carlo's company. The earlier rain had cleared and the stars were out, shining brightly, vying with the city lights; the hydrogen-fuelled constellations and asterisms refusing, after their monumental journey, to submit to radiance from a lesser source.

Dilemma

The morning following his visit to the garret, Marc woke at dawn. He was usually eager to get going, the creeping light acting like an energizing shot of adrenaline. This morning was different. He had spent a restless night teasing out the problem of Carlo—Carlo, a problem! He smiled, in spite of his disquiet, to think how Carlo would react to such a designation. He liked Carlo, and Carlo, obviously, liked him. Marc had not been open about his sexuality in words, but while he made no verbal admission, his body language spoke for him. It was not that he was embarrassed—Marc was under no illusion regarding his sexuality. It was not a problem for him when deciding to pursue a life in the priesthood, as celibacy applied whether one was homosexual or heterosexual. Whether or not he would make the same choice now that the attitude of the Church had hardened towards homosexuality was a moot point. However, having made his commitment he intended to stick with it, as long as... What would it take to derail him? Certainly not friendship with Carlo that, pleasant though it might be, would end when he had to leave Rome. Consequently, their relationship was going nowhere. In fact, they could not have a relationship. The more he thought about it, the more he doubted that they could even be friends. The thought brought a flash of regret. Inevitably, Carlo would want more than friendship. In time, Mark too might feel a platonic friendship inadequate. That could not happen if he were to remain true to his vocation. It would be advisable not to see Carlo for the time being. Circumstances would take care of that, as he would be busy with his thesis for the next while. Avoid temptation at all costs—he knew the drill. However, he had not practised it last evening. He felt guilty about that, but Carlo was so charming. That, of course, was no excuse for dropping his guard. To stimulate his resolve, he reflected on his youthful interest in the ancient texts.

Marc had first become aware of the scrolls, their discovery and subsequent history, through a television documentary. He was about ten years old at the time and knew little about Israel. He was aware from readings and sermons at Mass that Israel was the 'Promised Land', but that was about it. A less serious and studious boy would have eagerly switched over to *The Simpsons* to escape this boring stuff, but for Marc it was high adventure.

He thrilled to the dramatic re-enactment of Bedouin herders lobbing stones into a forbidding-looking hole in a rock face in search of a stray sheep (or was it a goat?) and stumbling upon a cave that they feared might shelter an evil jinn. The prospect of hidden treasure prevailed over their fear of dubious spirits. Their excitement, however, evaporated like morning manna when they saw what it contained.

Many of Marc's young contemporaries would have been equally disillusioned at finding a hoard of ancient manuscripts but, for Marc, it was akin to Jim Hawkins's treasure map. The Bedouin soon discovered that there was money in old texts. That single discovery would have been exciting enough, but it was just the beginning. It set in motion a race, thrillingly dramatized for television, between archaeologists and Bedouin to find further early material in the caves that peppered the region.

The initial find in late 1946 or early 1947 (the precise date is uncertain) led to a succession of discoveries that culminated in 1956 with the discovery of the eleventh cave. It contained, almost intact, the longest scroll of all, the Temple Scroll, allotted the symbol 11QT.

While his peers were busy committing to memory the fortunes of Premier League clubs, Marc was memorizing the documents discovered and their identifying labels. Books, videos and later DVDs relating to the scrolls and their discovery began to accumulate in his bedroom. His passion consumed his life and left little or no time for social interaction with his peers. The past animated him more than the present. Overtures to friendship went unreciprocated. Fergus came to mind. He was one of many, but probably the most tenacious, who had sought to cultivate his friendship. A keen tennis player, Fergus frequently invited Marc to join him on the court. Marc's responses were usually negative, but on the few occasions when he had agreed, his active participation was so lacking in enthusiasm that eventually Fergus lost heart and gave up. Like constellations in an expanding galaxy, they slowly, almost imperceptibly, drifted apart. The memory of Fergus cast a new pall over the gloom already shrouding him. Was he doing the same thing again with Carlo? Why the extremes? Did it have to be all or nothing at all? He had enjoyed the few hours with Carlo yesterday. Why could they not continue to be friends?

His appointment to meet with his supervisor to discuss his thesis, was fast approaching. He knew Monsignore Martini to be a demanding professor, and wished to have an impressive outline to present on this their first one-to-one meeting. Going over his notes, he believed that he knew as much as anyone could know about the scrolls, but he also knew that his knowledge was limited. Most texts of earlier times had come down to us gradually, with copyists and later printers producing the latest editions of the original, usually accompanied by commentaries and critiques. However, the Qumran scrolls arrived suddenly into the modern age. The biblical texts, of course, had their commentators through the ages, but the documents unique to the Qumran community had no earlier voices to offer insights into their meaning. This could be an advantage. With no flawed copies or zealous interpreters there was no possibility of misinterpretation. Yet, understanding them was not easy. Would he be able to grasp their full significance even if he could travel back through time to witness the scribes at work? He would still take his prejudices with him. The intervening millennia had altered the cultural setting and rendered it impossible to understand the scrolls in their cultural setting. The interpretation of the Hebrew Scriptures, or *Pesharim*, as the writers of the scrolls referred to it, was their primary interest. Marc was aware of the theory, but experiencing it viscerally was another matter.

2: The Time of Trajan

Lazarus was my name, a long time ago. However, I received a new name, Johanan, which means God is Gracious, at the time of my initiation into the Anointed One's saving mystery. After that, Lazarus retreated into legend. A fact less widely known, I am the disciple that many communities of believers have come to know as the 'beloved'. I do not make the claim boastfully—I am the recipient of a gift. My new name, like the actor's mask, obscures in order to reveal. My intention was to proclaim, through metaphor, mime and myth, a mystery long hidden in the mind of the Holy One and unintelligible in common language. Now, at the end of my days, I wonder if it is intelligible in any language.

My voyages have not always been pleasant experiences. Some were violent with howling winds and seas as turbulent as the clash of armies—I expected to end up not only in the watery depths, but also in shadowy Sheol itself. By contrast, this vessel is transporting me home with the ease of a soaring gull, affording me the leisure and tranquillity to think. After a life of teaching and writing, my thoughts inevitably return to the problem of conveying a message, especially one that transcends the scope of language.

The problem of revealing or interpreting the divine mysteries is not new, or unique to followers of the Way. Devotees of the ancient Mystery Religions faced a similar difficulty—how to explain them in a way that mere humans would understand. Isaiah, the prophet beloved of our founder, the Teacher of Righteousness, recognized the challenge when he put the following words into the mouth of God: *My thoughts are not your thoughts, neither are my ways your ways.* There! I have fallen into the same trap by giving a 'mouth' to the Eternal Spirit, whose voiceless Word created the heavens. We can see where this leads. The saviours of the Mystery Cults, like Osiris, Dionysius, Mithras and others, are seen as human-divine beings in order that the Mystes, the followers of the cult, would more readily understand them. As if the Eternal Spirit has need of human or semi-human intervention, to accomplish Its designs. I say 'Its' because the divine energy transcends all known categories.

Inevitably, followers of the Way are pursuing the same pattern. Many generations before my time, our founder taught his New Covenant by word of mouth. His teaching expanded as his successors' understanding of the eternal Mysteries, as revealed through the ancient scriptures, developed. Soon, we wrote it down, but always in the form of exegeses of the holy writings. Our library, abandoned in the caves around our sanctuary by the Salt Sea, was full of scrolls showing how the ancient writings enlightened our times. Such aids from competent mystics, like our Teacher, were necessary to understand the Divine Mysteries hidden in our Holy Scriptures. The Hebrew word for these interpretations is *Pesharim,* and our Teacher, being a true Jew, interpreted our history strictly according to the Torah.

Later, other mystics, like Philo of Alexandria, also a faithful Jew, but open to other wisdom, drew from Greek as well as Jewish writings for his *Pesharim.* According to him, the literal interpretation of the ancient writings was incapable of revealing God. Only through allegory and symbolism could we come to know a deity indescribable in featureless terms. Such a One, perfect, pure and incorruptible, could have no contact with base matter, not even as its creator. The creator would have to be an intermediary between corruptible matter and this sublime and incorruptible deity. The Greeks called this intermediary *Logos*, the Word.

In an effort to make this Greek *Logos* understandable to Jews, Philo identified It with the Firstborn of God, which Jewish Scriptures call '*Wisdom*'. He wed the two concepts of *Logos* and *Wisdom* in his *Pesharim* of our ancient writings. However, Philo did not see his *Logos* as a sacrificial offering atoning for sin. Nor did Apollos, a masterful preacher of the Way, who came from the same centre of Hellenized wisdom as Philo, and whom Paul accused of preaching 'worldly wisdom'. Paul, never one to underestimate his position, claimed to preach the Wisdom of God, which was a Christ Crucified. He accused Apollos of preaching a *Logos* other than Christ Crucified.

Coming from the Hellenistic city of Tarsus and ministering in the great cultural centres of the Roman world, Paul was well acquainted with the concept of *Logos*, but he never used the word. He chose instead to use the term *Christ*. For him the *Christ*, the anointed one, the Son of God, was the *Logos*. He developed a radically new understanding of the mystery, introducing a mythical *Christ*, who died on a cross in atonement for sin. Perhaps Isaiah's Suffering Servant inspired him in that direction, as it did our earlier scribes who wrote of a pierced Messiah. He was doing what poets and mystics have done since we first sought to understand the meaning of life.

Paul's *Pesharim* fell on good ground—a metaphor frequently used by my Master. Graphic stories appeared depicting the life and death of an Anointed Saviour—appropriately called *Jesus*, signifying saviour, and *Christ*, signifying the anointed—as taking place in time, and as an historical event. Such stories were allegories. The authors intended them to be mere illustrations of a spiritual truth, just like the ancient myths. However, I could see that simple-minded people read them as history. Only someone with an extended lifespan like mine is in a position to witness such a pattern unfolding over the span of years. Advancing years is like climbing to an ever-higher plateau from which to observe the true contours of life's journey. Only the years reveal the work of days, and decades that of years.

The first such gospel, as far as I am aware, is one purporting to come from Peter. I still remember my astonishment. A scholar probing scriptural texts evidently wrote it, but instead of merely interpreting the sacred texts for our time, he composed a story to explain the divine plan at work in human history. For Paul, God's saving action through His atoning *Christ* took place outside of human history, beyond time, but his method of interpretation, his *Pesharim*, lent itself ideally to historicizing a spiritual event, which is not an 'event' in the usual sense of the word, as I discovered when I began to preach the Way. To find an appropriate term is difficult, if not impossible, and only highlights the problem of describing the mystical in human terms. Nevertheless, this new method of describing it became so popular that many other gospels followed. In spite of the dangers inherent in historicizing a spiritual event, I could see its merit.

I found this method useful in describing the Divine Spirit's Great Work of Salvation, but I also knew that mysteries such as these are understandable only through that Spirit. My present problem is not with the *Pesharim* describing the Saving Mystery. What I cannot understand is the delay in bringing it to fulfilment. My Master seemed certain that the Lord would come in glory in our lifetime. He died without experiencing it, as did many of our followers. I retain that hope only because my life has continued far beyond normal expectation. My death has acquired significance far greater than that due to the dissolution of my physical body. It results from my Master's unguarded reply to Peter: 'What is it to you, if he should remain alive until I come?' As a result, a belief has developed that my existence guarantees the reality of the promised *Parousia*. If I should die before that fulfilment, many who follow the Way will fall away. Through no fault of my own, I will have failed them.

3: Growing up in Ireland

As he grew older, Marc's reading became more intensive and he began to appreciate the significance of the discovery of the scrolls for the new state of Israel. The scrolls had been abandoned just when Israel was about to fade from history. Their discovery coincided with the United Nations' proclamation of an independent Israeli state. Both Israel and the scrolls had spent two thousand years in exile. He read with consuming interest of the efforts of a man called Eleazer Sukenic, an archaeologist at the Hebrew University in Jerusalem, to secure the first scrolls discovered in what would become known as 1Q (Qumran cave number one). He began to appreciate Professor Sukenic's passion and the scrolls' enormous symbolic significance for the emerging state of Israel.

While Marc was becoming more familiar with the political and cultural fortunes of Israel, he was also expanding his knowledge of its geography. That region of the Eastern Mediterranean was vastly different from his own green, misty isle. The caves, he learned, were located in the Judean desert, northwest of the Dead Sea and 20 kilometres east of Jerusalem. The area is 420 metres below sea level, whereas Jerusalem is 750 metres above. It is a dry and arid region that contributed to the preservation of the fragile material for two thousand years. A desire to visit the region took root in Marc's mind.

Following their discovery, politics, religion, war, conspiracy theories and money combined to make the unfolding story read, for Marc, like a literary thriller. If that were not enough, 3Q (cave three) produced the Copper Scroll, which cryptically described the location of hidden booty and held out the intriguing possibility of a treasure hunt. Marc fantasized about undertaking his own search, in spite of the fact that a similar venture had already proved fruitless.

Many scholars considered the scrolls to be the most important manuscript discovery ever—tens of thousands of fragments amounting to something in the region of 800 documents, written in Hebrew and Aramaic. 7Q even yielded up some Greek texts.

4Q contained about 40 percent of the entire material discovered, something in the region of 520 texts in 15,000 fragments. 4Q also gave rise to conspiracy theories because of the delay in publishing the material from that cave. This was the subject of another television documentary, which further stimulated Marc's interest. The members of the team working on the material from that cave (4Q) were very slow in publishing their findings. They refused access to other scholars. This attitude made many in the scientific world wonder what they were hiding. In the 1990s, international pressure forced them to publish the material from that cave, and release it for international inspection. Among the manuscripts discovered were biblical and apocryphal texts as well as legal and sectarian works from about 250 **B**efore the **C**ommon **E**ra to 68 of the **C**ommon **E**ra. Marc noticed that most of the scholars writing about the scrolls favoured the abbreviations **BCE** and **CE** over the more familiar **BC** and **AD**. The obvious questions that followed were: where did these texts come from, who placed them in the caves and why?

Near the caves stood a ruin, which gradually attracted the attention of the archaeologists hunting the scrolls. Père Roland de Vaux, a Dominican priest and director of the École Biblique in Jerusalem, began excavating the first cave in 1949 and, in 1951, was the first to excavate the site at Qumran itself. From his work on the scrolls and evidence gleaned from the site, de Vaux concluded that the Qumran site was a religious settlement of Essenes—a sect that was new to Marc.

He soon discovered that they were a religious group equal in importance to Pharisees and Sadducees, both of whom he had heard of from the gospels. Essenes flourished from the second century BCE to the first century CE. He learned that they were at the extreme end of religious observance, living celibate lives in communities, usually separate from society, though they were also found among the general population. However, the New Testament does not mention them, which explains why he had never heard of them. They were, nevertheless, recorded in the historical accounts of Pliny, the Roman statesman; the Alexandrian philosopher Philo; and the Jewish historian Flavius Josephus.

Father de Vaux's conjecture that Essenes occupied the Qumran site seemed plausible and enjoyed general acceptance for years. However, as work progressed on the site and the scrolls, scholars emerged with opposing views. The bewildering plethora of opinions that emerged confused Marc. Qumran could indeed have been a sort of monastic settlement—it might also have been, according to various scholars, a military fort, a luxurious villa, or a pottery factory. A caravanserai, which sounded very adventurous and exotic to the youthful Marc, was another suggestion. The scrolls could have been the work of a nearby community of Essenes, or some other group, but they could also be the remnants of a Jerusalem or Temple library, hidden away in desert caves for safekeeping at the approach of the deadly Roman Legions hell-bent on quelling the Jewish revolt. Marc began to appreciate that dissecting history can be a challenging undertaking.

It was during this period that Marc had discovered Joseph Ross through the latter's publications.

Joseph Ross

Giuseppe Rossi, as Carlo called him—a name that briefly puzzled Marc—was in fact Joseph Ross. He was born in Ireland, but lived so long in Rome, had a face weathered by the Roman sun and spoke Italian with such a flourish that, in time, he fitted, like the other ancient monuments, into the landscape of the city. A famous name is always a welcome addition to a city's pantheon, and Giuseppe had a name, not household perhaps, but his reputation extended well beyond the margins of academia because of the questions he raised regarding the origins of Christianity. However, the biographical blurb on his many writings never hid the fact that he was born in Dublin in 1923.

Joseph attended Belvedere College, a Jesuit second-level school in Dublin. The Jesuits, ever astute at spotting young, promising talent, soon added Joseph's name to an unofficial list of potential recruits into their ranks. Whether his decision was completely free or made under the subtle influence of his teachers is uncertain but, upon graduation, he entered the Jesuit Order as a novice. At that time, Europe was at war, so he continued his studies in Dublin, taking Bachelor degrees in Semitic languages and archaeology from both the National University and Trinity College. He continued with postgraduate studies and duly achieved Master degrees in his chosen subjects. After the war, he left Dublin, oblivious to the fact that he would never return, and continued his studies at the Catholic University of Louvain, where he achieved doctorates in both his chosen subjects. He then undertook further postgraduate studies at the Biblical Institute in Rome. On receipt of an urgent request from Jerusalem for promising young scholars to work on the newly discovered Dead Sea Scrolls, he was ordained a priest and dispatched forthwith to Jerusalem. His subsequent work on the scrolls won him an international reputation. As Carlo had pointed out, Giuseppe was a prominent scholar. His translation of the scrolls into English was one of the first books on the topic that the youthful Marc had bought.

He remembered showing the book to his mother, expressing his longing to be able to read the scrolls in their original language. 'You probably will, one day,' she said quietly, as she took the book from him and turned it over to the biographical detail and thumbnail photo. Marc recalled that moment a few years later when, after announcing that he wished to study for the priesthood, his mother made the astonishing revelation that Joseph Ross was his granduncle. He could hardly believe it. By that time, the scroll scholar had become his icon. Why had the family virtually written such a prominent scholar out of its history? His mother knew little beyond the bare facts—Joseph had left the priesthood while working in Jerusalem, and married outside the Church. His parents had severed all contact with him, forbidding even the mention of his name. Marc expressed the opinion that such reaction was harsh. His mother was noncommittal, simply saying that it was the 1950s. Even in the context of a conservative Ireland, Marc thought that the family had overreacted, but he was viewing it from a later period—a perennial problem for historians. Joseph had simply dropped from family conversation and the mist that then began to gather around his name thickened as the generations passed—he almost slipped from memory. Marc suspected that his mother had volunteered the information as a final but futile attempt to change his mind about the priesthood. In spite of the criticism Catholic apologists levelled against his granduncle, Marc had high regard for his scholarship.

His mother's prediction proved true. Marc's reading of the scrolls in translation was so dedicated and intense that he was soon able to identify some of the ancient symbols and, gradually, to string them together in coherent phrases. Ancient Hebrew was not the usual plaything of modern youth, but that is exactly what the symbols were for Marc. He played with them until he forced them to surrender their meaning. This he found intensely satisfying. In secondary college, he concentrated on the classical languages of Latin and Greek, as well as Italian. In university, he perfected his knowledge of Hebrew, achieving a BA in Semitic languages, followed a year later by a degree in archaeology. He continued his studies in Rome and was ordained a priest there. At the time of his ordination, his bishop decided that he should continue his doctoral studies in Rome.

Marc's first sighting of his granduncle was in the library, chatting with Carlo as he checked in. His own meeting with Carlo in Saint Peter's Square occurred a few months later. Although he had never come face to face with him before, he readily recognized Joseph from photos and video clips on the Internet. Instinctively he wanted to approach him and introduce himself, but he feared a rebuff—after his family's rejection, such a response would be understandable. Joseph frequently visited the library, and Marc found himself choosing a reading position that afforded a clear view of his granduncle. However, this situation could not continue; he was concentrating on his relative to the detriment of his studies. Marc knew that any initiative would have to come from him since his granduncle knew nothing of his existence, so Carlo's offer to introduce them was timely and propitious.

4: The Time of Gaius Caligula

My Master was unique. At least, I thought so. His appearance, commanding but paradoxically docile, was sufficient to arrest one's attention. His speech, usually gentle but with the power to subdue the wind, was compelling and convincing. He taught me to seek God's purpose, and to pursue it faithfully, just as the water below our sanctuary follows the contours of the rocky wadi. That pursuit became my objective, my primary aim in life. However, it had not always been so...

I was born into a family rich in material goods. My parents, recognizing the importance of education, sent me, as a youth, to study in Alexandria. In spite of having a natural aptitude for learning, I could have done better. I squandered my time and their money on idle living. There I became acquainted with the teaching of Philo. His objective of harmonizing Greek philosophy and Jewish wisdom made little impact on me at the time. His principle Greek influence was Plato, but he also drew from Pythagorean and Stoic sources. As a faithful Jew, he believed that all wisdom comes from God, as revealed through Moses. As a result, he believed that Greek and Jewish wisdom could and should be reconcilable.

I also became acquainted with Apollos, a fellow student at the time, who followed the teaching of Philo with keen interest. His dedication to learning showed up my lack of commitment. My interest was superficial—it did not penetrate to my spirit. In spite of our differences, we became good friends. Apollos was a follower of the Therapeutae, a community of Jews living in exile in Alexandria who followed the Way—the New Covenant of our Teacher. A similar community following the same beliefs was living by the Salt Sea. At that time, I knew nothing of either community or of the New Covenant they espoused.

On my return home, I could discuss philosophy in Greek and Latin, and bamboozle simple Jews by demonstrating the relevance of Greek philosophy to Jewish scripture. It was a shallow veneer, a vulgar display of knowledge. In truth, being rich, I was dead, quite dead, to things of the spirit. Even my sister despaired of me. In desperation, she pleaded with a passing magus, a wise teacher from the community by the Salt Sea, to work his magic on her brother. Angered by her persistent pleading, his companions would dismiss her. To their surprise and further anger, the magus acceded to her plea.

I shall never forget that meeting. I was dead to the world, sleeping off the excesses of the night before, when a touch animated my spirit and resurrected me to conscious life. I groaned loudly, even angrily, thinking that my sister was trying to rouse me. Reluctantly, I opened my eyes, and the countenance that I beheld sent a message to my heart that brought serenity to my resurrected spirit. I grasped the hand stretched out to assist me and rose from the bed transformed, transported, in a heightened state of emotion that was new to me. I was in love. I begged him to stay with me, to teach me the way of life. He looked on me, and I sensed that he returned my love.

A week of instruction followed, culminating in my initiation into the ancient mysteries that theoretically I knew so much about, but whose spiritual significance I did not comprehend. From then on, my life was changed. A renewed man with a new name, I returned with my Master to live with the followers of the Way by the Salt Sea. There I spent two years studying our literature, contemplating our Teacher's New Covenant and exploring the developments that had occurred since his time.

Jesus, our Teacher of Righteousness, whose wisdom led us into the wilderness, was a man of faith and vision. His was an age of wrath.

No age is free from terror, as I should know, but his was more fraught than many; the very soul of the nation was at risk.

Seleucid power from the north had conquered our land, stolen our freedom and trampled on our customs, all of which steeled our resistance. The arrival of Antiochus IV Epiphanes, who profaned the Temple and corrupted the office of High Priest by selling it to unworthy and profane candidates, provoked open and organized hostility, led by the Maccabees.

On the accession of Antiochus as ruler of Syria, another Jesus, who preferred the Greek name, Jason, offered to buy the office of High Priest. This profanity resulted in the deposition of his brother, Onias, a truly worthy High Priest. While Jason was an unworthy, but legitimate candidate for the office of High Priest, Menelaus, who slyly outbid Jason for the position, was both unworthy and illegitimate. Antiochus found money more persuasive than legitimacy and installed Menelaus, who subsequently plundered the Temple treasury to meet the cost of his treachery. He also murdered his opponents, crimes he subsequently paid for at the hands of Antiochus's successor. Kings were also subject to the intrigues of rivals. A subsequent usurper established another illegitimate candidate, Alcimus, to the holy office. He did not live long to enjoy his coveted position. Then, out of the chaos, order emerged.

Our beloved Teacher, sublimely fitting and as legitimate as Zadok himself, followed in the holy office. His holy and happy tenure did not last. Corruption was so endemic in the country that holiness mattered little. Jonathan Maccabeus, forgetful of his noble past when he and his brothers fought to liberate the country, illegitimately accepted the role of High Priest and deposed our noble Teacher. Jonathan was self-seeking, pursuing his own aggrandizement. Followers of the Teacher called him *Apphus*, the Liar, and we wrote many harsh things about him under that title. We also referred to him as the Wicked Priest. However, he was not the only one. We met many liars and wicked priests during the years of our exile.

Shaking the dust of a decadent Jerusalem and profane Temple from his feet, our noble Teacher led his followers into the wilderness, to prepare the way of the Lord, as Isaiah, the prophet, had instructed. The Book of Isaiah is one of our favourite scrolls, copied repeatedly down through our years in the desert. There, our Teacher began to formulate his ideas for a New Covenant with God, as prophesied by Jeremiah: *I will make a New Covenant with Israel ... I will set my law within them, and write it on their hearts.* However, smarting at the Teacher's opposition, Jonathan pursued him to his place of refuge and killed him.

Since then, we have had many *episkopoi*. Before my Master, there was Johanan, called the Baptizer, whom Herod Antipas executed, fearing his influence with the people. Johanan could draw followers, like a flower draws bees, but he was no flower. Nor was he a reed shaking in the wind, as my Master used to say. He was as rugged as the wilderness that surrounded and shaped him. His headless body lies buried by our sanctuary.

Our Teacher's New Covenant did not envisage a break with the Temple, simply its renewal. He certainly would not countenance abandoning the Torah, the Law of God, handed down through Moses. Many developments have taken place in our understanding of the New Covenant since his time, but Saul's innovations were the boldest. He rejected the Torah, and insisted that new believers did not have to submit to circumcision or follow its dietary laws. He fumed against us for following such laws, telling us in so many words that since we were so attached to circumcision we should go the whole way and castrate ourselves. He was in open revolt with Peter, against whom he had some very harsh things to say. He set himself in opposition to my Master, asserting his special revelation. At one time, he roused the rabble in the Temple against my Master, who was lucky to escape with his life.

Another time, he caused a riot in Jerusalem when he brought foreigners into the Temple, the very thing we opposed.

Saul, a self-proclaimed Pharisee, had originally persecuted our followers for not obeying the Torah, since we had abandoned the Temple. Then on his way to Damascus, a code name for our place of exile, to 'discipline' us, he had some kind of revelation, which made him adopt our beliefs. Soon he began to threaten us again, this time for obeying the Torah. After his so-called revelation—we were never too convinced of his claim—he changed his name to Paul, and insisted that our Teacher's New Covenant freed us from the Torah, which he had previously upheld so vigorously. Paul's innovation met with opposition from my Master, who was a faithful follower of the Law. He even wrote a letter challenging Paul, calling him a 'foolish person', and telling him that a person is righteous by what he does, not by faith alone, as Paul asserted. However, Paul insisted on his view and shattered our previous unity. He and Peter were irreconcilable, and even his friend and colleague, Barnabas, parted from him.

His bold suggestions would have horrified our Teacher. Even my Master had difficulty with them, though he was beginning to relax his own attitude to Sabbath restrictions, much to the annoyance of the Pharisees. Neither our Teacher nor my Master could have imagined the beliefs that have developed among the various communities of believers since then. I expect that even Paul would be surprised, and perhaps not pleasantly. In my long life, I have come to realize that change is an undeniable and persistent feature of existence.

Even when Paul adopted our way of life, our followers did not trust him. We wrote harsh things about him, calling him a liar, a deceiver, which is probably true. He dissembled, and seemed proud of it. He claimed to be a Jew to the Jews and a Gentile to the Gentiles, in fact, all things to all people. Even after he became a follower of the Way, he still claimed to be a Pharisee. We should not have been surprised. What were we to expect from a member of the Herod family? Changing his name to Paul, he had hoped that a new name might hide an old allegiance. Some maintained that he was not even a Jew, which is also probably true since Herod and his descendants were Edomites. They tried to pass themselves off as Jews, by marrying into our Royal Family, but we knew where they came from and where their allegiance lay. It was with Rome.

5: Modern Rome

Marc worked diligently on his thesis in preparation for his meeting with his supervisor; time seemed to fly. The complexity of his topic had developed as his studies progressed. His head was reeling; his notebooks and hard drives filled with all of the possible scholarly explanations and interpretations he had first encountered as a young enthusiast and others that had arisen over the years. His own research—examining the scrolls to see if he could establish a link with the early Christian community—was adding to the confusion.

Most scholars dismissed a direct link; all would admit however that the scrolls reflect that period in Jewish history into which Jesus and Christianity were born. Marc was encouraged by some in the field, like José O'Callaghan, a Spanish Jesuit and biblical scholar, who believed they could establish a direct link. They argued that a fragment found in the seventh cave, catalogued as 7Q5, was a small fragment of the Gospel of Mark. That gave Marc hope that his relentless study of the texts would reveal a phrase, a word, or even a single symbol that would put the question beyond doubt. He was mindful of the fact that great minds had already tackled the question without success, but he was not discouraged. Marc would not claim to speak the biblical languages of ancient Hebrew, Aramaic or Greek as well as English, or indeed Italian, his present vernacular, but he could read them and more importantly interpret them with razor-sharp precision. The meaning of the words was important, but not as crucial as the shade of meaning in the mind of the author, which the bare word might have difficulty in always conveying. Marc had quiet confidence in his ability to decipher the various nuances of meaning that lay locked behind the ancient symbols. He could feel the rhythm of the writing and interpret not only the meaning but the melody behind the words. He thought of it as reading between the lines. In much the same way that the listener interprets music, he felt that the reader must decode words, especially symbols from a different age and in another language—the surface perception is not sufficient.

In pursuit of his objective, he was examining the Gospel of Mark for possible links with the scrolls. He chose this particular gospel because it was the earliest of the four gospels, as many, if not most, modern scholars would accept, though that opinion too has its critics. Mainstream scholars of scripture now generally accept that an unknown hand wrote this gospel around 70 CE—the same time that other unknown hands abandoned their writings before the advancing Roman Legions. The coincidence seemed uncanny, and Marc wondered if perhaps that crisis might have been instrumental in the writing of that gospel.

A more recent disputed find gave rise to the intriguing possibility that the author of the gospel attributed to Mark had written a second, more spiritual gospel for those initiated more fully into the Way. This latter document, known as 'Secret Mark', had been lost or outlawed. Like many other writings of the period, such as the Gnostic gospels, it did not accord with the orthodoxy emerging from the confused plethora of beliefs reflected in early Christian communities. However, in 1958, Morton Smith, professor of ancient history at Columbia University, was cataloguing the library of the monastery of Mar Saba near Jerusalem. There, he discovered a document claiming to be a copy of a letter of Clement of Alexandria, the second-century Father of the Church, which refers to 'Secret Mark' and quotes from it. Professor Smith photographed the letter and returned the original to the shelves of the library. Later, the original went missing. The find was the subject of heated debate. Although the photos did not carry the same weight as the original would, Marc with many other modern scholars was inclined to accept its authenticity.

In the early years, the Christian community was protean. There were as many opinions as to what was authentic Christianity as there are today. Then, no Mormons, Seventh Day Adventists, Jehovah Witnesses, Pentecostals, Methodists, or other familiar evangelists of today travelled around the ancient Eastern Mediterranean from Rome to Alexandria to Jerusalem preaching their brand of Christianity. However, Adoptionists, Arians, Gnostics, Montanists, Marcionites and others did. Just as is the case today among warring evangelists, they all claimed to be followers of the Christ, but preached doctrines remarkably at variance with each other.

The range of beliefs held by members of the different groups was vast: Jesus was human, not divine; divine, not human, and every possible degree of variation in between. As is evident from the letters of Paul, the Christian communities of the first century were as fractured as the Judaism reflected in the scrolls and from which it developed. Marc wondered how Sadducees, Pharisees and Essenes could belong to the same body of faith since they were at great variance with each other. The Sadducees did not believe in an afterlife, resurrection or the spirit world. If Jesus had been a Sadducee, resurrection would not have entered into his ideology; of course, according to some modern commentators, it did not!

A major shift occurred in the fortunes of the Christian Church when the fourth-century emperor, Constantine, began to favour it. The story goes that before a major battle that would determine his fate, he saw a cruciform sign in the sky and a voice assured him of victory if his army fought under that symbol. The reality was probably much more political. He wanted a united empire and decided that the best way to accomplish that was with a united religion. However, since Christianity was not united, he set about unifying it. He convened the First Council of Nicaea in 325 to thrash out the differences that existed between the various groups, and orthodoxy was born. With the power of the state behind it, one group, Constantine's group, was able to silence the rest. The Church that began to emerge from the chaos of the early Christian centuries was all-powerful, thanks to its adoption by Constantine. Since the victors invariably write the historical accounts, soon little remained of the unorthodox doctrines. The little we knew of them had come from the polemic of early Christian writers until the chance discovery of the Nag Hammadi documents in the Egyptian desert in 1945 revealed the extent and variety of the doctrines that existed in the early Christian world.

Marc was becoming restless at his desk. His head was spinning from the endless scholarly questions and possible answers on offer … and the silence. Silence, usually so conducive to study, was smothering him. The silence of a convent is more enervating than the silence of a library. He so wanted to get back to that more stimulating ambience, to further his research, but perhaps Carlo's presence there was the main attraction.

He had to drag his thoughts back to his topic. He was convinced that Jesus and his followers must have had contact with the group behind the writing of the scrolls. It was quite impossible to imagine that two important religious groups in such a small geographical area could have co-existed without exchanging ideas. Marc was convinced that a closer examination of the scrolls and the New Testament would reveal certain links between them.

Certainly, the New Testament does not mention Essenes, but equally the scrolls do not refer to Jesus or his followers. However, some of the terms used in the scrolls to identify their adherents are: Sons of Light; the Poor; Followers of the Way. The New Testament uses similar designations to identify its own followers. He thought it telling that the 'Poor Ones' was the name associated with the followers of James in Jerusalem. All of these similarities, sufficient for Carlo, were not scholarly proofs. As he pursued his research, Marc was becoming more and more convinced that a greater closeness existed between the two groups than a nod of the head as they passed each other on the dusty roads of Judea. Moreover, where had Jesus spent the years prior to his public ministry when the gospels introduce him as an acknowledged teacher? No offence to carpenters intended, but is a workshop the obvious school for docents? Of course, some scholars hold that Jesus was uneducated, unable to read or write. The conflicting images of Jesus that emerge from scholarly investigation of the gospels confused Marc, and sometimes, in their wake, brought a flutter of doubt to upset his tranquil faith.

In a fragment entitled 4Q246, the scrolls refer to a coming Son of God, saying: 'He will be called great, Son of the Most High; His kingdom will be everlasting; He will judge the earth in truth'. An unknown hand had written those words a hundred years before another anonymous scribe, now referred to as Luke, had heralded the annunciation in very similar terms. Marc thought this remarkable, and unlikely to be mere coincidence.

Jesus and his followers were Jews, immersed in the atmosphere of first-century Judaism. They were part of the culture of the day, so they must have been members of one or other of the contemporary religious groups. It would be difficult to imagine Jesus a Pharisee considering the way he denounced their many failings. Identification with Sadducees also seemed remote, as he did not share their spirituality. What was left? It appeared more likely that he was an Essene, at least spiritually— Jesus's attitude to the Temple was as ambivalent as theirs. There was no doubt in Marc's mind. Instinctively, he favoured Carlo's conclusion that one group grew organically from the other. If only he could find irrefutable proof that would end the controversy.

Sophia

'Faith is hard to swallow. I have great difficulty with the Resurrection. It is not my only problem with faith, of course, but it is somewhat pivotal. Birth is all too real, especially for a woman, but rebirth borders on the nonsensical.'

43

The statement came with the frankness of a thoroughly modern young woman. It was Marc's face-to-face introduction to Sister Sophia—he had been introduced to the community in general on his arrival. The young nun was also a medical doctor and consequently could pronounce with authority on matters medical, including birth. In addition, since modern nuns received courses in theology, Sophia was in a position to probe the problem of resurrection from both a medical and theological perspective and put forward convincing arguments.

Like Sophia, Marc was young and, he hoped, frank and modern. He was therefore willing to admit, to himself at least, that she had a point. Resurrection was a problem—a continuing challenge to faith. Not just Sophia's, it was also his, but he had resolved it by taking it *cum grano salis*! At least, up to the time of their meeting.

Marc did not like the role of spiritual director, not because it interrupted his work on his thesis, he just felt incompetent. He was more at ease divining the meaning of ancient texts than erecting signposts for someone else's spiritual journey. He sometimes wondered if perhaps he should have been simply an academic without the trappings of priesthood. Consequently, he was delighted to see the position of spiritual director retained, de facto, by an old retired priest who had previously been chaplain to the community and who retained the respect and confidence of the Sisters. On Marc's appointment, the Mother Superior who, in post-Vatican II fervour, had shed her title with the original cumbersome habit, explained the status quo to him as adroitly as possible. She feared that he might feel slighted to see the nuns forsaking their newly appointed chaplain to seek elsewhere for their spiritual roadmap to perfection. He assured her that he understood perfectly, without letting her see his exhalation of relief that accompanied her explanation.

However, in these days of declining numbers, Sister Sophia had been a recent and rare addition to the community and, consequently, highly treasured. She, like Pharaoh of old who 'knew not Joseph', did not know the older chaplain and opted to entrust her spiritual wellbeing into the hesitant hands of the younger priest. Marc soon discovered that he was ill prepared to deal with the range of female emotions, physical and spiritual, in ferment within the bosom of this young, energetic and attractive woman.

The issues she elaborated on with beguiling honesty and with what Marc could only perceive as gender-related complexity were his also. Issues long since put to rest, he believed, by accepting that faith was in essence inscrutable. Tertullian, the acclaimed second-century Father of the Church, wrote in *De Carne Christi* that the Resurrection was absurd. Its absurdity was the reason he believed. It was not much of a reason— in fact, it was anti-reason—but it is all there is, in spite of the mental gymnastics of some renowned scholars in making it appear reasonable. You simply accepted it and got on with life. Marc found it telling that the Gospel of Mark, in its original form at least, as far as that can be determined two thousand years after the initial quill stroke, has no resurrection appearances. It simply ends with an empty tomb. There could be many reasons for an empty tomb, as critics are eager to point out.

He was undoubtedly naive, but Marc thought that an explanation which brought quietude to his brooding Celtic male consciousness would work equally well on the exuberant, volatile psyche of an Italian female. When he tried to propose his solution or resolution to Sister Sophia, she would have none of it. 'God gave us the capacity to reason. Unique in nature,' she insisted. 'Is it logical to think that He would will us to suspend its function? If Tertullian,' she announced with vigour, 'was satisfied with such non-sense, I am not. Besides,' she added with controlled feminine irritation, 'I have no confidence in the facile meanderings of such a pathetic misogynist.'

Misogyny is a commonly used word; misandry is not. That fact speaks for itself. Tertullian was not an exception in his day, nor would he be in today's society. Sophia's use of the word forced Marc to reflect on his own attitude. Was he projecting a caring, understand attitude? Was it natural, not forced? Respect for another is not a consequence of

45

sexual attraction alone. Some in the field of human behaviour suggest that sex is at the root of discrimination. Marc noted and admired her beauty, but it did not threaten him as Carlo's did. He would not spend the night wondering what to do about Sophia as he did about Carlo, which under the circumstances was a good thing.

Sister Sophia's outburst, though contained, was another of those increasingly frequent moments that unsettled some core value in the inaccessible vaults of Marc's consciousness. At that moment, however, he was more concerned with Sister Sophia than with himself. He felt increasingly that he was waging a losing battle in this campaign—he hoped he would not lose the war. He had enough human vanity to fear that blame would accrue to him if the community lost this particular member—she was their hope into an uncertain future. Consequently, they battled, like gladiators of old, one for the pre-eminence of reason in the pursuit of faith, the other for the Augustinian concept of faith seeking reason. However, he was learning. After Tertullian, he did not dare raise the name of Augustine, who had mesmerized the theological world by conjuring up, from thin air, the concept of Original Sin and woman's deplorable involvement in not only its inception in the Garden of Eden, but also in its ongoing transmission, as child-bearers. The name Augustine would not sit well with Sophia's passionate feminism.

With Carlo and Sophia, Marc wondered if ambivalence towards the Church and faith might be a cultural phenomenon—perhaps all Romans displayed it. In any case, the result was that together they were causing Marc's conveniently hibernating problems with faith, Church and religion to stir.

Monsignore

Marc's mood was sombre as he made his way towards the Vatican Library to the office of Monsignore Santino Martini, the supervisor guiding his doctoral work. He was apprehensive about the meeting—a lot depended on it. The man in question was difficult, not one of his favourite lecturers. Mark feared that he might not accept his preferred

46

topic. He often spoke critically in class of the attention paid to the Dead Sea Scrolls. Still, he reasoned, it was down to himself. If his work was good, it would compel his director's approval.

The Vatican had settled back into normal mode after the election. As he crossed Saint Peter's Square, Marc glanced up at the papal apartments and imagined the pontiff at his desk advancing, with all the energy of a 'new broom', the spiritual concerns of the Catholic Church and the civic business of the Vatican State. Marc wondered which would take precedence in the new Pope's mind. Of old, popes were more warlords, leading their papal armies, than pastors.

Weeks had passed since the papal election and Marc's meeting with Carlo. He had worked conscientiously during that time ordering his research into an outline that would sway his director, but he missed seeing Carlo. That was the nub of the problem—Carlo was a distraction. He would not be pleased with such a label, and Marc willingly admitted that he was a pleasant diversion. His various facial expressions— enticing, challenging, appealing, and joking—would intrude agreeably, but detract, nevertheless, from Marc's concentration. He had experienced similar problems before. However, this time the charm of his new friend threatened not only his single-mindedness. Carlo had more than charm, he had sexual magnetism and that could endanger Marc's vocation. He had a year to work on his thesis. He would have to deal with the distraction, if he had any chance of success with his demanding director. Dealing with the erotic appeal of Carlo would be another, more difficult, matter.

The monsignore was one of Marc's professors at the Pontifical Biblical Institute, founded by Pope Pius X in 1909 as 'a centre of higher studies for Sacred Scripture in the city of Rome and of all related studies according to the spirit of the Catholic Church'. The declared aims of the college troubled Marc. Surely, he thought, a university pursues knowledge through intellectual means, wherever it leads. He, along with many others, had mixed feeling about Pius, whose adamant refusal to promote the critical and scientific study of the Bible stifled Catholic

47

scholarship in that field for generations. Pius seemed to put Church before truth. To be fair, he supposed that from the Pope's point of view the two were synonymous. As a dedicated Catholic, Marc shared that same conviction, but was willing to put his confidence to the test by investigation. He often wondered what he would do if he discovered a dichotomy between the two. However, he put the thought from his mind—there could be no conflict between Truth and Church Teaching—Catholic faith was in accord with reason.

He felt that Sophia would not acquiesce so easily. That in turn caused him to wonder if faith was simply a form of acquiescence. The thought reminded him again of Tertullian. Was Marc's solution to the mystery of the Resurrection simply to acquiesce? He shook his head as if to rid himself of the thought. Carlo and Sophia were both, in their respective ways, subverting his singularity of purpose. Sophia, the questioning believer, was forcing Marc to rethink his ready acceptance of the mysteries of faith. Though provocative, it was of a different quality from that posed by Carlo. The handsome, muscular, smiling atheist stimulated in Marc more than a questioning mind. Carlo's presence, even his absence, stirred Marc's body in a way that would lead inevitably either to surrender to the lure of love, or rejection of the lover. Both were unthinkable. Even as he walked towards this important meeting with his professor, his mind was on meeting Carlo afterwards.

It was early, but queues were already forming for the Vatican Museum. It would be nice to be a tourist for the day, he thought, as he sat down on a nearby bench to force himself to concentrate on his work. His supervisor was certainly acquainted with that other Jesuit with the Spanish—Irish name, José O'Callaghan Martinez. He was Marc's trump card. His mentor could hardly dismiss the findings of a fellow Jesuit and former professor at the Biblical Institute, who suggested that the scroll fragment 7Q5 might be from the Gospel of Mark. That idea had ignited Marc's initial interest in exploring a possible link between Qumran and Christianity.

The Jesuit, a renowned papyrologist, had been a professor with the Biblical Institute from 1971 (he made his controversial suggestion in 1972) to his retirement in 1992. He died in 2001. His opinion, if proven, would establish an earlier date for Mark's gospel as well as raising the intriguing possibility that other Greek fragments from the same cave might also be from Mark—Professor O'Callaghan Martinez had already proposed such a possibility. All of which tied in very well with Marc's hypothesis that there was a direct link between Qumran, Jesus and the burgeoning Christian community. He hoped that the suggestion posed by Professor O'Callaghan Martinez would persuade his director to accept his topic. He was satisfied that he had done as much as was reasonable in preparing his outline, so he got up and continued on his way.

In addition to his professorial post, Monsignore Martini was Prefect of the Vatican Library. His apartments were adjacent to the Library and it was there that he had invited Marc to meet with him to discuss his thesis. In his fifties, he was an imposing man in the mould of Pope Pius XII with features not unlike those of that wartime pontiff. Whatever his inner personality might have been, his exterior was cold, calculating and austere. He carried his purple-trimmed black cassock with grace, the purple sash encircling a slender waist. The face was Roman, no doubt sculpted by vagrant imperial genes, and uncannily similar to many imperial profiles that grace ancient coins.

The Biblical Institute and the Gregorian University were Jesuit-run academies and consequently most of the professors were members of that order. Marc was admitted to the professor's office by a young cleric. His supervisor's welcoming smile was so fragile it was in danger of cracking.

'Welcome, Father. I see you have something for me.' He took the document from Marc's outstretched hand and indicated a chair. The smile vanished as his keen, unaided eyes scanned the pages. Marc looked away anxiously. 'I am not happy with your choice of topic.' The cold unqualified statement deflated Marc. 'Surely all major scholars have abandoned the idea of a connection between the Qumran community and Jesus or the early Christian community.'

'That is true, Monsignore, but Professor O'Callaghan Martinez would be a notable exception,' suggested Marc politely. There were others, but Marc though it wiser to refer to the orthodox exceptions.

'Hmm,' murmured his tutor, as if about to contest Marc's suggestion. 'The professor was an excellent scholar, of course.' The softer tone encouraged Marc. 'However, his view, as you point out, is an exception. I fear that you will find little of substance to back up your thesis. Would you not consider another topic better served to reflect glory on the Church?'

'Surely the pursuit of truth in whatever area can only serve the Church.'

'Hmm,' purred the monsignore again, as if not totally in agreement with Marc's statement, but at a loss as to how he might challenge it. 'Perhaps, in a general sense,' he finally conceded. 'However, I am still not convinced. In fact, I am not an admirer of the Dead Sea Scrolls. I believe their historical value inflated. They have been used, as you know well, by many crackpots, including Ross, your fellow countryman, to bring discredit on the Church.' He looked searchingly at Marc. 'You are not going to be another crackpot, are you?'

His look and his question unnerved Marc. The reference to his 'fellow countryman' left him reeling, if only his mentor knew the full extent of their relationship. However, in spite of accelerated heartbeat and trembling legs, conveniently hidden beneath his cassock, he persevered. 'That is surely a reason for pursuing our study of the scrolls. We must continue analysing them repeatedly until the undeniable truth regarding them is established. I do not expect my work to be definitive, but I hope it might prove useful in advancing our understanding of the scrolls. After all, scholars have been studying the canonical gospels for two thousand years.'

'I hope you are not equating the two.'

'Certainly not, Monsignore, I am just pointing out that the study of ancient documents is ongoing. We can never assume that we have exhausted their meaning.'

'The results of such scholarly investigations are often unfortunate, to say the least. I think that the saintly Pius X was very wise to curb the zeal of scholars in investigating the Word of God.'

'Certainly, the Word of God needs no probing,' replied Marc diplomatically. 'It is the human expression through which God's Word is conveyed that requires scrutiny. You have taught us as much in your lectures. After all, where would the Church be without her scholars, such as you, Monsignore?'

The ghost of a smile haunted his lips. 'I am hardly a Church luminary,' he replied, the natural urge for recognition battling contrived virtue. Marc knew that he had scored. 'I suppose, for a doctoral dissertation the topic itself is not that important' he continued. 'Its purpose is to help us to evaluate the intellectual and investigative ability of the candidate. Of course, contributing to the eminence of the Church would be a bonus. You could do that, of course, by definitively disproving your thesis.' A thin smile accompanied his last statement.

Playing on his advantage, Marc posed the question tentatively. 'Would you think that a visit to Qumran to study the scrolls *in situ*, as it were, would be advantageous?' He did not expect a positive reply, however appeased his director might be, but because of his long-standing desire, he felt compelled to ask.

Ever since that first televised documentary, he had longed to visit the sites of the finds. He yearned to see and investigate the ancient caves and wander through the ruins of Qumran. While his peers were fighting intergalactic wars with the Jedi, Marc's imagination was probing the dusty caves and the crumbling ruins of Qumran with Professor Joseph Ross, long before he knew he was a relative.

'I should think not,' replied his mentor decisively. 'The scrolls are well documented. They are readily available in hard copy and on the Internet. Going to the site would add nothing to your investigations, and being such a volatile area, could well put your life in jeopardy.' He looked up at Marc, his gaze implacable, as if to forestall further discussion of the matter. Marc inclined his head in submission, glad at least that his chosen topic had survived his director's negativity. 'We should meet regularly now. Shall we say on the last Saturday of every month at this time?' He handed back Marc's papers with the same fragile smile that had opened the meeting. 'I look forward to your findings, but keep in mind that all our efforts should be directed to the glory of the Church.'

Meeting Giuseppe

Marc left the monsignore's study with that final admonition pulsating annoyingly, like the drip of a tap, through his brain; it did not sit well with him. It was another of those refrains, oft repeated as gospel, which irritated him. Was his faith so shaky—built on a quagmire as Carlo suggested—that such remarks unsettled him? The thought reminded him of Carlo and the prospect of meeting him after a couple of weeks sent a flutter of pleasure through him. However, disquiet shaded his delight. He was in dangerous territory. He knew it, but the lure of the charismatic Carlo was strong. He even found his provocative remarks strangely engaging. However, where would it lead? As he approached the reception desk, he found Carlo in conversation ... with Joseph Ross.

It reminded Marc that the first time he had seen his granduncle, they were similarly engaged. There seemed to be a bond between them that went beyond the professional. He paused, and was about to check in with another member of staff when Carlo saw him and beckoned him over. He felt a quiver of anticipation. He was unsure whether the flush he experienced was generated by the presence of Carlo or at the prospect of meeting his relative. A glow radiated from Carlo. Marc wondered if, like beauty, the glow resided in his own eye, or if perhaps his presence had sparked something in Carlo. He turned his attention to his granduncle, who was gazing expectantly in his direction. He presumed that Carlo had mentioned his interest in the scrolls and consequently his interest in Joseph Ross, or Giuseppe as Carlo referred to him. He could forgive the impatience he thought reflected in the professor's eyes— there must be many aspiring scholastics seeking to interview him. However, Marc's interest was much more than academic, which added another dimension to the emotions that collided within him. He wanted to express his appreciation for his writings that had sustained his fascination with the scrolls. He also wanted to make amends for the harsh treatment meted out by a conservative family. Settling old scores might amount to nothing more than an expression of regret on his part, but he felt that this, in itself, was important. Of course, his relative might simply reject him and his apology. Certainly, if the hurt inflicted by the family went deep enough, he might retaliate by meting out a reciprocal punishment. However, although the man he approached did not radiate vindictiveness, Marc braced himself.

'Marco, I would like to introduce Professor Rossi ... Mi scusi, Professor Ross.'

On closer inspection, the ancient eyes exhibited only patient interest in this intrusive young academic. 'I am very happy to meet you Professor,' said Marc. 'I too am Irish. I expect Carlo told you that I am preparing a thesis on the Dead Sea Scrolls. I admire your work ... on the scrolls,' he added, as a rather cumbersome exclusion of his more contentious writings. He bit his tongue and hoped that his slip passed unnoticed.

It did not. The shadow of a smile played on the old man's lips. '*Go raibh míle maith agat*,' he said in fluent Irish, his smile broadening. His eyes, resting on Marc for a moment, had a magnetism that blew the young cleric away. The professor then turned to Carlo, 'I was thanking Marco for his kind words,' he explained, concerned to keep Carlo in their conversation. Then leaning towards Marc, he said, 'I hope you don't mind me calling you Marco.'

Few words had been exchanged, but it was sufficient to show that the man had charm. Marc had already suspected as much from his writings. It was difficult to make a scientific tract 'charming', but Joseph

Ross managed it. He was far from the 'crackpot' his supervisor had denounced, and Marc was now glad that Carlo had initiated the meeting. He was an impressive person. It was difficult to explain—a few words in Irish, an enchanting smile, an awareness of others—all combined to lay charisma bare. Even his body radiated magnetism. He was certainly old, but age did not define him. He had a look of serenity that sometimes comes with age, if one is lucky enough to escape the abstracted look of dementia. He was tall, but his body was frail, so frail that he seemed more spirit than matter. His lined face reminded Marc of a battlefield. The image was plausible, as intellectual warfare must have raged across those deep, torturous trenches. His eyes of indigo indicated a final accord with whatever conflicts had arisen in the course of scholarly scuffles. Marc felt confident that he harboured no bitterness towards his family either, so broaching the subject of their relationship seemed less fraught.

'I have been involved with the scrolls for many years. If I can help you with your thesis, I would be happy to do so.'

'I would hesitate to burden you, Professor, but I would like to meet you again.' Marc's thoughts were on reconciliation more than studies.

'It would be a pleasure, Marco. I presume you have one of these contraptions,' he said pulling out a smart phone. 'If you give me your number, I will send you mine.' Marc obliged. 'My time is my own now, but I can remember the pressure of student life. I will be able to accommodate myself to your busy schedule, if you should wish to discuss your work.' He smiled at Marc and Carlo, picked up his books and made for the reading room.

'What a gentle man,' said Marc as he handed his reader's pass to Carlo.

'He likes you,' said Carlo.

'You think so?'

'Of course, you don't think he gives his phone number to everyone he meets. Even I never got it, and he likes me too,' concluded Carlo with a winning grin.

54

'I have a reason, other than studies, for wishing to talk to him,' confided Marc.

'Yes?' Carlo was all ears.

'You know that he is Irish. He is also my granduncle.'

Carlo's eyes popped in surprise. 'Your uncle does not seem to know you.'

'Granduncle,' corrected Marc.

'Whatever! How come he did not recognize you?'

'It's a long story. I need to talk to him—to tell him who I am ... and more. I will tell you about it sometime.'

'How about over lunch? Where have you been for the past few weeks?'

'Working! Preparing an outline for my supervisor. I have just come from discussing it with him.'

'Who is he?'

'Monsignore Martini.'

'Poor you!'

'You know him?'

'Of course! He is one of my bosses here—a real stickler.'

'Then you know why I had to work hard.'

'OK! Explanation accepted. Now, how about lunch?'

Marc knew that he should be keeping a rein on their relationship, but figured that lunch in a public place was hardly a recipe for disaster. He agreed with a nod and a smile and headed for the reading room.

Apology

Marc enjoyed research; he had a taste for it. As kitchen aromas were to one's appetite, the library ambience was to Marc's hunger for study. Now, however, it failed to work its magic of capturing his attention and keeping it focused on the subject at hand. Too many plots, ancient and contemporary, competed for his attention; current concerns dulled the older voices. After a few hours of battling to exclude Carlo and his granduncle from his mind by concentrating on the ancient symbols, he decided to abandon the effort. Damn it! He may as well admit it—he was also looking forward to an hour with Carlo. He gathered up the books and made his way towards the reception desk.

'Can you give me a few minutes?' asked Carlo apologetically.

Marc nodded and laid his volumes on the counter. As he waited, his granduncle approached with his armful of folios.

'We need a rest from books for a while,' he commented, as Carlo relieved him of his burden. 'Would you care to join me for lunch, Marco? We could discuss your thesis, or not, as you wish.'

'Thank you, Professor,' he stammered in reply to the welcome but unexpected invitation. He looked questioningly at Carlo.

Noticing the hesitation and the look, the older man continued: 'If you are free, Carlo, perhaps you would care to join us.'

Now, it was Carlo's turn to look confused and uncertain. Normally, he would have been eager to accept, but he knew that Marc had private issues to resolve with his granduncle, and this might be a good opportunity to do so. 'Thank you, Professor, but I won't be able to get away for about an hour; another time, perhaps.'

Marc threw him a grateful look, as he left with the professor. A short while later, they were seated, al fresco, at a nearby restaurant. A large green parasol protected them from the sun, which was warm for April. The professor looked cool in a light summer jacket, but Marc felt prickly and hot in his cassock. A waiter poured chilled white wine into their glasses and left to fulfil their order.

'April in Ireland does not usually lend itself to open-air eating,' said Giuseppe. He noticed his companion's discomfort and hoped that reflecting on a cooler ambiance might contrive to make the Roman atmosphere feel fresher.

'If we had days like this in summer, we would count ourselves lucky,' replied Marc. 'Have you returned to Ireland recently, Professor?' he continued, undecided as to his approach. He wanted to prepare the ground for his disclosure.

'No!' he answered. 'I have not been back for many years.' He paused and reached for his glass. The green of the sunshade coloured the wine and the condensation slipped down the side of the glass in lime-coloured droplets. 'I have received requests to lecture from all over the world, but never from my homeland. I suppose that was understandable in the Ireland of the past. Perhaps it would be different now, if I were still involved in the lecture circuit.'

'Do you have any family in Ireland now?' Marc posed the question tentatively—he was hoping to create an opening into which he might conveniently drop the news of their relationship.

'I don't know.' The glow seemed to fade from the old man's eyes, as he looked at Marc. He continued with a sadness that was all too evident: 'That may seem strange, but it is the truth.'

Marc was pained at forcing the man to relive such hurtful experiences. 'I am sorry, Professor. I did not intend to open old wounds.'

He looked kindly at Marc. 'It is my fault, Marco, I should not be so sensitive—it was a long time ago. My views and my life did not match my family's expectations, at least, not back then; I believe things are changing now. You probably know something of my life from your reading, especially as a student of the scrolls. In modern times, anyone with even a limited public image is subjected to considerable scrutiny.'

Marc seized the opportunity. 'I am aware of more than you might imagine,' he began quietly. 'I know, for instance, that you are my granduncle—my grandmother's brother.'

The old man was stunned and Marc feared that his revelation might have been too sudden. Perhaps he should have chatted around the subject for longer before making the relationship known. The waiter arrived with salads, creating a lull in the conversation, and giving his granduncle time to adjust to the news. The waiter fussed around them for a few minutes, then left with a gracious '*Prego*'. The shocked stare softened into a look of curiosity. The old man searched Marc's features, as if trying to find proof, written in the curve of his chin or the colour of his eyes, of the relationship he had just announced. A geological age seemed to pass, but in fact, it was little more than a normal gap in conversation.

'Anna's grandson,' he said, as if he had found the validation he sought.

'Yes,' confirmed Marc softly, though no affirmation was necessary—Joseph had only one sister and one brother.

'Marco, I cannot express how happy I am to meet you.' The expression of contentment that lit up his face endorsed his statement. 'Is Anna still alive?'

'I'm sorry, no. She died about ten years ago.'

'I see,' he said softly. 'She was the eldest, and I, though younger, have passed the normal finishing line. My brother was younger. Is he still alive?'

'Uncle James died in his forties, without marrying.'

'So, only Anna carried the family into the future. Reflecting on family history is a fraught activity —a bitter-sweet venture.'

'Professor, I have been looking forward to this meeting to express my sorrow at the way the family treated you and, as far as I can, to make amends.'

His granduncle looked at him kindly, 'Marco, it was a long time ago and you certainly had no part in it. My family's reaction saddened me more than it hurt me, but I thank you for your kindness. By the way, call me Giuseppe—Carlo does. In Rome do as the Romans,' he added with a winning smile.

They continued chatting about the family—as they nibbled the salads and sipped the wine—Marc filling in the gaps for Giuseppe, and bringing him up to date regarding Marc's own family. They were drinking coffees when they finally got around to studies.

'Now, tell me about yourself, Marco. What is the topic of your thesis?'

'I am investigating the possibility of a link between the people of the scrolls and Christianity.'

'That is an interesting theme, and one that needs addressing.'

'My moderator disagrees. He thinks that I might have chosen a more … worthwhile topic.'

Giuseppe's gaze rested on Marc, but he was viewing his own life. 'I see,' he said. 'Who is supervising your work?'

'Monsignore Martini,' Marc replied, as if naming his executioner rather that his research guide.

'I think it is a very pertinent topic. Perhaps your moderator thinks it might be too pertinent. He is, I believe, the Prefect of the Vatican Library.' His granduncle made the final comment as if it had significance beyond the obvious.

'He says that the question is settled.' Marc commented. 'Most scholars would agree with him that there was no connection, apart from the obvious—they were contemporaries.'

'It is true that many scholars discount any connection between the Qumran community and Christianity, but they are, in the main, committed Christians, anxious to maintain, however instinctively, the unique character of the Jesus message. Others, without any such affiliation, would be more open to the possibility of Qumran influence on the emergence of what we now call Primitive Christianity.'

'Still, those against are in the majority.'

'Majorities may win elections, but the lone voice is often the herald of truth.' The professor was pensive as he made his comment. 'Marco, I would like to show you my library. I have a lot of material that might prove useful to your research. Would you be interested?'

'Of course, Giuseppe, I would be very eager to study anything you consider relevant.'

'Would Sunday be inconvenient for you? You probably have duties.'

'I say Mass for the community early in the morning. Time is my own after that.'

'I rise early also, so come over whenever you like. I will be at home. Do you know where I live?'

'Yes,' replied Marc, with a hint of guilt. He then smiled. 'I must confess that I was curious about my famous granduncle, so I followed you once.'

An amused twinkle lit up his face and Giuseppe embraced his grandnephew as they prepared to part. 'Marco, I am so happy to have met you, and happier still to have found a grandnephew. I look forward to Sunday.'

Pleased with the outcome of the long-anticipated meeting, Marc watched as his granduncle departed in the direction of Campo de' Fiori.

Eureka Effect

After his lunch with Giuseppe, Marc returned to the library to thank Carlo for standing aside. 'It gave me the space to open up to Giuseppe,' he added gratefully.

'You owe me,' countered Carlo.

'Perhaps we could have lunch tomorrow.' suggested Marc.

'It's Saturday' replied Carlo. 'Luigi and I plan to go to the beach. Care to join us?' he added invitingly.

'I'm not much of a beach person,' replied Marc. 'I would not want to intrude.'

'You could do with a touch of sun,' commented Carlo critically contemplating his complexion.

'It's too early in the year to think of tanning.'

'Just what your tender skin needs—gentle and frequent. Also, you have to meet Luigi. You will like him, and he you.'

Certainly, Luigi's unusual career choices—Swiss Guard and would-be opera singer—intrigued Marc. He would like to meet the person that harboured such ambitions. However, his old problem with socializing stood in the way.

'Another time, perhaps,' he offered by way of excuse.

'Come on,' said Carlo encouragingly. 'You will enjoy it. Besides, you owe me. Remember?'

Marc agreed with the usual conflict of emotions—delight and apprehension—that attended any decision concerning Carlo. He then returned to his room in the convent anxious to continue his research. Handwritten notebooks and a profusion of print-outs littered his desk. In spite of the mountain of material, he was not happy. He tried to convince himself that it was still early days, but he was impatient. As of yet, no clinching fact, no *coup de grâce*, emerged from the mound of research to establish his thesis beyond doubt. Considering the human condition, perhaps there never was absolute certainty when re-evaluating the past. Prevailing influences distort the picture in each successive age. It is also possible that his supervisor might be right—you cannot prove a non-event. On the other hand, does absence of evidence indicate evidence of absence? He was tapping aimlessly on his keyboard, hoping that the action might trigger a flash of insight. It was not a recognized scholarly method, so he stopped and laid his head on his arm on the desk and mentally reviewed his work. He tried to visualize the ancient scribes working on their scrolls in the desert retreat. Had they experienced frustration and discouragement, if their work was not progressing well? From a distance, their lives of quiet industry seemed serene and trouble free, but that vision is far from the reality, as we know from history—the Roman Legions were breathing fire and vengeance on them, the people of an insignificant province, for defying the mighty power of Rome. If only he could penetrate the layered mists of time and see with greater clarity into their daily lives and read their minds as well as their scrolls.

6: The Time of Claudius

My years of peaceful reflection on our turbulent history ended when my Master suggested that I should further my education. He was a true Jew, but believed, like Philo, that all genuine seekers are one. He prevailed upon me to go to Antioch to study the Greek spiritual way. There, I studied with Apollonius of Tyana, a mystic and spiritual tutor, who followed the teaching of Pythagoras and consequently had much in common with Philo, the Jew, whose writings I had already studied in Alexandria. Apollonius abhorred animal sacrifice, and his reverence for all life would not allow him to kill animals even for food. He would be horrified to witness the Jerusalem Temple at festival times—it resembled a slaughterhouse more than a place of worship, rivers of blood flowed from the altar of sacrifice. I could identify with his convictions, as our community by the Salt Sea had rejected the Temple and its animal sacrifices. Following the teaching of Pythagoras, who developed the idea in Egypt, Apollonius taught that God is the most beautiful being and, as pure mind, is attainable only by our mind. He convinced me that prayer and sacrifice are meaningless instruments in our quest for God. He would have been unimpressed by Paul's emphasis on sacrifice.

To my great delight, I was there reacquainted with Apollos, my friend from Alexandria. He had to get used to my new name and my new, more spiritual, outlook. Consequently, I was able to share more fully in his deep insights and discuss with him at a more profound and experiential level than my former shallowness had allowed. Our friendship became more firmly rooted during that time. He also told me of his confrontation with Paul. The same Paul who had chastised our followers for not following the Torah, and later castigated us for following it too closely. After his vision, Paul stayed at the sanctuary by the Salt Sea for some time, and then set off to preach the Way according to his declared revelation. He preached his own wisdom whereas Apollos, true to Philo, based his understanding of the New Covenant on Jewish Wisdom literature. Consequently, he rejected Paul's idea of a suffering, sacrificial Messiah. Apollos wandered into Paul's territory and, much to the latter's alarm, proved very successful with the people of Corinth.

Paul undoubtedly felt intimidated by Apollos, who was tall and magisterial-looking. His neck, like a Grecian column, seemed designed specifically for the admirable head it supported. He had long yellow hair and startling green eyes, like the god Apollo, which seemed to blaze forth his profound mysticism. His words were as golden as his skin. Paul, on the other hand, was dark and squat, and his appearance inconsequential. He wrote well, which probably accounts for his frequent use of that medium, but by his own admission, he was a poor speaker. Playing on his advantage, he wrote a diplomatically worded letter to the Corinthians, but his ire, accusing Apollos of preaching worldly wisdom, was detectible behind the smooth words. The truth was that Apollos based his preaching on sacred scriptures, whereas Paul drew his out of thin air.

When I returned to our desert sanctuary, I had a deep understanding of Greek culture, which helped me to interpret our own Holy Books in the light of the Greek Mysteries.

We had members who chose to live in the community by the Salt Sea. Their work, apart from the physical labour necessary to survive, consisted mainly in writing. We copied the holy words of the prophets and wrote of our own way of life. Others went out to the towns and cities of Judea and beyond, to preach the Way. Many referred to us as Ebionites, the Poor Ones. My Master had a deep respect for the poor and the dispossessed. With our associates, the Therapeutae in

64

Alexandria, we were highly regarded for the gifts of prophesy and healing. My Master was adept at both.

I accompanied him on his journeys into the wider community to prepare the Way of the Lord—the prophecy of Isaiah that our desert community eagerly embraced. It was a cardinal influence on our desert way of life: it was the purpose of our existence. Paradoxically, part of that preparation was for war. That may seem like a contradiction, but my Master, a peace-loving man, said that he had come to bring the sword. It seemed part of our history. The Holy Books speak a great deal about war. If we were not fighting to defend ourselves, we were waging wars of conquest. What a savage, but apparently necessary, way to progress. How are we to blame when Yahweh taught us the fierce art of war, leading our ancient armies into battle, as the Holy Books tell us? We have our own scroll, envisaging our Holy War, which ends in victory for our sublime God and His people. Though we lived isolated in the wilderness, we were not alone. We had many followers in Jerusalem and the cities and towns of Judea and beyond, ready to support us in our efforts to purify the Temple, the city and the country.

Our war against the Romans did not have the outcome that we had expected. That was another hope that went unfulfilled. We had written confidently of victory. Perhaps we could interpret the destruction of Jerusalem and the Temple as punishment for abandoning His law, but the laying waste of the whole country and the destruction of our own sanctuary—the sanctuary of the true followers of the Torah—we found difficult to accept and almost impossible to understand. Whatever the reasons for the nation's trial, the results were all too obvious—the country in ruins and its people scattered and abandoned like chaff on a cornfield.

7: Modern Rome

Sunlight, mellow and honey-sweet, filled Campo de' Fiori. Its source would soon descend behind the buildings that enclosed the Campo. Giuseppe sat on the balcony of his apartment, his eyes following the descending orb. The sun, deified almost since the dawn of human consciousness until demoted to just another star by the Bible and subsequently by the Church, began its rehabilitation with Copernicus, who restored it to the centre of our solar system. Copernicus knew he was playing with fire, and refused to publish his findings until, towards the end of his life, his student, Rheticus, prevailed on him to do so. Copernicus escaped the fire, but Giordano Bruno did not. Giuseppe's eyes moved from the sky to the monument below his balcony. The sight saddened him. Yet, he chose to live here because of the memorial.

As a post-graduate student at the Biblical Institute, he would often come here, gaze up at the statue and wonder how such an intelligent man could fail to see the reasonableness of Christian faith. Such bewilderment had long since given way to admiration for the man's capacity to see through the faith-fog that shrouded sixteenth-century Europe. As a student, ruminating on the puzzle that was Giordano Bruno, Giuseppe did not realize that his own life would mirror Giordano's in many ways. When, years later, he returned to Rome a disillusioned but well-to-do intellectual, he decided to settle within sight of the statue. He had never regretted his decision. Looking down on the figure, he reflected on his innocence at that distant time. His question now was how could any intelligent person find Christian faith reasonable?

The last rays of the sun were stretching the shadow of Giordano farther and farther along the Campo, as if injecting his influence into the wider world—the sight encouraged Giuseppe to hope that ultimately reason would overcome humanity's dalliance with myth. He had nothing against myth. He admired it as an art form that told the story of humanity's consciousness. Some considered Giordano the first martyr for science and free thought. Giuseppe may have suffered distress and inconvenience for his convictions and, worst of all, family alienation, but not inquisitorial fire. That would certainly have been his fate had he lived in an earlier age. Religion had broken so many lives, past and present, and would continue to do so, no doubt, well into the future. And for what? A lie? Certainly a fiction. He believed that during his career, he had presented his opinions without rancour. However, he had found it difficult. Writing was easier; one had time to calm down and compose a measured critique. When lecturing, however, where words were often spontaneous and emotions high, he would frequently feel like screaming at an importunate interrogator, 'Open your eyes, you gullible people!' At such a time, he had only to reflect on how closed his own eyes once were, to restore not only his calm, but a baffled admiration for the tenacity of faith.

The statue of Giordano below on the Campo was dark and austere. Even in the mellow and warm glow of evening, it projected a gloomy prospect. The figure stood erect, brooding, a Shakespearean spectre, a hood falling in folds over his forehead, obscuring his face, his crossed hands resting on a book. Giuseppe always felt that the hood should be thrown back to reveal a vibrant face defiantly facing the Vatican, arms outstretched to command the attention of all who passed below. Perhaps Ettore Ferrari, the sculptor who executed the monument in 1888, thought that the shrouded figure more aptly conveyed his tragic, but heroic, end.

There was no cloak to cover his naked body on that February day in 1600 when his accusers tied him to a stake and burned him alive in this *field of flowers,* 'for holding opinions contrary to the Catholic

Faith'. Of course, Giuseppe did not agree with all of Giordano's views—like much of human knowledge, time has expanded on some of his ideas and rendered others obsolete. For example, Giuseppe did not hold with Giordano's belief that the devil would ultimately find salvation. He did not agree, because he did not believe in the devil, or for that matter, salvation. However, Giuseppe did accept it as an indication of the compassion that resided in Giordano's humane heart, when the Church itself was all too willing to consign not only the devil to hell, but dissenting humans to torture and penal fires. However, for his time, Giuseppe mused, Giordano Bruno was extremely perceptive. He was one of the few of his age to hold Copernicus's heliocentric planetary model, which maintained that planet earth revolved on its axis around the sun. He went further than either Copernicus or Galileo by asserting that our planetary system existed in an infinite universe. He also proposed the possibility of multiple worlds, a bizarre idea at the time and for many generations afterwards that has gained new momentum in the light of modern cosmology.

As a young man, Giordano had joined the Dominican Order and, in time, was ordained a priest. The inquisitorial Dominicans, who ultimately condemned him, handed him over to the secular authorities for execution. He showed greater courage and conviction than Galileo, who recanted out of fear, and denied what had become obvious to his scholarly mind—that the sun was at the centre of the solar system, and the earth moved around it. Who could adhere to such nonsense when the movement of the sun was clearly visible to our eyes and proclaimed in the Bible? However, Giordano had stood firm, on that and more contentious issues. He dismissed the divinity of Christ, the notion of the Trinity and the Virgin Birth, all of which were bound to upset the upholders of orthodoxy. His response to his sentence was an admirable indication of his profound courage and unshakable conviction: 'Perhaps you, my judges, pronounce this sentence against me with greater fear than I receive it'.

Giuseppe himself, like Giordano, had begun his priestly life believing all of the conventional doctrines. However, not long after his arrival in Jerusalem and launching into his work translating the scrolls, he had come to view primitive Christianity in a very different light. Giuseppe did not agree with the experts who claimed that the scrolls were not Christian documents. According to them, they were Jewish writings and merely reflected the time and place of Christianity's birth. For Giuseppe, that fact alone made the scrolls supremely important for understanding the intricacy of Christianity's origin. However, his growing awareness of the complexity that surrounded the formation of Church doctrine did not immediately disturb his faith. He found his work of translation stimulating and enlightening. He handled the ancient materials with awe, reverence even. The thought of a scribe scratching the symbols on animal skin not far from the place where he, two thousand years later, was trying to make sense of them, was awe-inspiring. At first, the similarity that was emerging between these writings and the New Testament texts simply intrigued him. The lifestyle of the community that produced the scrolls was considered the 'Way' and they themselves 'Sons of Light'. Water initiated them into the Way and shared communal meals strengthened it. As he submerged himself in the spirit of the people of the scrolls, Giuseppe became more and more fascinated.

He was quite happy and content deciphering and translating, identifying and transforming the ancient symbols into intelligible, modern idioms. However, as he quietly and diligently worked with his colleagues in the scrollery reassembling the precious fragments, he sometimes fancied going out into the field and involving himself in the actual search for further caves that was proceeding at a frantic pace. He longed to get in at the very beginning of the process—to search and find—to kneel in the dust of the ancient caves, dig his hands into the sandy residue and, with bated breath, unearth a fragmentary scroll hidden from sight for two thousand years. However, he had little time for daydreaming. His work was complex. He had to examine, conserve and authenticate the fragments, then reassemble them like a jigsaw; only it was more complicated than a single jigsaw. There were multiple versions of the same book. For instance, there were 22 versions of the Book of Isaiah alone. Imagine trying to fit a single fragment of perhaps one character back into its proper place in, not only the Book of Isaiah, but into the correct edition of the book from which time and impatient hunters had ripped it. In the case of the books unique to Qumran, no template was available to guide their reconstruction. There was no picture from which to work on those boxes. Only when he and his colleagues had concluded all this work, and done so successfully, could translation commence.

Isis, his cat, sleeping on a cushion beside him, raised her head as the music filling the room reached its crescendo. With eyes that seemed to divine the story behind the music, she looked at Giuseppe, sitting at a table on the terrace. He paused in his writing. He loved that music—*Ariadne Auf Naxos* by Richard Strauss. It was a complex composition, beginning life as a play and an opera, later adapted to a play within an opera. It combined farce and glorious music, resulting in teasing competition between high and low art. He had first seen it when a student in Germany. He loved it then, but it was only later that Ariadne and Bacchus became a balm for his shattered spirit. Isis and Ariadne! He smiled, a playful but thoughtful smile, at how myth had underpinned much of his academic work. He waited until the music, having reached its climax, dwindled phrase by phrase, note by note, instrument by instrument into resolved and satisfying silence. It is no wonder that the concept of spirit holds humanity in thrall—myth and music articulate that uniquely human element. He found it difficult to return to the mundane, but gradually, his fingers began to move again over the keyboard. He was engaged in writing his memoirs, not with any determined intention in mind, but simply for his own interest and as an aid to recovering his past. As he sat there reflecting on the music and the life of Giordano Bruno his own past lived again as he committed it, bit by bit, to the hard-drive.

8: Jerusalem: 1950

My name is Joseph Ross, archaeologist, palaeographer and onetime Catholic priest. Arriving in Jerusalem on my 27th birthday, I was extremely excited to be working in a city of such antiquity and cultural significance. I would have been even more thrilled, if that were possible, had I known then the extent of the subsequent textual discoveries, and that I was to be intimately involved in one of the great archaeological discoveries of the age. The ultimate, sensational extent of the finds was not yet evident in 1950, but even the thought of one wilderness cave, nature's secure vault, surrendering its two-thousand-year-old hoard was enough to render palaeo hyphenated scientists of every field breathless in anticipation. I was fortunate to get in at the beginning. Professor de Vaux, director of the École Biblique de Jerusalem, had just recently scoured Cave 1 with the thoroughness of an industrial vacuum cleaner and the delicacy of an artist's brush. Further tantalizing fragments, emerging from this process, arrived at our long table to start the difficult process of preservation, identification and finally returning them to the text from which time, corrosion and the abuse of eager treasure hunters had ripped them.

In the years immediately following my arrival, further caves released an avalanche of documents that would require the ingenuity and skill of more scholars than the few among whom I was fortunate enough to work. That work was challenging enough on a purely scientific level, but there was more involved than science. We had not only to preserve, identify, date and decipher the ancient symbols clinging to fragments already crumbling at our touch but, in addition, we had to race the Bedouin, not always successfully, to new discoveries and, at the same time, excavate the ruins of the Qumran settlement. This work would have been demanding in a peaceful setting, but war waged around us, with rival combatants anxious to get their hands on the newly discovered documents. By the time of my arrival, the seven relatively intact scrolls from Cave 1 were in divided ownership. Four were in the hands of the Syrian Orthodox Archbishop of Jerusalem and three purchased by Professor Sukenik of the Hebrew University.

Jerusalem itself was a bewildering fusion of old and new, somewhat similar to Rome my most recent domicile. The difference was that the 'new' in Jerusalem looked old—battered by climate and conflict. Subsequent to the Armistice Agreement of 1949, it was a divided city with both sides more concerned about national survival than architectural embellishment. Since Jerusalem held such vital significance for the three major religions, the original United Nations' plan was to declare it an international city administered by that world body. The pity was that that original plan had not prevailed. The Arab-Israeli conflict of 1948-49 ended that dream. The Armistice Agreement of 1949 had brought an end to open warfare, it also divided the city; a solution that satisfied neither side. It served only to perpetuate simmering unrest, mistrust and dissatisfaction that frequently boiled over into violent expressions of that discontent in the form of demonstrations, riots and localized bombings.

There was a detectable anti-Israeli pro-Arab bias among my colleagues, who were nearly all Christians of one persuasion or another. I found this bewildering. Following the prevailing logic, Christians were spiritual Jews. Why this endemic prejudice by Christians against them? Jesus was a Jew; if indeed He was anything. However, such doubts about the Saviour's status and even his existence, which Protestant scholars, such as Bruno Bauer, expressed in the nineteenth century, had not yet penetrated the bastion of mid-twentieth century Catholic seminary education. As for the scrolls themselves, since they reflected

Israel's ancient culture and their ancestors had secured their survival, I felt they rightfully belonged in Israel's keeping.

In the context of the ancient city, the museum, situated just outside the north-eastern corner of the old city wall, was an impressive modern building. My colleagues and I worked there as in the eye of a hurricane. Inside, the only conflicts were scholarly, while around us the battering winds of civil rivalry raged.

On my arrival in Jerusalem, I found accommodation in an ancient house inside the old walls that American efficiency had transformed into an adequate hostel in the midst of a strife-torn city. It was a convenient location, midway between the Holy Places of Christian interest and the Rockefeller Museum—where the scrollery to examine the scrolls was eventually set up. As a priest, the Holy Places associated with the death and Resurrection of Jesus were significant for my faith, but the buildings also held enormous cultural and historical interest. At the time, many of Jerusalem's ancient sites were located in Arab-controlled areas of the city. However, to complicate the situation further, the relentless surge of history had added an Islamic dimension to many of the sites—a significant example was the Dome of the Rock, built on the site of Israel's ancient Temple. History had made of Jerusalem a city of bewildering complexity that defied and continues to defy human ingenuity in brokering an agreeable *modus vivendi*.

I was thrilled with my living quarters. Only one subjected to the constant supervision of religious training regimes can understand the liberating experience of having one's own place. The building was old, but well maintained. My single room was large, serving as bedroom, sitting room, study and whatever. It had a French window that opened onto a flat roof with the ancient city spread out before me like an open scroll ready to be read. It was breathtaking! In the distance to the northwest, I could make out the hexagonal tower of the museum, while slightly to the northeast the gleaming Dome of the Rock dominated the skyline.

However, despite its buildings with their compelling antiquity, it was the history of the city, bloody and prolonged, that grabbed me with almost visceral interest. King David's assault on the Jebusite city in the eleventh century BCE lived on, not only in history but also in the very environment that enveloped the city. The cries of war never fade—encrypted on the atmosphere like information on a silicon chip. Solomon's influence still lingered; if nothing remained of his temple, the Temple Mount was the emotional heart of the city. The thrill of triumph and the dismay of defeat still resonated on the airwaves. Hope and despair still hung tangibly over the city. The despondency associated with national disaster continued through the centuries. After the Babylonians came Greeks, Romans, Arabs and Crusaders. They were all indelibly written into the history of the city and, even more intimately and intrinsically, into the very flesh and blood of its people. Its turbulent history continued. The present inhabitants survived as best they could. They bought and sold, laughed and cried, moved cautiously but courageously through the city's narrow streets on their daily errands, hoping for the best, fearing the worst. Who would willingly choose to be God's elect?

Who would willingly choose to be God's elect? That refrain was a sort of mantra for Leah Strauss. Slightly older than I, she was a mixture of physical and emotional contradictions: petite yet strong and muscular; pretty yet tough and severe looking; femininely attractive but capable of fits of masculine aggression. She seldom wore make-up and treated her hair with disregard, as if ashamed of its dark but soft attractiveness. She usually bound it tightly under a triangular black scarf. If you expected flattery, you were in for a shock. She was brutally frank. When we first met, she told me to expect only suspicion from the inhabitants of Jerusalem, herself included, as I was, quite naturally, an outsider to all, a *Kufr* to the Muslims, a *Goy* to the Jews. Initially, I was shocked, but later realized that her 'advice' was simply a statement of fact intended to save me subsequent distress and disappointment. All the attributes and contradictions I noted were understandable as her story unfolded.

Leah and her twin brother, Daniel, were born in Germany in 1922—probably the worst possible time for a Jew. Their parents were rich. However, riches were no defence against what was to come—quite the opposite. With the rise to power of the Nazi party, their parents took action and sent the twins, in their early teens, to the United States. To further their education was the declared intention, but the real reason was to get them out of harm's way. The parents sent a sizable fortune with the twins, with the intention of joining them if matters got too bad in Germany. In the event, the parents left it too late. Their letters stopped coming and all contact was lost. When I met Leah, she was still trying to find out what had happened to her parents but she could not trace them. It was as if they had ceased to exist in the 1930s. They probably had.

When the war ended, the twins, in their early twenties, decided to move to Palestine. Their own experience and that of Jewish history convinced them that the establishment of their own state was the only hope for the Jewish people. They decided to dedicate themselves to making that hope a reality. In Jerusalem they stayed at the Hostel Mordechai, owned and run by Joel Weiss, an American friend who had preceded them to Palestine. When asked about the name he had given his establishment, he told them that he had worked in a kibbutz of that name when he first arrived. The twins were impressed and soon found themselves working in *Yad Mordechai*. It was a dry, arid area with little vegetation, but the Kibbutzniks transformed it into an oasis. However, when the United Nations announced the establishment of the new State of Israel on 14 May 1948, they knew that the surrounding Arab States would not accept it.

War broke out within days and 2,500 Egyptian assault soldiers attacked *Yad Mordechai* with its 130 defenders. It held out for three days but finally fell to the Egyptians. Daniel died defending the Kibbutz but

Leah escaped and made her way to Jerusalem, where she took up residence once again with Joel. It was there that I met her.

War was as endemic to Israel as malaria to a mosquito-ridden swamp. Hostilities surrounded my associates and me as we worked on the scrolls. We also discovered warfare written into the texts themselves, especially in the War Scroll with its carefully delineated preparations for the final battle—the eschatological confrontation between light and darkness.

9: The Time of Nero

We had written about our glorious and victorious war for many generations, but the murder of my Master finally precipitated it. He, like our original Teacher, suffered at the hands of another reprobate High Priest, Ananus, appointed by the second King Agrippa. Ananus was a man of violent temper and immediately set about eliminating his critics. Foremost among them was my Master, against whom he brought false accusations of transgressing the Torah. The people were outraged when he was executed by stoning and forced Agrippa to remove that impious High Priest from office. We recovered my Master's holy body and brought it to the Salt Sea Sanctuary for purification, anointing and burial. Special stone formations mark his grave.

During the subsequent conflict, his murderer, Ananus, took the side of the Romans and Agrippa, but he suffered for his treachery at the hands of the dagger-wielding Sicarii, the most extreme of the Zealots. My Master's stoning to death ignited our resistance. Initially, it was slow burning, taking four years of further aggression and trampling on our sacred customs to erupt into a conflagration. In the seclusion of our desert retreat, we were confident of the outcome: we would rid the country of the Romans and their puppet king, Agrippa II. Then we would purify the Temple, purge it of foreign idols and restore the legitimate priesthood. That, at least, was the plan. We even had a design for a new Temple. The reality was different. War against the Romans was violent, chaotic and bloodthirsty. The memory of it still brings tears to my eyes and an involuntary shudder to my body. Its horror has not been dimmed by time.

Fighting broke out in the north during the reign of Emperor Nero with victories that astounded us—generating a vain confidence that our destiny was at hand. We became puffed up with pride in our ability to subdue mighty Rome. The war we wrote about in our scrolls did not reflect the reality—our war against the Kittim was orderly and victorious more by the hand of God and the might of His princely angel than the clash of weapons. Our successes in the north motivated the Romans to increase their aggression and Nero sent his most experienced general to subdue the country. Vespasian landed his legions in the turbulent north, where his son, Titus, joined him with his legions from Alexandria. It was a massive army, tens of thousands of men, well trained, armed and disciplined. They quickly subdued our northern armies, and then marched south. About this time, Vespasian returned suddenly to Rome. Nero was dead, and Vespasian saw his chance to step into his imperial shoes. He left Titus in command of the campaign. If anything, the son outdid the father in his brutal pursuit of victory.

In my long life, I have witnessed many momentous events. The most terrifying was my flight before the Roman Legions. First, from our refuge by the Salt Sea and later from Jerusalem as Titus ravaged the city and razed the Temple. That latter catastrophe was so terrifying that it defies description. I was fortunate to have Apollos at my side.

When the fortunes of war turned against us, and the Roman menace advanced in our direction like an unstoppable forest fire, razing all before it, Apollos arrived from Alexandria, where he had been witness to the preparations underway by Titus and his legions. He knew our situation was critical and set out with some of his fellow Therapeutae to stand with us. The futility of our position soon became obvious. Our fragile wilderness sanctuary could not hold out against the mighty Roman Legions. With the exception of a few who decided to die there, we abandoned our haven by the Salt Sea. Some went north to defend Jericho while Apollos and I joined those rushing to protect

Jerusalem. In spite of our antipathy towards Jerusalem and the Temple for indulging foreign customs, we had a natural impulse to rush to its defence. We had barely entered the city before Titus and his legions surrounded it. It was a terrible time. Food was in short supply, and to make matters worse, the Sicarii burned much of what we had in order to stimulate, as they saw it, our spirit of defiance and aggression.

We lacked the unity and leadership of the Romans. After defeat in the north, the vanquished leaders came south to help us in our defence of the city, but instead only succeeded in dividing us by clashing with the southern commanders. We had too many separate factions—the general population, the Zealots, and the Sicarii. Their respective leaders began to disagree among themselves. They were zealous in their defence of the country, but clashed over tactics. As a result, they spent more time bickering among themselves than fighting the Romans. It proved futile and ultimately fatal.

The inevitable end came when the Romans breached our defences and entered the city, killing all before them. They stormed through the city on foot and on horseback, swords swinging indiscriminately at anything that hindered their surge towards the Temple. Ferocious fighting around the area continued for many hours. We, the defenders, began to feel the pressure on our diminishing numbers until the aggressors finally broke through our resistance and set fire to the sacred precincts. The mayhem was terrible to witness, women trying to protect their children from arbitrary thrashing swords as they sought shelter on holy ground, but the Romans allowed for no spot to be a place of sanctuary. Their screams ring in my ears to this day. Men, fleeing inevitable retribution, knew there was little hope of escape. The thousands crucified provided a hideous backdrop to the ravished city. I thought that I would die that day, and I likely would have but for the strength and quick thinking of Apollos who, on one occasion, swept me from the path of their fearsome chargers. Together with other survivors, we made our escape through the tunnels that ran under the Temple and brought us into the open countryside. All defenders knew of the subterranean channels in case the unthinkable happened. Even in open country, we were not safe as Titus hunted down those who tried to escape and either killed them on the spot or captured them for the ultimate humiliation, crucifixion. However, a few of us managed to survive. Apollos and I made our way south under cover of darkness, putting as much distance as possible between us and the enemy. Eventually, we reached Alexandria and the sanctuary of the Therapeutae. There, we had time to recover from the ordeal, patch up our superficial wounds and consider our new position. The catastrophe gravely wounded our understanding of the Mystery. The glorious interpretation of our history did not become reality. Apollos and I discussed our new situation repeatedly over the period we tended our wounds, physical and spiritual. After the calamity, we had more in common with Paul's Suffering Christ than the glorious image presented in the Prophets and Wisdom Literature. Gradually, we came around to Paul's way of viewing and proclaiming the Mystery.

10: Modern Rome

Saturday morning and Carlo, the distraction, was still present in Marc's mind. Was he letting his guard slip? Seminary discipline was set implacably against what was termed 'particular friendships'. They were at best an obstacle and at worst a threat to the pursuit of Christian perfection. Was friendship with Carlo such a danger? It was inconvenient on a practical level—he was thinking of Carlo when he should be concentrating on his work. Where was his old fascination for the scrolls? Was passion for Carlo replacing his enthusiasm for the scrolls? Perhaps he was more of a threat than a mere obstacle to Marc's commitment. Dedication to a cause, especially if it demanded the denial of basic instincts, is all well and commendable if one is certain about the cause pursued, but faith is a leap in the dark. Did he see more clearly in that darkness than Giuseppe, the acclaimed scholar and self-proclaimed non-believer; or Carlo, the well-informed and engaging Gnostic? Had he greater certainty about his beliefs than the questioning Sophia? He felt as if he were at the end of a domino effect, poised and waiting for the first tile to fall and topple a series of values that amounted to his life.

He was still confronting his demons when he heard a car pull into the car park and emit two quick beeps. He grabbed his backpack, already packed with the requisite items for a beach outing—towel, swimming trunks, sun cream, sunglasses, sunhat and books. Books? Maybe not, he decided. He extricated them, zipped it up, swung it over his shoulder and left.

'I hope you don't have books stowed away there,' said Carlo with a suspicious glance at the bag. Marc was relieved to be able truthfully to deny it. 'This is Luigi,' he continued, nodding to an impressively built young man in the front seat.

'*Ciao, Luigi. Buongiorno. Come stai.*'

'*Bene, Padre, grazie.*'

Luigi got out of the car not only to shake Marc's hand but also to leave the front passenger seat free for him, much to Marc's embarrassment. Luigi stretched out his hand as a flash of jade escaped from his eyes. Standing outside the car, he was even more impressive. He was tall with closely cropped blonde hair, and a muscular body that vied with Carlo's. A black T-shirt hugged his torso like a second skin, accentuating rather than obscuring well-defined pectorals, which Marc would later discover were as golden as the neck. Sculpted bronze calves extended below black shorts, his feet fitted neatly into black sandshoes. The studied ensemble—black on bronze—was striking. Amid protestations from Marc, Luigi insisted on folding himself into the back of the little car already loaded with beach towels and a large lunch box.

'Get in,' said Carlo, rather gruffly, thus ending his protestations. 'I'm glad you lost the cassock—*L'abito non fa il Monaco!*'

'Shakespeare might not agree,' said Marc, smarting at Carlo's brusqueness.

'Who?' Carlo's smile and feigned ignorance of the English poet cleared the air.

Carlo, being a Roman driver, whisked them smartly into a main thoroughfare. As the city with its historic monuments sped by like a slide show, accompanied by a strident soundtrack of city traffic, Marc began to unwind. He allowed the ancient past and current concerns to recede from his consciousness, as Rome—ancient and modern—retreated from view. He was determined to relax and enjoy the day.

Turning back towards Luigi, Marc asked, 'Your term of duty with the Swiss Guard is soon to end?'

'*Si, Padre,*' was Luigi's formal reply.

'Please, Luigi, call me Marco.'

'He has been trained to kowtow to the clergy,' said Carlo, with contrived distain.

'Ignore him, Marco,' said Luigi playfully. 'He might take the hint. Anyway, I won't kowtow much longer.'

'Will you miss it? It's a very glamorous career.'

'It's not so glamorous behind the scenes,' replied Luigi with a hint of recollected exasperation.

'The guards are great favourites with the tourists,' added Marc.

'And our Luigi laps it up,' interjected Carlo. 'You should see him flaunting his manly physique for the cameras.'

'I'm hoping to flaunt before a different audience, as my publicist probably told you, Marco.'

'There are some secrets I can keep,' said Carlo with a display of mock indignation. 'However, this was not one of them,' he continued with a grin.

'An opera singer,' said Marc, with feeling. 'I admit that I am in awe of artists. They keep us sane. It won't be easy,' he continued. 'Anything worthwhile seldom is.'

Apprehension showed on Luigi's face. 'I know, but my voice trainer thinks I should give it a go.'

'I look forward to hearing you,' said Marc with obvious anticipation.

'I may be taking part in a concert soon. I will let you know.'

'Please do,' said Marc with enthusiasm.

The beach was isolated, but obviously an established favourite spot with Carlo and Luigi. The ever resourceful Roman found a shaded spot for the icebox and laid large beach towels on the sand, while the Swiss Guard peeled off his T-shirt, dropped his shorts to reveal a rounded buttocks that fitted tightly into black swimming trunks and ran into the sea. Marc gazed after him in stunned admiration.

'Well! What do you think?' asked Carlo, taking in Marc's reaction.

Embarrassed by his lack of control, Marc tried to regain his composure. 'He is a fine man,' he commented coolly.

'Oh! Come off it; is that all you can say?'

'OK then; he is gorgeous, with a body to die for. Is that what you want me to say?' Marc was becoming more frustrated and embarrassed. 'I should not be here. It was a mistake, and now you are making fun of me, just because I am trying to be what I should be.'

Carlo reached out and took Marc's hand, 'I am sorry. It's OK, there is nothing to be embarrassed about. Anybody with eyes would have to admit that Luigi is gorgeous.'

'It's not OK,' Marc flashed back, pulling away his hand. 'I'm a priest. You know what that means.'

'Even priests have feelings,' said Carlo quietly. 'Covering them up can lead to all sorts of ... difficulties. I should know.'

'What do you mean?'

'You told me recently that I was well informed. It's not just because I am a librarian. I experienced religious life from the inside. You would not think it now, but I too studied for the priesthood. So did Luigi—we met there. At least one good thing came out of it.'

Marc's frustration and anger were receding. He sat on the towel. 'Would you like to tell me about it?' he asked diplomatically.

Carlo slipped out of his white shirt and sat beside Marc. In spite of his recent embarrassment, Marc could not help admiring his friend's physique. It was the first time he saw Carlo shirtless and even beside the 'gorgeous' Luigi, he was by no means outclassed. They were different. Luigi was blond, and tanned to a golden hue, whereas Carlo's complexion was dark—his hair and eyes as black as tar and skin that the sun's rays turned to ebony. It had slipped Marc's notice that Carlo also dressed with attention—all white to contrast with his dark pigment. In the presence of such colourful physicality, Marc felt decidedly monochrome with his nondescript clothing and Celtic pallor on which even the Italian sun made little impact.

'I don't want to hurt or offend you, Marco' began Carlo tentatively. 'If you want to know, you must let me speak freely, without taking it personally.'

'Of course,' said Marc with more conviction than he felt.

Carlo did not like reliving his past. He did not even like thinking about it. He sometimes wished that he could forget it, but it had its uses—it helped to give assurance to subsequent convictions. 'I hate talking about it,' he began broodingly. 'Even thinking of it is stressful, but it taught me a lesson or two. Whether one balances out the other is questionable. When I was twelve years old, I enrolled in a minor seminary, initially against my parents' wishes—I was a stubborn sod,' he added, with a dismissive shake of his head. 'They gave in, probably thinking that I would change my mind by the time I reached seventeen. In my first year there, my body began to change.'

Carlo paused, considering his words. His phrase, he felt, was too bland to express the visceral explosions that certain sights and sounds elicited, and too mild and gentle to denote the surge for release that such explosions demanded. But he knew that a natural and universal phenomenon needed no elaboration.

'You know what it is like,' he continued. 'However, the feelings I experienced were not only new, they were different, not just different, but condemned—love and be damned, as I said before. You understand that also, I am sure. I began to realize just what this much-flaunted commitment to celibacy really involved and that custody of the eyes was not just a curb on curiosity.'

Carlo's statement reminded Marc of his recent failure in that regard. He looked towards the sea—a mirror reflecting the cerulean sky above. Luigi was ploughing energetically through the calm water. 'Yes,' he agreed softly. 'I understand.'

'At some point early on, the prefect of students—a middle-aged priest, but he seemed old to me—took me to his room.' The memory forced Carlo to pause in his narrative. 'Ostensibly, the purpose was to introduce me to physical penance—*nothing severe*, he insisted, *just a little stroke to help curb our unruly impulses.* I was astounded at his insight. How did he know? I was too naive, at the time, to realize that my new feelings were common to all at my age. He produced a small whip—a few leather thongs hanging from a platted handle. It looked harmless enough, but was sufficient to raise welts if used with vigour. He told me to undress.'

Carlo paused and looked out at the swimming figure. Marc slipped his hand over Carlo's and squeezed it reassuringly.

'I hesitated, and looked at him. His reassuring smile prompted me to comply. He snapped the whip. It barely touched by skin. *There now*, he said. *That was not too bad.* As he spoke, he rubbed the flesh that stung slightly from the stroke. He continued kneading my back, moving gradually downwards. He cupped my bottom, squeezed it and continued down and under, until he reached my balls. He fingered them and squeezed gently. I felt stimulated, but also bewildered and frightened.'

'What did you do?' Marc posed the question as Carlo gazed out at the energetic swimmer gliding through the water parallel to the shoreline.

'I didn't know what to do,' he replied, eyes still on the distant swimmer. He turned towards Marc. 'So I did nothing.' He lay on his back and looked up. A helicopter was hovering above them, disturbing the tranquillity of the scene. 'I was glad I didn't. The prefect vanished from our lives without a word a short time afterwards. I was relieved that he was gone, and that I was not the cause.' Carlo fell silent again, following the flight path of the helicopter. Marc began to wonder if he had finished his story. The sound and sight of the aircraft faded, and Carlo sat up again. 'I was reminded of the incident when reports of clerical abuse began to emerge. The criminal callousness that ruined so many young lives shocked me. My experience was unsettling, but not in the same league. My memory was of an old man, so frustrated by the demands of his calling that he had to seek furtive relief in such a pathetic manner.' He looked at Marc, his dark eyes trying to read Marc's expression. 'I'm not saying that every celibate reacts the same way,

88

Marco. I am not a psychologist, but recent revelations of abuse would indicate that repression of natural instincts is psychologically damaging. Why should you not be here, enjoying yourself with friends? Why should you not admire Luigi? He is admirable.'

'So are you,' said Marc, surprising even himself.

Before Carlo had time to react, Luigi came jogging up, bringing with him glistening pellets of the Mediterranean sliding off his bronzed skin. 'What's going on?' he asked, looking from one to the other. 'You look gloomy.'

'I was telling Marco about our time in the seminary,' explained Carlo.

'That explains it, then,' said Luigi, matter-of-factly. 'Aren't you coming in for a swim?'

The question, directed at both Carlo and Marc, contained a tone of incredulity that a conversation on their blighted seminary experience should take precedence over the inviting waters of the Mediterranean Sea. The trio quickly remedied the situation. They took to the water with enthusiasm, swimming, diving and splashing about. Marc, the least energetic, eventually began to tire. He sat at the water's edge, watching his more energetic friends playfully engaged, like frisky dolphins. They wrestled, throwing each other into the water, and launching one another, like acrobats, into the surf. They were uninhibited—touching, embracing, kissing. Marc looked on spellbound. He knew from Carlo how they felt about each other, but did not expect to see it expressed so openly and spontaneously. There was a refreshing innocence about it. Passions, usually tightly controlled, began to awaken—he wanted to be part of it. However, discipline and training asserted themselves, and he retreated to the towels and lay down. He looked up at the dome of heaven, into endless vastness ... and wondered, as a child of the universe, if his life of restraint and discipline had any meaning. Would looking at Carlo and Luigi—admiringly or lustfully—or even joining them in their affectionate play alter the path of the stars or change the course of human destiny?

Sophia

Arriving home from the beach, Marc felt out of sorts. He was reliving the revelations of the day and confronting the emotions they induced. His skin tingled. Exposure to the sun was a contributing factor, no doubt, but not the only one. His body was hot with desire and frustration—his memory tantalizingly rerunning the intimate frolicking of his friends, his imagination careering into dangerous territory. He had hoped to spend a few hours on his thesis, but his mind rebelled against any check on its recklessness. Then, he received Sister Sophia's call. Initially, he was impatient at her request for a meeting, but it might be the appropriate bridle to restrain his wilful memory. However, it reminded him yet again that he did not like the role of spiritual direction. He felt it arrogant in the extreme to think that one could enter into the core of another person's consciousness and direct it to greater fulfilment. He believed anyone could successfully direct his or her own spiritual life. Perhaps the real reason was that he did not feel competent, or even interested, in playing the part.

However unwillingly, he found his duty reining in his unruly reflections as he made his way to the room set aside for confessions and spiritual consultations. The room reflected the nuns' fastidiousness with order and cleanliness. It had a circular walnut table, polished to a mirror shine, with an assortment of chairs set down with military precision. The bookcase defied the visitor to a finger inspection for dust, while aesthetic formation rather than library science prompted the arrangement of the books. Apart from a prie-dieu, which afforded those so inclined a more penitential posture in which to receive absolution, the only other special feature was a glass-panelled door. The rules of the convent prescribed it to protect both parties and discourage certain wanton urges that privacy might otherwise encourage.

Sister Sophia was waiting for him. She rose to meet him as he entered. Her smile disarmed him. In spite of the spiritual challenges she presented, he liked her. She was sincere and had a bubbling personality. He knew she was pretty, but now, as Marc looked at her, he realized she was an Italian beauty smothered in an indefinable way by her vocation. He recognized that with a redistribution of his hormones, the glass door might prove the necessary deterrent it was designed to be. Like most modern nuns, she was dressed in simple, contemporary clothing—he wondered what Gucci or Armani would make of her figure. The only obvious sign of religious commitment was a small cross dangling from a silver chain that encircled her neck. History and association had transformed a hideous instrument of torture into a fashion accessory.

'I hope I have not disturbed you, Father,' she said softly.

'Of course not, Sophia,' he replied, as they sat down. 'Please call me Marco. Have you managed to reach an accommodation with Tertullian and the Resurrection?' His question was teasing. He immediately reproached himself. It was not the way to conduct spiritual direction. Perhaps that was why he disliked it so much. He had to be himself. He did not believe in putting on false airs—pretending to be other than what he was. In any event, he did not think such pretence would find favour with Sophia.

She laughed softly, remembering her previous outburst. 'I suppose we must be tolerant of Tertullian. He lived in a vastly different age.'

'True,' said Marc, thoughtfully. 'Time and place make captives of us all. How can a modern mind truly understand an ancient one? Words help, but only so far. We might translate a symbol into a corresponding modern word, but to understand the nuance of meaning that resided in that ancient mind, you have to read between the lines.'

'Such as the Resurrection,' she added pointedly.

'It would be interesting to know exactly what the gospel writers meant by it. Did they have in mind an historical, physical event, or something spiritual, or indeed a merging of the two that defied the capacity of language to convey? It is a problem, nobody would deny that, not even Tertullian,' he added with a chuckle. 'That was the very point of his argument.'

'Do you believe it? I am sorry for putting you on the spot, but it is crucial.'

91

'Don't be sorry. You are quite right, it is fundamental. Do I believe?' He shook his head in thought rather than denial. 'If I say Mass, I suppose I do.'

'That is hardly a resounding affirmation.'

'Religion and mystery are intimately bound together. If you believe in one, you believe in the other.'

'That is back to Tertullian again ... blind faith. I am sorry to be so picky, but the truth is, I have met someone. He is a patient in the rehabilitation centre, which raises ethical questions, but let me stress, nothing has happened. So, let us stick to the theological problem for the moment.'

Sophia's comment released the wayward memory, that of his friends kissing in the sea. The memory reignited his earlier frustration.

'A patient?' he queried, trying to regain his composure.

'He is a wounded, fragile person, but warm and caring. I am beginning to feel more than professional concern for him. From the way he reacts to my presence, I suspect he has feelings for me. Do I turn my back on him for Tertullian's absurdity? His needs and our mutual attraction are real. The other! What is it? Some vague phantasm, residing somewhere beyond reason? What do I do, Marco?'

'That decision is yours alone, Sophia. All I can suggest is that you pray—not mere formulaic words. Think about it. Turn it over in your mind. Absorb the problem into your innermost being, and let it ferment in your subconscious until a solution emerges. If you think it would help, talk to me anytime. The spoken word often clarifies the thought.'

'Thank you, Marco. A spiritual director of a former age would probably have recommended sackcloth and ashes.'

'Now, why did I not think of that,' said Marc with a smile, his own issues unresolved.

Giuseppe's Library

Marc recognized the music as he entered the apartment—*Ariadne Auf Naxos*, an opera by Richard Strauss, one of his favourites. The music, together with Giuseppe's welcome, put Marc at ease, as his granduncle, wearing a caftan, escorted him onto the terrace overlooking Campo de' Fiori.

'You cannot begin to understand what meeting you means to me, Marco,' said Giuseppe as Marc sat down. The morning air was pleasant and Marc, who had chosen to discard his cassock, was wearing black trousers and a white, short-sleeved shirt. 'We will have something cool to drink,' suggested Giuseppe, as he left the terrace.

'I love your music,' Marc said, as Giuseppe returned with a pitcher of fruit juice and two ceramic drinking tumblers, featuring scroll fragments in the glaze.

'I'm glad you like it,' Giuseppe replied, as the music increased in volume. 'Music has been a support in dark days,' he commented pensively. He set the items on the table and sat down. Marc eyed his fragment as if inspecting an original and discovered that is was the famous, or infamous, 7Q5—the disputed fragment that might, just might, be from the Gospel of Mark. He wondered if Giuseppe had intentionally chosen it for him.

'Is the 7Q5 for my benefit?'

'I know you must be very familiar with it, but I thought it the most appropriate of my Qumran kitsch. Have you been to Jerusalem?'

'No,' replied Marc sadly.

'When you go there, you will find many street traders selling them.'

'I won't be going,' said Marc with a shrug.

'Why not? I would have thought it essential for your research.'

'My supervisor, Monsignore Martini, does not think so.'

'That seems odd. Surely he must appreciate the value of such experiences for your studies.'

'He claims that all I need is readily accessible.'

'The scrolls are available in many forms, it is true, but to stand on the Qumran plateau, to visit the caves, to view the scrolls and just to breathe in the air of the place brings its own unique insights. It gives

93

you new perspective and ultimately new understanding of the scrolls and, more importantly, of the people who wrote them and hid them away.'

'Monsignore Martini does not see it that way.'

'I do not usually interest myself in Vatican personalities, but I did meet your monsignore once.'

'When was that?' asked Marc with interest.

'The Student Union at the Biblical Institute—there was no such thing in my day—invited me to give a lecture, at a neutral venue, I might add.'

'That was daring of them,' said Marc with a chuckle.

'Monsignore Martini obviously thought so too. He was there, presumably to protect the students from the rush of rationalism.'

'I'm sure he had something to say,' suggested Marc.

'He took me to task on a number of issues, which he was entitled to do. However, I felt his concern was with demolition rather than construction. I suspect that your thesis will have a difficult passage.'

'If I make a valid case, he can't deny it.'

'I have found that commitment to a cause provokes bizarre defence mechanisms.'

'Such as burning at the stake,' said Marc, looking down at the memorial in the piazza.

'Some are more subtle than that.'

'Giordano met with a sad end,' added Marc.

'Sad,' replied Giuseppe with emotion, 'but inspiring, significant and above all courageous. How many of us will have a monument erected to our memory? How many will be remembered five years after death, never mind five hundred?' As he was speaking, a cat leapt into his lap and began to bed down into the folds of the caftan he was wearing.

'What is it called?'

'Isis,' replied Giuseppe, 'after the Egyptian goddess, sister and wife of Osiris, and mother of Horus the resurrection god.'

94

'Born during the winter solstice,' reflected Marc thoughtfully. 'Paganism seems to underpin much of our religion.'

'It is hardly remarkable when the origin of religion lies in the sun—its daily and seasonal dying and rising. The winter solstice was particularly significant. In our technological age, we are no longer restricted by darkness and, as a result, we may have lost sight of our reliance on the sun for providing light, but as the sustaining force of life, we are as dependent as the ancients were.'

'We are just not as conscious of it,' commented Marc thoughtfully.

'If my studies have taught me anything, it is that Christianity is not unique. Few would deny that it grew out of Judaism.'

'Even Monsignore Martini would agree with that,' said Marc, with a chuckle.

'The gospel writers indicate a further dependence—on the ancient Mystery Religions.'

'A new version of paganism,' added Marc.

'Christ—like Horus, Dionysus and Adonis—was just another incarnation of the human and divine resurrection deities that resided in the religious consciousness of the ancient world.'

'The Christian myth endured and appeared unique because of Rome, the Empire as distinct from the Church,' added Marc. 'Carlo does not see any distinction between the two.'

'Carlo is an insightful young man,' commented Giuseppe. 'It is obvious that he likes you,' he added. 'You like him too, I think.' Giuseppe observed Marc closely as he made the statement.

Silence followed, as Marc wondered how best to respond. Sophia had no problem declaring her attraction—why should he? How open would his granduncle be to the idea of a same sex attachment? Did it matter? Whatever the outcome, it was his life. The beach scene played again in his mind. He could not deny that he liked Carlo, but what did that mean? He could say the same about Luigi and Giuseppe, even Sophia. But no! He could not. Liking Carlo had within it the potential to deconstruct his life. That was the source of the conflict raging within him.

'You are very observant,' he finally admitted.

Giuseppe could see the distress he caused Marc and thought a little levity might help. 'I am a palaeographer,' he said, with a smile. 'We are a nosey lot.' Becoming serious again, he continued, 'Love is precious, Marco, value it. Now, let me show you my library,' he offered, diplomatically closing the Carlo segment of the conversation. Now, Marc knew where he stood, if he wished to revisit the topic.

They moved from the terrace into Giuseppe's living room. It was a spacious and gracious area, and gave no indication of the complexity of corridors and multiplicity of living space that lay beyond. He directed Marc through a suitably palatial doorway into a corridor with three doors. Behind one was a well-equipped kitchen. Another led into a large, modern bathroom, where an open doorway revealed a bedroom beyond. The third door led into another room—larger, higher and more ornate, in every way more palatial. It had a frescoed ceiling of phallic gods and mammary goddesses with a few indulged-looking putti added to complete the celestial family. Densely packed bookcases, covered most of the walls. Assorted tables and chairs, some probably from the original palazzo, were scattered throughout the room, some piled with more books. A modern computer sat on an antique desk, ready to flood the ancient surroundings with electronically-generated information from the twenty-first century at the touch of Giuseppe's fingers.

'This is my world,' said Giuseppe. 'Beyond here, I rarely venture.'

'It is an impressive library,' commented Marc. 'An imposing room,' he added, looking up at the ceiling.

'You might like to see the rest of the apartment before inspecting my books.' Giuseppe opened a window to allow in a refreshing flow of air. 'This building was a palazzo in the old days.' Under the watchful gaze of the celestial troupe, Giuseppe led Marc across the library to yet another door, which opened into a bright vestibule. 'When offering the property for sale, some astute agent suggested making each floor a self-contained unit.' Marc went to the French window and stepped onto a second balcony that also looked down onto the Campo. 'Many years ago, I bought the top floor, and refurbished it to suit my needs. As you will see, it is more extensive than you might imagine.'

Giuseppe then moved across the vestibule under another frescoed ceiling of celestial beings to a further doorway, which opened into another corridor. Throwing open some doors, Giuseppe revealed extra bedrooms, fully equipped with antique furnishings, including enormous canopied beds. 'There is a bathroom and a number of other rooms. Initially, when I divided off my own quarters, I thought about renting this section but, since I did not need the money, I lost interest in the idea.' He pointed to another doorway in the vestibule. 'It even has its own entrance.' He produced a key from his pocket and handed it to Marc. 'If you are ever in need of sanctuary, you are welcome here.'

Marc was stunned. 'That is very kind of you, Giuseppe. A refuge is attractive ... especially now,' he added pointedly.

'You don't have to explain yourself to me, Marco. I want you to think of this place as yours—to come and go as you please.' They returned to the library, and Giuseppe activated the computer. 'You might like to have a look at this' he said indicating a file. 'I have started writing reminiscences of my time in Jerusalem. It might interest you while I see about lunch.'

Giuseppe left, and Marc, settling in front of the computer, began to read.

11: Jerusalem: 1950

Saturday, the day after my arrival in Jerusalem, I got up early, heart beating in anticipation of the exploration ahead. I was living in the city that bore witness to the Resurrection. That belief was the oxygen that sustained the glow of Western civilization. I could scarcely contain my excitement at the prospect of visiting the physical site of the event, the spot where time merges into eternity and space into infinity.

Weekends in Jerusalem can be disconcerting. Friday, Saturday and Sunday are holy days to one or other of the three main religions that live proximately if not amicably under the single Jerusalem sky. You might expect that the *mono* personage of monotheism could have decided, without disrupting the smooth running of the heavenly Jerusalem, on a single day acceptable to all to indulge His or Her vanity. However, as of yet, such prickly questioning had not broken through the carapace of faith.

I was leaving my room, going in search of a café to which Jewish Sabbath restrictions did not apply when I had my first meeting with Leah. She looked dubiously at my religious attire. It certainly could not have been a surprise to her, as Jerusalem was full of clerics of a bewildering variety, each with their own distinctive garb. She eyed me from top to bottom, eventually returning to my black hat on a head of unkempt hair. She remarked that I looked more like a Hasidic Jew than a Christian. I was surprised, but not hurt. In spite of her bluntness, she had a sincerity that softened the harshness of her comments. However, the remark reminded me that I did indeed need a barber. Perhaps I should also think about the hat. I smiled warmly at her, thanked her and said I would give the matter my consideration. She walked away with a smile that was difficult to decipher.

By accident—I would come to wonder if indeed it was an accident—we met up again. I had just ordered coffee and rolls when she entered the cafe. She looked around. The cafe was crowded, but not full. She feigned surprise at seeing me and made her way to my table. The pretence was so obvious that she evidently wanted me to be aware of it. She suggested that as we shared the same hostel, we might share the same table. Her suggestion made sense in a crowded cafe, so I invited her to join me. By the time we finished our breakfast, she had elicited from me all the relevant facts regarding my life and work. Apart from her name, I discovered virtually nothing about her. As we prepared to leave, I told her that I was going to visit the Christian sites, and asked her if she would care to accompany me.

'Not my scene,' she informed me.

'You are not a Christian, then,' I persisted. 'A Jew, perhaps?'

'Ethnically,' she stated curtly, leaving me with the obvious conclusion.

'I see,' I said. Unsure of what it was that I saw. 'You are probably busy.'

'No, I am not.' She paused then, as if weighing her options. 'Perhaps, I will join you after all.'

We set out on our way to the Church of the Holy Sepulchre, also known as the Church of the Resurrection. The names highlighted for me, even then, the different approaches of the Churches to the redemptive event. Roman Catholicism, in the spirit of Saint Paul, looked to atoning death, whereas the Eastern Church looked joyfully to the skies for redemption. As we entered through the ancient arch that led into the square before the church, I could not help comparing it to the massive piazza of Saint Peter's in Rome. There was no similarity. This space was inferior, and yet as far as significance went there was no contest. Here was not the tomb of just an apostle—this site had everything. It was a place of triple significance: Crucifixion, Burial and

Resurrection of the Lord of history. The mystery of redemption energized the area just as the cosmic rays of the sun pummelled the weather-beaten walls of the ancient edifice, but a greater rising than that of the natural sun had taken place here. The very fabric of the structure was history in stone. I could hardly contain my emotion.

We entered through an unimpressive doorway. In my mind's eye, I returned to Saint Peter's in Rome. The entrance to the disciple's mausoleum was so much grander that the very thought of weighing one against the other was futile. However, this space, encompassed by successive piles of stone and mortar, was unique, or so I thought at the time. I would later muse on the conflict that might have arisen between the deities when the Emperor Hadrian built a temple to Venus on the site. However, on that first, poignant occasion, I could have joyfully spent the whole day prayerfully exploring the interior that smelt of incense and burning wax, but it was not just redolent with aromatic spices, it was fragrant with the atmosphere of heaven. Even the light was celestial, I thought; whatever I perceived celestial light to be in those remote, simple and naive days. However, since my companion did not share my faith-fuelled emotion, I resolved to return alone another day and indulge my interest to the full. Therefore, forcing limbs that longed to linger to move rapidly around the tantalizing interior, I proposed that we move on.

When we emerged from the church, Leah suggested that, since we were myth tracking, we should also visit the Dome of the Rock, from where, she pronounced facetiously, Muhammad too ascended into heaven. I was familiar with the myths associated with the Temple Mount. As well as the site of Muhammad's mythical, equestrian flight into the heavens, it was also where the world was formed, Adam was created and Abraham, good father that he was, would have plunged a knife into his young son had not an angel prevented him. I was not amused. Putting the Jesus event on a par with the Muhammad myth was just too much. This time she had gone too far. I looked at her, anger smouldering in my eyes. Unabashed, she held my gaze, silently challenging me to defend my position. For a moment, nothing happened. I simply continued looking defiantly into her testing eyes. Then something jarred within me, as if the quiver of a mild earthquake had shaken my stability. In the days, weeks and years that followed, I would ponder Leah's defiant remark and the effect it had on my faith.

Meanwhile, I immersed myself, with consuming interest, in the work of salvaging and transcribing the ancient texts. The challenge was monumental—an excellent opportunity for any archaeologist or historian. I threw myself wholeheartedly into the task, brooding thoughtfully over the archaic writings trying to define their meaning, but more importantly seeking to liberate the scribe's thoughts imprisoned within the antique markings impressed on strips of animal hide.

12: The Time of Vespasian

I was always a wanderer. Initially as a student in Alexandria and Antioch and later bringing the good news of salvation, first with my beloved Master and, after he departed, with other companions. But, after the fall of Jerusalem, I was a homeless wanderer. After spending some time in Alexandria, trying to make sense of our faith in the wake of the destruction of the Temple and our former way of life, I parted from Apollos and made my way to Rome. I arrived in time to witness their arrogant victory celebrations, which they call the *triumph*—the final humiliation of my people. But victors are typically arrogant.

It was dark when I woke that morning from a fitful, trouble-filled sleep. Since the war, my sleep was rarely tranquil. Stars danced in the inky void of the Roman sky. It seemed as if the heavens had entered into the celebrations. However, it was not a day of festival for any Jew. I was not there to partake, but to bring the good news of salvation to my demoralized people now scattered throughout the empire. Since the war, it had become more difficult to understand and explain that 'good news'.

Our firm expectation of victory proved illusory. Now, the citizens of Rome with their emperor were ready to flaunt their success through the streets of the city; a conquest they attributed to Jupiter! The shocking, incomprehensible shame of it! How could Israel's God, the One and the True, permit his Holy Name to be defamed and humiliated before a lifeless idol? Could it be? I shuddered at the thought that slipped through my mind, well-guarded and disciplined though it was against such ploys of the Evil One. Is it possible that the God of Israel is less powerful than Rome's deities? I came to a sudden halt as confusion, like an obscuring fog, stalled my steps. Excited Romans on their way to the spectacle collided with me, berating me for impeding their progress and, taking stock of my countenance, ridiculing me for being one of the vanquished.

I was present at Octavian's Walls, to witness the arrival of our conquerors, the Emperor Vespasian, *Pontifex Maximus,* and his son, Titus, the despoiler of the Temple. Remembering the horror of Jerusalem, I shuddered to see that countenance again. Crowned with laurel and robed in imperial purple, they met the senate. A tribunal was set up, with a pair of ivory chairs for father and son to receive the soldiers' acclamation. They then made their way to the Gate of Pomp from where all such processions begin. There, they partook of some food, changed into their festive robes and witnessed the sacrifices prepared for the gods. Then the pageant in all its tragic magnificence proceeded through the streets towards the Temple of Jupiter Capitolinus.

The Legions carrying their standards were impressive even to the eyes of the vanquished. Trumpets taken from the Holy Temple blared, frightening animals and captives alike, who were reluctant participants in the spectacle. Pageants of gold, silver and ivory, depicting their victories, passed by, followed by the spoils taken from the cities of Galilee and Judea. Treasures taken from the Holy Temple came last— the Golden Table, the Great Candlestick, called the Menorah, and finally the Holy Torah. As a follower of the Way inaugurated by our Teacher of Righteousness, I had moved away from Temple worship, but still the sight was a grievous one to the eyes of any Jew. We criticized the abuse of the Temple, not the Temple itself.

The parade paused at the Temple of Jupiter, where the conquerors of the Jews awaited news of their final victory. Out of sight, over by the Tarpeian Rock, Simon Bar Giora, the captured leader of the revolt, was dragged to the edge of the precipice and thrown to his death. The cry of acclamation reached the Temple and ended that part of the celebration.

The emperor, his sons, family, senators and aristocrats repaired to the various feasts prepared for them.

For me, the soul searching initiated by Apollos in Alexandria continued. All our former hopes and beliefs were ash in the ruins of the Jerusalem Temple. I could see no salvation except by adopting the teaching of the dissident, Paul, and putting our faith in the Holy One and His will to save us.

13: Modern Rome

Lunch was simple and appetizing. It was pleasantly warm, so Giuseppe prepared an inviting salad with cheese, fruit, asparagus and a variety of other vegetables on a bed of lettuce, sprinkled with mint and olive oil. A platter of breads—ciabatta, focaccia and chunks of a baguette— occupied the centre of the table. An ice bucket with a bottle of chilled white wine completed the table. Giuseppe surveyed the table and, satisfied with it, returned to the library to call his grandnephew.

Marc was engrossed in reading Giuseppe's account of his time in Jerusalem. It was a fresh insight into the personal, as well as the professional, life of his granduncle. He found it intriguing. He regretted the call to lunch—he would have preferred to continue reading.

'Your memoir is fascinating.' Marc was back on the terrace nibbling a piece of cheese. 'As a general reader, it gives a new awareness of the time and place. As a relative, it is even more captivating.'

'I print it out as I proceed. You can take what I have done so far with you, if you wish.'

'Thank you, I would like that. You are very forthright about your private life. Might you be inhibited, knowing that your grandnephew will read it?'

'By now, I should have outgrown such reserve. Besides, as a biblical scholar, you must already know much of my life story, professional and private. It might help you to know that I have experienced life and love.'

'I don't want to anticipate events, so I won't ask about Leah. She was very blunt. I suppose her experiences made her that way. I found your reaction to her subtle challenge to the Resurrection very interesting. Initially, you were offended, and then something altered within you.'

Giuseppe reached for his glass and held it thoughtfully to his lips before sipping. 'That was a pivotal moment in my life of faith, the moment when life changed gears. It felt physical. Her comment was provocative, which was doubtless her intention. Initially, I felt indignant, but it impelled me to scrutinize more critically convictions often naively held. Marco, it is not my intention to plunge you into a crisis, but I do speak my mind. I respect your genuinely held beliefs, and trust your maturity to accept mine also.'

'Don't worry, Uncle, I have had some similar challenges recently.'

'Carlo?' Giuseppe posed the question gently.

'Among others,' answered Marc. 'He sometimes angers me, but behind it all, I realize he has a point. His comments make me rethink aspects of faith that I took for granted.'

'Faith is like a comfort blanket that surrounds us from childhood. As we go through life, doubts arise which cause us to wonder if faith really makes sense, but the blanket is so reassuring that we snuggle down and bury our doubts in its folds. Then something happens.'

'Like the incident in the Church of the Resurrection,' suggested Marc, choosing the optimistic name of the church.

'Yes! It may be nothing spectacular in itself, but its effects are. It provokes a radical shift of vision. We slowly but surely begin to view life from a different perspective. In my case, my attitude to the reading of scripture changed. Previously, even as an academic, I read the gospels with the eyes of faith without being aware that I was doing so.'

'Yes, I know what you mean. We realize that they are not firsthand, eyewitness accounts of the life of Jesus, but we read them as if they were. Even scholarly papers often refer to events in the gospels as if confident of their historical reliability.'

'That incident with Leah prompted me to be more critical in my reading. Was the recorded ascension of Jesus into heaven any more credible than the ascension of Muhammad? Why did I believe one and reject the other? Was Jesus himself any more substantial than Orpheus? I could pick out layer upon layer of the oral and written traditions from which the gospels developed over time and by different interest groups or individuals. Consequently, they are full of contradictions. Bizarre attempts are made to reconcile them, but they defy such efforts.'

'Like the developing idea of Mary's virginity,' suggested Marc. 'The early traditions knew nothing of a Virgin Birth, and then the idea was born—it was appropriate, and developing doctrinal issues required it. Later contributors to the gospels ran with it.'

'Yes, that is a good example. It should be obvious that there is no sincere way of reconciling the early and later traditions. The infancy narratives, another example, are rife with contradictions. Early traces of an acceptance that Jesus was illegitimate are detectable. In time, this developed into a belief in the Virgin Birth. *Mary was found with child.* Horror of horrors! Until a solution presented itself ... *of the Holy Spirit.* It is true to say that practically everything of significance in the gospels is open to challenge. That is why we have so many branches of Christianity today.'

'All claiming an historical Jesus as the founder,' added Marc.

'Was Jesus himself historical?' Giuseppe pointedly asked.

'Paul is vague on the question,' said Marc. 'His expression *according to the flesh* is hotly debated among scholars.'

'The original kerygma is so obscure that some scholars have built an adequate case claiming that an historical Jesus never existed. They claim, as we discussed earlier, that the gospels are presenting another mystery religion based on a myth. Some hold that the Jesus presented in the gospel derives from a number of similar teachers. Other scholars accept the possibility of an historical Jesus, whom tradition mythologized as it did Pythagoras, Apollonius of Tyana and others. All that you know, Marco, I am not telling you anything new.'

Marc understood exactly what Giuseppe was saying. It was nothing new. Only his attitude to it was changing. Of late, he was experiencing many moments of doubt, but so far nothing definitive that altered his view of life or provoked him to abandon his faith. He could still *feel* his soul. It was not, perhaps, a profound way of expressing his awareness of something beyond the physical, but it was his way. However, he knew that he was going through a process of change that could end with him abandoning his faith. Remembering the beach, he already had intimations of what might tip him over the edge.

Tourists

Marc's second meeting with his supervisor was discouraging. His research showed that he was not workshy, but he produced nothing new that was relevant to his topic. While Giuseppe's memoir was compelling on a personal level, so far, it did not advance his proposition that Qumran directly influenced Christianity. He was simply going over old ground, presenting yet again the former opinions. He felt deflated, while Monsignore Martini made no secret of his satisfaction at Marc's disappointment. He did not actually say, 'I told you so', but his attitude implied it. Marc left the office feeling demeaned, not by anything the professor said, but by his self-satisfied manner. He returned to the convent wondering despondently if he should give in, and abandon his chosen topic.

It was with relief that the familiar horn of Carlo's car penetrated his gloom. With renewed buoyancy, he went to the window and saw Carlo smiling up at him.

'Marco! Marco! We need some diversion,' he shouted. 'Let us be tourists for the day.' Carlo was dressed more like a combatant in battledress than a tourist—a camouflage-patterned tank top defined his muscular chest while military-style fatigues hugged his buttocks. The

110

sight and the suggestion came as a welcome relief after a disappointing morning with the monsignore.

After briefly conferring, they decided to leave the car and walk to the Borghese Gallery. Meandering by the Tiber, trees cast a welcome shade along the footpath.

Marc was disappointed that Luigi was not with Carlo. 'Where is Luigi?'

'Showing off for the tourists,' replied Carlo.

'You can sound insensitive,' said Marc. 'Does Luigi ever take offence?'

'Of course not, Luigi knows me. He knows that I love him.'

'That is obvious.'

Carlo flashed a challenging smile. 'Are you jealous?'

'No,' replied Marc. He liked Luigi. He could not be envious of him. On the other hand, Luigi might resent his intrusion into their close friendship. 'I just wonder where I fit in.'

'Do you want to fit in?'

'Let's not spoil the day by getting into that. I have issues to work out.'

They continued walking in silence, the bustling traffic to their right, the tranquilizing river to the left. Caught between chaos and calm, Marc was experiencing both. He wanted to enjoy the day with his friend, but Carlo's question reminded him of the concerns that needed addressing.

Arriving eventually at the Borghese Gardens, they sat on a bench. Marc looked hesitantly at Carlo, who responded to the inquiring look by asking, 'What's on your mind?'

'I just wondered if you lost your faith because of the incident you told me about.'

'No! That just showed me the frustration that develops from denying our basic instincts. I continued on to the novitiate.'

'And then?'

'You know—prayer, work, study and endless meditation on the "the great things of the gospel". I began to wonder if it was not just a tiny bit over the top.'

'Why?' Marc was genuinely interested.

'Any competent deity would not have made such a mess of things in the first place. You only have to look around to see the unholy mess this so-called creation is. Assuming that Mr Know-All did miscalculate, which is a ridiculous assumption to begin with, could he not have devised a less lurid remedy? I could not see much love in that plan for the salvation of the world. Meditating on the crucifixion is enough to make a sane person psychotic. It's sheer nonsense.'

'That is hardly a theological conclusion. Life is a mystery, not a self-evident proposition. Even scientists find it difficult to explain many of the problems related to the physical world. If we followed your reasoning, we would still hold that the earth is at the centre of the solar system.'

'Theology was not much help in that debate.'

'You know what I mean,' said Marc with exasperation. 'If you follow the obvious, you are liable to be wrong.'

'So you think it's obvious,' said Carlo teasingly.

'You are twisting my words.'

'If the deity played fair, I would think that a matter of such importance as the salvation of the world would be obvious to all, not just a few high-powered theologians.'

'So you left the novitiate,' suggested Marc, impatient with his inability to counter attack, or even mount an adequate defence.

'Not immediately—I did not rush to follow my instincts. My unscholarly conclusions led me to question the purpose of prayer and penance. What was so commendable about frustrating our natural urges? My eyes began to wander and landed on a fellow inmate from Switzerland.'

'Luigi?'

Carlo nodded. 'I wondered what he made of it all. Was he totally committed, or was he having doubts also? You know how it is. Silence and banning particular friendships make it difficult to get to know another.'

'Nevertheless, you did succeed.'

'We were robust young studs, so one day we got the job of sawing a few fallen trees in a nearby forest.'

'I'm surprised—two alone together.'

'Maybe they were short of manpower that day. At any rate, we worked in the shade of the trees, but were soon sweaty from our exertion—an old-fashioned crosscut saw was good enough for novices. Good candidate that I was, I kept my shirt on. Luigi however, showing a defiant independence that delighted me, threw aside his shirt. Even then, he was naturally muscular.' Carlo paused, and closed his eyes, recalling his undisguised admiration at the muscular physique and the smooth, bronze skin that glistened in pearl patches where the sun's rays managed to penetrate the thick, high tree canopy of the forest.

The pause lengthened, and Marc thought that Carlo had finished. 'Well,' he encouraged.

'Well, it was not the time to investigate Luigi's frame of mind— his body was too inviting. I was taking a chance. He was bigger than I was, if I miscalculated I could end up with a broken nose. But, he was irresistible. I reached out and fondled his nipple. His smile was a mixture of surprise and welcome—I was encouraged. He responded by unbuttoning my shirt and fondling my chest. Next, we were in each other's arms, caressing and kissing with the pent-up energy generated by years of restraint. Nature took its course, which ended in an explosion of pleasure. My first experience, apart from what is clinically termed "nocturnal ejaculation". Believe me, there is no comparison.'

'And that brought closure to all your uncertainty,' said Marc, dismissively.

'Yes!' Carlo was elated. 'You should try it.'

Strolling through the extensive parkland of the Villa Borghese, Marc was trying to imagine Carlo's earlier life, while his friend was amused at the effect his commentary had on Marc, who appeared scorched by a source other than the sun. On their circuitous way to the Borghese Gallery, they came upon the Villa Giulia. A mischievous glint lit up Carlo's face as he elbowed Marc and nodded towards the villa.

Marc knew the reason for Carlo's interest. His course in Church History touched, but did not dwell on the pontificate of Julius III, but his own interest filled in the gaps. He had already visited the villa, which was no longer the playhouse that Pope Julius had envisaged, but an Etruscan museum. He was well acquainted with that pope's life, but feigned ignorance when his cynosure began to sound off.

'Julius was pope from 1550 to 1555 and affairs of Church and State took second place to this, his Pleasure Dome. That is not to say that he was ineffectual in matters of Church and State. He was, however, primarily a connoisseur of the arts, the last of the High Renaissance Popes.' Carlo paused, like an accomplished guide, to give his audience time to admire both narrative and the skill of the narrator. 'He dismissed the criticism levelled against him for the time and money invested in building and embellishing his villa.' Carlo paused again, this time to give dramatic import to his next disclosure, which he proceeded to divulge with simulated furtiveness. 'Further condemnation arose over his love for a beggar boy that he picked up from the streets of Parma. Public censure did not deter him. Quite the opposite, it appears. On his election to the papacy, he created 17-year-old Innocenzo a cardinal, conferring on him the title Cardinal Nephew (*Cardinalis Nepos*, from which the concept and the term *Nepotism* comes). I admire Julius's attitude,' concluded Carlo with undisguised esteem.

'I don't see much to admire.' Marc was uncomfortable. 'The young man was ill equipped to fill such a role.'

'He was open about his sexuality in the face of criticism. Don't you think that admirable?'

'There was no need to flaunt it,' observed Marc.

Carlo did not comment. They continued their tour silently observing the Etruscan artefacts at ground level, while above their heads a swarm of winged Putti cavorted in primal innocence. Marc began to wonder—if he judged Julius not to be admirable, he had to admit that he was honest. To be oneself in the face of unrelenting criticism is never easy. Leaving the villa, they continued in silence towards the Borghese Gallery. Carlo found his voice once again.

'Cardinal Scipione Borghese built, embellished and adorned the villa,' he began, trying to revitalize his ill at ease companion. 'His uncle, Camillo Borghese, was elected Pope in 1605 and promoted his nephew to the College of Cardinals—another *Cardinalis Nepos*. As Cardinal Nephew he was perhaps the most powerful man in Rome. One of his first acts was to invite his friend Stefano Pignatelli to join his court in the city. Scipone's affection for Stefano was such that he allowed him a free hand in exercising all the power that resided in the office of the Cardinal Nephew. Naturally, scandal ensued and the pope ordered Stefano out of Scipione's house. However, the separation so affected the cardinal that he fell ill. The pope had to allow Stefano to return and nurse his nephew back to health.'

'What is it with Cardinal Nephews?' Marc felt exasperated, not by new information, but a new dawning.

'In time, Stefano himself went on to take his place in the College of Cardinals,' continued Carlo. 'Undoubtedly, Scipione loved Stefano, but he also loved art. Due to his patronage, the Borghese Gallery houses some of the most exquisite works of Gian Lorenzo Bernini whose touch could seemingly transform stone into pliant flesh.'

On entering the gallery, commentary was no longer appropriate or necessary. The works of art spoke for themselves. They gazed in awe and admiration at the *Rape of Prosperina* where Bernini's astonishing artistry succeeded in sinking the fingers of the rapist convincingly into the marble thigh of his victim as if into delicate flesh. Many connoisseurs of art refer to his sculpture of David as marble in motion. Contrary to the apparent motion of the stone David, the ferocious

115

concentration on the face of the youth with the sling immobilized the very fleshy admirers, just as it did the unfortunate Goliath.

When they left the gallery, Marc was subdued sauntering down the Viale Museo Borghese towards the Porta Pinciana. When they reached Via Veneto, Carlo broke their silence.

'Would you like some lunch?'

Marc was too preoccupied to eat, but did not want to disappoint Carlo. 'Not here,' he suggested. 'It is too expensive.'

The Veneto itself is touristy and expensive, so they turned into a side street and soon found an inexpensive trattoria frequented by locals. They ordered a salad and wine. Conscious of Marc's disquiet, Carlo made light conversation. Marc was reflecting on Pope Julius, Scipione and art. Music and art had a way of making him focus on what was real in his life. Julius and Scipione identified the specific reality he was focusing on.

'I have been thinking,' began Marc.

'So I noticed.'

'About Pope Julius. I do not think him admirable, but he was honest.'

'Why not admirable? He had the courage of his convictions.'

'He was a priest—a pope. Saving a youth from a life of poverty was admirable, but he should not have made him a cardinal. He should not have made him his catamite.'

'Perhaps people thought differently in those days. Perhaps, in the time of Julius and Scipione, their roles and beliefs were not as well defined as today.'

'I agree. If I have learned anything from research, it is that reading minds from the past is notoriously difficult.'

'Let us leave Julius to history,' suggested Carlo.

'And Scipione.'

'And Scipione,' agreed Carlo.

They returned to the Via Veneto and continued walking down the long, curving, tree-lined sweep of one of Rome's most elegant streets right into the Piazza Barberini, where they decided to rest and have a cool beer within sight of the Fontana di Tritone.

'Rome would not be Rome without Bernini,' said Carlo, looking over at the fountain.

'He certainly left his mark on the city.' Marc was thoughtful. 'I don't feel like going back to the convent just yet.'

'Come to my garret. We could listen to some music and later I will prepare dinner. After that, I'll walk you back to the convent and pick up the car.'

'It sounds good, but you must have other plans.'

'I enjoy showing off my lovely city.'

'It is magnificent,' agreed Marc, as they left behind the Fontana di Tritone and headed in the direction of Bernini's far more unusual monument—his obelisk-supporting elephant—and the basilica of Santa Maria sopra Minerva, which contained the tomb of Cardinal Stefano Pignatelli.

Secret Gospel

Leaving the convent at the start of another week, Marc considered availing of Giuseppe's library but, in spite of his granduncle's encouragement, he feared that he might appear forward. Instead, he made for the Vatican Library. He felt a rush of delight at the prospect of seeing Carlo again. The anticipated pleasure reminded him that his problem with the relationship was unresolved. He was letting it drag on from one meeting to the next, knowing that inevitably it would end either in bitterness or in bed.

Seeing Carlo brought the expected surge together with the resultant emotional stress. He suspected that Carlo might suggest lunch. He would ultimately have to take the matter in hand and bite the bitter bullet, but not today.

'Are you free for lunch?' asked Carlo, as Marc was about to retreat to the reading room with his requested volumes. Marc nodded with a smile and departed.

The morning passed in effortless concentration, reminiscent of his pre-Carlo focus on study. He did not notice Giuseppe's arrival and successfully contained all thought of Carlo. He was surprised, as the concerns that recently distracted him continued to dog him. Even the anticipated lunch with Carlo did not dilute his attention to his reading. He gathered his books and returned them to Carlo. As they chattered quietly, Giuseppe approached.

Addressing the two friends, he said, 'I would like to invite you both to join me for lunch?' They instinctively looked at each other and, reading the signs, the palaeographer, realized that they had made their own arrangements, and regretted his intrusion. 'If it is not convenient, we can arrange it for another day,' he added quickly.

'Thank you, Professor.' Carlo was the first to recover. He suspected that Marco would appreciate another meeting. 'I would like that.'

They found the same table at which Giuseppe and Marc had eaten the previous week with a similar green-shaded parasol to protect them from rays already pulsating with summer energy. They ordered and waited for the wine to arrive.

'Carlo,' began Giuseppe, as the waiter arrived with the wine, 'Do you know that Marco is my grandnephew?'

'Yes,' replied Carlo. 'It is a small world.'

'Very small,' said Giuseppe. 'Were we go back far enough, we would find that you and Marco are related. We all come from the same source.'

'Adam and Eve,' said Carlo, with a testing tilt of his head.

'It is as good a stab at it as any, I suppose,' offered Giuseppe.

'Probably not one that a modern biologist would create,' suggested Marc.

'Probably not,' conceded Giuseppe. 'But the ancients did not enjoy the benefits of a Darwinian education and a lab full of specialist equipment.' There was a pause in the conversation as the waiter arrived with the food.

'It is easy to see the light when you stand on the shoulders of giants,' offered Marc, continuing the topic.

'Not that easy,' suggested the librarian. 'There are many that dismiss Darwin, in spite of his tireless research.'

'And the subsequent experiments that substantiate many of his claims,' added Giuseppe. 'Giants help the process of acquiring knowledge in various fields, and then it's down to the individual. "It is true that truth is esteemed in the utterances of all the nations—yet is there any tongue or language that grasps it?"'

'1Q27,' said Marc, the symbol for the Book of Mysteries, from which Giuseppe quoted.

'You know your scrolls. I am sure you are also familiar with the Secret Gospel of Mark.'

'Yes,' replied Marc hesitantly, perplexed by Giuseppe's sudden shift from the scrolls to a disputed text allegedly used by an early heretical sect to support their homosexuality. 'It is a letter ostensibly by Clement of Alexandria, in which he refers to a secret gospel written by Mark.'

'In it Clement has strange things to say about truth. He suggests that true things are not necessarily the truth. Such an idea is odd to us, but he is promoting the primacy of faith over human opinions in the pursuit of truth. Of course, we would agree that opinions are not necessarily true. Human reason is a better guide, better than faith, I would contend.'

'I agree,' affirmed Carlo.

'Not everyone would,' continued Giuseppe. 'I know of a physicist who chooses to reject the undisputed claims of his science that do not agree with his faith.'

'Faith is tenacious,' suggested Marc 'It is not easy to break free and follow your ideals.'

'I agree,' said Giuseppe, softly. 'Is your lunch not to your liking, Carlo? You are not eating.'

'The food is fine,' he replied, taking his fork to the salad. 'I'm just interested. I must admit that this secret gospel escaped my attention. What is it?' Carlo directed the question to Giuseppe, who, with a flick of his eyes, redirected it to Marc, who was beginning to understand why Giuseppe had introduced the disputed letter.

'Morton Smith,' he began, 'an American scholar, claimed to have discovered the text while working at the Mar Saba monastery near Jerusalem in 1958. The document in question is a seventeenth-century copy of a letter purporting to be from Clement of Alexandria.' Marc looked at Carlo. 'You know that Clement's life straddled the second and third centuries. There is, obviously, a fair interval between Clement and the text in question. The professor photographed the letter, which subsequently went missing. It quotes two passages from this secret gospel and even directs where the passages quoted should fit in Mark's canonical gospel.'

'I must look it up,' said Carlo. 'Do you have any suggestions?'

'A good source is: *early Christian writings.com*,' suggested Marc.

'I know it. It's great, but it contains so much that the secret gospel slipped by me, unnoticed. Does the letter give any indication as to why Mark would have written a second gospel?'

'Yes! It was intended for those more advanced spiritually—for those striving for perfection. He wrote in fanciful language of the gospel stories leading believers into the innermost sanctuary of truth hidden by seven veils. I'm sure you know that Clement had Gnostic leanings—a circumstance that saw him removed from the list of saints. This letter would support that.'

'You said that he quotes from the gospel.'

'Yes! Two passages. One is very short. The longer narrative is a story of Jesus raising a youth from the dead—similar to the raising of Lazarus in John's gospel. It contains oblique indications of a homosexual relationship, which the Carpocratians espoused as supportive of their lifestyle. The fact that the letter disappeared has led to scholarly scepticism,' continued Marc.

120

'But the photographs exist,' insisted Carlo.

'Still,' suggested Marc, 'without the original to examine and test, doubts will linger. There are doubts as to its very existence.'

'It certainly existed,' said Giuseppe.

'How can you be so sure?' Carlo asked the question, but Marc was equally curious.

'I saw it,' replied Giuseppe as casually as if referring to the morning newspaper. He laid down his fork to explain. 'I was enjoying a break—a busman's holiday—examining documents and texts at Mar Saba. That was in 1958, when Professor Smith was cataloguing the books. I met him there and he showed me the text that he had just found.' Marc and Carlo were all ears. 'As Marco explained, it is a handwritten copy of a letter which appears to be from Clement of Alexandria. Consequently, the writing did not claim to be Clement's, but from a cursory examination at the time, I would say that the language and style were. The gospel excerpts quoted also seemed to me to be genuine Mark.'

'That should settle it then.' Carlo was emphatic.

'Thank you for your confidence Carlo, but not all would be so quick to accept my judgement,' said Giuseppe, with a patient smile. 'It is unfortunate that the original went missing. It is important to have the original of any disputed text. You will never get universal consensus, but rigorous tests would result in greater certainty.'

'Why did Clement write the letter?' Carlo was intrigued.

'We have many ancient texts that reflect various "interests" of the early Christian communities. In this letter, the Carpocratians and their homosexuality troubled poor Clement. It has the air of authenticity, because licentiousness frequently sent the same gentleman rushing for pen and paper.'

'Were the Carpocratians licentious?' Carlo's interest was evident.

'We don't know. Such writings showed us clearly that there were Christian communities that promoted sexual freedom. Their opponents eventually silenced them, together with their writings. We know of them now only through their critics, who chose to quote from their writings the passages most suitable for their denunciation. As a result, it is difficult to determine whether such early communities were licentious or merely liberal. Standing on the shoulders of giants, we can reliably conclude that not all early Christians were as sexually inhibited as today's Church.'

'I second that.' Carlo's emphatic endorsement reminded Marc of his friend's championing of Pope Julius and Scipione.

'We should approach all ancient texts, including the Bible and the Dead Sea Scrolls, with caution. Your supervisor, Marco, agreeing with Clement, would suggest that you study them with faith. I would prefer to examine them aided by reason. And live life with openness.' The message was not lost on Marc. Carlo too was pleased but unusual for him, restrained.

The meal continued to the accompaniment of everyday chatter. Knowing that Giuseppe would be interested, Marc told him about Luigi and his operatic ambitions. He expressed a wish to accompany them to the concert whenever it took place. However, towards the end of the lunch, Carlo returned to the topic that so gripped him.

'What could have happened to the letter?'

'If it still exists,' replied Giuseppe with a playful twinkle in his eye, 'You have the best chance of finding it.'

'Me!' exclaimed Carlo. Then Giuseppe's insinuation dawned on him. 'You think it might be in the Vatican Library?'

'If it is anywhere.' Enjoying his tease, Giuseppe sipped his wine.

14: The Time of Titus

A jagged shaft of crimson began to seep through the cracked shell of the eastern sky and drip its hesitant light into the early morning gloom that hung upon the whispering sea. The wind was slight, but sufficient to stretch the sails and propel the ship moderately towards the Egyptian coast. It was early spring and the night air was cold, but I was snug, wrapped in a warm cloak in a sheltered corner of the deck. Three companions lay curled up in sleep nearby.

I had not intended to stay on in Rome, but our followers, dejected in the wake of Rome's arrogant victory spectacle, prevailed upon me to prolong my sojourn with them. They longed to hear, repeatedly, the ever-welcome words about the *Parousia*—the longed-for vision of Daniel's Son of Man coming in his might and glory to establish his kingdom and overthrow established tyranny. In my efforts to console and strengthen, I drew upon the memory of my Master. His compassion was true and his words uplifting: *Blessed are you when you are hated and persecuted; wherever you have been persecuted, no place will be found.* My preaching was simply a reflection of his more sublime words. Paul's teaching about the passion of the Christ also strengthened the spirits of my persecuted fellow believers.

In the years following the war and its devastating consequences, it was difficult to see meaning in anything. It was then that the vision of Paul came into its own. There were many reasons to be suspicious of Paul, but in the light of subsequent events, he may have been right. In the wake of the war, our community was scattered. There was no

Temple and virtually no Jerusalem. What value did the Torah have without the Temple? In the aching heart of our dispirited and dispersed people, only Paul's Suffering Saviour and our resurrection with Him to new and eternal life made any sense. Paul got this idea of rising with the Messiah to new life from our writings, adapted it and made it his own. Only such a one, not adherence to the ancient Law, could put the maimed world to rights. It became the core of my preaching. Even Apollos, in spite of his many arguments with Paul, had to concede that his suffering Christos was more relevant to our shattered communities than all the wisdom of the ages. Of course, it had its problems. Presenting Paul's spiritual Christos in human terms inevitably seemed to humanize and historicize it. Time and language combined to dull the original message. After years of preaching and teaching, it was difficult to distinguish between the reality and the hyperbole that explained the reality. The only language available to speak of mysteries beyond human experience and understanding is the language of images—allegories, as Philo and Apollos called them. However, it frequently happens that the image used to reveal the mystery becomes the mystery itself. When I studied in Alexandria and Antioch, our masters taught us the ancient myths, but insisted that they were only representations—allegories. However, simple-minded, sincere followers of the Mystery Cults, believed that Dionysus or Mithras were actual people. That may be well and good if it encouraged their faith, but the better educated knew that such tales were only allegories. The same is true of Paul's Christos. We, the teachers, know that the stories relating to Paul's Christ figure are fiction, allegories, an aid to understanding, but many now believe them to be real events.

Looking up at the breaking dawn, I thought for a brief moment, that the jagged crack might rupture and explode before my very eyes to reveal the *Parousia,* and put an end to the problem of trying to reveal it in human language. That expectation was becoming a frequent fantasy now. Did that mean that the great moment was close, or that I was a hopeless optimist? Dawn, a time teeming with expectation and the hope

124

of new beginnings, seemed the perfect time for such a cosmic event. How long more would we have to wait? I had been waiting in expectation of that event all my life. The Master told us that it would arrive soon, in our lifetime. Now, with so many believers already dead, I began to wonder if it would ever arrive. The thought that my own continued survival perpetuated the expectation, brought on depression that grew more intense as the years passed, sadly unfulfilled.

As dawn began to surrender to morning, I smiled to recall the time when Peter, always intrigued and a little in awe of me, asked my Master, 'What of him?' His enigmatic reply gave rise to a belief among our followers that I would live to see the *Parousia,* but at that time, we all expected to witness the great day of the Lord's coming in glory. Now, many are dead and I look expectantly at the sky. I have lived long, too long, in expectation of that coming. The delay is incomprehensible. My Master and Paul, who agreed on little, did agree on the imminence of that great event.

The sun, already high upon our arrival, reflected from the mirror on top of the great tower on Pharos that identified the port of Alexandria. After many visits to the city, I still stood in awe before the magnificent lighthouse. It must surely be taller than the Babylonian Ziggurat, the arrogant building of which, the Holy Writings tell us, cast human communication into confusion. I was, from my constant travels, very aware of that confusion, but knowledge of my own native languages, Hebrew and Aramaic, together with Greek and Latin helped me through most linguistic difficulties. No matter how obscure the local dialect, someone was usually on hand, sufficiently familiar with one of the main languages, to act as interpreter. In preaching, my problem was not with a particular language, but with language itself. It simply is not adequate to the task. Even Paul was frustrated with language. We see through a dark glass, he said. The dark glass of language obscures more than it reveals of the eternal mysteries.

The city evoked many memories: student days with Apollos; contemplative days with my Master as we endeavoured to assimilate the spirituality of the Therapeutae; the weeks of recuperation following the horrors of war. It was a therapeutic place, for me more salutary than Gilead, though it did experience outbreaks of disorder. I, like my Master, had come to hold the Alexandrian Community in high regard. Upon our arrival in the city, it was to this centre that my companions and I directed our steps.

There was an air of excitement. A new book had been circulating among them. That, in itself, was not surprising, as all writings eventually found their way to Alexandria's great library. The news stirred my expectations, as I was already familiar with the work called the Gospel of Peter, which had dramatized, perhaps even historicized, the spiritual message of salvation. This new work was, in fact, two books—one a special, secret book for those more advanced into the mysteries of the Way—both said to be the work of Mark. I knew a Mark briefly in Jerusalem. Later, he and Paul spent some time with the brothers by the Salt Sea. They made some journeys together, but their relationship was sometimes fraught, as so many of Paul's relationships had proved to be. Perhaps he did write the books in question. When at our sanctuary, he spent some time writing about our Way. Nevertheless, I was intrigued and wished I could retire to my room to read it, but the brothers and sisters had many questions and wished to hear once again my understanding of the faith we held in common. Eventually, but with reluctance, they allowed me to retire.

As I handled the document, I wondered, as with the scrolls, what its future might be. It was different from the scrolls, written as it was on individual sheets of papyrus, and in Greek. I was intrigued to see that the book began with that greatly loved quotation from Isaiah, 'A voice crying in the wilderness prepare the way of the Lord,' so full of meaning for the community by the Salt Sea. The work reflected the spirit of the Teacher's New Covenant, but the author was not the Mark I knew. It was obvious that the author did not know Judea, and Mark certainly did. The gospel contained much from the *Wisdom Sayings* with which I was familiar. There were already various versions of them abroad. However, this book followed the narrative pattern of the Gospel of Peter. It began with a baptism by our earlier Episkopos and ended with a crucifixion and an empty tomb. It retained the characters that Peter's gospel had introduced into our teaching, but whereas Mark just alludes to a resurrection, Peter's earlier depiction was dramatic—it described a gigantic Jesus, supported by two cosmic figures, emerging from the tomb accompanied by the cross itself. Such hyperbole was plainly allegorical—expressing a mystery that was clearly beyond human understanding and consequently beyond our ability to express it. The new gospel was less obviously figurative and consequently more dangerous—it might lead people to believe that salvation was not the work of the Eternal One, but of a mere mortal. I am sure that was not the author's intention. It just highlighted again the difficulty we faced in presenting a message that clearly transcended language.

This new method of historicizing the spiritual was obviously a useful pedagogical tool, but the mystery of salvation enacted, as Paul stressed, before time began and in the realm of spirits must supersede the storytelling. That night, I resolved to produce a gospel that would retain the graphic descriptions introduced by these new gospels, but without ever losing sight of the eternal and unfathomable mystery that was the Eternal Father's gift of salvation. It was a difficult challenge that I had set myself.

The 'special' gospel for those initiated into the deeper mysteries, I found particularly intriguing, perhaps because I featured there. I recognized my meeting with my Master behind a highly dramatized event that appeared to make him into a God. Who but God can give life? He would not be pleased. Still, the story, bizarre as it was, stirred emotions and awakened memories of a once loving relationship. I have chosen to include it here.

And they came into Bethany. And a certain woman whose brother had died was there. And coming, she prostrated herself before Jesus and says to him, 'Son of David, have mercy on me.' But the disciples rebuked her. And Jesus, being annoyed, went with her into the garden where the tomb was,

127

and straightway a great cry was heard from the tomb. And going near, Jesus rolled away the stone from the door of the tomb. And straightway, going in where the youth was, he stretched forth his hand and raised him, seizing his hand. But the youth, looking upon him, loved him and began to beseech him that he might be with him. And going out of the tomb they came into the house of the youth, for he was rich. And after six days Jesus told him what to do and in the evening the youth comes to him wearing a linen cloth over his naked body. And he remained with him that night, for Jesus taught him the mystery of the kingdom of God. And thence, arising, he returned to the other side of the Jordan.

15: Modern Rome

Sitting on a bench, looking across the Tiber at the island dedicated to healing since ancient times, Marc reluctantly put aside Giuseppe's reflections. He found his granduncle's memoir very interesting, but was unable to give it his full attention; recent events kept intruding on his reading.

He normally found this place by the river soothing, but its magic failed today. He often came here to read and think. Inevitably, memories of the River Corrib at home came to mind. The Corrib had its charm, but the Tiber had history—blood was spilt into it, the odd pope ended up in it, and the Milvian Bridge, site of Constantine's 'miraculous' victory over his rival, straddled it. That bridge lived on in Christian consciousness almost on a par with the Church of the Resurrection in Jerusalem. Indeed that victory proved to be a sort of resurrection for the then outlawed and suspect Christian communities. Constantine's patronage raised a repressed religious sect into a Church Triumphant. He gave a suppressed alien cult something it did not have up to that time—prestige. It became glamorous and desirable—the emperor's religion. With status, came power; it became an arm of the state—in time it became a state. The thought disturbed Marc. He found many ideas disturbing lately.

Reflecting on the Roman Church of today he wondered if its external display of pomp and ceremony was, perhaps, more imperial than devotional. That the Church was the surviving rump of the Roman Empire was Carlo's constant jingle. Perhaps there was something to that. He pondered on a possible question for a theology examination: Today's Church—the legacy of Constantine or Christ. Discuss!

To Marc's back was the Jewish synagogue, built in 1904 when King Victor Emmanuel demolished the Jewish Ghetto and granted Jews full civil rights. From reading the reflections of Giuseppe so far, he could confidently infer his attitude to the Church's treatment of the Jews. It was bad enough that one Pope in the person of Paul IV (1555-1559), intolerant, fanatical and crazed though he was, should have herded Jews into a ghetto, it is incomprehensible that it took so long to correct such an atrocity. When the correction finally came, the civil power, not the Church, initiated it.

'Marco,' a familiar voice intruded on his thoughts.

'Sophia! What a surprise.'

'I am disturbing your studies,' she said apologetically.

'Don't let the books deceive you,' he replied, moving his backpack. 'Please sit down.'

'I am coming from the hospital,' she said, nodding across the river.

'Of course,' commented Marc, realizing that she spent much of her time there. 'It's surprising that we have not met here before. I spend a lot of time here. Asclepius helps to focus my mind on the ancient world.'

'Marco, meeting outside the convent, it seems the appropriate place to tell you that I have made a decision.'

'Oh,' said Marc with an apprehensive shudder.

'In spite of your valiant efforts to make sense of the Resurrection,' she placed her hand on Marc's hand. 'I have decided to leave religious life and concentrate on the present one.'

'I know your decision is a considered one, Sophia, but perhaps I should have advised you to seek another counsellor. I fear I added to your doubts.'

'Would that be such a bad thing?' She smiled as she posed her question. 'You challenged me. I would say that is the role of a spiritual director.'

'I am sorry,' sighed Marc.

'Don't be sorry. I am not. I was going to tell you at our next meeting.'

'Are you sure?' Marc's question was full of concern and some guilt. Her news made him aware of his own unresolved situation. At least, Sophia had made her decision.

'Yes!' Her simple assertion conveyed more assurance than any number of verbal embellishments and challenged Marc still further. 'You know that I have difficulties with faith. There is also that other matter. I told you I was attracted to someone. Well, we made love. It would probably have happened sooner, but he was a patient, and the medical profession too has its taboos. We could hardly wait for his discharge.' Her smile said it all.

'Is he fully recovered now?'

'Is an addict ever fully recovered?' A pained expression accompanied her question.

'An addict?' Marc's apprehension was evident in his tone.

'Julian was in rehab undergoing treatment for drug addiction. He had a very difficult time. I like to think that I might have helped.'

'Sophia, are you sure …?'

'Marco!' Sophia interrupted him. 'Rehabilitation is my field. I know exactly what I am getting into. I know what addiction can do to a person, but Julian is a thoroughly good person. That is his problem—he is too good. He cannot cope with life—endless wars, our inhumanity to each other, mankind's brutality to animals, our abuse of the environment and greedy rape of the planet. He tried to block it out, but his solution compounded the problem, as recourse to addictive drugs inevitably does. I know that in the future a solution more final might arise. Maybe, I can help him, but apart from all that, I love him.' Her statement was compelling in its simplicity and honesty.

Marc wondered if he would be strong enough to take on such a weighty commitment.

'Do you have time for a chat? I would like to know what you really think. Surely, you don't go along with Tertullian.'

Her comment amused him, and he chuckled softly. 'I am not being evasive, Sophia, when I say that I truly do not know. When I first wrestled with the problem of the Resurrection, Tertullian seemed an easy way out. It is such a crazy idea that it must be true.' The topic reminded him—'Have you heard of Rudolf Bultmann?'

'I think I recall the name from some of our lectures.'

'Our courses in the seminary treated him with caution. Of course, I read the great man—for a biblical student not to do so would be akin to learning to swim without going near water. I read his words, but did not listen to his ideas—my own preconceived convictions would not allow me to swim beyond my depth. Bultmann was an early advocate of form criticism.'

'Now, I remember him,' said Sophia, gratified to be able to 'box' him. 'Form criticism has something to do with getting to the core of the gospel message.'

'Exactly! Stripping away the layers added to the core gospel message in the course of oral and written transmission. Bultmann called it demythologizing the gospel. Strip away the myths to find the kerygma, the original message, at the heart of the gospel. Now that I am swimming in deep water, I may as well admit that I think if we analysed our beliefs they would fade into the mythical night from which they were drawn.'

'Where does that leave you now?'

'There are different interpretations of the Resurrection, ranging from absolute historicity to pure fiction. Throughout my student years, I believed that the story represented authentic, reliable reportage of the event. Being modern students, we accepted that the gospel writers themselves were not eyewitnesses to the life and death of Jesus, but we believed that they got their facts from eyewitnesses. Now, I find my conviction slipping from the most conservative interpretation to ... I don't know where.'

'It is necessary to face problems honestly,' said Sophia, seeing Marc's distress.

'You are a better counsellor than I.'

'Don't underestimate yourself. Religion is a minefield—difficult to traverse.'

'Miracles are always a problem, but as part of our religious legacy we accept them. If somebody told you of a person that came back from the dead recently, your reaction would be predictable. Many scholars suggest that Paul, the earliest New Testament writer, described a spiritual resurrection, but the Dead Sea Scrolls seem to have been developing the idea of a resurrected Messiah. Perhaps Paul got his idea from them. Mark, the earliest gospel, throws in the tantalizing notion of an empty tomb, to see how his readers would react. They evidently loved the idea, since the subsequent gospels ran with it and embellished it, like modern tabloids squeezing a particularly juicy and compelling storyline. The witnesses metamorphosed between men and angels, and varied in number in the later gospels.'

'I know that scholars now regard the last few verses of Mark's gospel as later additions. But the ending we have depicts a young man in the tomb speaking of a resurrection.'

'That is true, but there are no post Resurrection appearances described. The women fled the tomb afraid and bewildered. For such an extraordinary event, we need something more compelling.'

'I still find Tertullian unconvincing.'

'Many have followed his lead. Kierkegaard, the Danish philosopher, was even more pessimistic and with good reason. The corruption and evil we see in life can be overwhelming, and what we witness is only the tip of the iceberg. Our news bulletins are a daily witness to the atrocities that exist in our world, manmade and natural. Kierkegaard found life so absurd, corrupt and meaningless that faith alone made sense of it. He had no rational reason for his faith—his pessimism alone compelled him to take that leap. It is an understandable

133

position to take,' concluded Marc, his expression reflecting his own confusion.

'The leap of faith,' she added thoughtfully. 'He sounds a lot like Julian. "Creation's ceaseless, anguished sigh", he calls it.

<blockquote>

"I try,
But cannot dim the cry.
Creation's ceaseless, anguished sigh.
It reaches low, it stretches high,
Far, far beyond the seamless sky,
While down below ... I die."
</blockquote>

Poor Julian! You can see why he needs love, to give it and receive it.'

'Sophia!' Marc's voice reflected the misgivings evident in his eyes. He was concerned for Julian, without ever having met him, but also for Sophia and her uncertain future. At their first meeting, he feared the challenge she presented to his perceived inadequacy, but his admiration for her continued to grow with their friendship.

Sophia broke the protracted silence. 'Marco, do you really think that the misgivings we have are ours, plus a few others. Do you think it possible that the "great ones" in the hierarchy are immune to such doubts about the doctrine they preach with such casual certainty? Surely, they are aware of the problems associated with faith, yet there is never the slightest indication that there is any problem. They make their pronouncements as if everything were as clear as day and beyond dispute. I doubt their sincerity.'

'They are human. Expressing their doubts would unsettle others. The higher they rise the farther they have to fall. Self-preservation is strong in all of us.'

'That is true. If I thought it would help, I would encourage Julian to take Kierkegaard's leap. I would even take it with him—a less harmful therapy.'

'Is it?'

Marc's quiet comment elicited a surprised reaction from Sophia. 'Do you think that religion can be as dangerous as drug addiction?'

'History—Crusades, Inquisition and more recently Islamic terrorism—would make one wonder. Anyway,' he continued dismissively, 'you seem happy with your decision.'

'I am very relieved,' she replied, sensing that Marc did not wish to dwell on his comment. 'Since making the decision, I have wondered why I did not make it sooner. In the end, not doctrine or sex provided the push I needed. It was the abuse scandals—they shocked me. I did not believe that an institution that covered up such horrors could be of Jesus. The image of adults abusing young children and frightening them into silence was just too much.'

'That is a challenge for all of us,' said Marc sadly.

'Julian!' Surprised, she stood up. 'What are you doing here? Is anything wrong?'

'No,' he replied, embracing her. 'I thought you might like a coffee before returning to the convent. I thought I had missed you. Your colleagues at the hospital said you had left.' He held on to her hands and looked at her with such love that Marc felt a tremor run through him.

'Julian, I would like you to meet Marco, my very good friend.'

Marc stood up to shake his hand and found himself smothered in a tight embrace. Responding to Julian's friendliness, Marc could feel his shoulder blades through a light summer shirt. He was thin to the point of gaunt and of average height. His soft brown hair was curly and his eyes dark and searching. Marc could read there the truth of Sophia's statement that he needed love—to give it and receive it. Empathy, like a fragrance, emanated from Julian rendering Sophia's comment that he was a thoroughly good person superfluous. His magnetism was tangible, as was his vulnerability. He could feel in Julian's touch and see in his compassionate eyes a human who was not at one with this world. If he had lived in the first century, he would have been ideal material for initiation into the Mystery Religions of the time where knowledge (Sophia) would lead him to mystical understand and peace.

135

'Sophia's counsellor,' he said, as he released Marc and slipped his arm around Sophia's waist. His voice was a perfect accompaniment to the personality. Feeling his inadequacy in the role, Marc silently acknowledged it with an almost imperceptible nod. 'She thinks highly of you,' added Julian.

'Julian and Sophia,' reflected Marc as he looked at the complementary couple. Julian, the emperor defamed by Christian historians with the appellation 'Apostate' because, coming after Constantine, he tried to restore the Mystery Religions to the empire, and Sophia, the sublime Wisdom to which such religions aspired. 'Julian, you are a philosopher.'

'No,' replied Julian, assuming Marc's statement to be a question.

'Phil-o-so-pher,' stated Marc, enunciating the syllables distinctly, 'lover of Sophia.'

Julian's thin lips formed a shy, whimsical smile. 'Then I am a philosopher.'

They continued chatting for a few minutes, the body language between Sophia and Julian mesmeric. Then they departed, leaving Marc, captivated by their togetherness and disturbed by his own dithering—Sophia found resolution, why not he?

He pondered the encounter for some time. Meeting Sophia calmed him. He was now able to concentrate, so he took up Giuseppe's reflections and began to read.

16: Jerusalem: 1951-52

Reality that appears so concrete, resides in a moment so fleeting that its actuality seems insubstantial. Caught in the furious flow from past to future, the delicate present has barely time to exist. Teetering on the edge of two eternities, the *now* might be said to have an even flimsier claim on reality than the Higgs boson elementary particle that evaded detection by the enormous Hadron Collider for nuclear research for so long. It is only memory that gives substance to our present, providing it with the anchorage it would otherwise lack. If we had no memory of our past, we would have no knowledge of ourselves. Life would be meaningless successions of disjointed moments, rudderless and without the compass of identity. It was only in retrospect that the direction of my relationship with Leah became clear. Day by day, as if by stealth, our casual acquaintance became something more.

In spite of its inauspicious beginning, Leah and I grew close over the months that followed our initial meeting. From that first morning, we formed the habit of having breakfast together. Soon, walking me to the museum after breakfast became routine. It seemed natural to find her waiting outside the museum one evening to walk me home. That too became habit. Towards the end of the first year, I began to wonder just where that pattern would lead. I was aware of the 'dangers' or 'possibilities' as I came to think of them. My training had equipped me to recognize them and erect adequate barriers against them. However, since that first day in the Church of the Resurrection, something had changed in me. Leah's provocative comment about resurrection had unsettled me. My direction was no longer singular, my commitment no longer secure.

When it came, it was not a surprise. It seemed as natural as all the other stages in our relationship that had become routine. On our way home in the evening, we frequently stopped for dinner at a convenient restaurant along the way. After our meal, we would spend some time in one or other of our rooms. I was doing all the wrong things, but there was bravado in flouting the prescribed precautions. During those intimate chats, I would tell Leah of my day's work and she would relate instalments from her life story. During such exchanges, the vulnerable, loving Leah would emerge from behind the defence shield that life's misfortunes had erected around her. Her voice trembled as she spoke of her parents and the dread provoked in the family by the increasing power of Nazism. Her loathing for that regime was pathological. At first, she could not speak of her brother. It was only after months that she tearfully broke her silence on the topic, and spoke of their closeness, interdependence and his death. The grief of that tragedy drove her to protect her vulnerability by adopting the hard shell that I first encountered.

I also discovered that Joel, the hostel's owner, was not just an American friend, but a former lover. They had continued their relationship for a time after Leah arrived in Palestine, but it stopped after Daniel's death. Many things stopped then. His loss seemed to be the last straw, which proved too much. All the rest she bore with stoicism: the rise of Nazism and the suffering it caused her family; flight to a new country, learning a new language and adapting to a new culture; the unknown fate of her parents; another new culture and language, war and finally the death of the one who had shared all that with her. That loss overwhelmed her. So, when she took my hand and led me to my bed, it was no surprise, I had come to know the loving, vulnerable Leah lurking behind the shield of cynical woman of the world.

I was no Lothario. I was a bundle of nerves, guilt and fumbling inadequacies. Leah was the expert. Her patience with my ineptitude, her

138

tenderness and her love guided me to an adequate culmination. It was not an explosive climax. To call it adequate was to take liberties with the word, but it was a conclusion. That in itself was something. She did not stay the night. She left me in the early hours, abandoning me to a riot of religiously fuelled guilt. She probably knew that I had to face my conscience alone. However, such moral badgering did not stand in the way of further lovemaking. It too became a habit.

Frequent repetition dulled the voice of conscience, but did not silence it. Silence came through my work on the scrolls and the impetus they gave me to inquire objectively into, not only the canonical works, but all the available literature pertaining to the emergence of the Christian faith. That inquiry finally and irrevocably silenced that pestering whisper and freed me from servitude, as I came to see it, to a flawed and inadequate system of understanding and attaining transcendence—the flower of our consciousness.

My professional work on the scrolls continued. In November of 1951, Father de Vaux started excavating the ancient ruins that stood as a silent witness, shrouded in dust and sand, near the caves. A few weeks later, a colleague who worked on the site, asked if I would like 'to have a look'. I was as thrilled as a child promised a treat. We drove in a clapped-out pickup that suffered from overuse in difficult terrain and harsh climatic conditions. We descended from Jerusalem 750 meters above sea level to the basement of the planet 420 meters below sea level. Whatever semblance there was of January weather we left in Jerusalem and descended into the dry, arid region of the Dead Sea—the perfect atmospheric conditions to ensure the survival of manuscripts. It was a relatively short journey, but it seemed long. What roads there were, were in poor condition. The memory of the recent World War was still vivid, and its conclusion had only brought a new war to this region. We travelled through the West Bank, at that time annexed to Transjordan by King Abdullah, who apparently preferred a Jewish state as his neighbour to a Palestinian one run by the Mufti. That preference undoubtedly led to his subsequent assassination. Some biblical stories brought the region a measure of fame. Who has not heard of Jericho, where the walls came tumbling down? But the discovery of the caves and their intriguing contents had suddenly brought the area to international attention that left the legend in the shade. We arrived at the excavation site, the ancient ruins of Qumran, thought unimportant until then. The possible importance of the site in understanding the origin and history of the scrolls had saved it from its sand-layered grave.

It is an elevated spot, a plateau, redolent with atmosphere, resounding with history, and radiantly beautiful. What is so delightful about scattered stones and broken-down walls emerging from a barren and brittle landscape? Beauty resides in the eye of the beholder, and I beheld it that day with the Dead Sea, shimmering like blue crystals, clearly visible in the distance. Some of its attraction undoubtedly lay in its mystery. Father de Vaux's work was already bearing fruit and his conclusions regarding the site were forming. In time, he would announce to the world his theory that the site, probably built during the reign of John Hyrcanus, 134–104 BCE, was a Jewish sectarian settlement. The Qumran community, as he called it, numbered among its members the authors and copyists of the scrolls found in the surrounding caves. Later, other voices would question his conclusions and present their own. To this day, controversy continues to cloak the site, and indeed the scrolls, in seductive mystery.

My colleague, busy with his helpers, left me to my own devices. The atmosphere of the place, reminiscent of a bombed-out cathedral, fascinated me. I could have spent my time walking around the crumbling walls that were emerging from the dust and sand that had accumulated over millennia. The phoenix, an appropriate emblem, came readily to mind. However, I was afraid of getting in the way. I left the airy plateau and descended a precarious declining slope into the dry wadi that twice a year had carried precious water to the long-ago inhabitants of the settlement. I walked some distance along the dry riverbed enthralled by the views of the high, fragile-looking bluffs that contained the numerous caves that were fast becoming international icons of the region. I could not resist. I struggled up the escarpment, hoping eventually to reach an accessible opening into one of the caves. The climb was more difficult than I had anticipated, and more hazardous, but I was young, lithe and enthusiastic for adventure.

My foolhardy exploit brought me to a ledge. Above it was a hole in the marl. By stretching, I managed to reach the bottom of the opening—my above average height an undoubted boon. Wart-like accretions pockmarked the surface of the rock. I saw them as stepping-stones to a kind of immortality. Fame for its own sake did not interest me, but I was young enough and sufficiently idealistic to want to make a mark: *footprints in the sands of time*! Stretching fully, I grabbed at the base of the aperture and pulled myself up, allowing my feet to find the lower knurls. I looked inside and saw that the base of the cave was lower than the ledge. I swung my legs over the edge and lowered myself cautiously onto the floor. The interior was welcoming, like the atmosphere of a favourite room. I sat down in the dust of ages. It was easy to imagine the community members, if you accepted Father de Vaux's theory, living in caves like this around the central building. Perhaps some sheltered in this very cave, listening for the disciplined but deadly tread of the Roman Legions, and waiting, hearts pounding in counterpoint to the thud of the approaching army, for annihilation. It was also possible that this convivial atmosphere had never in its long history witnessed a human presence. Could it be that it was waiting, its hospitable ambience renewed day by day over the millennia, for my arrival to give it purpose, fulfilment and completion? The thought intoxicated me. I dug my hands into the dust and sand that covered the floor more fittingly than a Persian rug, revelling in my own relevance … and touched something. It was a small object. I wrapped my fingers around it as my imagination framed all sorts of exotic possibilities. I opened my hand and gazed down at a coin. It was not even an old coin, from an ancient civilization. It was a modern French coin of the late 1940s.

It was an irrelevant find, an insignificant event. A non-event, really, but it taught me a lesson that I have never forgotten, and which ruled my professional life thereafter. My immediate reaction was one of deflation—it pricked the bubble of my pomposity. Obviously, I was not the first person to occupy that space. But more importantly it taught me that *eureka* moments are rare in humanity's journey towards enlightenment. We make progress through mundane probing and reasoning, sifting and challenging our ideas until we see as clearly with our mind as we do with our eyes. I pocketed the coin, returned to the plateau and waited for my colleague to conclude his work.

17: Modern Rome

Another Saturday, and Marc had spent much of the previous week in Giuseppe's library. As expected, he found it contained numerous works pertinent to his studies. Giuseppe's own reflections on his years working on the scrolls were interesting, especially to a family member. They were also important for Marc in that they gave him the feeling of actually being part of the event that always fascinated him.

He left the convent early and, on his way to Giuseppe's, he stopped at his favourite spot by the river to read another extract from the manuscript. However, he was unsettled. His meeting with Sophia and Julian the previous week, recurring in his memory like a repetitive promotional plug, left him drained and inert. To add to his emotional distress, Sophia had finally departed the convent and religious life during the week. Now, it was Saturday again, and there was every chance that Carlo would phone. Formerly, Marc was so single-minded that friendships or their lack did not disturb him. However, he sensed that he was changing. He felt invigorated by his continuing friendship with the engaging and provocative librarian and did not want to lose it, but the question was whether he was ready for its logical consequences. Concurrently, his doubts regarding his vocation were increasing. He feared that he would end up without faith or friend. That was a lonely prospect indeed.

Marc was not surprised when his phone rang. He retrieved the cell phone from his backpack and saw that it was Carlo calling.

'*Buongiorno, Carlo.*' Marc tried to inject more cheerfulness into his greeting than he felt.

'*Ciao, Marco.* Can we meet?'

The very sound of Carlo's voice stirred up such emotion in him that he knew this could not continue. Balancing two balls would have to stop. Decision time had come. He hesitated for a moment, 'Yes, of course.'

'Where are you?'

'Ponte Fabricio.'

'When you are a renowned Doctor of Theology, we will have to erect a monument to you there. Wait for me.'

A Doctor of Theology! The dream was becoming a mirage, slowly but surely dissolving like a vapour in the desert heat. In his mind, chaos prevailed, but in the tree-lined pathway beside the Tiber, tranquillity reigned, dripping with green droplets of sunlight through the leaves.

Reading Giuseppe's reflections had disturbed him, but he was also intrigued. He was disturbed, because his life seemed to be reflecting that of granduncle—love and a crisis of faith. He was intrigued by what he considered Giuseppe's brave and candid portrayal of his most intimate feelings. Marc wondered if he would have the courage to be so revealing—so far, he did not have much to reveal. The thought depressed him.

On an academic level, his life was successful, but on a social level, it was empty. He wondered if it were a life at all. He was beginning to think that his was a life without the *f*. Study had been the dominant feature of his twenty and more years so far. That had never troubled him before, but now he wondered if it were not all just an illusion, another mirage. When the illusory oasis in a desert disappears, what is left but sand. He already had a Master's degree, with competence in many languages, ancient and modern, but was that the essence of life?

Giuseppe was an intelligent man and if he, a supremely well-informed person, found belief intellectually dissatisfying, it must surely be suspect, to say the least. Their recent discussion on the topic continued to replay in his mind. If, after a life of sincere dedication to faith-inspired discipline, you were to die and find it was all for nothing, you would not even have the satisfaction of knowing that you had been conned—that you had conned yourself. He smiled in spite of his gloom at the absurdity of his thoughts, but it had its origin in the remark of a priest. As a second-level student attending one of the school's annual spiritual retreats, he was bemused by a comment the officiating priest made, jokingly perhaps, that 'belief' was the 'safer' bet. After death, the believer was a winner no matter what. If the afterlife proved to be a fact, the believer could rejoice, if there were no afterlife, he would know nothing of his mistake. Marc did not derive much satisfaction from the idea. Later, as his studies progressed, he discovered that the idea originated with Blaise Pascal, the seventeenth-century philosopher. Attaching it to a renowned name did not make the proposal any more acceptable to Marc. Bizarre as it may seem, he felt that some satisfaction would cling to his dead consciousness for prevailing against the almost universal rush to believe.

He rose from his shaded bench and walked across the tree-lined footpath to look down on the river—its water brown, and its movement sluggish. What a contrast with the river that flowed through his hometown, which always seemed to be in full flow, even in the height of summer. But what history had unfolded here on the Tiber's banks! It flowed serenely by when Brutus and company dispatched Caesar, when Titus passed victoriously with his trophies from Jerusalem. Its tranquil movement did not pause during the sack of the city in 1527 and its convenient depths willingly welcomed the mutilated bodies of unpopular popes and inept politicians. It diluted the blood of armies and provided refreshment for generations of countless Romans. Romulus, if there ever were a Romulus, palmed its water to slake his thirst. In spite of its history, Marc's thoughts now turned to that other river, far away in his homeland.

He reflected on his own early years growing up there; his attraction to a solitary, studious life, from an early age. He was the type

145

of boy and youth that should have been the target of bullies, but was not. His quiet disposition attracted friendship, but he did not respond. He did not actually spurn friendly advances, but from inertia rather than design, he just did not encourage them. His real interest lay at home in his room among his DVDs, books and computer, where he was already trying to distinguish and identify the letters of the ancient languages and draw meaning from the apparently random and meaningless scratches on the ancient scrolls. Such friendly advances gradually ceased, killed off by the unprofitable effort it took to penetrate his apathy.

Fergus and his attempts to engage Marc in his interest in tennis came to mind again. His persistent efforts to cultivate Marc's friendship died ultimately of frustration. Now, he was doing the same with Carlo … and for what! Did he consider himself a self-sufficient entity, the first in the history of humanity? Was he afraid of the demands friendship would necessarily bring? Or, was he afraid of … sin?

Life and training had conditioned him to fear sin. In the seminary, an essential tool in the formation of character was a little book into which the students were encouraged to enter their every failing, misdemeanour, great and small and every infringement of the rules. Such concentration on the negative, he always felt, was bound to wound the psyche. Was such conditioning valid? Was it healthy? Marc treated it with a degree of scorn, convinced that it was much ado about nothing. Was his present disquiet a result of such training? He had done nothing to compromise his priesthood, but in spite of his innocence, he felt that his attraction to Carlo was in itself a sinful act, alienating him from the celebration of Mass. In addition to feeling unworthy, the ceremony itself was beginning to irritate him—it appeared ridiculous. The vestments, which may have some symbolic meaning, were to modern eyes simply idiotic—even gross, when viewed in the full panoply of a televised papal Mass with the poor and dispossessed worldwide looking on. But it was the prayers, so cringing and repetitive, as if God were a hard-of-hearing tyrant, that he found increasingly difficult to articulate. Even the mystery behind the whole rite was losing its credibility. His pious congregation of nuns did not help matters. Their worshipful attendance was a challenge to his growing scepticism. He had discarded the cassock. Like Sophia, he too felt ashamed of what it represented. He wanted to throw off much more. However … what would he do? Where could he go? How could he continue his studies? Did he want to continue with them? His life was suddenly, and it seemed irretrievably, spiralling out of control. Pressure, almost physical in its intensity, was building within him, like floodwaters behind a dam.

The river, moving sluggishly but calmly along, could conveniently put an end to his problems, but he was not suicidal. However, he was desperate. A gentle beep of the horn put an end to his reverie. He continued to stand there, facing the river, wondering what to do. Would he revert to type and walk away yet again from another friendly overture—back to the life he knew, the life that offered security and a clearly defined path. There was still time to pull his life back together. Perhaps what he was experiencing was the Dark Night of the Soul, which so many mystics had experienced. A week's retreat would put it all right again. Then, he remembered Giuseppe's advice regarding retreats: challenge yourself, don't simply acquiesce in a miasma of contrived spirituality.

Another beep sounded, more urgent this time. He turned around and faced the car. He thought for a moment that he was looking into the face of Fergus, but Carlo's smile, both welcoming and urgent, superimposed itself on the fading image of Fergus. Marc did not move, seemingly impervious to Carlo's traffic problems. He had the feeling that the river behind him was witnessing another historic moment, perhaps not as grand in scale as past events, but decisive in his personal history. Like Giuseppe in the Church of the Resurrection gazing into the challenging face of Leah, this was his pivotal moment. The precipice loomed. He picked up his backpack, looked at the car, then back along the path towards the convent. He paused, a moment of indecision, and walked, inexorably as time … to the car.

Mars

Carlo looked enquiringly at Marc, tense and unsmiling, as he settled into the seat beside him.

'Where would Marco like to go?' Sensing Marc's fragility, Carlo spoke quietly.

'Mars!' Marc had no destination in mind, he simple wanted to be off the planet and out of orbit.

Carlo put his foot down and hurtled into the ever hectic traffic as if he were indeed about to blast off into space. He negotiated the traffic maniacally, but expertly, challenging other equally maniacal drivers for disputed spaces. Marc, regretting his desire for planetary change, was holding on to his seat as if gravity no longer prevailed—his earlier worries lost in the greater anxiety for self-preservation. He looked at Carlo and wondered what had ignited this urge to possible extinction, but he did not think it the appropriate time to distract the driver with questions. Carlo eventually slowed and pulled into the spot before a crumbling mound of antiquity, which, to the chagrin of many city modernists, littered far too much of Rome's contemporary landscape.

'Well?' Marc was bewildered.

'Mars,' replied Carlo. 'You wanted to go to Mars. Here we are, *Campo Marzio* – the Field of Mars.'

'Crazy clown.' Marc broke into a hearty laugh. 'It's not exactly the Mars I had in mind.'

'The original *Campus Martius* extended right down to *Ponte Fabricio*, so we were already in Mars, but Marco looked as if he needed some excitement.'

Moved by his friend's concern and by his way of addressing it, Marc's 'Thank you,' was heartfelt and with a depth of feeling rarely displayed. 'You are a good friend.'

'I want to be Marco's best friend.' He tapped gently on Marc's knee. 'Now, tell me what's wrong.'

'Oh! Nothing and everything,' said Marc, his words expressing the confusion he felt. 'My life is a mess. It seems to be crumbling to pieces around me, like that decrepit ruin over there.'

'That "decrepit ruin" is, as you know well, the last resting place of our illustrious Emperor Augustus, who ruled the world when your Jesus was born, assuming that the latter was ever born. There is no doubt about the former. In an atypical excursion into your area of expertise I stumbled upon the intriguing fact that a number of specialists in your chosen field are investigating the possibility that your Jesus started life as a myth, later acquiring a miraculous physicality and subsequent biography.' Carlo adopted the exaggerated tone of knowledgeable tour guide in order to lighten the mood.

'I'm impressed. You are a palaeographer now?'

'No! Just an enquiring terrestrial seeking illumination.'

'Maybe we enquire too much.' Marc's discontent with his life and studies was still evident.

'It comes with the package—built in, we can't avoid it. It's entertaining, so long as we don't let it get out of hand.'

'You think I let it get out of hand?' Marc was questioning not confrontational.

'It's not your fault. We all are prisoners of our environment.'

'I have never felt imprisoned before, but I do now.'

'Let's go home and you can tell me all about it.'

Carlo drove back at a more moderate pace, continuing to act as the larger-than-life tourist guide to his foreign friend. His intention was to lessen Marc's dejection rather than add to his already abundant knowledge of his adopted city.

'Our illustrious Augustus would not be too pleased to see the state of his last resting place,' observed Carlo.

'He does not really rest there anymore,' said Marc.

'No! Alaric thought more of the containers than the divine ashes within.'

149

'All the gods seem to be crumbling to ash,' growled Marc despondently.

'*Piazza Montecitorio*,' Carlo remarked by way of distraction. 'Did you know that that very obelisk once told the time? It was the gnomon for Augustine's massive timepiece, so designed that its shadow fell across the *Ara Pacis* each year on the emperor's birthday. It was a very elaborate way of proclaiming Rome's victory over Egypt. The Egyptians had dedicated the obelisk to Ra, the sun god; in Rome, it told the time by the sun. And later, Constantine, the founder of the Christian Church, as distinct from the Christian faith, decreed that Sunday be set aside to honour the sun god … not the Resurrection.'

'You are very well up on your history,' said Marc, impressed by his knowledge of Church and State.

'I'm a Roman. All Romans are proud of their history. Besides which, I am a librarian.'

'So you keep telling me,' replied Marc glibly.

They arrived at Bernini's *Elephant*, parked and made their way to the garret.

Inside, Marc sat down at a small table just beside the window that led to the 'roof terrace' as Carlo dubbed it. When his friend disappeared into the kitchen, Marc took in the neat interior once again. A degree of pride mingled with embarrassment settled on him when he observed his own countenance looking back at him from another corner of the room. Carlo returned with a frosted bottle of Orvieto Classico and two glasses, which he set down on the table.

'Now,' he said, pouring out the wine before settling down in the chair opposite Marc. 'Tell me all about it.'

Marc was glad of a receptive ear, and no ear was more receptive than Carlo's was. He described, as best he could, the confusion he felt, the doubts, the recent irrelevance of his studies and the effects Giuseppe's writing was having on him. However, Fergus and the gnawing fear that life was passing him by, he avoided.

Carlo listened with keen attention until Marc had exhausted both himself and his topic. 'You can stay here, if you want to get away from the convent.'

'Thank you,' said Marc with a mixture of sincerity and inexplicable panic.

Carlo laughed at his expression. 'Don't worry! I can control myself. If my naked body beside you is too gross for you to contemplate, I can sleep on the floor.'

Marc reached across the table and took Carlo's hand in his. 'That is not so, and you know it. You are a good friend, I don't deserve you. You should forget me. Luigi is a better friend.'

'Luigi is a good friend and I love him dearly too. Life is for living, Marco; live! Why don't you talk to Giuseppe? He is a man with a lot of experience—theoretical and practical. And he is your granduncle. He is interested in you.'

'Perhaps I will. I have spent a lot of time at his place recently. He has an interesting library. He knows that I am unsettled, but he is very diplomatic. I suppose he does not want to influence me.'

'Let's go then,' urged Carlo, who did not believe in dawdling.

18: Jerusalem: 1954-55

My years in Jerusalem were turbulent. The hostilities that flared between the new state of Israel and the Palestinians were explosive, but just as charged, albeit of a different order, was the academic conflict. The intellectual peace of earlier months ended when extra scholars arrived to cope with the influx of new material and international scholars became aware of the finds. Strident verbal battles raged over the texts, daily coming to light, and their interpretation. Some commentators proclaimed them hoaxes, elaborate and ingenious, but forgeries none the less. The weight of evidence in favour of their authenticity has long since silenced all but the most obdurate.

In archaeological terms, the decade following the discovery of the first scrolls was extraordinarily rich. My colleagues and I were just about coming to terms with the vast richness of the discoveries at the Dead Sea, when news began to filter through of another important find in the Egyptian desert. Though discovered in 1945, the importance of these texts only began to emerge in the subsequent decades. Known as the Nag Hammadi Library, the thirteen codices contained over fifty documents. In contrast to the Dead Sea Scrolls, which are ostensibly Jewish-related manuscripts, the Nag Hammadi books are largely, and undeniably, Christian. They include such works as the Gospel of Thomas, the Gospel of Philip, and reflect the controversies that raged within the early Christian communities. They highlight the reality that it was indeed a time of travail, with a number of groups vying with each other for primacy.

The codices are, in the main, third and fourth century copies of earlier Gnostic writings, but also include works of ancient secret wisdom. Some writings of Plato are included among the Nag Hammadi codices, which would indicate that Christian Gnosticism drew from the vast reservoir of Greek philosophy.

The scrolls were beginning to reveal with blinding clarity the fractured nature of Judaism during the time of the second Temple, the period in which Christianity was born. The Qumran texts do not mention Christianity; the name did not exist at the time. However, from them we can deduce that Christianity was not a 'new' religion that came down from heaven with Jesus. It grew organically from ideas circulating around the whole Middle East at the time.

The codices from Nag Hammadi emphasize the same point. For them the Jesus Mystery was simply a flowering of the Mystery Religions that pervaded the Eastern Mediterranean. They also expose with equal clarity the diversity of theological opinion that splintered the early Christian community. They reveal with arresting vividness the diversity that existed among the early communities and the variety of interpretations put forward to explain the so-called *kerygma*, the Proclamation of the Good News. Ultimately, imperial backing gave one group the edge over the rest. At the Council of Nicaea, orthodox Christianity became a political entity more than a religious one.

The victors, with the power of the state behind them, soon silenced all opposition. Forgetting their own recent persecution, they hounded the so-called heretics and demanded the destruction of their books. However, at least one group of monks so revered their alleged 'heretical' books that obliteration was not an option. They carefully and lovingly stored their leather-bound papyrus books in an earthenware jar, sealed it and hid it in the Egyptian desert. The books remained there for some fifteen hundred years before emerging from their sandy tomb into a world no longer bent on their eradication. Far from being threatened by paranoiac hostility, they were carefully preserved and restored and are now housed with care in the Coptic Museum in Cairo, their contents a secure part of our journey towards understanding our cultural heritage.

The knowledge gleaned from the two discoveries was not exactly new to me. I knew of the Jewish cultural scene from my studies. I also had a one-sided view of the controversies that swept through the Church in its formative centuries through the polemic of early Christian authors. It was the scale and vividness of these recent revelations that I found profoundly unsettling to my faith.

By August of 1952, my *affaire d'amour* with Leah was well established. It was the month that cave 4 was discovered—very close to the Qumran ruins. The deputy controller of the work, a non-cleric, with whom I had become friendly, arrived at the museum elated and seething. His joy derived from the apparent volume of fragments found there—ultimately it proved to contain more fragments than all other caves together. His anger resulted from the fact that the Bedouin got there first. They had removed a vast amount of material, the purchase of which the museum would now have to pursue. It was at this point that more labourers became necessary for this very productive vineyard. However, the increased numbers did not mean a diminution of individual work. The workload was increasing daily, but that only added to the excitement.

In view of the experience I had acquired over the previous two years, the deputy invited me to oversee the work at the site of this latest find. I was delighted at the prospect. When we arrived at the site, I was surprised to see just how close the cave was to the Qumran excavations. It appeared to be less than a few hundred metres, which raised the question as to how the Bedouin managed to locate and remove so much material with the archaeologists working nearby.

The vast volume of material found in cave 4 together with its proximity to Qumran suggested the possibility that this cave acted as a library for the Qumran community. Cave 4 is actually two caves, cut by hand from the marlstone, thus adding weight to the library theory.

I was dressed for the dust and sun in my shabbiest khaki and the *keffiyeh*, which Leah had given me to replace my western hat. It is an Arab headdress, but though Leah was staunchly Israeli, she was not anti-Arab. Nazism had voided 'anti-ism' from her system. She suggested that it might be a more suitable headdress for my work, which involved the collection of the fragments from cave 4 and their safe transportation to the museum.

Due to the visceral thrill it gave me, I spent much of my time in the cave. To say that it was dry within that confined area is an understatement. The atmosphere there was more effective at drying our sweaty faces than the most absorbent handkerchief. That atmosphere had preserved the scrolls for two thousand years. After restoration and publication, it seemed the obvious place to store them into the future, but that would never happen. Plans were already afoot to build a suitable edifice in Jerusalem to house them.

The final reckoning for cave 4 revealed that it contained over eighty per cent of all the scrolls discovered, around fifteen thousand fragments representing five hundred different texts. Consequently, our work was slow and painstaking, and continued over several seasons. We swept it clean, and as a final flourish, we swept it again, just to make sure that we found and removed every fragment. As the final trays of this treasured find were on their way to Jerusalem, I lingered, reluctant to leave what had become for me a sacred space. I sat in the dust, hugging my legs, absorbing the atmosphere and fantasizing on the far-off events that had conspired to safeguard these ancient writings and bring them, battered but sufficiently complete, through two thousand years of darkness into the light of our time.

How ironic that their concealment began during a time of war as the Jewish state was approaching its end only to be retrieved again during a time of conflict when the new State of Israel was being established. It seemed fortuitous, and I wanted to believe so, but the cold light of reason indicated prosaic chance.

I sat on, reluctant to leave this cathedral of history. My eyes swept the walls of the cave. If only those walls could speak. If only a hidden camera could have recorded the comings and goings of two thousand and more years ago. In a sense, we did have the roll of film from such a camera. Thanks to the care and ingenuity of the individuals involved, we had the scrolls—a verbal snapshot of the time and the people that occupied that fraction of history.

Eventually, I had to rise and drag myself reluctantly away. I was sitting in a corner, and as I stood up, I put my hand on the wall for support. Something fell at my feet. It was a potsherd; such items were usual in the other caves, but scarce enough in this particular one. All the activity within the cave over the past seasons must have loosened it from its secure hiding place. I picked it up and examined it. The shard seemed to be from a rather small pot or jar; nothing as big as the jars that secured the scrolls found in other caves. I continued examining it for a few moments, and could tell that the break was new and instinctively looked up.

The top of the cave was not high, but the walls and roof were rough, especially where walls and roof met. There were numerous gashes and abrasions in the stone but, guided by the position of the fallen piece, I probed in one such fissure above my head. The motion of my hand broke the brittle marl and revealed a ledge on which stood the remains of the pottery jar. I carefully removed it and gazed at it with awe. I knew instinctively that it was ancient.

My heart skipped a beat when I saw that it contained a small scroll. A rhythm played out on the timpani of my spine. Whose hands had placed this scroll in the jar and concealed it here? What prompted him, if it were *him*, to do so? What story did he have to tell? My mind took flight once again on its magic carpet, imagining various probable and improbable, but always dramatic settings. However, only the scroll itself could reveal the answer, if indeed it would.

My body trembled with anticipation. Discoveries to the archaeologist are like notes to the musician—their multiplicity and complexity only add to the magic of the melody. And *I* had found it. It would not go into the general pool of fragments. I would examine it alone and decipher its contents. I returned to the museum in a state of concealed elation and with a sense of achievement. However, with all the work accumulating for our attention, I knew that it would be some time before I would get to unlock the secrets of this artefact, my own precious message in a bottle. Even if its message proved prosaic, its simple existence was precious to me.

19: Modern Rome

After re-reading his latest Jerusalem instalment, Giuseppe pressed the save key. The exercise provoked an avalanche of memories—segments of his life toppling willy-nilly from the distant reaches of recollection like a meteor shower from the darkness of space—bringing, in unequal measure, pain and peace. The phone bleeped and restored him to the present.

Marc could access the apartment with his own key but, as he and Carlo walked through the Campo, he decided to phone ahead to ask if Giuseppe were free for a chat. Giuseppe's response was predictably affirmative. As they made their way, Carlo stopped outside a cafe. 'It is best that you talk to Giuseppe alone. I'll wait here for you.' Marc was disappointed, but he could see Carlo's point; as a relevant other in the present circumstance, his presence might make both feel awkward. With a forlorn look, he nodded his head in agreement, and made for the entrance to Giuseppe's apartment.

Giuseppe received Marc with his usual warmth and, on this occasion, a touch of concern. Marc felt guilty about intruding on his granduncle's serenity and loading him with his problems. Giuseppe had gone through all this in his own life, the last thing he needed was to face it again in the life of another—a member of a family that had shown scant support when *he* needed it.

'You are very welcome, Marco.' Giuseppe led them out onto the terrace. 'I noticed that Carlo stayed below. I hope he is not afraid of me,' he added jokingly to detract from what, he suspected, would be a serious conversation.

'No! He thought I should talk to you alone.'

'I see.' Giuseppe's gaze was penetrating. 'Would you like some wine, Marco?'

'No! Thank you, Giuseppe. I already had some with Carlo.'

'Some fruit juice then?' asked Giuseppe.

'Not just now, thank you. I would like to get your advice.'

Giuseppe motioned Marc to a seat and sat down himself. It did not take a psychic to know what was on his mind. Giuseppe had noticed the signs since their first meeting. They became more marked as the weeks passed. As Marc began to speak, he looked … Giuseppe searched for the appropriate word … sad … confused. Neither was sufficiently compelling. His look suggested despondency deeper than either word conveyed, intensity beyond the scope of both to transmit. Lost—might be better. In spite of its contribution to humanity's social development, language can be inadequate. If a person could knead words as a baker the ingredients of a cake, a single word, *sui generis*, with just the right import might result. Lost would certainly be one element. Throw in sad and confused with an ample sprinkling of fear. Wrecked, devastated, shattered would also feature in the recipe. The resulting word would describe Marc. He was all of the above. He was the human equivalent of a ship that had lost its anchor and was drifting rudderless in a turbulent sea.

Whatever way you might express it, Giuseppe could identify with that look. His own mouth had once formed the helpless plea that Marc's now evoked. His eyes had once looked with hopeless appeal into an uncaring environment—seeking sympathy and understanding, but his quest was in vain. In those days, condemnation was the primary response to the symptoms Giuseppe had then displayed. Piqued condemnation is still there, but glossed over with a veneer of strained, pained understanding that is more concerned with institution than with the individual. That would not be Giuseppe's response. He knew from

160

his own experience that a resolution rested ultimately on one's own shoulders, but there were things he could do to help. The biggest problem facing one in Marc's position was loss of security. At present, he had a guaranteed future—the Church housed, fed, and educated him. It would continue to care for him in illness and old age and, at the end, honourable entombment. It was the best insurance policy anyone could have. Yet, like every such protection, it came at a price, one too exorbitant for some to meet. In Giuseppe's case, Leah had removed that fear. She had given him the security to choose his own road. He would do the same for his grandnephew.

Giuseppe listened silently. Marc's problems were clear, and as anticipated, their resolution less clear. Even Marc's research, which he had always enjoyed, was losing its appeal. 'I don't seem to have any eagerness for study anymore,' he said. 'I have always hated counselling. I feel incompetent. I am incompetent. Now, I find celebrating Mass abhorrent. It is not just that it is unpleasant; it is offensive to me. The vestments, the gestures, the prayers, they are all so futile, empty, meaningless. The reality is that I don't believe in it anymore. I suppose the obvious thing to do is to go home and talk to my bishop. I know my parents won't mind. They never wanted me to become a priest in the first place.'

'What about your studies?' It was Giuseppe's first interruption.

'My studies are finished. I can't study as things are, and if I leave the priesthood, I will have to find a job. Anyway, I am not making any progress on my topic.'

'You have too much insight and knowledge into your topic to give it up now. Your voice should be heard, it may be more pertinent than you imagine.'

'People don't want to know. They are happy with their myths.'

Giuseppe looked sympathetically at Marc. He frequently experienced the same pessimism. 'It is not a matter of destroying people's comforting illusions. It is pursuing truth. That is the essence of rational life. To abandon it is to die intellectually. I would like you to continue that work.'

'I am good for nothing at the moment.'

'Don't make a decision yet. Take your time. Relax!'

'Relax is the very thing I can't do in my present frame of mind. The thought of going back to the convent even for one more night is painful, and the morning ritual is repulsive. I know it sounds crazy, but that is how I feel.'

'You don't have to explain it to me, Marco. I know only too well how you feel. That is why I want you to stay here with me. Consider this your home. Go down now and ask Carlo to drive you to the convent, pick up whatever you need, and come back here.'

'I could not intrude on you, Giuseppe.'

'Marco, you are not intruding. I can think of nothing more delightful than having my young grandnephew living with me. After a few days of peace and quiet, you will be in a better position to make a decision.'

Stars and Galaxies

A tiny fissure triggers a flood, and Marc felt himself carried along with increasing and frightening rapidity like a white-water rafter, not knowing exactly how his adventurous ride began or where it would end. However, after his talk with Giuseppe, he was trying to be positive, but was still in a daze when Carlo drove into the convent car park. The Fiat Punto had many advantages in a bustling city, but transporting goods was not one of them. However, Marc was glad to have it. Carlo, thinking ahead, had brought some empty cardboard boxes in which to transport Marc's few belongings, while Marc himself moved as if in a trance. How quickly life's circumstances can change. When he set out that morning, to read at Ponte Fabricio, he had no idea that he would be returning to pack. Carlo stayed with the car as Marc, carrying the two boxes that would carry the totality of his possessions, walked towards the convent. He also felt wasted, like a scarecrow buffeted by the

162

elements, finding it difficult to discipline his mind to concentrate on the needs of the moment. He would have to inform the superior, as she would have to arrange for someone to celebrate Mass in the morning. Sophia's earlier departure relieved him of the duty of informing her directly; he had her phone number and would call her in a few days with his news, which she would no doubt be expecting. Her only surprise would be at the suddenness of his action. Compounding his difficulties, was a residual guilt concerning Sophia's decision. He felt that he should broach that subject with the superior also, but was not relishing the prospect.

His supervisor, the monsignore, would be more difficult, but he would have to let him know. He could try contacting him to arrange an appointment for the following day, but religious are protective of their Great Silence, a period of reflection that precedes Sundays and major feasts. There was little chance of contacting him before Monday, which suited Marc just fine.

Marc went to his room, packed up his belongings with a sense of relief rather than nostalgia and returned to the car. 'There is no need for you to wait,' he suggested. 'I have to see the superior,' he explained. 'I don't know how long I might be. Besides,' he added quickly to forestall Carlo's reluctance to leave him, 'I need a walk and a breath of air to get my head around all that has happened.'

He returned to the convent and, as luck would have it, he met the superior at the front entrance. 'Sister, may I have a word,' he asked apologetically. She was always a gracious woman and no less so now at his intrusion into the convent's Great Silence. She led Marc to her office, where she invited him to take a seat before sitting herself.

Marc tried to explain the situation, which was not too clear in his own mind. His explanation, he felt, was making the circumstances more confused and even incomprehensible. 'I will be staying with my uncle— my granduncle actually, who lives in Rome—for a while. I am very sorry, Sister, for the inconvenience. I am giving you very little time to find a celebrant for Mass in the morning.'

'Do not worry about that, Father. Your well-being is more important. As you know, our former chaplain celebrates Mass here every morning. It is a small matter to rearrange the times.'

'Thank you, Sister … for trying to make me feel less guilty about disrupting your schedule.' Marc paused to consider his next remarks. 'There is another matter weighing on my mind. I feel that I have contributed to Sister Sophia's decision to leave the convent. My inadequacies and my own confusion, I feel, have compounded whatever problems she was confronting.'

'Please, Father, have no misgivings there. Sophia is a fine person and a skilled doctor. She will do commendable work in her chosen profession. However, I knew from the beginning that her place was not here. One develops an instinct for such things after years in a position like mine. Sophia was very happy with her decision, and I, quite frankly, was relieved that she made that choice; she would never have been truly content and fulfilled here.'

After expressing his gratitude for her consideration in his present position, Marc walked back to Campo de' Fiori, wondering if the superior had also made up her mind about him. Far removed from the Great Silence of the convent, Romans, like citizens of all great cities, were in a frenzied end-of-week rush for diversion. Above, all was tranquil—no apparent rush among the spheres. The timeless message of the stars flashed across the universe. The source is old, but the starlight that reaches our searching eyes is ever new, renewed every second, photon by photon, at the end of its multi-million-year journey to our planet. Some had set out from their source when Augustus ruled the empire, and others millions of years before. The photon surge that reached the scribes writing bench at Qumran was two thousand years younger than the light that played around Marc in Campo de' Fiori. All looked calm, yet a close encounter with a supernova would be far from a tranquil experience. There was surely a message there for Marc— tranquillity in the midst of turmoil—both calm and chaos were competing in his consciousness, though he was sensible enough to realize that his confusion was far from cosmic. With a refreshing lightness of heart, he put his key into the lock and let himself in.

'Welcome home, Marco,' said Giuseppe, embracing and kissing him in the Roman way. 'I want you to think of this as your home. Carlo was kind enough to put your things in one of the bedrooms, but you can choose any room you like.'

'Thank you, Giuseppe. The meanest room in a palazzo is more than I am accustomed to, and more than I deserve.'

'Nonsense, Marco. I invited Carlo to stay the night. I thought you might like to go out for something to eat. I suspect that you have not eaten all day.'

'I am not hungry.'

'Probably not, after the day you have had. But you should eat something. Besides, I am sure Carlo is hungry.' Giuseppe nodded encouragingly at Marc.

Marc looked bewildered. He suddenly felt the full impact of his dependence. He had no money, and he did not want Carlo to have to pay for the meal. Equally, he did not want to be a financial burden on Giuseppe. It was one thing to share his uncle's home, but to expect him to support him was quite another.

Giuseppe recognized his gaffe and rushed to repair it. 'If you would prefer, we could have a take-away delivered inside half-an-hour.' Marc was relieved, in spite of the realization that Giuseppe would still be paying.

Carlo smiled in welcome as Marc made his way onto the terrace. 'Giuseppe has just been telling me that he is writing about his time in Jerusalem.'

'Will your manuscript be ready for publication soon?' Marc was glad that Carlo had diverted attention away from him.

'It could be, Marco,' replied Giuseppe. 'I was undecided about publication. My primary objectives were to retrieve my past before it is lost forever and to keep myself engaged. I don't expect it to have a profound impact but, as I told you earlier, we must keep pursuing truth.'

'Perhaps I can help,' suggested Marc, hoping to make some return for Giuseppe's kindness.

'There is much you could do, Marco, but I hope you will continue working on the scrolls.'

'I can't see how. I will have to see the monsignore on Monday. He will certainly drop me. Probably order me to return to Ireland.'

'You don't need your supervisor to continue your research.' realizing that Carlo probably felt out of the conversation, Giuseppe concluded the subject. 'Think about it over the weekend,' he suggested.

The food arrived and ended the conversation for the moment. A sort of musical chairs followed until they finally settled themselves around the table on the terrace. The stars that attracted Marc's attention earlier continued pulsating photon-by-photon, colliding with the manmade particles of light illuminating the Campo; intense activity that went unnoticed by the casual observer—we live quietly in the midst of tumult. After the meal, Giuseppe suggested that Carlo and Marc go for a walk before retiring for the night.

Outside, the night sky still captivated Marc. Its expansiveness seemed to suit his present mood. 'A light-year is a measure of distance, not of time,' reflected Marc, knowing that Carlo was well aware of that fact, but he found expressing it strangely comforting. 'Some expanses are so mindboggling that it is easier to understand them in terms of time. It is difficult to understand how some people still think all that is just a few thousand years old,' he reflected, looking up, trying to penetrate the artificial light of the Campo to the ancient sparkling tapestry beyond.

'There is no accounting for people's beliefs,' replied Carlo, more conciliatory than normal in view of Marc's present problems.

'Can they really be sincere?' asked Marc, reflecting Sophia's recent puzzlement.

'I guess so,' Carlo said with more than normal restraint. 'I was sincere in my former beliefs.'

'I was also, but religious fundamentalists are different,' said Marc. 'They ignore evidence. At least, we tried to accommodate our beliefs to

166

the facts. Today, with so many scientific facts proven beyond doubt, among them the incomprehensible age of the universe, it is just too ludicrous a position to hold.'

Carlo bit his tongue. He sympathized with Marc's situation and did not want to be insensitive to his feelings. Still, he could not restrain himself. 'Some might find the Virgin Birth incredulous, as well as the Resurrection, doctrines on which faith rests.'

Marc glared at Carlo, and then relaxed. 'You are right, of course. I don't think they are exactly comparable. They are mysteries beyond reason, not contrary to it.'

'I'm sorry. I know what you are going through. I don't mean to twist the knife, but some would disagree.'

They moved out of the Campo into a quieter area. 'I know,' said Marc. 'I question them now. I probably have wondered about them for some time. I was afraid to admit it, even to myself.'

'It gets easier.' Carlo was at pains to be encouraging.

'I can feel it.' Marc looked brighter. 'I have a lot of sorting to do. For starters, I have to see my supervisor on Monday. I am not looking forward to that, but I can feel my mind moving into a new gear. I am lucky to have Giuseppe. Let's go home. I am tired.'

'Giuseppe invited me to stay the night, but if you would prefer, I can go home.'

'I would like you to stay, if that is convenient,' said Marc. 'Will Luigi mind?'

'I'll let him know,' replied Carlo. 'He will understand, besides he spends a lot of time training—voice and body. He will hardly miss me.'

'There are plenty of rooms,' Marc added—a subtle clarification. Carlo smiled at the delicate hint.

As they made their way home, star-filled galaxies continued to bombard the city and the planet with their impartial light, leading some to irrational assumptions and others to balanced seeking. As he lay in bed, Marc's earlier reflection on the Qumran scribes, whose lives were illuminated by the same celestial source, returned. In spite of his present disillusionment and his formerly declared apathy, the scribes and their scrolls were never far from his mind. As his eyes closed in an effort to induce sleep, his mind and imagination opened on another more distant prospect. 'How I would love to get inside their heads,' he whispered to himself, as the melody of their words seemed to resound around him.

20: The Time of Domitian

Once again, I found myself in Rome. Domitian, brother of the despoiler of Jerusalem, ruled. Perhaps it was divine retribution on the desecrater of the Temple, but the rule of Titus had been short and troublesome. He had hardly assumed power when Mount Vesuvius erupted burying the cities of Pompeii and Herculaneum. The following year, fire had consumed much of *Campus Martius.* There was no sign of the fire as I made my way through the area, rebuilt by Domitian. He developed the nearby *Circus Agonalis* to satisfy the people's lust for games, and no doubt, his own.

I had no interest in their games, but I viewed with fascination and a degree of compassion their vain quest for the divine. Their many temples to a variety of gods were evidence of this; there was even one, commissioned by Agrippa, the Roman general and friend of Augustus, to *all* the gods, Pantheon; yet they ignored the One, True God.

My feelings towards Rome and its Empire were ambivalent, as might be expected from one who had witnessed, at first hand, its brutality and its achievements. Its network of roads certainly eased the burden of travel. Their motivation in this regard was not, of course, to facilitate my journeys to bring the Good News, but to make it possible to move the massive Roman armies quickly and efficiently in order to maintain the *Pax Romana*—the peace won and maintained by Augustus. I stood, impassively viewing the mausoleum of the same Augustus, impressively flanked by a pair of obelisks, its arched entrance adorned with the Emperor's own *Res Gestae divi Augusti*; a record of the deeds of the divine Augustus. After his death, the Senate deified Augustus.

169

The idea puzzled me—could mere mortals make a god? Could a mortal become a god? Now, the 'divine' ashes lay in a golden urn within the mausoleum. Could a god die and crumble into ash?

Since the Gospels of Peter and Mark that I have already mentioned, further narratives kept appearing in various communities of believers. They seemed intent on outdoing each other with extraordinary claims and bizarre exploits. I became more resolved than ever to produce a well-balanced account that more fully revealed the mystery at the heart of the story. For me, salvation was the result of a cosmic struggle between Light and Darkness. My Anointed One, the Christ, would be totally in control of all events, even his ultimate sacrifice, which I would depict according to the model of the recent stories. The previous gospels concentrated too much on the human, as if God needed mortals to bring about His salvation. He did not. His wisdom alone, His Word was sufficient. As a result, every mortal shares in that salvation, not just us, Jews. Because of that, we mere mortals can reach out directly to God. Since God dwells within us, no intermediary is necessary, as Apollonius of Tyana taught me so long ago. We were slow to realize that. We saw ourselves as the chosen of God and grudgingly allowed gentiles to share it with us, but at a price. They had to follow our laws and customs. Whatever else we might think about Paul, he persuaded us to broaden our understanding of God's salvation. You may detect ambivalence in my assessment of Paul also—his treatment of my Master still rankles after all these years—but it makes sense that God would not create people without hope of salvation.

Augustus may have brought peace to the empire, but his successors brought the sword to my native land. Why, I wondered, is peace so alien to human life that armies are necessary to establish and maintain it? Some of the new writings claim that this Jesus of Nazareth came to bring the sword, a saying frequently used by my Master, and probably many others. In those days, before our bitter experience of defeat, we were all straining for war.

Space and time did not exist for the Christ that I preached; why should they? He was from eternity. It was the birth of the Eternal One, not the physical birth of His symbolic substitute that concerned me. I tried not to dismiss such writings out of hand. When dealing with truths beyond experience, I understood the need to express it in human terms; I did so in my own preaching, and would continue to do so in the gospel I intended to compose. Even the authors of the *Res Gestae divi Augusti* used rhetoric—and they were writing about mundane achievements. However, I was now beginning to fear that in the recent writings the messenger was more important than the message. Paul never allowed that to creep into his writings. For him the message was always foremost, though his creation of a Christ crucified and resurrected did lend itself to unfortunate interpretations. Now, there are further letters appearing, written in his name, and in which I do not recognize the voice of Paul.

I turned from the mausoleum and the recorded deeds of the Divine Augustus and made my way towards the *Ara Pacis* and the giant *Solarium Augusti*, which tells the time with the aid of an Egyptian obelisk brought to Rome by Augustus as a victory trophy. Again, my ambivalence was evident. I found myself reluctantly admiring Roman skill in constructing such a masterful horological instrument. I paused to follow the almost imperceptible movement of the obelisk's shadow across the marble paving indicating the passage of time. It almost seemed as if the Romans had usurped a divine power—penetrated a celestial secret—as the device, harnessing the light of the ethereal orb, counted out the passage of time on earth.

Time! The relentless measure of fleeting moments! A tide of endless but invisible motion that never stops, never falters. Willing or unwilling, we are carried along effortlessly in its ceaseless wake. Suddenly, I felt old. I was certainly getting older, time's inevitable consequence, and I was making little progress on the gospel I had resolved to write that day in Alexandria. Since then, I had settled in Cyprus, becoming Episkopos to our followers there. The same title that my Master once held in our refuge by the Salt Sea, though the community I guarded had grown vastly different from that unique, original gathering in the wilderness. Paul's vision of the New Covenant had prevailed, but it did not stop there. New insights were constantly challenging our understanding of the Mystery. It seems that change is as relentless as time. I sometimes wished that Apollos was by my side, to draw on his profound wisdom to extract the gold from the dross of the new interpretations, but he, like so many others, had departed without witnessing the fulfilment of his hope—how cruel the deity sometimes appears to be!

Since I did not expect the relentless nature of time to slow for me, and allot me greater measure, I resolved to engage a scribe to commit my thoughts to papyrus. On making inquiries, I learned of a young man from our community, gifted in calligraphy who worked for a Roman Senator. He had made known to his family his desire to return to the island if a suitable position arose. Turning from the almost mystic time machine, I made my way to interview the scribe to assess his suitability.

On my way, I pondered how I might express the inexpressible— what finite words might best reveal an infinite mystery. It was not something new to me, I had been preaching about it all my adult life. However, the spoken word that hangs on the air like a delicate soap bubble differs from the written word that could outlive the author, as Paul's writings have. In spite of Paul's good example, I feared the written word. There was danger there. Others could alter your words and put forward ideas that were quite alien to you. Even the spoken word can be risky; it is sometimes misinterpreted. However, we are mere humans, and if we wish to communicate, we must use the tools at hand.

I had put the message into many different words, revealed it through a variety of hyperbole. At times, my own rhetoric might have induced me into believing that the hyperbole was the Mystery. In spite of my misgivings, I must find the right expression, the one enduring word that would encapsulate all I had ever preached—the word of words that would reveal the essence of the Mystery, rather than usurp it. How does one describe a beginning that had no starting point; a salvation that began outside the restriction of horology; upon which unrelenting time had no influence?

The ancient scriptures open: 'In the beginning, God created heaven and earth...', but that was not the true commencement. Far beyond the edge of time, lay another. A beginning that never began, that always was. How does one express that? Words, inadequate words, the only satisfactory one is God's word. The Greeks call it Logos, the scriptures call it Wisdom—the tangible expression of the ineffable. Suddenly, an idea formed in my mind. The Word was not born under a star, as some of the new writings would suggest. It was born before the stars existed. It had no beginning. It has no end. It simply *is*; way outside the current of time; the Word the Father proclaims eternally and which continually proclaims the Father is outside the influence of the divine Augustus's massive gnomon.

In the midst of my reflections, language began to form around my thoughts ... *In the beginning was the Word, and the Word was with God, and the Word was God. In the beginning, He was with God...*

21: Modern Rome

Frustration was the measure of the night. In spite of initiating measures to address the problems that recently tortured him, Marc's life was still in turmoil, but that was not the main cause of his restlessness. Carlo was in bed in a nearby room. He could not get the thought out of his mind, his flesh tingled and his heart raced, as if suffering an allergic reaction to that proximate presence. The comfort of his surroundings could not lure him into relaxation and sleep, that other bed more tempting than the one in which he tossed. When the fiery glow of dawn singed the edge of the curtains, he felt relieved that darkness was retreating together with the fantasies it spawned. Despite the sexual tension rippling through his loins, there was some relief in that he did not have to celebrate Mass for the nuns or anyone else for that matter. Nor did he feel any urge to attend Mass even though it was Sunday, the day of Ra, as Carlo was quick to point out. That sense of letting go was, at least, one positive, resulting from the upheaval of the recent past.

The thought energized him and he hopped out of bed, not with the keenness of former times, but with a little more eagerness than of late. He shaved in his room—the circular heads of his electric shaver razing the light, blond-tipped stubble with ease. He then went to the bathroom to shower. Carlo was there, towelling himself off after his shower.

The sight reactivated the desires he had experienced throughout the night. Despite having fantasized about him all night, the sight of a naked Carlo was unexpected. Marc was immobilized. This strong reaction surprised him, as he had seen Carlo naked on the beach. The ambience made the difference. Carlo appeared in the vapour of the

175

bathroom like a divine manifestation, his black hair glistening and dripping water, the droplets running tantalizingly down his muscular back and over the curved rise of his buttocks. For a classical scholar like Marc, Carlo enveloped in mist was the perfect stand in for Poseidon, the sea god of Greek mythology. Marc simply stood in admiration, but residual guilt emanating from years of combating temptation still gripped him. He felt he should be controlling his eyes. Carlo himself was unconcerned; he looked at Marc with an amused expression, and when Marc turned to leave, he said, 'It's all yours.' What was he referring to? Was it another of his friend's double entendres? Marc was perplexed, and then Carlo shook his head and with an amused expression left the bathroom.

In the shower Marc could not forget the 'divine manifestation'. Indeed, he did not wish to erase the memory, in spite of feeling that it was sinful. What was immoral about it? It was wrong if you took pleasure in it. 'Damn it!' he muttered into the jets that pummelled his body. 'Of course I took pleasure in it—it was divinely pleasurable.' He tried to reason himself into replacing his artificially acquired conscience for one more authentic, based on the natural standard of good and evil. The ancient gods were more liberal as was evident from their myths, which were so integral to his studies. He thought that he was as conversant with them as he was with the Bible myths, Old and New Testaments, but he was beginning to realize that his understanding of Greek and Roman mythology was superficial. He gave them a condescending nod, acknowledging them, but only as inferior guides in humanity's search for meaning. Now, with growing awareness of the shortcomings of the Christian myth, he was appraising the pagan stories in a new light. Having once stepped away from allegiance to one side, he was conscious not only of its deficiencies, but also of the positive contributions of the spurned others.

Poseidon, the god of the moment, was the god of the sea. Marc was familiar with many of the deities that the ancients created to rule over the various elements and conditions of life: sea, mountains, life, death, harvest and so forth. That was the way until the idea of 'one god' evolved. However, even Christians found it necessary to divide that 'one' into three to identify more readily the various functions of the 'one'. Was that more enlightened than the old way? He wondered. The ancient Greeks had their trinity, representing the known elements of air, earth and sea: Zeus, god of the sky, Hades, of the underworld and Poseidon, the immortal of the sea.

Like all ancient Greek deities, Poseidon was a sexual being. He had many lovers, among them a number of males. One of them was Nerites, and from their mutual love came Anteros, who became the god of requited love, and consequently the avenger of unrequited love. How tolerant they were of all love! Marc paused in his reflections to let that thought take hold. Unlike the biblical god, they were not homophobic. Marc had not considered that before. The Bible's negative attitude to human sexuality seemed so barren and repressed by comparison. Christianity continued the Hebrew Bible's aversion to sex. Even Paul, the apparent liberator of Christianity from biblical proscriptions, followed the same dour path. He would liberate the new followers from Leviticus 12:3, but not from Leviticus 20:13. The result was a Western Civilization with a negative view of human sexuality that was only now beginning to change. For two thousand years, Jews and homosexuals suffered victimization which, initiated by the Church, had entered into the consciousness of the age. This had continued into modern times. Recently, various civil authorities have made efforts to correct both, but the Church, while making overtures towards one, seemed to be hardening its attitude towards the other. The Church's vitriolic opposition to homosexual love verged of the pathological—love and be damned, as Carlo so often reiterated. One of the reasons, according to the Catholic Catechism, was that it did not proceed from genuine affection.

Towelling himself off, Marc felt deeply offended, affronted, cut to the quick by such an accusation. He did not feel just affection for Carlo; he loved him. Did the love of a wife-beater proceed from genuine

177

affection? The Church would not entertain a loving same-sex union, but it vigorously upheld, under pain of sin and its consequences, a loveless union. At least, it had done until quite recently. The fact that it relaxed its attitude would seem to indicate that it was not too sure in the first place, which was little comfort to those who suffered under its harsher regime. Would other rigorously held views meet the same fate when developing mores find them intolerable to support? Would the time come when the doctrine of the Virgin Birth would be too preposterous to find support? Perhaps it already had, as Carlo had indicated last night.

He put on his bathrobe, and returned, not to his own, but to Carlo's room.

Duet

Carlo was surprised. Marc held him in his gaze, trying to access Carlo's thoughts as he would the symbols on a scroll. However, the mind was more difficult to read. Words would have to suffice.

'Do you love me?'

Carlo could see that this was not a time for frivolity. Still, it was difficult to break the habit of a lifetime. With an amused glint, he asked, 'Would you like a biblical answer?'

'I would like a straight answer.'

'You know that I love you.' The frivolity had departed from Carlo's expression. His Petrine response was deadly serious.

'Show me.'

He looked at Marc with undisguised astonishment. 'Now?'

'Now,' repeated Marc, as he walked decisively towards the bed and dropped the robe. He just stood there, his back to the approaching Carlo, his mind a swirling galaxy of complementary, confusing and contradictory thoughts and emotions. His body trembled with anxiety and … lust, but not just lust—Carlo was not a mere body to him, he was a person whose love he desired and appreciated as much as he craved his body.

A first sexual experience is a sensitive, awkward affair, but for a dedicated celibate there can be the impediment of breaking what he regarded as a vow to God. Marc sensed Carlo's approach and felt his hands as they rested on his shoulders, but was unable to turn to face him. He struggled to demolish the obstacle that stood between them, his vow to a presumed deity. What did it mean in the light of his present belief? Would a vow to Poseidon, Hermes or Apollo be binding? A vow made to the planet Jupiter would elicit a wry smile from even the most legalistic mind, but at least the planet had some reality. If there were no object, then surely there could be no vow.

As Carlo's arms encircled him from behind, his tantalizing lips touching the sensitive tissue of the back of his neck, Marc recalled a recent description of blasphemy as a victimless crime. It was a simple revelation, but it did the trick—no victim no crime—no deity no vow.

He turned to face Carlo and devoured him with his eyes and then with his mouth. Intense pleasure surged through him as their tongues played. Carlo, still partially dressed, slipped quickly out of his clothes.

The sensitive hands of the librarian alighted like butterflies on chosen, charged petals of Marc's flesh, releasing pulses of electrifying pleasure that he never knew existed beneath the folds of his Celtic skin. The mouth and tongue ranged passionately, subtly over Marc's secret places, probing, licking, setting off within him explosions of exquisite delight. Marc, for his part, was amazed at how nature transformed him from maladroit novice to smooth lover. Their lovemaking, growing in intensity and urgency, eventually reached its explosive climax. Sex had reached its goal, but love continued. They lay in each other's arms, wishing that the universe would dissolve and leave them there forever. They had found paradise, but not in the faded, cracked writing of ancient texts.

Monsignore

Monsignore Martini looked displeased.

'You should have consulted me before taking precipitous action. I fill the place of your absent bishop. You should have shown me the courtesy of conferring with me.' As he spoke, his colour heightened and his displeasure escalated into anger.

Marc no longer cared. He and Carlo had repeated their lovemaking on Sunday night—this time in Marc's bed. The effect on Marc was profound. It gave him a new outlook on life. He would be polite to the man, but he did not give a toss for his display of anger. 'I am sorry, Monsignore. It was a sudden decision, and I did not wish to disturb you over the weekend.'

'You did not mind disturbing the Sisters over the weekend. The superior was at her wit's end trying to find a replacement at such short notice.' Marc felt like smiling at this evident exaggeration, but controlled the impulse. 'What is the problem that required such immediate and drastic action?'

Marc could have told him that he had decided to leave the priesthood, but he did not think that it was any of his business. He would write to his bishop in his own time. 'I just need time to reflect on my studies and my future.'

His supervisor's anger moderated. 'A retreat perhaps,' he suggested. 'I can arrange one immediately with a monastic community. I am sure you will emerge a happier and more committed priest.'

Again, Marc almost smiled—could he bring Carlo? 'Thank you, Monsignore, but that won't be necessary. I just want some time to myself.'

'You will do as you are told,' his anger was again beginning to mount. 'You have not abandoned obedience with everything else, have you?'

Marc was enjoying this. If his moderator knew what 'everything else' included, a monastery would seem an ineffectual solution. 'I am sure my bishop would favour my request, Monsignore.'

'He is far too lenient with you. Where do you propose to live during this period of reflection? How do you propose to support yourself?'

Marc was looking forward to this, but he kept a straight face. 'My uncle has kindly offered to put me up.' With full consent of the will, he teasingly revealed the information that would lead to the identity of this convenient uncle. He could hardly believe his callousness and that he was taking such pleasure in it.

'Where does your uncle reside?'

'Here in Rome,' replied Marc, hoping the questions would continue.

'Is he a priest, or an academic perhaps?'

'He is retired,' said Marc, avoiding disclosing too much at once.

'If he is your uncle, he can't be that old.' His inquisitor was becoming impatient.

'He is my granduncle.'

'What is his name? Perhaps I know him.'

The old Marc would have felt guilty at this stage, but not now. 'Giuseppe,' he said, feeling like a mouse getting the better of the cat.

'Giuseppe,' he pondered the word. 'Is he Italian?'

'No, Monsignore, he is Irish.'

'How did he acquire the name Giuseppe?' The priest's irritation was rising with the questions.

'Living so long in Rome, it sort of acquired him.'

'His name is evidently, Joseph,' snapped the professor, his impatience mounting again.

For a moment, Marc thought of teasing him still further by saying that his name was '*Seosamh*'—the Irish language equivalent—but decided against it. He was tiring of the game. 'Yes, Joseph Ross.'

'Your uncle is ... Joseph ... Ross.' His supervisor was incredulous. 'Has he been prompting you to pursue your ridiculous thesis? You are going to reside with, not only, a heretic and an atheist, but one disciplined by the Church. In your fragile state of faith, it is a recipe for

181

ruin, and your bishop would certainly not approve. I will contact him and advise him to recall you immediately.'

'I will inform him, Monsignore.' Marc was not going to submit to the man's coercion.

When he returned home, he decided to write to his bishop to inform him that he had decided to leave the priesthood. The man had always been friendly and courteous to Marc; he would return the favour. However, not yet, he decided, putting off the letter writing. Finding relief in Giuseppe's similar experiences, he returned once again, like a distressed patient seeking an analgesic, to his granduncle's narrative.

22: Jerusalem: 1955

Subsequent to my first lovemaking with Leah, Western guilt asserted itself and soon propelled me towards the confessional—the refuge of sinners. I should have known better, but environmental influences stick like a tick and suck the liberating fluid of rational reflection from our minds. Initially, my confessor, within the emotionally charged surroundings of the Church of the Holy Sepulchre, was understanding and sympathetic. However, when he offered absolution, it was on the inevitable condition of fleeing the occasion of sin. As a priest I was aware of that. So why did I pursue it? One of the imponderables associated with rational living is that sometimes our actions seem far from rational. At any rate, I balked. My feeling for Leah and her love for me had enriched my life and, as I saw it, deepened my spirituality. How could I label it an 'occasion of sin'? My confessor's sympathetic understanding evaporated in such a passion that I wondered if my situation reminded him of such an 'occasion of sin', regrettably lost, in his life.

I was fortunate to have an academic position, not a pastoral one. My religious exercises were expressions of personal devotion—no congregation depended on my ministry. After our first tentative lovemaking, I stopped celebrating Mass, not for want of faith—though wounded, that was still substantially intact—but through the pressure of acquired guilt.

I found myself in new and bewildering territory where natural innocence and derived guilt collided. On the one hand, deep down at the anatomical level of my being, where the subatomic particles of existence sparked and fired, I found my relationship with Leah good—that word does not do justice to the conviction I had. The assurance, passion and fervour I felt was primal. It scratched at the quarks, neutrons and electrons that dragged me out of the abyss into, not only existence, but also consciousness. That cosmic *good* stood in defiant opposition to the *evil* that my acquired nature and cosmetic conscience proclaimed that union to be. To abandon that *good* would be to tear out the nucleus at the core of my atoms and allow my miraculous birth into this new life to seep into the chasm of non-existence. Instead of abandoning Leah, I abandoned Mass.

The growing awareness that, like a mist, cloaked my religious beliefs did not develop in isolation; it found gradual but insistent confirmation in the writings emerging from the rock caves near the Dead Sea and the sands of the Egyptian desert. Two thousand years of Orthodox Christian influence had formed my conscience and convictions. In the same way, the happenings of the previous millennia determined the perception of the inhabitants of the Fertile Crescent in the first century of the Common Era.

Paul was a first-century man, but a complex one. As a Jew, his cultural influences were Palestinian, but coming from Tarsus, he was also influenced by Greek ideals. Alexander the Great had conquered, not only the territory of the Eastern Mediterranean, but the hearts and minds of its people. However, Paul was also a Roman, as he was proud to assert. Therefore, Paul thought like a Jew—a Palestinian, Hellenic, Roman, Jew. So did the inhabitants of Qumran who secreted their precious library safely out of the way of the approaching Roman army.

That does not mean that they were all the same, like peas in a pod. Just as a family produces siblings of varying and, at times, conflicting opinions, passions and desires, so does a nation. However, the soil is the same; it produces cacti, olives, cedars and a variety of vegetation, but the cacti, olives and cedars all have the flavour of the soil from which they sprang.

As the scrolls began to multiply so did my work of deciphering them. Reading the words last read by a Palestinian Jew—influenced by Roman and Hellenic culture—produced one major effect on me personally. It made me realize that I could never really understand them. How did such a person think? The fact is, I did not know. I read their symbols through the filter of my own experience, never through theirs. True, I had a wonderful snapshot of their thinking in the scrolls. I could make out their features, as one might the features of grandparents and great grandparents in old, fading photographs. One could see their faces and their outdated dress, but know nothing of them beyond their surface appearance. They were alien beings, but mere generations separated us, not millennia. This awareness drove me back to a more critical reading of the New Testament and, with almost culinary delight, I began to appreciate their homogeneous flavour. I delved with consuming passion into an in-depth and, for the first time I would maintain, an objective study of these various writings. I had the added advantage of being able to read them in their original language and from the oldest extant texts available. I concluded that I could never know them. What I assumed I knew was the thought of subsequent polemicists, dogmatists and copyists who added to the ingredients to suit their own age and purpose. The meal that arrived at my table was an indigestible stew unsuited to my modern palate.

Nobody can deny the influence of the New Testament on our modern world, the Western world at least. With dismay, I became convinced that the authority we conferred on these works was misplaced. It, as a unit, was not the word of God—such a God would certainly be diagnosed schizophrenic. They were, in all their diversity, very much human words, varied and sometimes contradictory, emanating from human beings who were grappling with their own personal and cultural problems while pursuing their own agenda. We could become familiar with their features and their surface teaching, but we could never know them.

Why, then, did we accord them such authority, while spurning other writings of the time, such as the ones then rising from their Egyptian grave? Churchmen and Evangelicals of today would say, because they are true, and truth, like immiscible oil, always surfaces. I wonder! Their enduring authority is more likely the result of power. Constantine made Christianity. He took Paul's creation and designed it to fit his own purpose. It had no more validity than that of Mount Olympus. Their deities and decrees also had a political purpose, to direct the lives of the inhabitants of the Greek and Roman worlds. The Romans took over the Greek gods and Constantine took over a Jewish god, sanitized by Paul. What was good in both emerged from the moral perception buried deep in human consciousness.

While grappling with these disturbing and growing convictions that saw my faith vaporizing into the vacuum from which it was drawn, I tried to find time to devote to my own scroll. As I had discovered it, I wished to keep it as a personal project. I worked on it in my own time, but it was a slow process. However, I was in no hurry; archaeologists of necessity cultivate patience. I had already concluded to my own satisfaction that the manuscript was old—probably first century CE. The writing itself would determine the period more accurately. I was looking forward to the stage when I would be able to decipher the writing. The top edge had unfurled slightly, revealing a few letters. The writing was Greek, placing it in the minority of the Dead Sea canon. It was also unusual in that the writing material was papyrus, not parchment as with the scrolls.

186

23: Modern Rome

Resuming his reading of Giuseppe's reflections brought a surprise. What had he found? Intrigued, Marc stopped reading. His granduncle was a silent one. He had never mentioned his find either in conversation or in his writings. Perhaps its significance was slight. However, every fragment, however trivial, had its own unique importance. The whole library of Qumran had been in the public domain for some time now with the exception of a few texts that eluded identification, so Marc must have come across whatever it was that Giuseppe had found. He had no way of knowing which might be his granduncle's as each fragment was identified with the cave in which it was found, not with the individual who found it. Marc wondered if it might have a bearing on his own research, but he thought not as his granduncle would surely have mentioned it.

He wanted to continue reading, but decided to take a break. He left the library, walked across the vestibule and onto the terrace. Giuseppe was on the other terrace working at his laptop. Marc stood there pondering 'the find' as his granduncle's favourite music drifted towards him.

Giuseppe looked up and spotted his grandnephew on the second terrace. 'Care to join me for a coffee?'

'I'll make it,' replied the younger man and made his way to the kitchen.

Marc was fortunate, and he knew it. He had only been living with Giuseppe for one week and he already felt like a new man. After a memorable first day, he found his life reforming. Carlo stayed over a few nights during the week, and Marc could safely claim that repetition did not dull the thrill of their lovemaking. On each occasion, his attitude hardened towards the institution that outlawed such a genuine expression of affection. Love, and be damned, Carlo's refrain, with a subtle shift of emphasis that challenged the dire prediction of Church moralists, became his. After the chaos of the recent past, a new creation was forming.

The week passed peacefully and his granduncle was kindness itself. Marc had written to his bishop. The letter was polite but direct. He expressed his appreciation for the understanding the bishop had shown him in the past and hoped he would accept his decision to leave the priesthood with equal sympathy. He did not go into the reasons for his change of heart, beyond the mundane—he was not happy. The letter was concise. He had moved beyond discussion. He had drifted into a new unchartered orbit leaving behind the old gravitational pull that had ordered his former life. Even the looming difficulties of the unknown faded before his relative's kindness.

After the turmoil of the previous week he had returned to the scrolls with interest but without a definite goal. Where it might lead, however, was secondary to the satisfaction he found in the work itself. He also noticed a subtle but profound change in his attitude to study. There was no seismic shift but there was a difference. He was willing to entertain diverse interpretations without necessarily committing to any. Previously he had been sensitive to a subtle polemically induced constraint, like the imperceptible tug of the tide on a calm sea. It was nothing noticeable, lost almost in the nature of things, but now he was definitely aware of its absence.

As the coffee maker gurgled and steamed beside him he reflected on his good fortune. In spite of Giuseppe's willingness to help he did not wish to be a burden. He would stay only as long as he felt that he was making a legitimate contribution to Giuseppe's work. His granduncle no longer gave lectures or made public appearances but he received numerous requests for articles to various publications dealing with the origins of Christianity. To answer his correspondence alone was a sizable task with which Marc was more than willing to help. The virulent content in some correspondence shocked him, and not all was from a predictable minority.

He also viewed Carlo differently. He was no longer afraid of the demands that friendship might make, no longer apprehensive of where it might lead but enchanted by where it did lead. The spectre of 'sin' had joined the 'bogey man' in the closet of abandoned childish terrors. He had not suddenly become a libertine but had acquired a more mature morality based on sound virtue—justice, honesty and compassion—not on the changing mores of successive generations. Reviewing the week just passed he was amazed at the change that had taken place in him, so radical and, in the end, so smooth. He now knew what Giuseppe meant when he spoke of 'changing gears'. A smooth, but definite shift had altered his trajectory—thanks, in the main, to Giuseppe. He was the prop without which he would surely have slipped into depression and perhaps worse. When his demons began their assault he would not have believed it possible to put them to rest so thoroughly and so finally. Rather than the revelatory blessing it was proclaimed to be, he began to see faith as a blindfold that hindered the mind's true perception.

'You did not tell me that you found one of the scrolls.' Marc made the comment as he poured the coffee. 'Which one was it?'

Giuseppe smiled. There was a twinkle in his eye recalling the moment. 'It is an experience ... an event like that. It colours the rest of your life. You relive the thrill every time you remember the moment. It is like music. The ecstasy you experienced when a musical work first spoke to you returns at every hearing.'

'Is that true of the music playing now?'

'Ah, yes! *Ariadne* does it for me every time.'

'The music is beautiful, though the opera seems a bit muddled.'

'It went through a number of revisions.'

'You have a great appreciation of music.'

'Music, art in general, is the true revelation, and artists the authentic prophets.'

'More so than the Bible and its seers,' suggested Marc.

'We can't blame Jeremiah and company. However, art is more immediate—touches our essence. I often think that if the prophets and the Qumran scribes had expressed their searching and awareness in music instead of words, we might understand them better—it communicates directly, mind to mind.'

'It's strange that you should say that,' said Marc, thoughtfully. 'I have often felt the same. How can we expect to understand words written in a completely different context from that in which we read them? But directly, mind to mind, that makes sense—that intangible part of consciousness that we have been trying to understand ever since it emerged from whatever kind of awareness our pre-rational ancestors enjoyed,' suggested Marc.

'I find it intriguing to speculate on just how that leap into rationality occurred. Did one member of a family group stand out from the rest? Did he or she have a greater awareness of their surroundings and themselves?'

'Perhaps it was not a leap at all, just an awareness of the self, gradually developing over the generations from blurred image to higher definition, so that no single member ever stood out.'

'We simply do not know. However it happened, it has become the hallmark of humanity, the defining event. We have filled numerous temples with a variety of gods and built massive cathedrals in an effort to understand and explain it. Yet it remains elusive, forever out of reach, defiantly refusing our efforts to rein it in.'

'Fearing that revealing it would destroy its potency.'

'It would certainly destroy its mystery. Art is the most significant leap we have been able to make into that transcendent element.'

'I find that I fantasize on the past also, but usually within the Homo sapiens period. I would love to have a peep into the lives of the people that wrote the scrolls.'

'I find myself drawn to a much earlier period,' said Giuseppe thoughtfully, 'Way, way back.'

'To the fishy period,' suggested Marc with a grimace.

'No, after our ancestors took to the land,' continued Giuseppe.

'They were unpromising, scurrying little creatures, by all accounts, with limited prospects of survival.'

'You could not imagine one of them composing a Beethoven symphony. Yet one of their direct descendants did. I find that fact terrifying in its potential.' Giuseppe's awe was evident in his expression.

'One of their descendants composed *Ariadne* also, the myth as well as the music.'

'We are fortunate that our studies brought us into contact with all the great myths of the ancient world. I feel enriched by that awareness.'

'Poor Ariadne,' said Marc, simulating sympathy, 'Abandoned on Naxos by her lover Theseus.'

'And rescued by another divine/human being, Dionysus to the Greeks, Bacchus to the Romans. It is surprising how few realize how closely Christianity follows the ancient myths, Dionysus in particular.'

'Dionysus the resurrection deity, son of a god, but born of a human mother.'

'He was the god of wine, his followers celebrated in the Bacchanalia, all reminiscent of Cana and the Eucharist. But, I listen to the opera for the music. "I would have the eternal stars die rather than have you die in my arms". The final entreaty of Bacchus has a special resonance for me. But, what Richard Strauss did with it... that you have to experience.'

Marc, the linguist, had understood the German words before Giuseppe translated them. He wondered what relevance they had for his granduncle. His quiet but passionate emotion filled their space as much as the music, but Marc chose not to pursue it.

'The story of the myth is high drama but Richard Strauss set it in a context bordering on farce, somewhat similar to the *Behind The Scenes*

191

segment that comes with many DVDs—yet the music is sublime. Maybe he is telling us something,' said Giuseppe thoughtfully.

'Treat all myth as farce,' suggested Marc. 'That reminds me, you did not tell me which of the scrolls you found.'

'I thought I had successfully deflected you,' said Giuseppe with a chuckle. 'Continue reading, you will find out. Then we can talk.'

24: Jerusalem: 1956

During the 1950s, the flow of fragile texts rising from their tombs in the wilderness was surprising—an inadequate word to describe the overwhelming amount of ancient material discovered. The increased number of experts engaged to deal with the volume of new texts discovered did not reduce our individual workload. I was frustrated not to be able to find time for my pet project. If I had included my scroll in the general pool of finds, the work would have progressed quicker, but I was selfish and egotistical enough to seek to do the work myself, and in private.

Evenings were also busy—my *affaire de coeur* with Leah continued. If anything, it intensified. The diminishing divine embrace seemed to propel me with greater passion and intensity into Leah's welcoming warmth. After a day bent over the ancient fragments, decrepit, discoloured and deformed by time, I could not wait to get back into arms that were youthful, lustrous and supple. She became my anchorage from the personal, academic and political storms that raged in and around me. I found it extremely disconcerting to see that wars still raged. In circumstances physically threatening and morally discouraging because of the apparent inability of Homo sapiens—the wise ones of creation—to live in peace, Leah's eyes stabilized me and focused me on another possibility. Her tranquillity calmed me, her body comforted me and her love supported me. She and her family had experienced the extreme of intolerance and she had emerged from it, wounded perhaps, but not deformed. She was a worldly person in the sense that she did not expect an afterlife to correct the inadequacies of this one. Her attitude was to work with what we have. She was intolerant of intolerance and intransigence. With her, my life had meaning. Her simple presence was more instructive and uplifting than all the so-called sacred texts ever written.

Inevitably, the question of commitment arose. At the time, I was in no position to commit to anything. I was in a mess. Then something happened which commanded my attention and compelled me to shift my notice from the confusion of the first century to the chaos of the twentieth. After yet another night of rapturous love, after which she lay, replete and fulfilled, in my arms, she informed me matter-of-factly that she was pregnant.

The news shocked me. What did I expect? Only a retard would have failed to consider the possibility, but that is exactly what I was—made so by prescriptions I allowed to rule my life. Leah was unperturbed. After her experiences, a birth was a positive. It was time for me to accept my responsibility. I would marry Leah despite clerical celibacy, a law that by then held as much relevance to my twentieth-century life as the Levitical laws of ritual purity. I would make explicit what was implicit in our shared life. My commitment to the priesthood had so weakened over time that leaving it was not the emotional trauma it might otherwise have been. However, my solution was not to Leah's liking. I could quit the priesthood if I wished, but she was not sure that she wanted to marry. I could understand her reluctance. Her experience had taught her to be wary. She wanted the child but suggested that we carry on as before, making the best of a challenging and volatile existence. To a degree, I agreed with her. My commitment to Leah was in my heart not on paper. However, I could not carry on playing a role that no longer made any sense to me. I would leave the priesthood. That decision presented its own problems.

Subsequently, I set in motion the necessary steps by writing to the Jesuit Superior General in Rome. Fearing the inevitable, I approached my non-clerical friend, the deputy controller of the project, to acquaint him of my situation. I knew that he respected my work and hoped that he, a professional with no clerical affiliations, would support my efforts to remain with the team in the likely event of my recall to Rome. The response to my letter came inviting me to Rome to discuss the matter. In reply, I pointed out that due to pressure of work a request for leave would not be welcome at present. In any event, I insisted that I had made up my mind and no further debate on the matter would alter my decision. That brought the predictable reaction—an order to relinquish my post in Jerusalem and to return forthwith to Rome. Neither the tone nor the context of the letter surprised me, it was the 1950s not the 1980s when the increased volume of defections compelled greater understanding for those involved. As it turned out, my position proved secure due mainly to my friend's efforts, the demands of the work and our limited numbers.

Signs of Leah's pregnancy were beginning to show, but only to the intimate observer. Her condition changed not only her body—it seemed to soften her resistance to marriage. While I did not attach much importance to the externals of the institution, I did appreciate its significance in strengthening the bond between two people. Consequently, when I noticed her opposition to the idea weakening, I supported it. In the fourth month of her pregnancy, we were married in a quiet civil ceremony, with Joel and a female friend acting as witnesses. It was not a time or a country for vacations, so we decided to postpone our honeymoon until after the baby was born.

Bliss defined the days that followed, but bliss in the midst of chaos. Then one day, as I was about to leave for the museum, Leah suggested that she accompany me as far as the market. I donned my *keffiyeh* and we left. As we walked, I was reminded that this was what our future life would be. Leah seemed to read my mind. Never one to be constrained by convention, she reached out and took my hand, as we walked contentedly through the narrow, bustling streets of Old Jerusalem. I have since come to rail against all religions that in their respective and restrictive ways put limits on expressions of love. At the time, still compelled by cultural coercion, I squandered the opportunity to give her a parting kiss. That lost opportunity I will regret to my dying day.

As I drew near to Herod's Gate, a tremendous explosion resounded and reverberated in the direction from which I had just come. Such blasts were common enough in Jerusalem at the time, but on this occasion, an icy hand gripped my entrails and tried to tug them out through my mouth. Panic seized me, and I rushed back to an unrecognizable and chaotic marketplace.

Over the years I have tried to erase the scene from my memory, but year after year it only grows more vivid. The air was thick with dust and vapour. Shrill screams vibrated on the air mingling with the cries of the ages. The blast shattered the wooden stalls and blended their contents to pulp. The buildings around the perimeter of the market suffered from the severity of the blast—it tore the plaster from the walls, and glass from the windows littered the street. The sight of the bodies, whole and broken, was almost too much to bear. Only anxiety and concern sustained me sufficiently to continue into the centre of the carnage of what, just a few minutes before, had been a lively marketplace.

To search seemed strangely futile, but terror and love, an unlikely combination, propelled me. I picked up an arm and then wondered why? Would I recognize it as Leah's limb? Would I be able to identify the flesh that I kissed and stroked, the arm that sheltered me from my worst demons? Conscious of the futility of my act, I replaced it reverently and moved on. Why presume the worst? Surely Leah had survived. Even now she was sheltering, shocked but intact, away from this carnage. In spite of my efforts to think positively, foreboding grew with every step I took.

The wounded were walking around, dazed and unable to comprehend what had happened. Screaming loved ones, out of their minds with fear, conducted their own frenzied searches just as rescuers arrived to initiate an organized sweep of the area.

I continued aimlessly through the chaos. How long was I walking? Time seemed irrelevant—I was moving through a place that time forgot. As if in a dream, I spotted a familiar-looking headscarf. It flapped slightly, as if trying to attract my attention. Red had seeped into the blue and yellow embroidery. Dread immobilized me. It seemed like forever that I stood there gazing down at her still beautiful face. At last, with a dazed and unnatural calm, I knelt and gathered the surprisingly intact body into my arms; she was as beautiful in death as in life. I held my entire family, my entire world in my arms and rocked them gently. I often think that I too died that day.

There are scholars who, guided (or misguided!) by what is termed *probabilistic reasoning*, accept the existence of God on the presumption that God's existence is as probable as not, therefore He exists. As I knelt that day in the chaos of a post terrorist attack, quietly sobbing and holding my world to my heart, God seemed very remote.

Later, while trying to rebuild the fragments of my life, I considered leaving the hostel. The building that held such sweet memories now provoked only bitterness. Work helped but I felt my loss keenly when I returned to my empty room. Joel and my non-clerical friend were my only supports during those difficult months, especially Joel, who shared something of the desolation I felt. He was anxious that I stay. I think that we sustained each other.

I was also tempted to leave Jerusalem, but my work was there. With the double loss of Leah and faith, work was all that kept me steady. I also enjoyed it, as much as one in my condition could enjoy anything. As a substitute to abandoning the historic city, I delved with greater intensity into its past. I cleaned and preserved the ever-increasing number of fragments landing on the table of the scrollery. I scrutinised their provenance in order to restore them to their original places in the brittle fabric of the relevant scroll. Then and only then followed the work of reading and translation.

International scholars were beginning to complain about the slow pace of publication. Dissatisfaction developed into suspicion that

Church authorities were hiding something. Certainly, arriving at the publication stage was a monumental task, and in spite of our increased numbers, we were still too few. However, the critics had a point. The coordinators were reluctant to release our findings to scholars worldwide who were willing to help. They seemed afraid that something damaging to the status quo might surface. I wondered what they would have done in that eventuality.

I was fortunate that the work was absorbing but, no matter how deeply the ancient past preoccupied me, the recent past haunted me daily. My wound was too deep to heal quickly. I wondered if it would ever mend. On the surface my work continued as normal but I was not the same. I had lost the love of my life. Maybe I would love again but I doubted it. In the event I never did love again. If Leah had died intestate, as her husband I would have inherited her estate, but I discovered a will made before we were married leaving her substantial estate, the greater part of which was in the United States, to Joel and myself. The Nazis and the war had demolished the family's German assets. The birth of a child would no doubt have influenced her to make another will but, in the tragic circumstances in which I found myself, I was content to respect her previous wishes.

Jerusalem then was a city of death and destruction. Its turbulent history spanned the centuries. The unfortunate result of being Yahweh's chosen people, as Leah frequently pointed out. She did not believe in Israel's God but understood that the fiction had become part of Israel's unhappy history. That election, I was beginning to realize, was the fictive creation of so-called seers and prophets, megalomaniacal in the extreme.

The city also presided over the death of my faith, but in spite of the usual appellation *loss of faith*, I counted it as gain, and still do, a resurrection to rationality in this city of resurrection and other curious myths. I would that everyone addicted to the drug of faith could know the rush of release that I experienced at 'coming off' it. Leah's death had precipitated it, but her life had also been influential. Her deliberately provocative remarks had focused my mind not only on the absurdity of my beliefs but of all irrational convictions. However, the ancient texts themselves gradually extracted the poison from my system. How ironic that Christian faith should die for me in the same terrain that saw its birth!

My work of deciphering and translating the texts proceeded with greater assurance and clarity without the drug of faith, which can so often further cloud the already equivocal essence hidden behind all ancient script. A more fitting title for the Holy Bible would be the Equivocal Bible considering the vast array of exotic, esoteric and contradictory movements that claim it as their source.

25: Modern Rome

May the eternal stars die
Rather than that you should die in my arms.

Now he knew. Marc stood up to stretch his legs. He walked through the vestibule onto what he was beginning to think of as his terrace. Giuseppe was at work on the other, tapping away on his laptop keyboard. His compassion was almost physical as Marc looked over at his granduncle so industriously engaged. What a tragedy he had suffered! No family to support or console him yet he entertained no bitterness, as demonstrated by his kind attitude to Marc. How alone he must have felt in a distant city, a different culture, with indifferent colleagues and only Joel to share something of his emptiness. The thought provoked Marc to renewed resentment against his own family. He wanted to express his sympathy, but what could he say so long after the event. He was at a loss for words.

The music in which Giuseppe did find consolation reached Marc's ears: *Und eher sterben die ewigen Sterne, Eh denn du sturbest aus meinem Arm!* The German language was a *sine qua non* for a biblical scholar. Consequently, Marc had no difficulty following the vocal exchanges between Ariadne and Bacchus, who were exchanging faltering expressions of love, at times hesitant, other times fearful, lest love should prove an illusion. Ariadne had already experienced the pain of abandonment. Words and music, longing yet hopeful, were expressing the inevitable fear that accompanies love, the possession of which is so intense that its loss is a constant and consuming dread. He wondered, with a shudder, how he would react to such a crisis. Marc already liked the opera but, in the light of Giuseppe's experience, his appreciation of the music was growing. He found himself pausing in his work to listen, emotion building and climaxing with the music, and like Giuseppe, musing on the origin of consciousness and the capacity of a mass of cellular tissue to adapt sound into a meaningful and transforming experience. Love and music sustain each other, as is evident from the constant theme that accompanies music. Consequently, he felt that finding and expressing love brought a new intensity to his enjoyment of music, as if the experience unlocked some secret compartment in his psyche releasing new and arousing passion.

Marc looked across at Giuseppe, who had stopped typing. His head was resting on the back of the chair, his face slightly raised, looking up into the cloudless sky. It was obvious that he had paused to absorb the music. Marc could imagine what he was thinking, and his own vicarious shame resurfaced. He would have liked to call to him and offer to bring him a coffee, but he could not face him just yet. Instead, he returned to the library to continue reading.

26: Jerusalem: 1956

By the time of Leah's death, the rich vein of finds was ending. The archaeologists once again lost out to the vigilant Bedouin in the race to the final discovery. Of course, we did not know at the time that the discovery of cave 11 in early 1956 would be the last. Among the scrolls found there was the largest non-biblical text of the collection, the Temple Scroll, which restates and embellishes precepts regarding worship and the Temple. However, that particular scroll did not find its way into the hands of the archaeologists until 1967 when, because of Israel's victory in the war of that year, the scroll fell into Israeli hands, together with the caves themselves and the ruins of the Qumran settlement. Whatever about the political consequences, the Israeli victory simplified our work by gathering all the scrolls under one authority. I also felt it patently obvious that Israel had an unassailable claim on the scrolls since they formed part of its cultural history.

My evenings were void. Not just 'free', 'empty', 'vacant', but void. The word has that connotation of being not just unoccupied, but inescapably and indescribably so. Such were my evenings—craving for a touch that was no more; pining for a voice forever silenced. The crushing emptiness, like the irresistible pressure of a black hole, oppressed me. I had an urgent need to fill it. It was then that my precious scroll came into its own. Instead of returning to the abyss that was my room, I stayed on at the museum and worked into the night on my pet project.

I had previously managed to determine that the writing was Greek. It appeared to be a letter, but there was no designated recipient; it was more in the nature of an open letter to one and all. The closer I came to the reading stage, the more excited I became. I tried to restrain my wilder speculation, but human nature being what it is, extravagant fantasies kept popping surreptitiously into my mind. In my more restrained moments, I continued to hope; the professional in me knew that all ancient fragments had their place in elucidating the past. I repaired the little jar in which it had been so carefully stored and kept it in my office, separate from the other pottery fragments—not for any subversive reason—simply because it was my exclusive find and I wished to keep it near for as long as possible.

The tests to which I submitted the two items proved to my own satisfaction that they were ancient—as old, at least, as the later scrolls. When it was ready for reading, I held off, as a child might put off eating a candy, relishing the prospect as much as the reality. Then I could wait no longer. I unrolled the ancient papyrus, fearing that it might crumble at my touch—made from a water reed, it was more fragile than animal skin—but it proved resilient. I secured it with two stoppers to prevent recoil. I was accustomed to scanning texts briefly to get an impression of the contents before examining them closely. I registered the symbols for 'Beloved Disciple', a nom de plume for the author of the Gospel of John. It was early in our understanding of the Qumran scrolls, but there was little evidence so far of a Christian dimension, so this possible reference surprised me. Then my eyes alighted on 'Paul' and 'Tarsus'. There was little doubt now that this text had something to say about the early Christian movement. Fantasies again ran wild. I was about to settle down to a closer reading and examination of the scroll when one of my clerical superiors entered, wondering why the light was on when everyone had presumably left for the night. In my naivety, I told him about my find and, consequently, my interest in pursuing it to the end. He seemed to understand my excitement and the exclusivity it provoked, and nodded appreciatively. He asked me if I had identified the text, so I explained that I was just about to read and study it. He approached to have a closer look. He was much older than I was and, at the time, more skilled in reading the ancient symbols. I followed his eyes running down the text and suddenly he stopped and looked at me. 'Are you sure you didn't read it?' His abruptness surprised me. I assured him that I had not; I had just succeeded in unrolling it when he arrived. He looked relieved, and informed me that he would personally continue the examination. He rolled it up again and, as he left, assured me that he would keep me informed. I was shocked and, considering the symbols I had managed to translate, suspicious, but what could I do? He was a very senior member of the team. If I challenged him or indeed hinted that I had identified segments of the text, he would probably have dismissed me. He departed, leaving me to wonder what a fuller reading of the scroll might have told me.

Summer was departing with the weather displaying the usual confusion that accompanied the change of seasons. Some weeks had passed since I was forced to hand over my scroll and my colleagues and I had other matters demanding our attention. The political situation had once again ignited and with increased ferocity. Not only was Israel, yet again, in open conflict with its Arab neighbours, England and France were in dispute with Egypt over the Suez Canal. Before hostilities broke out, we had to move the scrolls to Amman for safekeeping, and we, the members of the international team of experts, had to seek a place of safety. I would have liked to go to Egypt to do some research on the Nag Hammadi manuscripts, but Cairo was probably more dangerous at that time than Jerusalem. I might have returned home to Ireland, but I was not welcome there, so I headed back to Rome. Unlike Giordano Bruno, who spent many years avoiding territory under the influence of the Inquisition, I had no fear of returning to the organizational centre of the Church. My former superiors would hardly welcome me with open arms, but I did not intend to call.

Growing numbers of pilgrims were returning to the Eternal City, as Europe continued to rebuild itself after the war. Unlike them, I did not rush to the tomb of the apostle. Instead I made for Campo de' Fiore to lay at the feet of Giordano Bruno my lately acquired Rationalism, Humanism, Agnosticism, whatever term one might use to describe my collected convictions. Various opponents applied all of them to me at different times. I hate that word—I do not wish to be anybody's opponent. I suppose all the classifications or appellations are just. I am all, yet I am none. I am merely a seeker after ... Truth? Reality? Whatever it is, I have not found it. I have found what it is not, but what it is eludes me. Perhaps the purpose of life, if indeed it had a purpose, was in seeking.

After paying my silent tribute to the great man, I walked around the Campo. Winter was in the air. However, a surprising number of people was strolling about, speaking a variety of languages and taking an animated interest in their surroundings. They were the vanguard of a phenomenon that would sweep Europe and the world over the coming decades—tourism.

Making my tranquil round of the Campo, identifying with the other tourists, I began to feel a wholeness that had evaded me since Leah's death. Rome was proving to be therapeutic after the endless strife of Jerusalem. I was fantasizing about settling in Rome after my work on the scrolls concluded when I noticed a sign—*In Vendita*—hanging from the terrace of an old palazzo, indicating that it, or part of it, was for sale. Something stirred within me. With a rush of excitement, I decided to buy it now that I was in a position to do so. Until that moment, I had not decided to make Rome my home. Since leaving the priesthood, Ireland did not seem a happy choice. What better alternative was there than Rome, and what better location in the city than within sight of the memorial to the man whose life had so inspired me?

I took the details of the selling agent and went directly to his office, which was nearby, to enquire into the details. The property market was not exactly booming at the time, so Signor Conti received me with gushing enthusiasm. I expressed a desire to see the property at his convenience. He assured me that he was at my service right then and there and, with the consummate skill of a herdsman corralling his animals, led me with seductive dialogue across the Campo to the property.

'Far from palaces he was reared', was an Irish putdown that certainly applied to me. My home in Dublin was fine, but not palatial. I had never imagined myself viewing a palazzo as a prospective buyer. However, the vendors were evidently conscious that such a property was beyond the reach of most, financially and socially, in the aftermath of the recent war. They had made some effort to divide the floors and offer them for sale as separate units. A single floor was vast, far too much space for me but, thanks to Leah, I could afford it. The property, with art, history and culture radiating from its stone, marble and frescos, impressed the antiquarian in me but the view of Giordano from the terrace sold it. I decided to buy the top floor. As the recent war had illustrated, one's future is never secure, so I reasoned that if I fell upon hard times, I could rent half of it as a self-contained unit. However, no subsequent cataclysmic event compelled me to adopt the role of 'landlord'. Signor Conti, in spite of his best efforts, could not hide his surprise at concluding a sale so quickly and effortlessly.

I moved in immediately and started work on what would eventually be my first published book. As I set down the outline I intended to follow, I felt inspired by the close proximity of Giordano. I was influenced by more than a mere lifeless memorial, I felt that his spirit had taken possession of me and moved me as a master chess player moved his pawn, and the words flowed freely. I recalled his passion for the written word in his pursuit of knowledge and truth. He sought books that were suspect by the Church and would hide in the monastery privy, away from prying eyes, to study them. This tactic was eventually discovered and, hearing that the Inquisition was preparing a case against him, he fled the monastery. Twenty five years later, his fugitive life ended in flames in the campo below my terrace.

My writing dealt with my recent professional work in Jerusalem. As it was technical and consequently daunting, I felt that it would not be a great seller. I could have written about Leah; that would probably have injected a popular and human element into an otherwise pedantic work with limited appeal. However, though I was beginning to come to terms with her death, I felt it might be prostituting her memory for financial gain. In the event, the book sold well and was translated into a number of languages. I had underestimated the lure of mystery and the appeal of ancient biblical-related texts.

Winter passed working on the book in my palatial surroundings. Every day I grew more attached to my new home. I read up on its history and investigated the lives of the various families that had inhabited its gracious enclosure. Delving into the lives of past generations is a sobering enterprise. As with all history, it emphasized the fragile and transitory nature of our fleeting years.

Archaeology is a vivid reminder of this as each layer of human habitation is built on a previously forgotten level, inhabited by individuals who considered their existences pivotal and, if not eternal, at least timeless, but which were brusquely and impassively erased in time, thus allowing another occupancy to rise and conceal, physically and mentally, what went before. My investigations into the generations of previous residents of my palatial abode had an unforeseen consequence in that it provided material for a later series of books on the families of Rome that I had, at that time, no intention whatever of undertaking. The series proved both popular and profitable in an era of increasing tourism.

In the New Year, hostilities ceased in the Sinai and by spring I was back in Jerusalem. I was naturally anxious to see what had happened to my scroll during the intervening months, so I approached my colleague to inquire about it. He told me that he could not find it. It evidently had gone missing somewhere in the course of the move to safety. I looked at him with scepticism but he merely shrugged and added for my consolation that it was not authentic. His tests had proven that it was a medieval forgery. I did not bother to ask how a medieval forger managed to hide it away in Cave 4 without finding the hoard of ancient documents stored there and alerting the world to his find, thereby finding fame and presumably fortune that his 'forgery' would never realize.

I was disappointed but most of all I felt bereaved. My voice from the past was no more. It was a scholarly and historical loss. Of course, it could have been genuinely mislaid. It was a chaotic time and, undoubtedly, fragments did disappear forever during the upheaval of that period. However, to declare it spurious convinced me that its loss was contrived, calculated and callous. I may have been disappointed, disillusioned even, but I was not surprised. As many, like Giordano, have found to their cost, dogmatic faith is the enemy of free thought and ultimately stands diametrically opposed to the pursuit of knowledge.

27: Modern Rome

Marc stopped reading. His reaction to the loss of the scroll reflected that of Giuseppe. As an historian, he felt it deeply. For any ancient witness to go missing by accident was always a tragedy, to silence one deliberately was a crime. What had it contained? What had happened to it? Obviously, Giuseppe did not have the answers to such questions. He knew little, apart from the possible Christian references he had managed to spot before his colleague whisked it away. Marc was intrigued by those allusions. It would seem to indicate that his thesis was on the right track. No doubt, that was the reason why Giuseppe continued to encourage him to persevere with his research.

Carlo, with an after-shower glow and aroma, joined Marc in the library. His arms encircled Marc in a gentle embrace that gradually began to intensify. His effortless display of emotion moved Marc to respond by embracing Carlo in return. He did not possess the same Mediterranean ease of expression as his lover and wondered if his origins by the windswept edge of the North Atlantic were the cause, as asserted by many social and biological scientists.

Giuseppe had gently hinted that as this was his home now, Marc should invite whomsoever he chose whenever he wished, and intimated that the presence of an ancient relative should not inhibit him in any way. 'If you have been following my reflections, you will know that I have some experience of love,' he hinted diplomatically. Marc was amazed by his granduncle's tolerance and understanding. He was an old man, born into a time and place where religious preachers tolerated marital sex, ranted against extra-marital sex and were, in the main, silent about same-sex activity, probably rendered speechless by—as they perceived it—its deviant and criminal nature. Giuseppe was a man out of his time, his acceptance more forbearing than the age into which he was born. Marc doubted his own broad-mindedness. Being an insider thrust acceptance upon him. He often wondered, if he were heterosexual, how he would react to homosexuality. He feared that a reversal of roles might find him wanting. The thought provoked him to respond to Carlo's embrace with greater warmth—kissing him with Mediterranean passion.

Marc was intrigued at how one event can trigger another without any evident connection. What could be farther apart than their embrace and a spiritual exercise? Yet, for no apparent reason in the midst of hugging Carlo, he recalled a devotional essay on the meaning of blessing. The word comes from the Latin *benedicere*—to say something well. It does not refer to perfect speech, but to effective assertion. When it is God's utterance, it is no idle word—it does what it says. It is life changing. That is a blessing. There is a number of such benedictions on the road to Christian perfection, among them—Baptism, Confirmation, Holy Orders. Marc had experienced all three, but for him none proved as effective as Carlo's embrace—none more life altering. The thought acted as a stimulus, compelling him to lock Carlo more firmly in his arms, snuggle into his neck, tongue his ear and whisper, 'I love you'.

'Whoa!' exclaimed Carlo, with surprise and delight. 'What brought that on?'

'I just realized what a blessing you are.'

'Then how about letting the Italian sun bless your white skin?'

'It's not white,' Marc objected, feigning offence. 'See how tanned it is.'

'Really!' Carlo placed his deeply tanned arm alongside Marc's honey-coloured skin.

'You are a freak,' retorted Marc. 'But a nice freak,' he added, gently kissing the dark arm. 'The beach sounds great. I long to see you naked.'

'You just had that pleasure.'

'That was over an hour ago,' replied Marc dismissively.

'I have created a monster!' Carlo's laughter resounded around the library. 'I invited Luigi. You like to see him naked too.'

'Great!' The remark subdued Marc, but did not surprise him. It was obvious to Carlo that Marc admired Luigi's physique. 'We better get started on breakfast'.

4QMMT

The aroma of coffee permeated the kitchen as Marc prepared a plate of croissants and toast, while Carlo fed a variety of fruits into the juice extractor. They carried the lot to Giuseppe's terrace. His granduncle was an early riser, but Marc knew from his short time with him that when he got involved in his writing or reading he promptly forgot about breakfast. Isis, observing from a cardboard box that she frequently favoured over the many cushions she appropriated as her own, watched with eyes of mystic wonder as they sat around the table on the terrace. Marc felt uncomfortable. He buttered a slice of toast and nibbled it thoughtfully. He should refer to Leah but just did not know what to say.

'I have been reading your Jerusalem journal.'

'I hope you don't find it too boring,' said Giuseppe apprehensively. 'Such writing can be very self-indulgent.'

'The opposite,' replied Marc enthusiastically. 'It's fascinating.'

'How far have you got?'

'I have finished all that you have posted to the library computer.'

'Ah!' sighed Giuseppe.

'Giuseppe, I don't know what to say.' Marc struggled with a variety of emotions: sadness for Giuseppe and renewed bitterness towards his own family. 'I feel the family let you down badly.'

'There is no need to say anything, Marco. It was long before your time. As for the family, well, it was a different age. What do you think about my little scroll and its dubious disappearance?'

Marc felt relieved that Giuseppe had closed the difficult topic, and Carlo, silent until then, picked up his ears. 'What scroll?' he asked.

'While working in Jerusalem, Giuseppe found a scroll in one of the Qumran caves,' explained Marc. 'It later disappeared.'

Carlo was showing great interest. 'Did it ever turn up?'

'I'm afraid not,' replied Giuseppe. 'It faded from sight just as the ancient Gnostic writings did—a more recent example of similar intolerance. I doubt that my little scroll will ever have its Nag Hammadi day.'

'Did you manage to read it, before it disappeared?' Carlo's interest was obvious.

'A number of events beyond my control intruded on my examination of the scroll, but I eventually arrived at the reading stage.'

'And...' Carlo's excitement was palpable.

'As a prelude to a careful study of the script, I let my eyes wander over the entire scroll. The symbols for "Beloved Disciple" and "Paul ... Tarsus" jumped out at me.'

'Yes ... Yes,' urged Carlo, his eyes popping with his curiosity.

'Before I could read any more, one of my superiors arrived, wondering why I was working so late at night. I told him about finding the scroll and since I had found it, I wanted to work on it myself. He seemed to understand my eagerness.'

'Then what?' Carlo continued his probing.

'He looked down through the script and whatever he saw provoked him take over the work of deciphering the text. That was the last I saw of it. All this happened at a difficult time. The Suez crisis had just erupted and we had to move the scrolls to safety and vacate the region. On our return, my superior told me that the scroll had gone missing during the upheaval.'

'Did he seem distressed about it?'

'Quite the opposite,' replied Giuseppe. 'As if to console me for the loss, he told me that he had it examined and it proved to be a fake. I was convinced that was untrue. If he could lie about its provenance, he could lie about its fate.'

Despite his scepticism regarding Vatican integrity, Carlo was surprised to find that a similar dishonesty might extend into related areas of Church interest like archaeology. 'Do you think that any archaeologist would wilfully destroy historical evidence?'

'I can't be sure that it was destroyed. It could be hidden away to prevent it from threatening the status quo. It could be in a secure vault in the Vatican Library,' he added jokingly, in view of Carlo's position.

'Do you think that it was a significant threat to prevailing beliefs?'

'I have no way of knowing,' answered Giuseppe. 'From the few words I had time to interpret and my colleague's reaction, it would appear so. As an archaeologist and historian, I mourn its loss. However, no matter how sensational it might have been, it was not necessary.'

Marc was baffled. 'If your associate was afraid to reveal it, surely it was significant.'

'Significant? Yes! Necessary? No! I never mentioned it because all the indicators are already there, as I have tried to show in my writings. Examining the texts we have with openness and honesty will lead to the truth about faith. We reach enlightenment not through *eureka* moments, but by the slow, determined slog of working it out by reason.'

The words rang a bell in Marc's mind. 'Maybe so, but sometimes reason needs a nudge.'

'Perhaps,' commented Giuseppe. 'But being forced to search for your own answers is probably more rewarding and the result more enduring. I am sure that you feel more confident in your present convictions because of your previous experiences.'

'That is certainly true,' said Marc, with conviction. 'Then when our reason recognizes truth, change follows.'

'Change follows very slowly. Authority is not interested in reason or truth, only power. That is why we have to take to the streets,' concluded Carlo decisively.

'True enough,' agreed Giuseppe. 'Nevertheless, adjustment does occur. Even the Church has modified its stance over the years. I have lived long enough to be a witness to changes in practices that were never part of your lives. Devotional exercises like Missions, Retreats, Processions, Benedictions, Rosaries, were part of the daily, weekly, monthly and annual cycle of the years. They were integral like the seasons.'

'My mother seemed to take delight in telling me how strict and severe fasting and other penances were in her day,' commented Marc.

'They were harsher in my early days,' said Giuseppe. 'Refraining from meat on Fridays identified you as Catholic. Even the laws surrounding marriage, a bastion of Church discipline, have changed. A Catholic of the early twentieth century would hardly recognize the Church of today.'

'The people of the scrolls also questioned their customs over time,' said Marc, 'and adapted accordingly. To question the Temple was an extraordinarily courageous stand to take.'

'Despite that they were passionately conservative, but change comes from tension with authority, and we know from this,' said Giuseppe, lifting up the goblet with scroll fragment *Ma'ase Ha-Torah*, 'that such pressure to adapt existed in the group.'

'4QMMT,' said Marc quietly.

'Are you familiar with it, Carlo?'

'I have read a few articles about it. It is an appeal from someone in authority, the Teacher of Righteousness perhaps, to a wayward colleague to return to the true spirit of the group.'

'The Guardian of the community was trying to persuade a fellow member to return to the strict observance of the Mosaic Law, as they understood it. It is not in the least fanciful to imagine a subsequent leader writing to Paul in similar terms.'

'James did confront Paul,' observed Marc, as he picked up Giuseppe's tablet, more convenient than his laptop, and tapped on 'biblegateway.com' to find the letters of Paul.

'Paul was seeking liberalization from the *Works of the Law* for his converts,' continued Giuseppe. 'Some scholars maintain that Paul's expression is a perfect Greek translation of these Hebrew words,' continued Giuseppe, again referring to the scroll goblet.

'The same experts also contend that they are found nowhere else in ancient rabbinic literature,' said Marc, addressing Carlo. 'They are unique to Paul and the Qumran scroll.'

'It would appear that Paul had this text in mind when he wrote to the Galatians. He uses the same terminology and persuasive tone, not to endorse the theology of this text, but to rebut it. Do you remember the text, Marco?'

Marc had already found the text. 'I have it here, "We ... know that we are not justified by the *Works of the Law,* but by faith... It is for freedom that Christ has set us free. Stand firm and do not let yourselves be burdened again by the yoke of slavery."'

'Thank you, Marco. Today, we think of Paul as the epitome of orthodoxy but, in his day, he was anything but orthodox, as we can see from his letter to the Galatians, in which he fought so energetically to change the discipline of the early Christian community—to free it from the Jewish Torah.'

'Paul's antagonism towards James over the matter is obvious in his letters and in the Acts of the Apostles.'

'Yes! It was probably more trenchant than either document would suggest,' commented Giuseppe. 'The letter of James in the New Testament, though not written by James, probably reflects his attitude to Paul's liberalization. In that letter, he denounced any attempt to replace the works of the law with faith alone—*faith without works is dead.* James, the observant Jew, lover of the poor and leader of the first Jewish Christian community in Jerusalem, was a powerful and immovable obstacle in Paul's path. James was in the way, and I suspect

217

that Paul would not have been too distressed to see him eliminated by the political scheming of Ananus. Basing their finding on the Clementine Literature, which is another highly complex and controversial document, some scholars claim that Paul had a hand in a plot to get rid of James. I suppose we will never know for sure.'

'Because of his uncompromising stance,' said Marc, 'Some have challenged Paul's Jewishness.'

'And there is some evidence for this' remarked Giuseppe. 'There is a few very confusing verses in his letter to the Philippians where Paul launches into a scathing attack on the Jews, calling them dogs, evildoers, mutilators of the flesh—referring to circumcision. He then calmly claims to be one of them, himself circumcised and faultless in observing the Law of Moses. Paul claimed to be all things to all men, but if you carry that dictum too far you end up contradicting yourself.'

'Paul appears to be aggressively self-confident,' suggested Carlo. 'He does not hesitate to tell the Galatians that the gospel he preached was entirely his own. "I did not receive it from any man, nor was I taught it; rather I received it by revelation." Paul had the arrogance of the Herods. Do you think he was a member of that family?'

'He drops a few names in his letters that would indicate as much. If you read the New Testament with an eye on the writings of Josephus and other writings of the first and second centuries, you might pick up some intriguing intimations. The Acts of the Apostles tells us that after Paul's conversion, the Jews in Damascus were out to kill him. To escape them, Paul's friends had to lower him in a basket over the city wall.'

'I often wondered about that,' interjected Marc. 'Paul's own account is different.'

'In his second letter to the Corinthians,' continued Giuseppe, 'Paul tells us that it was the Governor of the city, under instruction from King Aretas, who was going to arrest him. At that time, King Aretas was at war with Herod Antipas.'

'Herod had divorced the king's daughter in order to marry Herodias, the mother of Salome. Do you think Paul was there on some kind of secret mission for Antipas?'

'We will never know for certain, but on Paul's own words we know that his escape was not from the Jews but from a vengeful king. Josephus also speaks of a certain Saulos going on secret missions for the Herods and even for the emperor. Some modern scholars would identify Paul with that Saulos.'

'If Paul were involved in politics, what prompted his interest in religion?' Carlo looked perplexed.

'Separation of Church and State is a modern phenomenon. For the ancients, Carlo, religion and politics went hand in hand. They were two sides of the same coin. Rulers, like the pharaohs represented the deity and worked hand in hand with the high priests to keep the people in their proper place.'

'Their ancient legends were composed to promote the image of a divine ruler,' said Marc.

'The legend of Osiris goes back four or five thousand years. He is one of the foremost resurrection gods, brought back to life by Isis, his sister and spouse.' Giuseppe smiled indulgently in the direction of Isis, who looked in his direction at the sound of her name.

'That is true also of the "divine" Caesars,' said Carlo, enthusiastic about the topic. 'They were the physical representatives of the gods.'

'The Jews followed the same pattern,' continued Giuseppe. 'Theirs was a theocratic state. Their kings were "messiahs", the anointed sons of Yahweh. They did not always live up to it, but that was the idea.'

'The Roman Catholic Church is a bit like that,' suggested Carlo returning to his persistent theme. 'It is ruled autocratically by the Vicar of Christ on earth.'

'Don't forget that it is also a political entity; the popes once ruled a large segment of Italy and had moral authority over all other sovereigns of Europe. It was also a feature of life to find bishops governing various principalities throughout the continent.'

'If Paul were working for the Herods and the emperor, why was he executed in Rome?' Carlo posed the question with a look that suggested he had his own answer.

'Was he executed in Rome? Was he executed at all?' Giuseppe retrieved the tablet from Marc. 'The New Testament does not make that claim. The Acts of the Apostles concludes as follows: "For two whole years Paul stayed there in his own rented house and welcomed all who came to see him. He proclaimed the Kingdom of God and taught about the Lord Jesus Christ with all boldness and without hindrance!" Strange conditions for a prisoner, you would think. Likewise, there is no indication in Josephus that the Romans executed his Saulos. The martyrdom of Paul, and indeed that of Peter, is based solely on legends that grew up in subsequent generations.'

'Legends!' Carlo shook his head. 'Where would Rome be without them?'

'Short of a very profitable tourist industry,' replied Marc jokingly. He then continued. 'Early opponents of Christianity like Celsus and Porphyry ridiculed Christianity because, according to them, it attracted only the superstitious and uneducated. That can hardly be true when you consider the writings of the New Testament and other early authors like the philosopher Justin.'

'Don't forget the writers of Gnostic literature, like Valentinus, the poet. They were Christians also, and probably subject to the same criticism. At that time, writers of such quality were certainly in the minority. Even today, scholars are undecided about Jesus—some see him as a teacher, others as a peasant who could not read or write. If Paul were a member of the Herod family, his Roman citizenship "by birth" would be understandable, and he certainly would be well educated.'

'And the evangelists,' prompted Carlo.

'We know nothing of them, but it is intriguing to think of them as well educated members of the ruling class, carrying on the work of Paul, trying to sever the new faith's links with Judaism and mould a new mystery religion that would serve the empire. It did not take Constantine long to spot it.'

'You have to hand it to Constantine,' said Marc. 'He came up with a great idea when he adopted Christianity, and moulded it to suit his purpose.'

'Paul's shrewdness was even greater,' said Giuseppe calmly. 'Constantine would have had nothing to work on, if Paul had not laid the groundwork. He took a fanatical band of freedom fighters and craftily transformed it into an eventual arm of the very state it was fighting.'

'Historical events worked in his favour,' observed Marc.

'True,' said Carlo. 'The destruction of the Temple left much of the Mosaic Law redundant.'

'Paul created a synthesis of Hellenic and Judaic cultures, which became Western Civilization. Not bad for the tent maker he is reputed to have been' added Marc.

'Our culture rests, perhaps not solely, but certainly fundamentally on Paul.' affirmed Giuseppe. 'He could not possibly have imagined where his break with Judaism would lead.'

'Those who came after him,' said Marc, 'became more anti-Semitic, and prepared the ground for a Roman takeover.'

'They were certainly anti-Semitic,' said Carlo, with conviction. 'And the Church that developed from their writings was vehemently so. The apologies of recent popes are, in my opinion, far too little and far, far too late.'

'Well, I can see that our little chat has raised passions,' said Giuseppe, smiling in Carlo's direction. 'It is a beautiful day and it is your free day, you should get out and enjoy it.'

The friends needed no further encouragement.

On The Beach

Change, fundamental and far-reaching, was part of life, as Marc was beginning to find out—his life had undergone a seismic shift since their last trip to the beach. Guilt no longer induced him to look away as Carlo and Luigi shed their clothes. Instead, he revelled in the beauty of their manhood. Carlo, always the spontaneous one, threw his swimming trunks aside.

'We have the place to ourselves,' he said, by way of explaining his action to Marc. Luigi eagerly followed suit, indicating to Marc that nudity was normal for them on the isolated beach; beachwear had been in deference to his presence. Gazing at the nude Luigi, with his striking golden physique, blond hair and startling green eyes, Marc felt certain that he would be the first choice on any artist's list to model for Apollo, and he did have his Hyacinthus. According to the myth, Apollo loved a Spartan prince, Hyacinthus. Their happy union provoked the jealousy of Zephyrus, the god of the west wind, who also loved Hyacinthus, and in a fit of disappointed rage, contrived the death of Hyacinthus. The thought was disconcerting and made Marc wonder if the role of the troublesome Zephyrus might be his in threatening a harmonious relationship. However, his love for Carlo did not ignite in him an opposite emotion towards Luigi. In fact, he had feelings for him too, which he was so far unable to label; was it just admiration for his obvious physical appeal, and/or his musical talent and aspirations? For now, he continued to stare as the reincarnated deity ran into the sea. Between the gods Poseidon and Apollo, Marc, rejecting his earlier self-imposed identification with the god of the west wind, felt incredibly happy to be just his own mortal self in such attractive and stimulating company. He noticed Carlo watching him with that all-knowing expression he conjured up so well.

'He is beautiful,' affirmed Carlo.

'He is not the only one,' replied Marc by way of acknowledging Carlo's equally admirable presence.

'True! You are not bad either,' said Carlo, deflecting Marc's compliment. 'Coming?' He stretched out his hand and Marc, discarding his trunks, let him lead the way into Poseidon's watery kingdom. They sank into its depths, surfaced together and, as naturally as the tide flows, drifted towards each other and kissed.

A moment later, a shudder of guilt passed through Marc, but it was not his old conscience reasserting itself. He was not even sure that 'guilt' was the correct word to express the concern he experienced when he saw Luigi observing them. On their last outing, Marc had been in that position—he then sat apart on the beach watching Carlo and Luigi embracing, fondling and kissing. At the time, he did not feel jealous—he knew that they were old friends and Carlo never made a secret of his feelings for Luigi—he just wanted to be one with them.

Luigi, however, might well be jealous. Marc was a new intrusion into their lives, a possible usurper in Luigi's eyes, tellingly green. Marc did not know how their kissing affected Luigi, but seeing him looking on, seemingly isolated, made Marc sad. He dispelled the feeling by stretching his hand out towards Luigi, inviting him over. For a moment, he feared that jealousy might induce Luigi to ignore, or reject his gesture. He hesitated, then sank into the surf and drifted towards Carlo and Marc. They encircled him with their arms and drew him close. Observed by a European Shag poised on nearby rocks—its dark outline clearly defined against the blue of sky and sea—they hugged and kissed, one to one and all three together, as the gentle surge tickled their nipples. Marc felt transfixed as the hands of his friends travelled down his back, coasting his spine, setting off waves of delight, as if his skin harboured tiny explosive devices that discharged at their touch. Their fingers trickled down until each palm cupped the round of his bottom setting off further detonations and inducing him to impale himself more tightly into the bodies of his friends. He burrowed more deeply, desiring to become one with them, to be them—three in one. The intense pleasure building up inside him resulted in satisfying release. As his body relaxed, he clung to his friends' shuddering bodies, all three supported by the buoyant Mediterranean.

When they emerged from the sea, Carlo was in high spirits. 'What do you really think of the Carpocratians?' He directed the question to

Marc, as he retrieved the picnic box from its shaded location. 'Were they licentious or liberal?'

'Nobody knows,' Marc answered, pouring fruit juice into plastic cups. 'Not enough evidence.'

'Who?' Luigi was mildly interested, as he lay on the towels, waiting for the food to be unpacked.

'An early Christian sect that indulged in homosexual sex,' said Carlo, his voice and eyes dramatically conjuring up the perceived horror of their activity.

'Not only homosexual,' corrected Marc. 'According to Irenaeus, Church Father and heresy hunter, they believed that you had to experience everything life had to offer to avoid returning for a second attempt. If you exhausted every possibility the first time, you discarded the body and entered into union with the eternal, the Holy One. It would seem they had a poor opinion of the body.'

'Poor deluded fools,' observed Carlo.

'It would appear that they considered the body a burden that hindered the free flight of the spirit.' Earlier, up to his chest in the stimulating Mediterranean, in intimate bodily contact with his two friends, Marc had never felt his spirit soar so freely. Whether the spirit is a separate entity or radiates from the body via the brain was a question Marc was not about to address. He had simply experienced transcendence. 'We only have the commentary of their detractors. Without an unbiased account, we will never know what they really believed.'

'Does it matter?' Luigi asked the question, as he munched a sandwich. 'The world has moved on since then.'

'The voice of reason,' announced Carlo. 'Give the man another sandwich.'

'Do you have a favourite song?' Luigi posed the question as he paused between munches.

'You know mine,' said Carlo.

'Yes, "E Lucevan le Stelle". However, it might be less impressive with just piano accompaniment.'

'Does this mean that you are giving a concert?' Carlo was suddenly very interested.

'Not really,' replied Luigi. 'I have been asked to contribute one or two pieces for a concert being organized by hopefuls, like me, to promote our wares.'

'That's great,' said Marc. 'When is it?'

'In three weeks, at the Parco della Musica.'

'Very impressive,' said Marc.

'Don't get carried away, it's in the smaller Teatro Studio.'

'It's still impressive.'

'Even that will probably be too big for the numbers we will inveigle into attending. It's free,' he added timidly, as if otherwise they might not come.

'We'll be there,' was Marc's resolute reply.

'You did not say if you have any favourites,' Luigi reminded Marc.

'I have many,' he said. 'How about Richard Strauss? "Morgen!" has piano accompaniment. German is not a problem, I presume.'

'A flair for languages is as natural to the Swiss as it is necessary for opera singers. "Morgen!" is a good choice. I love it. Very appropriate also, considering where we are—*zu dem strand*—to the beach, under wave-blue sky. What do you think, Carlo?'

'It's a bit subdued if you're aiming to make a splash.' Carlo was reluctant to surrender his favourite. 'Still, I'm sure you would make it shine,' he added gallantly.

'Do you know any booking agents that you might snare?' Luigi contemplated the remaining sandwich as he posed the question.

'Go ahead,' said Carlo. 'You need to keep up your strength,' he added encouragingly.

'My granduncle has many contacts in publishing,' said Marc in reply to Luigi's question. 'He is very interested in music, but I don't know if he has any connections there. Why don't you come to dinner this evening? We can ask him.'

Giuseppe meets Luigi

Arriving back from the beach, Carlo dropped Marc home before continuing on to the garret with Luigi to shower and change. Before making a start on dinner, Marc told Giuseppe about Luigi and the concert. When they arrived back at Campo de' Fiori, Marc interrupted his preparations for dinner to introduce Luigi, and then retreated back to the kitchen. Giuseppe found Luigi fascinating. He was intrigued by the young man's unusual life choices. However, as a lover of music, what impressed him most was Luigi's ambition to pursue a career in that area.

'I would have loved to be able to fill an auditorium with my voice,' Giuseppe revealed.

'From what I hear, you have done just that on many occasions,' replied Luigi, the enthusiasm of one sparking a reciprocal emotion in the other.

'There is no comparison. The singer speaks to the soul, the lecturer to the mind.'

'Is there a difference?' Carlo looked coy as he posed the question.

'Good question, Carlo. I will leave the answer to mystics and neuroscientists. Whatever the conclusion might be, I find that the singer reaches a part of me that evades the lecturer. So, Luigi, you have a great future ahead of you.'

'I am just not sure it will be in opera,' replied Luigi. 'The next few months should tell. I hope you will be able to attend the upcoming concert.'

'I am looking forward to it,' answered Giuseppe. 'I have an old friend who might accompany me. Together, we have attended many concerts and operas over the years.' Wary of raising vain expectations, he refrained from mentioning that the 'old friend' was formerly an agent and critic—now, like himself, long retired.

'Was he a theologian also, or an archaeologist?' Luigi was genuinely interested.

'No,' replied Giuseppe evasively. 'Speaking of archaeology,' he continued, anxious to divert attention from his friend's former occupation. 'Did Marco tell you that I once found an ancient text while working on the Dead Sea Scrolls?'

'No,' said Luigi.

'Not exactly beach chat,' said Marc, who had just returned from the kitchen.

'Quite so! I am sure you have something more stimulating to engage you on the beach.'

'We were discussing the Carpocratians,' was Carlo's teasing repartee, as Marc and Luigi exchanged amused glances.

'Tell me about the scroll,' prompted Luigi. He was interested, as most people are about discoveries of ancient artefacts, and myths have a significant place in opera, but his experiences had made him doubt their relevance to modern life, except as a form of entertainment.

'There is not much to tell,' said Giuseppe. 'I was working in one of the caves, carefully transporting a vast amount of fragments to the museum in Jerusalem. I was about to leave when a piece of pottery fell at my feet. Looking up, I found a small jar hidden in the porous stone. Inside, I found a scroll. I was very excited.'

'I can understand that it is exciting to find something like this, but does it really matter?' In expressing his doubt, Luigi hoped he would not offend Giuseppe.

'Judging from our history, you are right to be suspicious,' said Giuseppe. 'We have given some ancient writings a status that they do not deserve. Voices from the past are important, if we learn from them rather than live by them.'

'What did it say?' Luigi posed the question.

'I don't know,' answered Giuseppe. 'I did manage to make out one or two symbols that might indicate a Christian connection, but then it went missing.'

'If it did,' added a suspicious Carlo. 'The Church was afraid that it would be to Christianity what the meteorite was to the dinosaurs.'

'But we don't know,' challenged a more reasonable Luigi.

'Why else would it go missing?' There was no doubt in Carlo's mind.

'No, we don't know.' agreed Giuseppe. 'However, Carlo might have a point. Religious hierarchies are political institutions and as such have a well-developed sense of self-preservation. Thankfully, we have artists to nourish the spirit.' He looked inquiringly at Luigi. 'How did you become interested in music? To move from the military to music seems ... unusual.'

'I suppose it does,' Luigi shifted uncomfortably in his seat. 'I am a weird mixture. Perhaps it is part of being Swiss. I also spent some time in a seminary—it was there I met Carlo.'

'You are both full of surprises,' said Giuseppe, delighted at the range of their experiences.

'I grew up with music,' continued Luigi. 'Both parents were singers with the Lausanne Opera. My mother gave singing lessons, so I was singing from an early age.'

'Why choose the priesthood over a singing career?' Giuseppe wondered aloud.

'I suppose I thought it was more ... meaningful.' Luigi gave a helpless shrug.

'Ah!' Giuseppe sighed. 'The idealism of youth.'

'The novitiate did not do much for my spiritual development. Quite the opposite, it turned me off religion, but I did have one beautiful experience that convinced me that the priesthood was not for me.' Luigi's fleeting glance at Carlo said it all.

'And then you opted for the military instead of music. Why?' Giuseppe was baffled.

'I was always very physical—developing my body as well as my voice. I always intended to try my hand at opera, but I thought a few years in the military would be interesting. Then, I was assigned to the Papal Guard and that was very exciting.'

'And how did your disaffection with religion come about, if you don't mind me asking?'

'In the novitiate, I was disillusioned. I am not like Carlo; I don't have well-resourced arguments. I just thought that it was all a bit in the clouds.'

'A good description,' commented Carlo.

'Then something happened,' continued Luigi. 'My mother became very ill. She suffered greatly, before she died. My father was in despair just watching her. I was still in the novitiate at the time. I requested permission to return home to visit her, but ... the retreat could not be interrupted.' Luigi shook his head, still unable to reconcile the refusal with professed Christian values. 'They did allow me home for the funeral,' he added, fighting his emotion. 'I never went back.'

'You poor boy.' Giuseppe went and sat beside Luigi and put his arms around him. It was an incongruous sight—the aged, thin arms trying to encircle the broad, muscular shoulders of the young man. 'Once again, the perceived values of the institution outweigh those of the individual. I am sure your presence consoled your father.'

'I don't know,' whispered Luigi. 'He seemed to fade day by day. He never really recovered from my mother's death. After I left for the military, he walked into Lac Léman and drowned.'

Marc was aghast. 'Lake Geneva,' he said, inaudibly, his heart swelling in sympathy with his friend. He was only now learning the details of Luigi's life. He wanted to go to him, as Giuseppe did, and display his support, but he just could not move from his seat.

Trio

The duet became a trio.

During the dinner, the mood began to revive, helped by Giuseppe's careful monitoring of the level of wine in each glass. Discussion of Luigi's past gave way to his aspirations for the future.

They fantasized about travelling with him to the great opera houses of the world. By the end of the meal, their spirits were again soaring in camaraderie and high expectations. When the night ended, and in view of what had gone before, it seemed heartless to let Luigi return alone to the garret, so Marc suggested that he stay the night. Together they dressed an old, canopied bed in a vacant room for Luigi and, after a nod and a wink from Carlo, all three ended up sleeping in it. Awareness of Luigi's past concentrated the minds of Carlo and Marc on giving him more than his due attention. They pampered him with hands and mouths, and Marc, the former celibate, surprised himself by the degree of abandon to which he was prepared to go to express his love for his friends. Afterwards, coiled together like clinging ivy, they slept soundly.

Marc woke as dawn light was filtering through the curtains to find that he occupied the centre of the bed. In memory he recalled the earlier scintillating experience of searching the smooth surface of his friends' bodies—the arm of one now lying diagonally across his chest, the other gently cupping his genitals. That memory and their actual presence beside him brought fresh arousal, but he reluctantly restrained his incipient lust and, gently dislodging both limbs, slipped out of bed and made for the shower. After showering, he went to his own room to dress, then to the kitchen to grab a coffee to take to the library, there to ponder how he might pursue his topic.

His earlier research on the scrolls, which he recently thought of abandoning, took on new and greater significance, buoyed by the possibility that there was a text, though lost, that might vindicate his position. Admittedly, it was all a bit dubious, but it, and Giuseppe's conviction, gave him the drive he needed to examine the available texts with the assurance that he was on the right track. He was happy, even anxious, to bury himself in his notes and battle with the ancient symbols to draw out the nuance of meaning that best suited the text, guided by his new-found confidence. Marc examined his outline to see how he might more convincingly proceed. Despite widespread rejection of a possible connection between the Qumran sect and the proto Christian or

Jerusalem community by virtually all mainstream scholars, most of whom had a religious bias, the indicators were impressive: geography, theology, lifestyle, and writings.

'Good morning, Marco, you are up early.' Giuseppe's entry into the library interrupted Marc's deliberations. 'I hope I am not disturbing you.'

'It is your home, Uncle. It is good of you to share it with me.'

'It's your home too, Marco, for as long as you want it to be. I enjoy having you and Carlo around.'

'I asked Luigi to stay over last night also. I hope you don't mind.' Marc was suddenly anxious that he might be taking his uncle's kindness for granted.

'I am glad to see you acting on your own initiative. Luigi is a fine young man and with such tragic experiences for one so young. I hope he succeeds in his chosen career. I would like to help. If he needs a place to practise, we have many rooms here—the vestibule is comparable to the salons that hosted many intimate concerts. If you think it appropriate, you could mention it. I will leave it with you.'

'He is staying with Carlo since he left the Guards. He certainly does not have much room there. His teacher may have facilities, but there may be many availing of them. I will mention it.'

'Good! Now, did my glimpse at the scroll give you more confidence in your topic?'

'It's a pity we don't have it. I would like to try reworking my thesis now that I am a little more positive about it. That's what I was doing just now. As you know, there are four main areas which could indicate a possible link between Qumran and the primitive Christians: geography, theology, lifestyle, and writings.'

'The region was not vast,' affirmed Giuseppe. 'Despite primitive modes of transport by today's standards, people journeyed a lot.'

'Religion, conflict and famine were major factors in the movement of people' suggested Marc. 'The New Testament, Paul in particular, reads like a travelogue.'

There was a large map of first-century biblical lands hanging on the wall. Giuseppe approached it. 'In a country where religion was a way of life, and religious sects the political parties of the day, it is impossible to imagine that one faction was unaware of what another was thinking and doing.'

'It would seem inconceivable that one messianic group with an impressive library would, at the very least, fail to attract the attention of another entertaining similar messianic expectations,' said Marc.

'Messianic expectation was widespread in the first century,' affirmed Giuseppe. 'However, the Qumran sect and the proto Christian group shared a unique apocalyptic messianism, as you know. You might say that their ideas in that area were not only similar but the same.'

'They believed that the end of time was imminent,' said Marc.

'In John's Gospel, Jesus confided to his disciples—in a little while you will see me again. Paul was also confident that the Parousia was just around the corner.'

'John's Gospel also indicated that there was a belief abroad that Lazarus would live to see the return of the Christ. That Gospel tried to dispel that idea. As time passed, with that hope unfilled, the developing Church laid less and less stress on it.'

'Geography and theology are good indicators of a possible connection between the two groups,' said Giuseppe, as he turned from the map and walked to the window. 'Add their respective lifestyles and their association becomes more pronounced.'

'At first glance, the strict lifestyle of the sectarians at Qumran may not seem to reflect that of the Christian communities depicted in the New Testament.'

'There are two possible explanations for that,' reasoned Giuseppe. 'The Qumran group was only one manifestation of that way of life. Other members, living in the towns and villages of Judea and neighbouring territories, did not follow such an austere lifestyle. It would be more accurate to contrast Qumran with present-day monastic discipline compared to the less rigorous life of the lay Christian.'

232

'And the second explanation,' probed Marc.

'The New Testament communities were already settling into a post Pauline spirituality, which was straining relations with groups like that of Qumran. However,' continued Giuseppe, 'in spite of the changes initiated by Paul, both groups reveal common elements.'

'Like the messianic and apocalyptic expectations we mentioned.'

'Not only that,' affirmed Giuseppe. 'They both considered themselves the True Israel, participants in a New Covenant with God; both rejected the Temple; pooled their resources; their leaders were bishops; they considered themselves Children of the Light; found purification through water; a ritual meal of bread and wine replaced Temple worship. The similarities multiply. What more does an unbiased observer need?'

'And we have not yet mentioned their writings,' said Marc.

'The textual similarity between the Qumran writings and the New Testament is the most telling of all.'

'We have already discussed 4QMMT, the *Works of the Law* text, which Paul had adopted, if only to refute it.'

'The smoking gun, as some scholars call it,' said Giuseppe. 'There is also 4Q246, often referred to as an Aramaic Apocalypse or the Son of God fragment. A skilled palaeographer can determine with reasonable accuracy the period from which the writing came. However, if the particular text was a copy, the original must be older still.'

'4Q246, dated around the middle to end of the first millennium BCE, is reminiscent of the apocalyptic language of the Book of Daniel,' said Marc.

'The Spirit of God comes upon a Daniel-like figure who prophesies that an end-of-time ruler, called the Son of God and Son of the Most High, will establish an eternal kingdom.'

'Compare that to the Annunciation scene in Luke's Gospel, where the angel Gabriel announces to Mary that her son's titles will be Son of the Most High, Son of God, whose kingdom will be eternal.'

'Only a hardened polemicist would deny a connection between both texts,' affirmed Giuseppe, reflecting Marc's conviction.

Noises from the kitchen alerted them. 'Our guests are up', said Giuseppe. 'Will we join them for breakfast? Then get out and enjoy the day. It's Carlo's day off, after all.' With that, Giuseppe handed Marc an envelope, which he took with a puzzled expression. He opened it to find it contained a bankcard. 'I opened a bank account for you—until you get on your feet.'

Marc handed it back. 'I can't, Uncle. You have done so much already. I just can't.'

'Marco,' his granduncle said gently. 'Everybody needs a helping hand at times, but you are not just a recipient, you are a contributor.' Marc's blank stare moved Giuseppe to continue. 'You have brought meaning to my end of days. I am, as the expression goes, a man of means. You have no idea how frustrating that can be when, as the end of life approaches, you have no flesh and blood to benefit from your good fortune. You are the son, the grandson I might have had. Do not deprive me of that comfort. Now, go and treat your friends to lunch.'

Overcome with emotion, Marc could not speak. He just embraced his granduncle.

Swiss Guard

Later that morning, walking leisurely along by the Tiber, they arrived at Ponte Sant'Angelo. 'Bernini,' said Carlo, adopting his favourite alter ego—tour guide. 'Being foreigners in the city,' he announced grandiosely, 'you may not know that in Rome you are never far from Gian Lorenzo.' Playing their part, his friends nodded appreciatively. 'Pope Clement the ninth commissioned him to sculpt the angels for this bridge, which in the event he deemed too beautiful to stand exposed to the elements.'

'He was interested in opera,' commented Luigi. 'He opened the first opera house in Rome.'

'He also commissioned Gian Lorenzo to design the colonnade encircling the piazza,' continued Carlo, as they made their way from Castel Sant'Angelo along Via della Conciliazione towards the colonnaded piazza that Clement had commissioned and Bernini executed. 'Coming from the fringe of the Empire,' he announced mockingly as they entered the piazza, 'you must be impressed.'

'The fringe never extended to Ireland,' said Marc with exaggerated pride.

'Sad,' lamented Carlo. 'You did not enjoy even a fringe benefit of what we, Romans, had to offer.'

'The piazza is impressive,' conceded Marc quietly. 'It seems to say something about the power of faith.'

'Or the genius of Bernini, who was a man of faith, of course, but I suspect that it would be just as impressive if he were a pagan. The Pantheon, commissioned by Agrippa and rebuilt later by Hadrian, emerged from a different set of beliefs and it is equally striking. Less exuberant, it is true, but some maintain that its sublime simplicity makes it even more remarkable than the baroque.'

Approaching the basilica, they paused. 'According to Giuseppe, it leaves the Church of the Holy Sepulchre in the shade,' said Marc. 'The disciple outshines the master.'

They made their way across the vast expanse of the piazza, and entered the basilica. Inside, the light from the cupola directed the eye to Bernini's baldacchino, its bronze glistening in the light from above.

'The notorious Barberini pope, Urban the eight, robbed the Pantheon of its bronze to pay this tribute to Peter—one pagan temple supplying the material for another. What a fixation we have with gods and goddesses, myths and legends! I wonder whose bones are here, marked with such distinction.'

'Many, I would suggest,' said Marc. 'It is, after all, built on an ancient burial site.'

'I know,' said Carlo impatiently. 'But whose bones are there, just there.' His eyes drifted down to the sunken crypt beneath the baldachin.

'Who knows?' Marc dismissed the question with a shrug.

'Let's get out of here,' suggested Carlo. 'I feel entombed.'

'You'd be so lucky,' said Marc, with a chuckle.

'It's the Tiber for my ashes. I'd rather mingle with the fighting legions of old than be entombed with the popes.'

'In the Tiber, you'd also mingle with quite a few popes, I expect.'

Emerging into the narthex of the basilica, which was flanked by two equestrian emperors, Constantine and Charlemagne, Carlo was prompted to remark, 'Constantine is still keeping an eye on this last segment of his empire. You have to hand it to him; he knew what it took to secure survival. Still, it's bizarre that a ruthless, murderous megalomaniac like Constantine is proudly ensconced in a Christian temple.'

As Carlo was going on about Constantine and the rump of empire, two flamboyant Swiss Guards approached. Marc allowed his gaze to linger on the masculine figures that inhabited the Renaissance-style uniform of the pope's personal guards. The rakish twist of the black beret he found particularly stimulating. Previously, guilt blighted his enjoyable admiration. Custody of the eyes had trained him not to look, or, in the event of an inadvertent glance, to look away. Now, that frustration of nature's sublime gift no longer applied. As he stood in the grand portico, he had no such feeling, just guiltless admiration and delight. 'I would love to have seen you in that uniform,' he confessed to Luigi.

'Would you like to meet them?' As the flamboyant pair approached, Luigi moved forward to greet them. Recognizing Luigi, they stopped amid exclamations of delight. Luigi introduced Lautrim and Silvan, who were just coming off duty, as two of his very good friends. Suddenly, there was a thunderous tolling, and conversation stalled for the duration of the bells.

'Would you like to join us for lunch?' Marc was surprised at his forwardness.

'Thank you, I would love to,' replied Lautrim, 'but, unfortunately, not today, I already have an appointment. Hopefully,' his intonation injected expectation into the word, while he eyes, directed at Marc, expressed their own invitation, 'another time.'

'Yes, of course,' replied Marc, taken aback.

'Thank you,' said Silvan, 'but I too have another appointment.' Turning to Luigi, he continued. 'We must all get together very soon.'

'Are you free three weeks from today? There is a concert in Parco della Musica.'

Silvan and Lautrim exchanged glances. 'We will check and see,' answered Lautrim. 'If you are singing we will do our best to be there.'

'I will call you,' promised Luigi.

The two impressive guardsmen departed, leaving Marc bewildered, in a nice sort of way. 'That Lautrim is a saucy bugger,' said Carlo, chuckling. 'Just because he wears colourful fancy dress, he thinks he is God's gift.'

They watched the retreating blue, yellow and red figures. They were an impressive pair. Maybe it was the uniform with its Renaissance flourish erroneously credited to Michelangelo that dazzled.

'Many features of the "fancy dress" go back a long way,' explained Luigi. 'But the present design of 154 coloured stripes dates from 1914. We may look like clowns,' he continued, forgetting that he was no longer one of them. 'But we are trained to face the most challenging situations.'

'I hope you two are free for lunch,' said Marc, as they meandered slowly around the gift stalls where tourist paraphernalia was displayed. Benign popes, past and present, smiled their plaster smiles, intent on seducing the pious pilgrim and enthusiastic tourist into believing their only interest was otherworldly. Artless reproductions of great art were on display. Carlo pointed to the collection that included the *Pieta* and the inevitable two *Davids*.

'There would be a Jesus-like cleansing of these stalls if the fiery Michelangelo spotted this lot. Just look at what they have done to our

237

sublime Gian Lorenzo's defiant *David*. Where is the resolute mouth, where the grim determination and fixed stare? Here he looks … well, I could put it indelicately, but I might offend your delicate ears.' Marc elbowed him good-humouredly. 'There is movement, though,' continued Carlo, with exaggerated academic gravity. 'Look at his hand, it's shaking, and about to drop the sling and make for the hills.' Marc and Luigi tittered at Carlo's whispered comments.

Leaving the Vatican, they wandered slowly into the secular streets of Rome. Clouds were gathering as they made their way across the Tiber once again. They had no particular destination in mind, simply happy to be together, wandering aimlessly. The Corso Vittorio Emanuele was bustling, as usual, but they were quiet, each savouring the presence of the others. Occasionally, their hands would touch, casually and intentionally—the subtle gesture of cautious lovers.

'Tell us more about the Swiss Guard.' Marc directed his request at Luigi. 'You must have all the inside information.'

'Their history is pretty well known,' replied Luigi. 'They are Swiss, of course; came into the service of the pope at the request of Julius the second, arriving here on 22 January 1506. Julius, being a Della Rovere, chose the family colours, blue and yellow for their uniform. A few years later, when Leo the tenth came along he added red to reflect the Medici colours. Some 20 years later, in defence of another Medici pope, Clement the seventh, the guards suffered their greatest loss of life when the troops of the Holy Roman Emperor sacked Rome. Some historians would claim that Clement was not worth 147 heroic lives. Their official language is Swiss German.'

'I was wondering more about their modern history?'

'The murders, you mean? It was a sad event. The commander, Alois Estermann and his wife were shot by halberdier Cedric Torney, who then shot himself.'

'There were rumours,' suggested Marc tentatively.

'It was before my time, but there were lots of rumours. Some claimed that Estermann was an East German Stasi agent and an

238

unknown fourth killed all three. Others suggest a power struggle between Opus Dei and Masons led to the murder, but nobody really knows. Well, I suppose somebody knows, but they're not talking.'

'There was talk of a sexual relationship between Estermann and Torney,' suggested Carlo.

'Yes,' replied Luigi. 'Torney appears to have been unhappy with the dominance of the Swiss German contingent in the corps. He turned to Estermann for ... comfort, only to be disillusioned later.'

'Whatever happened, it was tragic,' said Marc.

'Made all the more poignant by the fact that it was Alois Estermann who fell on the wounded John Paul to shield him with his own body during that assassination attempt in 1981, only to be gunned down himself less than twenty years later.'

'Why can't we live at peace with one another? We are such a crazy bundle of genetic information, warring at the slightest provocation,' concluded Carlo sadly.

They sauntered down Vittorio Emanuele, not saying very much, happy to be together, but subdued by Carlo's uncharacteristic melancholy. Eventually, they arrived at Piazza Venezia with its massive monument to King Victor Emanuel II.

'Rome has a love-hate relationship with the monument,' observed Carlo. 'But mostly hate. Its detractors concede that you get the best views of the city from it, not because of its elevation, but because you can't see the monument itself when viewing the city from its terraces. I like it. I am not too sure about destroying the historically rich Capitoline to make way for it, and maybe it *is* a bit over the top, but it is what it aims to be, the altar to the homeland, full of heroic imagery; perhaps not always true to history, but true to the ideal.'

A slight mist began to fall as they climbed the expansive steps to the tomb of the Unknown Soldier. Two modern-day soldiers stood guard, one on either side. Carlo, Luigi and Marc, heads bowed, paid their silent respect.

'Another unknown body,' said Carlo, reflecting back to their conversation in the basilica.

'Why are soldiers necessary?' Marc, in reflective mode, posed the question.

'Because of a fruit, according to the ancients,' replied Carlo sardonically. 'Life is cruel and unpredictable,' he continued. 'No competent and self-respecting deity would claim it.'

'The Gnostics recognized the incongruity,' observed Marc. 'Their solution, introducing a secondary incompetent deity as the creator of matter, only added to the confusion.'

'At least, they faced the problem honestly,' said Carlo. 'Not like others, who try to hold on to the competence and goodness of the creator of this shitty world.' Carlo spat out the words with such vehemence that Luigi and Marc paused to look at him. They rarely witnessed such depression and gloom on the face and in the words of their normally optimistic friend.

Two side stairways behind the tomb of the Unknown Soldier ascended to the base of the equestrian statue of the king that dominated the monument. The steps were high, steep and damp from the mist. They ascended slowly, keeping close to the outer balustrade, pausing frequently to look down at the tomb and out over the city.

'Poor fellow,' lamented Marc. 'Whoever he was, he ended up in a very prominent location.'

'Death being what it is, I don't suppose it matters to him now,' commented Carlo sadly. 'Life is for living, my friends, never forget that. Let's go to lunch.'

Morality and the Bible

Weeks passed.

Carlo's work and Luigi's tuition occupied their days leaving Marc free to develop his ideas and pursue his writing. His two friends had virtually taken up residence with him, creating evenings and nights of fantasy so removed from the life he had known that he sometimes wondered if he had slipped unconsciously into another dimension. He could not explain even to himself the smooth alignment that existed between them, as if individually they were not only incomplete, but also nonexistent, like a potential element waiting for the proper conjunction of particles to vivify it.

Marc's writing was progressing satisfactorily. He felt energized and his ideas were beginning to fall into place. Typing away on his laptop, he was aware of the vocal gymnastics of Luigi in a distant room, when Giuseppe entered the library.

'Carry on, Marco. Don't let my shuffling about disturb you.'

'Actually, Uncle, if you have time, there are a few ideas I would like to toss around with you.'

'My time is yours, Marco. What is on your mind?'

'Firstly, on a personal level, I want to ask if you are,' Marc paused to consider the word, 'comfortable ... with me, Carlo and Luigi around. It must be an intrusion into not only your life, but possibly also your sensibilities. You must know that we sleep together. Does it disturb you?'

'Are you happy, Marco?'

'I never thought I could be so happy.'

'Then, that is all that matters to me.'

'You are very understanding for an...' Marc paused.

'For an old man,' said Giuseppe with a chuckle. 'The general perception is that age makes us conservative. It seems to me more likely that the experiences of life should make us more tolerant and open.'

'Do you think that a person can love two people at the same time?'

'That is a difficult one for an old man,' replied Giuseppe light-heartedly. He continued more gravely. 'In theory, I don't see why not—I imagine silent admirers abound. To make such a relationship work in fact would be difficult, especially with the complication of mixed progeny. Even in same sex relationships, it might be difficult, not only to love equally, but to express it evenly. It would require very special individuals and an extraordinary mutual love' He paused, and then asked gently. 'You love Carlo and Luigi?'

Marc's demeanour was confirmation enough. 'They are amazing,' his words a mere breath that scarcely troubled the molecules of air that surrounded them.

A tremor passed through Giuseppe as the recollection of a similar but, in his case, a singular emotion escaped from the vault of memory. 'You will have to work on it,' he said kindly. 'Remember Apollo—he was in love with the beautiful and athletic prince of Sparta, Hyacinthus.'

'Lucky Hyacinthus—loved by two gods,' said Marc recalling his own identification of his friends with two deities.

'Unfortunate Hyacinthus,' declared Giuseppe. 'Zephyrus, his second admirer, was seething with jealousy because the object of his love favoured another. One day, Apollo and Hyacinthus were throwing the discus when jealous Zephyrus seized his opportunity. Being god of the wind, he blew Apollo's discus off course and redirected it at Hyacinthus, striking him dead.'

'The love of Zephyrus was flawed, if he could kill the one he loved, even if his love was not reciprocated,' declared Marc. 'It might have been different if he loved Apollo also, and they loved him, but I doubt it. Zephyrus was selfish.'

'It is just a reminder that we need to work on human relationships, but nothing worthwhile is achieved without effort. From my developing familiarity with all three of you, I judge your chances very positive.'

'I believe so too,' said Marc confidently. 'Now, concerning my project, I would like to bounce a few ideas off you—to clarify my thoughts.'

'I'm all ears,' said Giuseppe, settling into a comfortable chair.

'Earlier, I was listening to a debate between two academics whose attitudes to biblical interpretation are similar, yet they arrived at different conclusions.'

'That is hardly surprising, it is common among scholars,' said Giuseppe.

'I am not surprised, just puzzled that two reasonable individuals working from a similar premise could reach, not just a different conclusion, but an opposing one? There is more than reason at work here and I don't know how to approach it.'

'Tell me about this debate,' suggested Giuseppe.

'Like most mainstream scholars today, they accepted that the Bible developed over centuries, written by various authors who had reworked earlier oral and written legends to address problems that had arisen in their day.'

'So far so good,' commented Giuseppe.

'Both agreed that human authors produced the Hebrew Bible and the New Testament, a conclusion which led one debater to treat the combined opus as he would the writings of Shakespeare or any other literary work.'

'And the other,' probed Giuseppe.

'For him such works had a special resonance, in that they recorded humanity's search for the divine.'

'The eternal question,' sighed Giuseppe.

'I can't see how you can jump from the virtual to the real. Thinking or writing about our quest for God, does not make the existence of a divinity a fact or raise the written record of that search to a special and incontestable level.'

'For some, it does,' sighed Giuseppe.

'But why?'

'The "why" is a constant philosophical debate and consequently difficult to analyse. In this present context, I suspect that it is something in the readers even before they approach a biblical text. You did say that there is more than reason at play here. They *want* their investigation of the Bible to satisfy their longings, or instinct—the elephant, as an eminent and respected social psychologist depicted its enormous influence as distinct from its much smaller rational driver. The aura in which the centuries have cloaked the collective texts of the Bible have given it a mystical authority. Many individual pieces of art, be it

243

literature, painting or music, have become iconic symbols for one or other movement or event—the art of Andy Warhol has defined an age; Orwellian has become an accepted English adjective.'

'That is true, but they don't have that incontestable hold on our conscience and consciousness as the Bible has.'

'You are quite right, of course. For me, it is more sensible to address the ancient writings as art.'

'Like the works of Shakespeare,' added Marc.

'Or the cave paintings of Chauvet and Lascaux among others. As I have said before, art speaks to that intangible in every human heart. For that reason, I would have no problem swearing in a court of law on the Bible. Equally, I would be willing to pledge my word on the poems of Heaney or Yeats, or on the myth and music of *Ariadne*.'

'So you think that should be my approach—the Bible as art?'

'It's your work, Marco. Treat it as you see fit. I would suggest however that you don't tread the outworn path of selecting scriptural passages to prove your point. Such extracts were addressing different audiences in a variety of situations at various times. Consequently, you will find sayings to sustain and demolish the same moral dilemma.'

'True,' affirmed Marc. 'One of the debaters stated that the Bible is not a manual for right living. If you followed some of its prescriptions today, you would be accused of infanticide, child brutality, war crimes, even homophobia,' he concluded with a laugh, indicating that such a possibility was a barely credible fact in today's permissive society.

'Our mistake in the past was to use the Bible as just that—a manual for right living. It is, rather, a collection of myths and as such, it is an artistic reflection of life's mystery, similar to music and other forms of art. I am convinced that many interpreters of scripture are more poets than scholars. I don't mean to suggest that poets are not intellectuals. It is just that the realm in which they live and move and have their being has a different focus.'

Marc's smile indicated his recognition of his uncle's play on words from Acts 17. 'So there lies the difference between my two debaters,' suggested Marc.

'It would seem so to me. One is strictly rational in his approach. The other is captivated by the new world order that Paul composed—the Kingdom of God established by the Son recreating this groaning creation through the guidance of the Spirit.'

'You can hear the poetry in Paul's words and in the delivery of some exegetes, when commenting on them—their speech takes on a lyrical quality and their eyes mist over.'

'And understandably so. It is a beautiful and consoling concept in this very inadequate creation. Unfortunately, there is not much evidence of the presence of that Spirit in the past two thousand years of Christian history—even within the sacred kingdom itself. And why?' Giuseppe's pause was equivalent to highlighting his subsequent words. 'Because it all rests on the existence of a benign and competent deity for which, outside our poetic consciousness, there is not one scintilla of rational proof.'

'Thank you, Uncle, your ideas have given me a clearer direction.'

'I hear Luigi practising his art—he has a fine voice,' said Giuseppe.

'You are coming to the concert on Sunday?'

'I would not miss it,' replied Giuseppe. 'My friend, Matteo Augeri, will accompany me. We will find our own way. You have both been working hard all morning. Why not go and meet Carlo for lunch?'

Parco Della Musica

Though it opened to the public in 2002, pressure of studies had prevented Marc from yet attending a concert at the impressive venue, but he had once taken a guided tour of the facility. Designed by the aptly named architect, Piano, Marc recalled the guide declaring his creation more *forte* than *piano*. He was impressed by the three auditoria, with decreasing audience capacities of two thousand eight hundred, one thousand two hundred and seven hundred, which overlooked an open area designed like a Roman amphitheatre, and which fulfilled the dual purpose of public piazza and open-air theatre with capacity for three thousand spectators. The guide, at that time, explained that for acoustic reasons, the three concert halls were separate structures, entered from a curving foyer that connects all three at ground level. 'It was,' he proudly exclaimed, 'a complex worthy of the Caesars.'

'Thank you, Marco, for inviting us.' Sophia was exuberant. She had a way of making a mundane event singular. They—Sophia, Julian, Carlo and Marc—were enjoying a light meal in the venue's restaurant before the afternoon concert. Luigi was understandably too preoccupied, emotionally and physically, to engage socially before the concert.

'It is hardly a premier event,' chuckled Marc, trying to downplay his invitation, though the event with its potential for Luigi's future career was very significant to him. 'It is good of you and Julian to make the effort to attend. It means a lot to Luigi. His worst fear is facing an empty space.'

'A crowded venue would be mine,' ventured Julian. An engaged and engaging listener, he fixed his gaze on Carlo and Marc.

'Julian is more at home on the personal level, as indeed, I am.' Sophia reached out her hand to cover his.

'I can see that,' said Carlo, conscious of their empathetic natures. 'Is communication your field?' Knowing Sophia's profession, he addressed his question to Julian.

'I trained as a teacher, but worked briefly as a dogsbody with an NGO in Haiti.' Julian shifted his gaze fleetingly to Sophia, then back again to Carlo.

'Haiti! You went in response to the earthquake,' said Carlo, assuming the obvious.

'I was there when the earthquake struck,' replied Julian quietly.

'That must have been scary,' commented Carlo.

246

'Yes, I suppose.' Julian pushed his plate away and gripped the arms of his chair. 'That was not the worst part,' he continued, his memory scrolling, like a disaster movie, the catastrophic consequences of an act of God. Sophia, watching him with concern, flashed an uneasy glance at Marc. 'It was the ... the ... nonsense of it. The people there had little enough. Every day was a struggle. Out of the blue, their world disintegrated around them, killing the lucky ones outright, burying many more. The number of dead is unknown; estimates run in excess of two hundred thousand men, women and children.'

'Nature can be so cruel,' commented Carlo. 'How did you manage?'

'We worked around the clock,' continued Julian. 'We lost count of days, digging through the rubble, trying to free those trapped, but mostly finding only dead bodies.' Julian, usually reticent about himself, carried on like a man driven. 'Time passed and hope of finding more survivors was fading. Then, on the point of giving up, we located a young girl still alive under the rubble. In our efforts to free her, we worked frantically. Our haste was understandable but unfortunate—we dislodged the rubble that supported some of the surviving walls with inevitable consequences. The subsequent collapse killed three of the rescuers, but we managed to free the girl. In the middle of all this death and destruction a cry went up from the onlookers: "God be praised!".' Incomprehension floated in his eyes and choked his voice. 'Can you imagine?' He stared at Carlo with the penetration of an unimpeded neutrino. 'Can you imagine?' he repeated. '"God be praised". A few hours later, the girl died.'

Driven by compassion for his companion, Carlo got up from the table and stood behind Julian. Resting his hands of the frail shoulders below him, he kneaded them encouragingly. 'Don't let it get to you. Life makes no sense. There is no grand plan. It is simply the best that nature could cobble together atom by atom. We just have to make do with it, help each other out and, in spite of the mindlessness we call life, try our best to love each other. Accepting its senselessness is the only way we can manage to survive and live.' Julian reached up and grabbed Carlo's hand, as a drowning swimmer might. 'Now, let's go for a walk,' continued Carlo. 'And get in the mood to enjoy one of the good things nature has managed to conjure up.' Sophia looked at Marc with relief, and with what he could only interpret as immense gratitude for Carlo.

They left the restaurant and walked around the perimeter of the concourse. The afternoon was pleasant, the air therapeutic as they made their way around the crescent-shaped arena. Carlo's suggestion of a walk was felicitous—ideal for dispelling gloom and anticipating an artistic event. Groups of people, walking, talking—admiring, and possibly critical of the venue—were dotted around the piazza. They could not all be going to the concert, but one approaching group certainly was. Lautrim and Silvan led a cohort of, presumably, fellow Guards in casual wear. Luigi's friends were determined that he would not sing to an empty hall. Introductions were attempted, but names were lost in the energy of the moment. Relaxed conversation, with an undercurrent of excitement, followed. The atmosphere was friendly and jovial, chasing away the lingering shadow that had descended on the luncheon table. Sophia, her previous concern forgotten, was glowing with delight at finding herself surrounded by a brawny band of the Pope's own bodyguard. Julian's concern to maintain the interest of his beloved was sufficient to distract him, at least briefly, from his concerns with the wider world. Carlo's antipathy towards Lautrim that resulted from their previous meeting seemed to have dissipated in the conviviality of the moment. They laughed and joked together like old friends. Marc reflected on the stir they would have caused had the Guards turned up in their eye-catching uniforms. Cameras would click, challenging the accuracy of Carlo's former remark to Marc—*L'abito non fa il monaco*—the habit does not make the monk.

Together, they entered the large reception area and made their way to Teatro Studio—a room of adequate size, but small compared to the three main concert halls. The Guards made a good enough audience by themselves, as they settled en masse in the central parterre. Also

248

represented were the friends of other participants. Giuseppe and his friend already occupied seats to the side. Marc introduced Sophia and Julian, and Giuseppe introduced his friend to all four. Since the side rows contained only four seats, Marc and his friends sat behind Giuseppe. They settled down—encased in acoustic-friendly wood panelling—and amidst the subdued hum of conversation, waited for the concert to start.

Marc felt his anxiety mounting. Apart from the practice sessions in the apartment that reached him from remote corners, he had not really heard Luigi sing. Even if he were aware of the quality of his voice, he would still worry—a first in any field could conjure up demons of doubt not only in participants but also in those on the sidelines. An opera singer required more than a great voice. The performer, male or female, must fit convincingly into the role. Body language and voice were complementary. Luigi might be handsome and striking, but the interaction of that imposing presence with the part and with the audience was what distinguished the performer. Marc was hardly aware of the first few performers, he was in Luigi's skin experiencing the anticipation that, he was convinced, convulsed his friend. However, when he appeared on stage, Luigi was smiling and appeared unconcerned, which put Marc at ease and in the mood to float with the music.

Luigi's first offering surprised Marc, but it shouldn't have. He chose to open with Carlo's favourite, 'E Lucevan Le Stelle', arranged for piano accompaniment, in spite of his fear that it might lose something of its flair without an orchestra. Luigi's heartfelt rendition of Puccini's tragic aria made up for the lack of a fuller backing. The audience could feel Cavaradossi's despair as, under a starry sky, he waited for death when he was so much in love with Tosca and life— Luigi was living the event not just expressing it. The applause was exuberant, wild even, but Marc was gratified to see that even without the Guards, there was general delight at Luigi's performance.

'Morgen!'—Marc's suggestion—was his second choice; both pieces mythical in the sense of conveying a meaning beyond the obvious—significance only Marc and Carlo could interpret. Regarded as one of his most beautiful songs, Richard Strauss dedicated 'Tomorrow!' to his wife on their wedding. The piano accompaniment introduced the melody with gently repeated arpeggios executed in languid rubato, preparing the way for Luigi to enter with a gentleness that challenged the instrument. They vied with each other to produce a tone with profundity of passion that teetered on the edge of silence. Luigi's voice captured the almost heart-rending love expressed in the verse: 'The sun will rise again tomorrow, and unite us, happy ones, on this sun-drenched earth. To the wide, wave-blue beach we will go and looking into each other's eyes, silent happiness will descend upon us'.

Marc, choking with emotion, looked at Carlo, who sat transfixed, lost in that glow of fervour that music, above all other art forms, can produce. Voice and instrument faded so gradually, that the audience could hardly distinguish the moment sound gave way to silence. They just sat there, enveloped in an artistically created spell, unwilling to shatter the moment. The silence continued and Luigi, standing before hushed spectators, began to look anxious. Then a single voice from the midst of the Guards broke the spell. 'Bravo!' The audience, awakened as from a trance, joined in to make manifest its earlier silent expression of tribute.

Relaxation

The 'hopefuls' as Luigi had referred to them, were pleased with their self-help efforts to promote their prowess on the concert stage. Expressions of interest from various quarters gave encouragement to some of the participants including Luigi, who so impressed Signor Augeri, Giuseppe's friend, that he approached Luigi after the concert inviting him to participate in a benefit concert he was helping to organize. As the intention was to raise money, he would receive no payment, apart from his expenses.

'It has significant fringe benefits,' a delighted Luigi explained later to Carlo and Marc. 'Especially for someone starting out—experience, recognition, expanding my repertoire. On this occasion, however, Signor Augeri asked me to stay with the same pieces—this time with an orchestral backing. It will be such a blast!' he added, his blond hair, now liberated from military constraint, bristling at the prospect. 'You will come?' He looked expectantly at his friends.

'Try to stop us,' challenged Carlo, brimming with eager encouragement.

'When and where?' asked Marc, equally supportive.

'Three weeks from now in L'Aquila. I will have to spend some time there to practise with the orchestra. It is a well-known cultural centre, with its own symphony orchestra.'

'And lots of ruined and damaged buildings,' commented Carlo.

'That's the reason for the concert,' affirmed Luigi, showing them the flier. 'They need money to help restore the city after the earthquake. Signor Augeri does not promote such events any more, but he was born in L'Aquila and wanted to help.'

'I've never been there,' said Marc. 'The city may be damaged, but I believe its setting is striking, surrounded by the high snow-capped Apennines. You should feel at home there, Luigi,' he added glumly, sad at the pending separation, even a short one.

Marc recalled the conversation as he sat at the computer in the library. A Chopin ballade, sound fragrance, permeated the airwaves. Before he settled down to write, he had set the player on shuffle, releasing an eclectic mix from his music files. Music did not usually distract him—it stimulated his concentration. However, it did distract him when 'Morgen!' was randomly selected. Luigi was absent—he was in L'Aquila rehearsing with the orchestra—and he missed him. He sat back and gave himself to the music, contemplating the nature of love. It continued to hold him in thrall.

With Carlo on his annual leave, giving of his free time to assist Marc with his research, he could not claim to be lonely. When he first fell in love with Carlo, he thought that he had reached the fulfilment of life's desires. Carlo, beautiful in mind and body, satisfied his every expectation—their lovemaking seemed complete. Then Luigi entered, opening up a new dimension of exploration and desire. He fitted in like a perfect cadence, bringing their love to a harmonic resolution. Now, with Luigi in L'Aquila, they were alone again, the duet reinstated. They slept together, experiencing each other as they had in the beginning, content to a point, but they both admitted that something was lacking— the trio from *Der Rosenkavalier* with just two voices. Or, thought Marc, as the song faded into stillness, leaving transcendence tangible in the atmosphere, 'Morgen!' without the accompaniment.

'I thought you had issues, theological and historical, to resolve before our getaway,' said Carlo, as he quietly entered the library. 'That song has you bewitched.'

'It is not just the song,' replied Marc, rising to embrace Carlo. 'And we both are enchanted.'

'As he is,' commented Carlo. 'He just phoned me, wondering what time he might expect us.'

'What did you tell him?'

'We should be there for dinner.'

'And?' inquired Marc, anticipating a cryptic response from Luigi.

'His reply,' laughed Carlo. '"Just get here; I'm hungry, but not for food."'

'Aren't we all,' said Marc. 'Apart from that, I will be glad of the break. I sometimes think that I am living in the first century.'

'Are you making progress on your *issues*?'

Marc looked at the computer screen and the desk littered with printouts. 'The bytes are mounting, but I sometimes think it is a pointless exercise.'

'Such is life,' said Carlo matter-of-factly. 'We just fill in the time. What's your present problem?'

Marc switched to his 'favourites' file, and pointed to the list. 'I have been listening to many debates over the past few weeks, mainly around two topics—the Resurrection and the historicity of Jesus. Trying to explain the ineffable seems pointless,' continued Marc. 'It's like a tennis match. The same players do the circuit—venue by venue—bouncing their ideas back and forth.'

'But unlike tennis, there is no winner,' added Carlo.

'They just go through the motions and agree to differ. I am just adding another contentious ingredient to the mix.'

'I know how you feel,' said Giuseppe, as he entered the library. 'With enough such elements added, reason will prevail.'

'You seem very positive, Uncle.'

'The trends are there, Marco. We know from Charles Darwin that physical change occurs, but it takes a mesmerizingly long time. So does cultural change—it takes so long that we have to remind ourselves that it happens. It began when our ancestors sensed that life was a mystery.'

'It still is.'

'True, Carlo,' whose interjections Giuseppe welcomed when others might find them intrusive. 'Initially, humanity's challenge was twofold—to survive physically and prosper spiritually. We created multiple gods to take control of the forces that would ensure agriculture's salvation. In time, the many gods gave way to the idea of a supreme being with a court of divine helpers.'

'And at last, the one emerged—the master of the universe,' added the iconoclastic Carlo.

'But it was not enough to survive from season to season, this new spirit that resided in human consciousness craved to live forever,' said Marc.

'Most reasonable scholars and commentators agree on that development,' said Giuseppe. 'The ancients began expressing this longing for personal and eternal salvation in the form of myth and art—the surviving texts and cave drawings bear witness to that.'

253

'Each culture had its own stories of salvation—Egypt created Osiris; Persia, Mithras; Greece, Dionysus,' affirmed Marc.

'Then,' continued Giuseppe, 'three significant events took place which laid the foundation for Western Civilization. The Athenians' defeat of the Persians at the Battle of Marathon in 490 BCE gave them the breathing space to develop what we now call Hellenism. Alexander spread this Greek Culture throughout his vast empire, Hellenizing their myths along the way. Finally, in 70 CE, Jerusalem, with its Temple, was destroyed, freeing the Logos Myth of Philo from its Jewish roots, and concluding Paul's work.'

'Preparing a religion fit for empire and which became the root of Western Civilization,' continued Marc.

'So, to return to your original problem, Marco: the mystery of our consciousness, which gives birth to our spiritual awareness, continues to baffle us. There is a long, interminable history of influences at play here. They are not quickly or easily dislodged.'

'We are making progress in understanding consciousness. It is a natural phenomenon.' Carlo had no doubt.

'Neuroscience is helping to locate its source, but some people, especially those of various religious faiths, hold that its source is elsewhere—in a separate entity, the soul. United with or separate from the body, according to one's conviction, they accept that it lives forever. According to the Gnostics, its destiny is to soar, free from matter, back to its creator. Orthodox believers hold that it attains perfection united with the resurrected body.'

'They will have to jettison the fiction when scientists produce artificial intelligence.' Carlo's position was clear.

Giuseppe chuckled. 'It would certainly cause a tremor, but we are not there yet.'

'It is only a matter of time—a short time,' affirmed Carlo.

'What kind of intelligence will result, I wonder?' Giuseppe did not share Carlo's confidence.

'The equivalent of the human brain,' Carlo's excitement was palpable. 'It is already technologically possible to copy the human brain into such equipment.'

'But what kind of intelligence will that be? That is the question.' Giuseppe continued probing. 'Will it be capable of producing a symphony comparable to Beethoven's, play with feeling a prelude of Chopin, which says more than the notes tell, or be transported, as we were, by Luigi's singing? If it does, religious polemicists will face a challenge—but, as I said, we are not there yet. In the meantime, we debate, debate and debate!'

'I don't know about you two,' moaned Carlo, 'but I need a break.'

'You should be relaxing, Carlo,' said Giuseppe, sympathetically. 'After all, it is your vacation. Why not take off for L'Aquila now. I am sure Luigi will be more diverting than new technology and ancient myths.'

'We will have our own Bacchanalia,' announced an enlivened Carlo.

'Mind you don't over-lubricate his vocal cords,' advised Giuseppe light-heartedly. 'Enjoy yourselves. It is a spectacular region, beautiful mountain scenery. My friend, Matteo, and I will see you at the concert.'

28: L'Aquila

The crisp air of L'Aquila crackled like the ice that layered the crags enfolding the city—like the eagle of its name, L'Aquila floats on glacial currents. Carlo, hunched against the cold, looked up at the startling surround of the Gran Sasso. The wind, swirling around the icy peaks, cascaded down into the valley and penetrated the walls of the ancient city making the cold seem more piercing; the visitors could hardly believe that the summer heat of Rome was a mere hundred kilometres down the road. As well as a cooler climate, the mountains, formed by tectonic forces, brought spectacular scenery and less welcome seismic activity that inflicted on L'Aquila and the surrounding area a history of disastrous earthquakes.

'Do you know,' asked Carlo, speaking to both and to none, 'that Italy has the only active volcano on mainland Europe?'

'You mean Vesuvius, I suppose,' said Luigi. 'Is it still active?' Carlo shook his head, despairingly.

'What about Etna?' Marc knew that Carlo put a lot into sourcing interesting tit-bits for the trip and, while conscious of his mistake, wanted his friend to have his moment.

'On an island,' Carlo replied with the feigned forbearance of a guide responding to the challenge of a poorly informed tourist.

'It must have been a terrible mess immediately following the earthquake,' mused Marc, as he looked around. It was a few years after the earthquake, but he could see that L'Aquila was still severely scarred.

Struts and girders supported weakened roofs and cracked walls while the wind threatened to dislodge protective hoarding.

'It still is,' said Carlo. 'Look over there.' He pointed towards the cathedral, the Duomo from which the piazza in the centre of the city got its name. 'It appears unscathed, but aerial views show a partial collapse of the roof directly over the apse. As a result, that church and indeed much of the city remains shut down.'

'The damage to other buildings is very obvious,' Marc commented, surveying gaping cavities in surrounding walls and the collapsed dome of the Church of the Holy Souls, temporarily covered by a dome-like structure to hide its gaping wound.

'Around three hundred people died here.' Luigi's concern was obvious. 'That is the real tragedy. Buildings can be repaired.'

'Three, four and more thousands died in previous quakes,' observed Carlo stoically. 'You will have to do a lot of singing to repair all this,' he continued, gazing around the piazza. 'Why do they bother?'

'What do you want them to do?' asked Marc. 'Live in tents?'

'That's a thought,' replied Carlo. 'Tents would be safer in a region of seismic uncertainty.'

'Also colder,' said Luigi, snuggling into his woolly jacket.

'True,' Carlo agreed. 'But I was thinking of the churches. They have been repairing and rebuilding them regularly since 1315. By now they should have got the message.'

'Which is?' Marc was intrigued, as ever, by Carlo's ability to cut through centuries of conditioning and hone in on the essence of things.

'That the deity in whose honour they keep rebuilding them doesn't want them; otherwise why keep knocking them down. Nature, after all, is subject to his whim. Remember Julian's story about the Haitian earthquake: praise be to God, indeed.' Carlo shook his head, incapable of comprehending such folly.

'The divinity must favour the nude over there,' commented Marc, looking in the direction of the fountain that stood in front of the cathedral.

258

'You mean the Luigi lookalike,' said Carlo, jokingly provoking his friend.

'Give over.' Luigi, knowing Carlo, was neither embarrassed nor angered.

It could also be a Carlo lookalike, thought Marc. Aloud, he said: 'Since he is a feature in a fountain, standing in a basin supported by dolphins, water spouting all around him when in full flow, I suspect that he and his twin at the other end of the piazza represent Poseidon.' Since Marc never told Carlo or Luigi of his own Poseidon experience in the bathroom, he knew that his allusion to Carlo went unnoticed, but he was contented just to have made it.

'Maybe that's why he was spared,' suggested Luigi. 'One deity respecting another.'

'Whoever is in charge of earthquakes does not seem to have much respect for Christianity's Supreme Being.' Carlo walked towards the fountain as he spoke. 'Perhaps he took offence when a disgruntled archbishop deemed your man there an offence to morality.' He looked up at the nude that topped the fountain, now dry. 'The civic leaders of the city took a more tolerant view. Now, Poseidon stands unscathed while the cathedral, behind its intact facade, lies in ruins.'

'A coffee might warm us up,' suggested Marc.

'Good thinking,' said Carlo, looking around for a warm-looking cafe, out of the wind that was getting stronger by the hour.

They left the piazza and walked down one of the narrow streets that fed into it. The wind was even stronger there, channelled as it was into a narrower space. It screeched around them like a malevolent deity, sending casually abandoned beer cans and plastic bottles careering ahead of them. They ducked into a trattoria that provided not only coffee, but also an array of tasty tit-bits and an assortment of beverages. They settled for coffee, hard cheese and a plate of assorted breads.

'Were you happy with your performance yesterday?' Marc put the question to Luigi.

'Happy! I don't know. Is one ever happy with a performance? I enjoyed it, though. It was such a high having the backing of a full orchestra, better than a roller coaster. I felt as if I were being lifted up and carried on a torrent of sound.'

'You did Puccini proud,' said Carlo.

'And Richard Strauss,' added Marc. '"Morgen!" always moves me, but your interpretation ... took me to heaven.'

'I thought he only did that in bed.' Carlo aimed to be blasé, but his expression revealed his own rapturous memory.

'There are various routes to ecstasy.' Marc raised his coffee cup, toasting both. 'I saw Signor Augeri talking to you this morning before he and Giuseppe left for Rome. I am sure he was impressed.' Marc's suggestion was a thinly veiled nudge for information.

'*Tosca* is going into rehearsal for an end of summer production—the final open-air concert of the season. He asked me if I would be interested.'

'What part? Carlo asked.

'Cavaradossi,' replied Luigi, with a mischievous grin.

'You're joking!' Marc was incredulous that a principal role should come his friend's way so quickly.

Luigi laughed, 'Don't get carried away. It's only as the understudy. That means filling in during rehearsals, until the guest tenor arrives. Then he takes over and I wait in the wings for him to develop a sore throat. I told Signor Augeri that I would be delighted at the opportunity. I think he had that in mind when he asked me to sing the same pieces—he wanted to see how I would handle the Cavaradossi aria with an orchestral backing. I am so grateful to Giuseppe; it is all thanks to him.'

'I am sure that he would be the first to say that it is thanks to you, and your talent.' Finishing his coffee, Marc suggested that they make a move.

'It will be good to feel warm again.' Luigi rubbed his hands and blew into them.

'Not just yet,' interrupted Carlo. 'We must first pay homage to an icon.'

Luigi and Marc exchanged puzzled glances. 'I didn't think you would be interested in a papal tomb,' said Marc. While recognizing Carlo's penchant for history, Marc did not think that a thirteenth-century pope would be a major attraction.

'You mean Celestine the fifth, I suppose,' remarked Carlo. 'He deserves some respect. At least he did not lust after high office, like so many others. He was a hermit, living in a cave somewhere around here.' Carlo directed his comment to Luigi, knowing that Marc would be familiar with the details from Church History. 'When Nicholas the fourth died, the cardinals could not decide on a successor—politics again, the noble families of Rome vying for the position.'

'It dragged on for two years,' added Marc.

Carlo continued his commentary. 'Pietro, the hermit's name before he became pope, got impatient with them and wrote a letter telling them to stop playing politics and elect a pope, or words to that effect. A swift decision followed that probably made Pietro regret interfering—they elected him. He refused to accept the office, saying that he was not fit for such a role—he wasn't. He was too unworldly. The cardinals pressured him into accepting. Then after a few months, they realized their mistake, and persuaded him to abdicate. He was only too happy to return to his cave, but his replacement, Boniface the eight, a worldly monarch if ever there was one, would not let him. He confined him in a castle, where he could keep an eye on him. He died within a few months—at the hands of Boniface, many claim.'

'As the first pope in history to resign the papacy, he has become prominent again because of recent events.'

'That's right,' agreed Carlo. 'Though there were a few before him who, willingly or unwillingly, vacated the papal throne.'

'He formalized the process of resignation,' explained Marc.

'It sounds like Game of Thrones,' observed Luigi wryly.

'The real-life Game of Papal Thrones leaves the fiction in the shade. Pietro was admirable to shun it, though I would not rush to follow his hermetic lifestyle,' confided Carlo. 'I would like to visit his tomb though, but we can't. That church also is closed for repairs since the earthquake.'

Marc and Luigi looked at Carlo, their expressions more vocal than words—where then?

'Follow me,' he said, and led them out into the wind-swept street. They followed their leader through a succession of squares and thoroughfares, without comment, Marc and Luigi exchanging questioning glances. Eventually they arrived at the cemetery on the edge of the city. Carlo strode through the entrance and turned right with the assurance of a frequent visitor, though his friends knew that this was his first visit to L'Aquila. He evidently made many virtual visits to the site that meant a great deal to him. They arrived at a large mausoleum, but the object of Carlo's interest was a gravestone lying flat beside the larger tomb. To his friends' surprise, Carlo dropped to his knees, leaned over and didn't just kiss the cold stone; he *kissed* it with the intensity that a lover might display.

'I am nothing,' he declared, looking up at his friends. 'I am humbled beside the man whose bones lie here.'

Marc was too dazed to speak. Luigi asked: 'Who is it?'

'Karl Heinrich Ulrichs,' replied Carlo, rising to his feet, 'A gay-rights campaigner, long before it had a name.'

'Tell us about him,' nudged Luigi, knowing that they were in for a lecture anyway, but he was truly interested.

'He wasn't just a gay-rights campaigner, he led the way. There were one or two others writing on the subject at the time, but he stood out by declaring himself 'Uranian'—a word he took from Plato before the word homosexual was coined.'

'Clever derivation,' observed Marc, the mythologist, enthusiastically. 'According to various myths, Aphrodite had two births. According to one, she was born from the severed genitals of Uranus, which his mutilator threw into the sea. In another, she was born from the union of Zeus and Dione. That gave Plato, and later, as you say, Karl Heinrich, the idea to identify same-sex love with Uranus and heterosexual love with Dione. Sorry!' added Marc, 'I interrupted you.'

'He was German, obviously, born in 1825. He graduated in law, but soon lost his job because of his sexual orientation. He spent the rest of his life writing and pleading with jurists, in their own terms, for a change in the law that criminalized what he contended was an unchanging, natural urge. He fought his campaign on two fronts— natural law and civic responsibility. Nature is superior to law,' he affirmed, 'so no law that frustrates nature is just, and all law should reflect the state's duty to care for every citizen. He formulated many of the tenets that human rights activists use today.'

'How did he end up in L'Aquila?'

'Frustration,' replied Carlo. 'He was getting nowhere with his legal arguments, and his health began to fail. He moved south and eventually arrived here. He lived in poverty until the local marquis became aware of him. He housed him and helped him as far as Karl would allow. In the end, he saved him from a pauper's grave and arranged for his burial beside his own family tomb.' Carlo nodded in the direction of the larger mausoleum. 'We owe him so much.' Carlo's emotion was obvious. 'He started a movement that led to the relative freedom we enjoy today, still restricted in numerous places and in many minds. Beside him, I am nothing,' repeated Carlo mournfully.

To distract his friend from his gloom, Marc said, 'I am ignorant about the history of the Gay Rights Movement. You said there were others. Who were they?'

'Karl Maria Kertbeny, who gave us the terminology homosexual and heterosexual. And John Henry Mackay.' Carlo was watching his friends keenly as he pronounced the name. They looked at each other.

'The poet?' Luigi asked the question on both their minds.

Carlo was enjoying their surprise. 'The one who wrote "Morgen!"'

263

'I knew he and Richard Strauss were friends, but I didn't know he was gay.' Marc's surprise was obvious as he turned his back to the wind assailing them with detritus from the surrounding graves as an attention-seeking child might pummel a parent with toys.

'You must have noticed that the lyrics of the song are gender neutral. They could apply to any couple. I can make a shrewd guess as to who John Henry had in mind when he wrote the poem.'

'It's obvious who Richard Strauss had in mind when he wrote the music, since he presented it to his wife as a wedding present.'

'And I know who was in my thoughts as I performed the song,' admitted Luigi, embracing his two friends.

'Of the three, only John Henry Mackay lived to see the rise of the monster Hitler. Nazism put an end to their work. This gentle man here,' said Carlo, looking down at the grave, 'would have been outraged at a regime that showed no duty of care towards its citizens. Instead, it herded them into concentration camps and gas chambers. Mindless thugs ransacked John Henry's offices and burned his works. Ten days later, he was dead. What a crazy, incomprehensible world we inhabit.'

Carlo dragged himself reluctantly from the grave, and they made their way back towards the entrance. Gusts were howling through the tombs like pila-wielding legionaries rampaging through the streets of a fallen city. Carlo paused for one last backward glance at his hero's grave. He stood for a moment, reluctant to leave, gazing as if into infinity, and then turned to face into the full force of the cacophonous wind. Memorial bouquets were scattered around the cemetery, and Marc commented jokingly that something must have angered Zephyrus when the gales spiralling down from the high peaks of Gran Sasso caught a loose piece of masonry from one of the elaborate mausoleums and sent it flying through the air. With the precision of a discus thrower and the speed of a comet, it caught Carlo in the centre of his forehead. He dropped to his knees and rolled over, his vacant stare meeting the uncomprehending eyes of his friends.

29: Aftermath

Alone in bed, Marc could see the morning light teasing the edge of the curtains that so effectively blocked its entrance into the room. He had no wish to admit it. He did not want to see the sun, or the blue ocean above the biblical firmament, as if this were a day like any other. Without Carlo, how could any day be normal again? If he had the power attributed to Joshua, he would have forbidden the sun to rise at all. He just wanted to lie there in the dark, savouring what was left of Carlo's presence. He could no longer pick up that distinctive, affective fragrance. Perhaps he had just grown too accustomed to it, lying all night, as he had, in its sensuous aroma, or could it be that Carlo was vacating gradually and inevitably all former haunts.

The thought grieved Marc; he wanted Carlo to haunt him forever. The concept of paradise, where fellowship endures, was suddenly appealing. He could understand its hold on even the most rational mind—on his own mind until Carlo, like a diligent window cleaner, allowed the light of reason to enter and curb the rampant rush of environmentally acquired convictions. But the Christian heaven would not do. If Christian marriage were inappropriate in its rarefied atmosphere, the great abomination could hardly expect to feature. Carlo would certainly not settle for that, nor indeed would the new Marc, lately reborn in love. But now, he was not too sure—to be united with Carlo, whatever the conditions, was a compelling motive to endure whatever it took to ensure that end. In spite of the erotic appeal of the bed and the magnetism of the darkened room, Marc had to get out—out of the room, out of the apartment. He knew that Giuseppe's concern would inevitably bring him to Marc's room.

Outside, the searing light would, he knew, search out his vulnerability and open his wounds anew, but he could not face either Giuseppe or Luigi at present. His love of Luigi seemed only to accentuate his loss and he presumed that Luigi felt the same. When they returned home last night, after a harrowing day in L'Aquila, Luigi had gone straight to his own room—like Marc, he needed to be alone. His relationship with Carlo was of a much longer duration than Marc's few months. Consequently, the phantoms threatening to assail his sleepless night were more entrenched. Marc had room only for his own grief. In fact, it was swelling by the hour like a malignant tumour forcing from his usually compassionate heart all thought of others. It also filled him with doubt. Perhaps through the faith that he had abandoned to be with Carlo was now the only way to find him again.

In his confusion, Marc left the house without shaving. He had little interest in keeping up appearances, but his stubble was so light that the extra growth hardly shadowed his chin. Outside, even with sunglasses, which shaded more than the light, the sunlight assaulted him. In spite of its apparent normality, this was not *just* another day.

At Ponte Fabricio, he sat down, looked at the river and listened to its tranquillizing flow. Like any river, it had millennia of experiences, which it was willing to impart to those who took the trouble to listen. At this spot, the river had opened its arms, thousands of years ago, to allow the Tiber Island to form. Legend had it that when the despised Tarquinius Superbus, the last Roman ruler before the republic was formed, died around 510 BCE, his hated body was thrown into the river where silt gathered around it, eventually forming the island. Rome had a surfeit of legends. No doubt, every city shared in the phenomenon of cloaking its history in vivid imagery, but Rome excelled in the art.

Gazing on the river brought Carlo's recent comment to mind. Was it so lately that he jokingly expressed his resolve to have his ashes cast into the Tiber? He certainly did not think such an eventuality imminent.

In retrospect, it seemed uncanny; one of those eerie experiences that tend to lend legitimacy to some form of cosmic consciousness. His wish, however playfully uttered, now seemed in doubt, unless he had expressed it to his parents. But what young person so readily anticipates death?

From his first days in Rome, this spot had drawn Marc. He had absorbed its myth, legend and history. He looked across at the church of San Bartolomeo now occupying the site of the ancient temple dedicated to Asclepius, the mythical medical man, whose attributes were reminiscent of Jesus. Asclepius, the son of a god, Apollo, had a penchant for raising the dead, or so it seemed—his success in matters medical was so legendary. However, his phenomenal success provoked the wrath of the god of the underworld who petitioned Zeus to get rid of Asclepius or his underworld kingdom would soon be depopulated. Zeus obliged by having him struck by a lightning bolt. Apollo was not too pleased and intervened with Zeus to restore his son. His patient pleading, and less than patient elimination of the Cyclopes who fashioned the lightning bolt that killed his son, eventually met with success and Zeus not only raised Asclepius from the dead, but also made him a deity of medicine. The island's dedication to healing continued through the ages. The modern-day followers of Asclepius, the Brothers of St John of God, the Fatebenefratelli, still maintained a hospital there.

How easily, or so it seemed to Marc, had Carlo broken through the crust of faith, toughened, like a developing carapace, by two thousand years of religious indoctrination. How his gentle jibing had made Marc, the supposed scholar, realize that historicity was not the evangelists' strength. Floating on the sea of Eastern Mediterranean myths, Matthew, Mark, Luke and John, whom centuries of orthodoxy had cloaked in the mantle of historians like Herodotus, Thucydides, Suetonius and Tacitus had more in common, as Giuseppe had recently indicated, with poets and playwrights in the mould of Homer, Euripides, Virgil and Ovid. Marc, as a student of ancient history, knew well the myths relating to Osiris, Dionysus, Adonis, Mithras, Horus and the rest of the pantheon

267

of human/divine/resurrection deities, but refused to accept that such stories had any influence on the evangelists. It was only when he had met Carlo and began to reflect on the question anew that a connection seemed not only possible, but also inevitable. Or was it?

Grief was creating confusion in his mind and was eroding his previous conviction. Perhaps the myths, in exposing the longing of the human heart, were preparing the way for the evangelists, the bearers of the authentic divine message that would assuage all human yearning. Reflecting just now on Apollo reminded Marc that the god who fathered Asclepius was also the lover of Hyacinthus. The thought played on Marc's mind like a hallucinogenic drug creating bizarre associations between Carlo's death and that of Hyacinthus—deadly wind-blown objects and jealous gods. Was Carlo's death a lesson for him?

Reflecting on Carlo was a double-edged sword. It brought consolation, like the touch of cool steel on a summer's day, but it also brought to the fore the keen edge of loss. Even so, he could have continued to brood over him for the rest of the day, for the rest of his life. It was his first exposure to real bereavement and, at times, he felt that the loss, the sadness and the loneliness would physically crack the shell of his existence and wash him away just as the pounding surf gradually disposes of a beached wreck. That was exactly what he felt like; a beached wreck.

'Marco!'

The word balanced delicately on the edge of his consciousness, failing to penetrate his reverie. The proximity of another body standing by the bench gradually drew him out of himself. He looked up to meet the concerned gaze of Sophia, dressed in a light summer dress, her hair escaping under a wide-brimmed sunhat. She had lost that indefinable quality that identifies a 'nun'. Was it because she had now experienced physical as distinct from mystical love? Would its effects be so clearly visible? He wondered if it showed equally in his demeanour. She was not alone. By her side was Julian, looking just as anxious. Marc stood up, kissed Sophia and embraced Julian. 'What a surprise! A very pleasant surprise,' added Marc, desperately trying to cover his own despondency.

'How are you, Marco? You look … is anything the matter?'

Marc had to steel himself to cover his emotions. In spite of his efforts, he could feel his resolve peeling away like flecks of paint from that beached wreck that he felt identified him. His anguish would be evident to those less perceptive than Sophia and Julian. There was only one way to say it. 'Carlo is dead.'

'How awful, Marco!' She took his hand and sat down dragging him onto the bench with her. Her companion, equally stunned, sat beside him. 'What happened?' Her voice was strained with shock.

'He was killed yesterday in a bizarre accident.' Marc tried to describe the circumstances of the weird misfortune, but describing it only deepened his own curious conviction that he was in some way culpable.

'At times like this one misses the conventional platitudes.' Sophia looked at him through a helpless glaze. 'Can I help at all?'

'Thank you, Sophia. Time, according to ancient wisdom, heals all. I suppose it will, but right now...' His voice faded away.

Julian put his arm around Marc's shoulder. 'Carlo was an example of what it is to be human. I could feel his compassion. I too feel his loss.'

Sophia took Marc's hands and kissed them. 'Dear Marco, if there is anything we can do, please phone. You will let us know the funeral arrangements. We would like to attend.'

'You both are very kind. I will contact you. Meeting you and Julian has helped.'

He watched as they walked away arm in arm, and once again, demons of doubt descended on him. Was his apostasy the cause of Carlo's death?

Funeral

The church was a modern building in a northern suburb of Rome. When Marc and Giuseppe arrived, they took their places beside Sophia and

Julian. Lautrim and Silvan followed presently and joined them. Sergio, busy no doubt in the restaurant, was last to arrive. His inner conflicts over Carlo's death exacerbated by the surroundings in which he found himself, Marc knelt, stood and sat in unison with the congregation. He wondered if Carlo would be so accommodating. Giuseppe, wrapped in a contemplative aura, no doubt confronting in his own way the mystery of life and death—another death inevitably recalled by the present tragedy. Sergio looked bemused, as if unable to reconcile the rite with the one whose memory it celebrated. Lautrim and Silvan, accustomed to ritual, were at ease in the setting. Marc was the most disorientated, disillusioned and disturbed. A short while ago, conducting such a service would have been a normal part of his life. It would have brought him consolation, but now only recrimination. The stark, straight lines of the church itself hardly seemed appropriate to the character of a city of ecclesiastical Baroque, but the funeral service conducted within its walls was utterly inappropriate to the character of Carlo.

Luigi was present with the choir in the sanctuary. Carlo's family, who had known Luigi since his and their son's shared student days, had asked him to sing during the liturgy. It was a request of which Carlo would have approved, and one which might have comforted Marc, but for the fact that he was beyond consolation. A private cremation would follow the church service. Marc was gratified to know that at least part of Carlo's spontaneous wish would find fulfilment. He felt an urge to ask what they intended to do with the ashes, but judged it inappropriate. Besides, the thought of Carlo's beautiful body reduced to ash was too upsetting to consider.

After the service, Marc approached the family to express his sympathy once again and to introduce Giuseppe, Sophia and Julian. They thanked them for coming, but Luigi was the main object of their appreciation. Seeing another side of Carlo's life, made Marc realize how little he really knew of him and yet how profound was his influence on Marc's life. In typical Roman fashion, there were kisses all around, parents, sister and two brothers. One brother was so strikingly similar to

Carlo that kissing *him* was, for Marc, particularly charged. It took every gram of willpower to brush with his lips the deeply tanned cheek of Tommaso.

After some polite hesitation, Sophia and Julian accepted Marc's invitation to join them for lunch in Sergio's trattoria. Luigi had already invited Lautrim and Silvan. It was well past lunchtime so they had the place to themselves except for a few stragglers grabbing a late lunch in the midst of a hectic tourist round. Luigi looked uncomfortable. Marc wondered if a surfeit of admiration for his singing was to blame, or if, like him, a pleasure-bearing duct had erupted and drained all joy away. Sophia evidently thought it resulted from the former and sought to dispel Luigi's embarrassment by diverting the conversation from him.

'I wonder what you biblical scholars think of this new find.'

Marc was shuffling his food listlessly. 'What find?' he asked apathetically. He had lost his taste for more than food.

'I would have imagined that the whole world has heard of it by now,' she replied matter-of-factly. Marc, disillusioned with ancient texts, could not motivate his mind to search his memory banks for recent discoveries in the field.

'I suspect,' Giuseppe intervened, understanding Marc's diffidence, 'Sophia is thinking of the recently published fragment— the so-called "Gospel of Jesus's Wife".'

'Of course,' Marc replied, trying to generate some interest. His excitement at the time of the announcement subsequently evaporated as the usual proponents took up their predictable positions on either side of the argument. As usual, rational debate gave way to personal attacks—it was all so futile. All was vanity compared to the reality of loss and the phantoms it conjured up. He could not escape the image of Apollo and Hyacinthus whose discus throwing ended in a tragedy that has captured the imagination of poets and artists from ancient times. Even walking in the Borghese Gardens, reliving happier days, frisbee-throwing youths reminded him of Ovid, the Roman poet of the intertestamental period who was born in an Apennine valley—the

271

region in which L'Aquila stands today. One of the great love poets of the age, Marc recalled his epic poem on the death of Hyacinthus as he watched the frisbee flying from one to the other. Apollo blamed himself—declaring himself the agent of his young lover's death. According to Ovid, the god deserted his divine duties at Delphi in amorous pursuit of the youth that captivated him. A further twist to the story made jealous Zephyrus, the West Wind, the instrument of destruction. In Carlo's case, the wind was the driving force, but Marc could not shake off the growing conviction that he was the cause—guilt that follows love that loved too much.

The silence around the table became a force that reminded Marc that they were waiting on him, the acknowledged expert, to expound. 'Ah, yes,' he muttered, as Giuseppe looked on anxiously. 'It is a papyrus fragment, the size of a credit card. Most agree that the material is ancient, but the authenticity of the writing is in doubt. Nevertheless, the debate continues. My position would be to let the experts continue the work of validating it or not, as the case may be. If it proves to be genuine, then let the debate begin.'

'What does it say?' Lautrim was indifferent, but talk, even about ancient texts, was better than the painful quiet that silence provoked.

Hardly caring to hide his apathy, Marc replied. 'As with ancient texts, some words and letters are missing or illegible. As a consequence, it is garbled.'

'So, why is it important?'

'Because of a few words that are clear: "Jesus said to them—my wife".'

'So what's the big deal?'

'Exactly,' Marc managed a tired smile. 'Why should the marital status of Jesus cause such debate? It matters because of the stand the Orthodox Roman Church took in promoting celibacy as a superior state to marriage on the basis that Jesus was not married. It would also be difficult to explain how a divine being would be remotely interested in engaging in human sex.'

'Zeus did.' The amorous activities of the gods were something that did engage Lautrim.

'That is the point. They were trying to demonstrate that Christianity was superior to paganism.'

'It seems like a lot of fuss about nothing.' Luigi's comment reflected Marc's own attitude. He wanted not only the conversation to end, but also the lunch. Sophia and Giuseppe exchanged concerned glances.

Consequences

Giuseppe's anxiety continued through successive days and into the following weeks. During the first week after Carlo's death, he watched as Luigi and Marc moved about each other like visitors in a sickroom, afraid that their interaction might somehow disturb the fragile atmosphere to the detriment of the patient. After the first week, Luigi had to turn his attention to the rehearsals already underway and to which he had committed himself. Giuseppe, understanding the two friends' grief, was confident that Luigi's return to routine activity and a profession he loved would gradually restore him to normal life. His own interest in and work on the scrolls had helped him to come to terms with the loss of Leah—he hoped that the same would be true of them. However, as the weeks passed, he became more concerned about Marc, who showed no interest in returning to his research and writing—his former fascination seemed to have degenerated into apathy, even loathing. Giuseppe tried to encourage Marc to sit in on Luigi's rehearsals.

'Luigi would be encouraged by your interest and presence,' he suggested to Marc. 'It is a big step for him. He could do with your support.'

Marc returned a blank stare, which slowly softened. 'I love Luigi and I want him to do well, but I just can't. If we settled into a comfortable relationship, it would be like acknowledging that Carlo is no more.'

'But Carlo is dead,' Giuseppe said. 'He is gone. You have to accept that, if you are to live again.'

'No! I want him to live on ... in heaven ... nirvana ... in the stars.'

'That is your pain talking. "Suppressed grief suffocates," according to Ovid. "It rages within the breast, and is forced to multiply its strength."'

'Ovid is my nemesis; he also says that I was the cause of Carlo's death.'

Giuseppe looked aghast, fearing for Marc's sanity. 'That is nonsense.'

'It's not. The accident was too bizarre to be random.'

'Life is bizarre. People die every day in accidents and natural disasters of one kind or another.'

'This was different. It was a copy of Apollo and Hyacinthus. In Ovid's poem, there was no Zephyrus. Apollo blamed himself for neglecting his divine duties in order to indulge in the charms of his lover. I did the same. This is the consequence.'

Giuseppe was appalled. 'You are a reasonable man, Marco. You know that is not true. Your reason led you to reject faith.'

'Did it?' Marc was challenging. 'Was it not, rather, Carlo's dark, appealing eyes, ravaging me from a distance or his sensuous mouth with its engaging smile inviting me to taste its pleasures. Did his magnificent body as he stood naked on the beach, like a Greek god, have nothing to do with my defection? Is it not likely that I found reason to doubt because I wanted him so much?' Marc seemed to dissolve into a shadow as his anguish poured out.

'My dear boy,' said Giuseppe with the compassion of one who understood it all. 'We are human, creatures of an ethereal mind and an all too physical body. Both guide our decisions and actions. Not all the magnetism in the world would have diverted you from your convictions if your reason had not already led you to distrust them. Doubting made the physical presence of Carlo even more attractive, and he was a very engaging young man, always happy and positive.'

274

'Not always,' murmured Marc. 'He had a dark side also, which only surfaced recently—at the tomb of the Unknown Soldier and again in L'Aquila. He was pessimistic about life.'

'With reason,' said Giuseppe. 'Paul described it as creation groaning in travail, but after two thousand years, the birth—the new creation he proclaimed—has not proven to be the panacea he envisaged. I remember, towards the end of the Second World War, seeing newsreels showing the liberation of the death camps—Bergen-Belsen, Dachau, Auschwitz. The footage was blood curdling. After five years of wrenching and wretched war news, you might expect that the public should have become impervious to shock. But no; the cinema audience sat in stunned silence watching scenes not from war but from hell, unfolding frame by frame. How could one human being inflict such horror on another?' Giuseppe paused, as if recalling his own reaction at the time. 'The Nuremburg Trials followed, making the perpetrators face up to their crimes. When it was all over, we thought that the world was renewed and sanitized—such vileness could never occur again. Then came My Lai, Khmer Rouge, Srebrenica, Sarajevo, Darfur, Congo, Sudan, Rwanda, names that have become synonyms for humanity's depravity. The list goes on in various parts of the world, it continues as we speak. We have learned nothing from the past. To paraphrase Lucretius: If a god had designed this world, it would not be as frail and faulty as it is.'

'"No competent and self-respecting deity would claim it." That's what Carlo said.'

'True,' affirmed Giuseppe. 'But this life is all we have—a fragile bubble in a turbulent ocean of time.'

'Why do we bother continuing to live at all?' Marc, who in his recent struggle with the loss of faith experienced anxiety, apprehension, dread even—a mixture of emotions—but never suicidal tendencies, now gave his granduncle reason to worry.

'As well as the evil we perpetrate on each other, human beings are also capable of incredible goodness, heroic unselfishness,' said

275

Giuseppe, in an effort to raise Marc's spirits. 'Life has its dark side, a terrible dark side, but it also has its wonder. Do not let the evil obscure the good. Above all, remember Luigi. Think how difficult it must be for him to concentrate on his profession after what has happened. He is doing his part to fill our days with magic. Music doesn't just camouflage the darkness; like the dawn, it dispels it.'

'No! It doesn't.' Marc's words contained the flint-edge of bitterness.

'If you try it,' urged Giuseppe gently, 'you might find that it does. Luigi needs your love now more than ever. I know that you love him, but if you don't want to lose him also, go and support him in rebuilding his life. Maybe in doing that you will find your own.'

Giuseppe's words had healing potential, but they could not penetrate Marc's defence-shield against any accommodation with his new circumstances. Whatever promise they held waited like dormant buds for a favourable season.

30: The Time of Trajan

Forty years have passed since Vespasian and his son, Titus, devastated my homeland and our refuge in the desert. I have returned to that sanctuary, now wrecked and abandoned, with two disciples, expecting to die here. It all began in this place, among fellow messianic seekers, not under a lustrous star as a recent writing asserts, though the heavens constantly announce the wondrous works of the Creator Spirit, or so we convince ourselves. Is that an illusion?

The legs that bore me on so many journeys are, like the body they carry, thin but strong despite, or perhaps because of, their prolonged and frequent use. My skin is yellow, creased and crumbling, like ancient parchment, cured and tanned by sun and wind, and written with the script of years. I am an old man now; so old that my early life seems like a dream—perhaps it was, perhaps it is. Past events have blended into dreams and dreams into a dubious reality. The edge of certainty has blurred, leaving a diaphanous vision of the past that is insubstantial and open to comforting but fanciful illusion. Does old age bring wisdom, or is that too an illusion?

Forty turbulent years have come and gone since we had to abandon our refuge and our life's work—the scrolls we tended so carefully. On my return to the much-loved site, I made my way down into the wadi below the settlement to view the cave that earlier brothers, because of its proximity to the sanctuary buildings, had hewn out of the rock to act as a library. The rocky prominence of the cave, its entrance not visible from below, stood high and proud overlooking the wadi like a sentinel sphinx. My heart swelled at the sight. The ascent was difficult, even for a young person, but I made my way up the escarpment to find the entrance to the cave. Inside, it was a sad sight, but at least the Romans had not found it. Our scrolls still rested on the shelves and tables, covered with the dust and debris of forty years, but still intact. We used many surrounding caves for storage. I thought I knew where to look, so with the help of my companions, I tried to find them. In the course of a quick search, we discovered only one, which I am glad to say, also preserved its secret hoard safe from the Romans. Securely sealed in pottery jars, they too waited.

I stood with my disciples on the plateau that I once knew so well, and tried to convey to them the simple life that we had lived here before the advance of the Roman Legions. It is so different now; the sight of the ruined buildings saddened me, though the Romans did restore some buildings to use as a lookout from which to keep the peace. The only thing that remained unchanged was *Yam Ha-Melah*, the Salt Sea—the Romans call it *Mare Mortuum*, the Dead Sea; its depths void of life because of its high salt content. However, perhaps that also has changed. The sea appears farther away now than in the happy days of our simple life here when its tranquil surge seemed to lap at the base of the marl plateau that supported our refuge. That, at least, was my memory, but memory, I have come to realize, is a fanciful friend. However, near or far, it shimmers in the sun as it did in those days when my companions and I lived removed from the contagion of the Jerusalem Temple, and worked on producing and preserving our beloved writings and ... waiting—always waiting.

It was that expectation that directed our existence here in the desert. Our Teacher led his first followers to this isolated wilderness to prepare the way of the Lord. My companions and I awoke every morning hoping and fearing in equal measure that that very day would witness the Lord's coming. At night, we lay down to rest wondering if during sleep the heavens above would be ripped apart to reveal the Holy One coming in power and majesty. We thought that moment had arrived when the Roman Legions advanced towards us. We had built our expectation on defeating them—another vain hope. I am still waiting; waiting for the fulfilment when the Holy One would burst through the firmament, rending the heavens like an old rag, scattering the stars like useless trappings with no further purpose, and meting out his justice to all.

Depressed in Spirit, I made my way to our burial ground and stood silently beside his grave. There, I reflected on my life investigating the ancient wisdom revealed through the words of Apollonius, and the writings of Philo, Plato, Pythagoras and many others. I recalled my thrill at hearing Apollonius describe the Pythagorean idea that only the mind can know and reach out to God. Now, in what surely must be my final days, I doubt that even the mind could penetrate such sublimity. To know it would be to diminish it. I have come to identify with just one wise man from the distant past, Protagoras, who dismissed the question of the existence of the gods as too great to fathom. What were his words? 'I have no way of knowing whether the gods exist or not, the question is too sublime and human life too short.' Not having discussed Protagoras with my Master in life, I wished that I could now cross the great chasm, as my Master called the great divide between the living and the dead, to seek his counsel. Would he berate me for lack of constancy? Have I failed faith, or has faith failed me? Whatever the truth, I would soon lie beside him, united in love, if not in faith and hope.

The Salt Sea, speckled with sunlight, was acting as a sort of semaphore inducing me towards it. I told my disciples that I wished to be alone to think and, leaning on my staff, I directed my sandaled feet towards the shore.

Lying full length on the sand that edged the sea, I looked up into the infinite blue where the night jewels lay hidden. Would it happen now? Would it ever happen? The azure dome remained tightly sealed and defiantly unperturbed. Was our hope and expectation just empty vanity? Was our Divine Spirit as illusory and ineffectual as Zeus or Jupiter? Was the divinity of the Most High no more than that of

Augustus? As I lay there, faith and hope evaporated into the ether above. It was all a grand illusion.

Hardly conscious of my whereabouts, my mind reliving the past, I felt as I did that day in Rome, walking through *Campus Martius* on my way to interview the scribe. That collaboration proved successful. Most communities of believers had, by then, accepted Paul's symbol of a suffering Christos as the most meaningful to our suffering and dispersed followers, so I decided to adopt that same allegory. I wished to remain anonymous, so my gospel appeared among our followers in the scribe's beautiful calligraphy with only the most oblique references to the author.

I wrote according to my convictions at the time. I was long conscious that external change was a natural phenomenon, now I have to admit to change within my own consciousness. At the time of writing my gospel, the Pythagorean idea that the mind can know and reach God and his maxim—*not everything should be told to everybody*—influenced me greatly. Remembering Mark's two gospels, one for beginners in the faith and the 'secret' gospel for the 'perfect', I decided that my one gospel would contain both features. New believers could gain much from the surface stories, but only the initiated could understand the deeper spiritual meaning contained in tales, such as my own resurrection, which I endeavoured to make clearly allegorical. I also tried to counter the myth surrounding my own longevity—my Master did not say that I would live to see the *Parousia*, only *if* I should. My gospel was a stylized account, ordering various truths into discernible blocks. Salvation was the result of a cosmic conflict between Divine Light and Primordial darkness. The Christ, the Light, was directing events, not subject to them. From the outset, the place of the Logos outside human history is clear and unequivocal and his subsequent actions within human history are clearly that of the Master ordering his subjects. Even his final sacrifice proceeds, stage by stage, according to his will.

As to the crucifixion, I have witnessed many; all were horrible. That was not the case with my Logos, the Christ. He dies because he calmly surrenders life. In framing this allegory, I drew much from Philo. I trust that he would approve. I know Apollos would, because in our time together, we composed many such fables to illustrate the message we preached. There is also much of my beloved Master in the words and actions of the Christ. He, unlike Augustus, would not wish for apotheosis, which was another reason I wanted my gospel to be clearly and unequivocally allegorical. Canonization was not my purpose. A knowledgeable reader would not interpret it factually. If the less erudite understood it as history, where was the harm? I thought, at the time, that if it brought them solace in a comfortless existence, it would have achieved something. Now, I wonder.

I am done with allegory. I want to leave another message, clear and unambiguous, with those surviving in the surrounding caves—my last testament, uncorrupted by an intermediary. What to write? How would I compress a lifetime of faith and expectation, and final disillusionment into a tiny roll of papyrus? This time there would be no problem with words, no mystery beyond the capacity of language to describe, just the simple statement of fact, my preaching vanity, my hope illusion.

Back in the cave that the community had used as a library and where dust and debris already layered the scrolls, I paused to look about. I brought along a small jar in which I intended to put the scroll for safekeeping. I looked around for a suitable crevice in the gnarled rock of the cave—it may have to survive there for another 40 years. The permeable rock provided many possibilities. I reached up to a promising-looking crevice and pushed the urn in. I paused to inspect my handiwork and wondered into what kind of world it would emerge. Would that world even know of one called Lazarus or Johanan? Or anything of the faith that we professed and the hope we held, or would my words be meaningless in an age that has long since given up waiting for the *Parousia*? I withdrew the jar and laid it aside, waiting for its cargo. I felt I was entrusting my life to that little vessel. Would a human hand ever touch it again? Would my last testament crumble, unread, into the dust? Some might think that would be best. The human spirit, they would claim, needs hope. Is hope more important than truth? With that thought, I started writing: *Lazarus was my name a long time ago...*

31: E Lucevan Le Stelle

The stars are indeed shining brightly, not only the stars. The moon—bright and full, nature's own spotlight—illuminates the ancient ruins. The baths, opened to the public by Caracalla in the year 216, could accommodate nearly two thousand patrons. It was a huge multi complex. The main cathedral-like bathhouse was larger than Saint Peter's Basilica and contained three areas of varying temperatures. Patrons began in the hot-steam area of the caldarium and worked their way through the tepidarium to the frigidarium and on to the roofless swimming pool with its mounted bronze mirrors that deflected the rays of the sun down on the swimmers. Underground furnaces heated the water that an especially constructed aqueduct conveyed to the site. The resultant steam heated the floors and sneaked its way into cavity walls to create an efficient caldarium. It housed not only baths but also libraries, shops, restaurants, gymnasia, galleries, gardens for recreation and brothels for more basic pleasure. It was lavish, with mosaic walls, gold-edged marble floors, and decorated with paintings and monumental sculptures. Colonnaded porticoes and walkways connected the various areas and gardens, and it was all free. The gift of a kindly emperor to his people, one might imagine, but Caracalla's brutality succeeded in making the notorious cruelty of others appear almost benign. Now, it is a ruin, a spectacular one indeed, which hosts the summer production of Puccini's *Tosca*.

It is Luigi's operatic debut, an unexpected one, and consequently for Luigi terrifying. He considered it a coup to land the position of understudy to the guest tenor. He had been rehearsing the role of Cavaradossi for a few weeks in preparation for the arrival of the leading man, who would appear only for the final rehearsals, as befitted his status. In the event, the star broke a leg—a good luck wish that evidently backfired—and he had to cry off. For Luigi it was a stroke of luck, but he would have liked a gentler push into the top role. Consequently, Luigi is terrified, and with good reason—the Romans love their opera, and do not treat indulgently the artist who fails to meet their expectations.

I feel Luigi's anxiety. I also have confidence in his ability to captivate even the exacting Romans. Hearing him in the previous concerts when he captivated not only me but also the entire audience with his evocative rendition of 'Morgen!' was sufficient to convince one of his talents. The beauty of his voice alone would, I believe, take him to the top of his profession, but he also has that indefinable quality— charisma—which makes an artist, but not only an artist, special. I rejoice sincerely for him, but I am conscious of a jealous streak that wants to keep him to myself. However, no person has such a claim on another, as life, with bitter finality, has already taught me.

Revitalized by Giuseppe's advice, I took a renewed interest in Luigi's career. I sat in on some of the rehearsals, guiltily at first, feeling that I was betraying another, but seeing his dedication to a part that he had little hope of singing motivated me to row in more eagerly behind him. Though he never expected to fall into the role, he gave it his all, anxious to learn from the experience. I admired him, but did not respond when he returned one night exhausted by his efforts and in dread after hearing that he would have to sing in place of the fallen star. He needed companionship and love and, for the first time since that terrible day, he crept into my bed. His naked presence, like static electricity, provoked my unwilling body to respond. The hairs on my arms leaned towards him even before he touched me. I ached for him, I wanted him, but I refused him—something that was so perfect with three seemed flawed with two. He returned to his room lonely and frustrated, and left me feeling guilty and condemned to a restless night.

The scrolls no longer consumed me, as music did Luigi. The only past I wished to visit was my time with Carlo. I had not come to terms with his death, still convinced, in spite of Giuseppe's efforts, that I, like Apollo, was the agent of my lover's death. That guilt drove me to visit churches once again. I would skulk in, like a thief intent on raiding the poor box, and take my position in some dim corner, conscious that he whose memory precipitated my action would be disparaging in his criticism of my efforts to compensate for my complicity, as I saw it, in his losing his life. I needed to do something—something like Apollo in making a flower to grow from his lover's blood or giving his son, Asclepius, a place among the stars. But who am I to dispense such favours?

Lautrim, who sits on my left beside Silvan, squeezes my hand, as if expressing through me, not only his solidarity with Luigi's opening night jitters, but his confidence in his friend's talent, and in his will to succeed. Our party for Luigi's debut consists of Italian, Swiss and Irish. Sadly, the one who would have been his most ardent supporter is absent—an unnecessary reminder that Carlo lives on in my consciousness. Beyond Lautrim and Silvan is an excited Sophia, even the soothing presence of Julian cannot diminish her expressive enthusiasm. Past Julian is Sergio, with a friend who is unknown to me, but who evidently knows Luigi and is anxious to share his opening night. No doubt, he has many other friends, and perhaps lovers, scattered among the audience. I know that a contingent of his former colleagues in the Swiss Guard is present, ready to cheer on their compatriot and wield, if the need arises, their halberds in the face of disenchanted Romans. However, I am confident that it will not come to that. To my right, my sister and brother sit, suitably awed by the antiquity of our surroundings and by Rome's animated opera-going elite. Nearby is Carlo's family, enthusiastic for Luigi, whom they consider a member of the family. In front, my mother and father take their seats, one on either side of Giuseppe and his friend Matteo Augeri, the rift caused by the moralistic attitude of a previous generation forgotten in a kinder age.

Three ominous chords from the orchestra draw me out of my reverie. A furtive figure scurries across the stage and the music drama begins. The first act of Puccini's opera is set in the church of Sant' Andrea della Valle where Luigi, as the artist Cavaradossi, is working on a mural of Mary Magdalene. Luigi enters and engages the sacristan in light conversation, and then enters into his first aria. I discover an emotion that I never experienced before, a cocktail of fear, exhilaration, anxiety, petrifaction and others that defy classification. As Luigi's voice fills the open-air arena, once again Lautrim's hand, large and strong, grips mine, squeezing it to the point of pain. Luigi's voice is clear and pure. There is no sign of the anxiety that I know he is experiencing. He is in control, alluring the Romans with their own favourite fare. The aria ends, and the ancient ruins resound with applause. Luigi beguiles even the exacting Romans.

The opera continues to its tragic and melodramatic conclusion. The evil Baron Scarpia sentences Luigi's Cavaradossi to death by firing squad. Awaiting execution, he sings his final aria on the roof of Castel Sant'Angelo. He remembers his love for Tosca—the stars were shining then. Now, love is gone, he dies in despair. What a time to die, he laments, when he loves life so much. It was Carlo's favourite aria. Luigi's voice falters, the audience tenses—out of anxiety for the singer, or admiration at his ability to identify with his character. My heart leaps in trepidation. The lyrics remind him of Carlo. He steadies himself and carries on. A tear trickles down my face—the first since that tragic event. Now, the words and music seem to grab me by my entrails. I am shaking. I find I cannot wait to see the fictional death—thought of another death convulses me. I stand, push by a bewildered Lautrim and make for an isolated part of the ruins.

It is such a short time since I collided with Carlo. A collision it indeed was, proving to be the catalyst that led to the demolition of convictions and beliefs that I thought as secure as the foundation of Saint Peter's basilica. Perhaps it is significant that the church stands on an ancient necropolis.

A short time, but so much has been crowded into that space that it could have been a lifetime ago. Time, elusive and mischievous, seems to delight in constantly confounding our perception of it.

The music floats towards me. Tosca is telling Cavaradossi to feign death convincingly—unaware that Scarpia has duped her. Carlo had no need to feign death, it was all too real, and just when he loved life so much. How unconscionable life is, but nobody knew that better than Carlo did. 'Why are soldiers necessary,' I asked the ridiculous question at the tomb of the Unknown Soldier. I recall Carlo's reply: 'Life is cruel and unpredictable. No competent and self-respecting deity would claim it. Life is for living, Marco, live.' Tears begin to trickle down my face as I stand in this ancient site. How many soldiers have died in the innumerable wars that have taken place since this was a going concern of Caracalla. In that period alone, countless generations have perished in conflicts and disasters, natural and manmade, and the carnage continues—life is indeed cruel and unpredictable.

I recall the day that I stood alone and at a distance witnessing the scattering of his ashes. Understandably, Carlo's parents had decided to confine that moment to the family, the immediate family at that. They contacted Luigi to let him know the time and place, and hoped he would understand their decision. In the event, Luigi was not free to attend, had he been invited, so I, forlorn and alone, stood above on the tree-lined path, where I fancied I could hear the beep-beep of the Fiat, and looked down on the scene below.

I was, at least, gratified to see that Carlo's family had chosen the Tiber. I wondered at their choice, but speculation was futile. Also pointless was pondering the absence of a religious figure. Their choice of location was probably one of convenience, as the tip of the island with the current running past seemed ideal for such a sad enactment. To me it was not fortuitous, or so I liked to think. Some skilled stage designer had chosen the spot I had made my own—a place that Carlo identified with me. That thought made the sight even more poignant. The small group of parents, sister and two brothers huddled together at the peak of the Tiber Island where the river, split by the tiny landmass, united again and, carrying its new responsibility, continued its journey to the sea—so emblematic of life itself. I hoped, I think I even prayed that day, that like Asclepius of old, the Carlo I loved would find his own place among the stars. That was, after all, what I wanted, the assurance that out there somewhere he lived on.

However, under the starry light of the constellations that keep the ancient gods and myths ever before our eyes, but in a time far removed from fanciful mythology and exotic gods, and in the cold light of reason, I am now quietly convinced that death simply is *the end*. That is obvious to my rational mind and, however reluctantly, I must let Carlo go, but not without making a gesture to his memory. I will get back to the scrolls, but not just yet. After two thousand years, they can wait a little longer. I know that my efforts will make little difference. As Giuseppe often indicated, people will continue to follow their entrenched views. Jews will follow the dictates of a mythical Moses in their quest for the divine. Muslims will pursue the same end by adhering to the directives of one who, like Constantine, united the tribes of Arabia in a single religious polity. Christians will continue to place their confidence in an individual that scholars are fast consigning to the region of non- reality. There may have been an historical figure way back from whom the Christian Jesus grew, but to all intents and purposes, he is irrelevant— irretrievably lost behind the mythical gospel figure. Yet, we cling to them with indefatigable endurance. Enlightenment, like the poet's peace, 'comes dropping slow'.

I will return to my studies, not to change people's entrenched views, but to continue exploring our understanding of human consciousness, but for now, that can wait. Love takes precedence. Apollo inscribed his loss in a flower. What, according to Ovid, did Apollo say? 'Yet on my tongue thou shalt forever dwell; thy name my lyre shall sound, my verse shall tell.' My tribute to Carlo will be to compose a carefully researched biography of Karl Heinrich Ulrichs, the man beside whom he claimed to be nothing, just moments before he died. But Carlo was a significant person in my life. I will write about that also so that those who read it will know that he was not 'nothing'.

288

I will put my heart and love into the work, but I readily admit it is not equal to a place among the stars or even an annually blooming flower whose breath perfumes the skies. But, unlike Apollo, I am a mere mortal, incapable of such divine largesse.

I turn, and head back in the direction of the applause in time to see Luigi and the cast taking their curtain call. The Swiss Guards are on their feet, intimidating the Romans by their example. Luigi, smiling broadly, waves out at his enthusiastic friends. He has worked hard at a difficult time and has received his reward—my own expression of appreciation and love awaits him. Giuseppe was right; Luigi—his art and his love, not Paul's sophistry—is my light in this dark world, this groaning creation.

Epilogue: The Vatican

At his office bureau in the Vatican Library, Monsignore Martini finishes reading a scroll which lies unrolled on the desk before him. His index finger moves along the ancient papyrus, his eyes capturing the symbols, his mind releasing their meaning, until he reaches the end. Thoughtfully, he scrolls back to the beginning and reads it again... *Lazarus was my name a long time ago.* When he finishes reading it, he goes to the window and, with a look of chastened inevitability, he gazes out on the vast Bernini piazza towards the basilica.

ACKNOWLEDGEMENTS

This book is out there and available because of the persuasive skills of Lucia and Tony. I acknowledge that fact—gratefully, in spite of restless nights, laborious days, habitual eyestrain and a certain kind of dread.

Author Catherine Brophy with her native sound advice guided my early fumbling efforts. Writer and Humanist Celebrant, Joe Armstrong's enthusiasm and direction gave me the will to continue. Roger Derham, my former publisher, was a willing adviser on title, cover design, and related issues. My previous editor, Valerie Shortland, came to my assistance once again with wide-ranging advice from her abundant experience. My deep gratitude to Jim O'Crowley who, with forensic vision, kindly undertook a final sweep of the text to clear out the remaining detritus—any that might linger is the result of my negligence.

Sincere thanks to journalist, Bernie NiFhlatharta, and her friend, John Brophy, for their advice on the important subject of copyright. My great grandniece, Stacey Fox, has displayed her skill and cleverness in drawing together many of the book's themes in her cover design—the Dead Sea area, St Peter's in Rome, Giordano Bruno, more hero than heretic, Bernini's Elephant, also in Rome, and the Shrine of the Book in Jerusalem.

Other nieces and nephews, friends and neighbours have expressed their support and encouragement in various ways, all of which I acknowledge with gratitude.

Lightning Source UK Ltd.
Milton Keynes UK
UKOW02f2308180515

251808UK00001B/39/P